LINDA P. BAKE[...] decided to show her work to others within the past decade. She is the author of two DRAGONLANCE novels, *The Irda* and *Tears of the Night Sky* (with Nancy Varian Berberick), and quite a few short stories. Linda and her husband, Larry, live in Mobile, Alabama, where they indulge in Mardi Gras, flea marketing, hockey, and collecting books for their to-be-read stacks.

NANCY VARIAN BERBERICK wasn't quite born with a pen in her hand, but she does remember wanting to hurry up and learn to read so she could start writing her own stories. She cut her teeth on the Brothers Grimm, maintains a long and happy relationship with Beowulf, revels in Norse mythology, and is having a wonderful time with "Orlando Innamorato." Nancy is the author of eight fantasy novels, four of them in the DRAGONLANCE series: *Stormblade*, *Tears of the Night Sky* (with Linda P. Baker), *Dalamar the Dark*, and *The Inheritance*. Forthcoming is *The Lioness*.

DONALD J. BINGLE, a corporate attorney, is better known as the top-ranked player of classic roleplaying tournaments. In addition to being a writer of a variety of gaming materials and sanctioned tournaments for the FORGOTTEN REALMS, DRAGONLANCE, PARANOIA, CHILL, TIMEMASTER, BOND, and DREAM PARK game worlds, he has published a number of short stories, the most recent in *Historical Hauntings*. He has the good fortune to be married to a curious and delightful kender, named Lindakins, who makes all their adventures together entertaining. He can be contacted through www.orphyte.com.

This story is JEFF CROOK'S second foray into the world of the tinker gnomes and their diminutive accomplices (gully dwarves and kender), and if that weren't enough, he is currently writing a novel (*Conundrum*) about the hapless curmudgeons. When not fleeing in terror from their latest mishap, he works as a technical writer for the U.S. Postal Service. Come to think of it, things aren't much different there than in Mount Nevermind. He is the author of two previous DRAGONLANCE novels: *The Thieves' Guild* and *The Rose and the Skull*.

The author of over twenty novels and more than a dozen short stories, RICHARD A. KNAAK has been contributing to the DRAGONLANCE series since the first Tales Trilogy. Besides the New York Times best-seller, *The Legend of Huma*, he has written four other novels based on Krynn, the latest being *The Citadel*. In addition, he is the author of the popular Dragonrealm series and several independent novels, including the contemporary fantasy *Frostwing*. Most recently, he has written novels based on the popular computer games, Warcraft and Diablo. At present, he is in the midst of the first novel of a major trilogy concerning the future of both the minotaur empire and Krynn at large. More about the author can be learned at http://www.sff.net/people/knaak.

BRIAN MURPHY is currently the assistant editor of Science Fiction Weekly, the Internet's premier web site for SF and fantasy news, reviews, and interviews. He has also served as managing editor of Satellite Direct magazine and editorial assistant for both Realms of Fantasy and the late, lamented Science Fiction Age. He has written book, web site, and movie reviews for all of these publications. He lives in Alexandria, Virginia, with his wonderful wife Kerri.

NICK O'DONOHOE has been a mystery, science fiction, and fantasy writer. His novels about veterinarians treating fantasy animals include *The Magic* and *The Healing* (selected by the American Library Association as Best Book for Teens), *Under the Healing Sign*, and *The Healing of Crossroads*. His first science fiction novel was *Too, Too Solid Flesh* for TSR, about an all-android acting company performing Hamlet. He has also written *The Gnomewrench in the Dwarfworks*, a World War II home front fantasy. He has contributed to DRAGONLANCE short story anthologies since the first Tales.

DON PERRIN is a displaced Canadian, who went looking for heat. To him, Wisconsin was the deep south, and he's settling in nicely. He's the creator of Kang and Slith, the commanders of the Draconian Engineering Regiment made famous by he and Margaret Weis in *The Doom Brigade* and *Draconian Measures*. His new endeavor, Perrin Miniatures (www.perrinminis.com), is up and running, creating historical military miniatures, and will soon be making fantasy figures for the Sovereign Stone roleplaying game. Don is the author of the DRAGONLANCE novel *Theros Ironfeld* and the co-author, with his wife Margaret Weis, of *The Doom Brigade* and *Brothers in Arms*. He and Weis have also written *Knights of the Black Earth*, *Robot Blues*, and *Hung Out for Roc*. Don and Margaret live in a converted barn with an assortment of dogs, cats, computers, and books.

JEAN RABE'S life is books—fantasy, science fiction, mystery, whatever. When she's not writing books, she's reading them (and stuffing the ones she continues to buy under the bed, in the pantry, and behind the towels in the linen closet so her husband won't see just how many she has). In what amounts to her free time, she plays with her two dogs, watches the fish in her backyard pond, visits museums, plays war games and roleplaying games, and buys more books. She's the author of several DRAGONLANCE novels and short stories, including *Downfall* and *Betrayal*, and is the editor of two DAW anthologies.

KEVIN T. STEIN has contributed to the DRAGONLANCE series for eleven years. His first novel was *Brothers Majere*, in the Preludes trilogy.

PAUL B. THOMPSON is the author of a dozen books, including eight in the DRAGONLANCE series. With co-author Tonya Cook, his most recent titles are the Barbarians trilogy: *Children of the Plains*, *Brother of the Dragon*, and *Sister of the Sword* (2002). Paul has also published numerous non-fiction articles on military history, popular science, and the paranormal. He often contributes to the DRAGONLANCE and MAGIC: THE GATHERING anthologies. He lives in Chapel Hill, N.C., with his wife Elizabeth, several thousand books and videotapes, and a rapidly aging PC.

THE SEARCH FOR MAGIC
TALES FROM THE WAR OF SOULS

EDITED BY
**MARGARET WEIS
& TRACY HICKMAN**

THE SEARCH FOR MAGIC

©2001 Wizards of the Coast, Inc.

Distributed in the United States by Holtzbrinck Publishing. Distributed in Canada by Fenn Ltd.

Distributed to the hobby, toy, and comic trade in the United States and Canada by regional distributors.

Distributed worldwide by Wizards of the Coast, Inc. and regional distributors.

Made in the U.S.A.

Cover art by Matt Stawicki
First Printing: October 2001
Library of Congress Catalog Card Number: 00-191034

9 8 7 6 5 4 3 2 1

ISBN: 0-7869-1899-3
UK ISBN: 0-7869-2672-4
620-T21899

U.S., CANADA,
ASIA, PACIFIC, & LATIN AMERICA
Wizards of the Coast, Inc.
P.O. Box 707
Renton, WA 98057-0707
+1-800-324-6496

EUROPEAN HEADQUARTERS
Wizards of the Coast, Belgium
P.B. 2031
2600 Berchem
Belgium
+32-70-23-32-77

Visit our web site at www.wizards.com/

TABLE OF CONTENTS

INTRODUCTION

Although titled *The Search for Magic*, the stories in this anthology range far beyond an actual physical search for the magic that vanished with the departure of the gods. The stories in this anthology deal with magic in all its aspects.

"All For a Pint" by Brian Murphy tells the cautionary tale of two wizards who endeavor to use what small amount of magic remains to them in order to provide themselves with a livelihood by creating a brew that has a bit of a magical kick to it.

The elves use wild magic to help their people escape the ravages of the Dark Knights who occupy Qualinesti, as a young elf mourns an end of the elven way of life in "The End" by Nancy Berberick.

A god's magic calls down a fearsome storm upon Ansalon, causing the sea to return to Tarsis, thus fulfilling one man's tortured dream in "The Lost Sea" by Linda Baker.

"Some Assembly Required" by Nick O'Donohoe is a gnome story and there's a kender in it, too. Consider yourself warned.

introduction

"Go with the Floe" by Paul Thompson is another gnome story that tells of two entrepeneurs who come up with an interesting use for a glacier.

Jeff Crook devises a magical way to cure afflicted kender in "The Great Gully Dwarf Climacteric of 40 S.C."

Kevin T. Stein deals with a darker sort of magic in "Bond", telling the story of a group of Dark Knights who have bonded with wolves in order to fight a remnant of Chaos.

"A Twist of the Knife" by Jean Rabe is the story of an assassin sent to kill a Solamnic knight.

A Baaz draconian finds that someone is trying to steal the magic in a powerful artifact in "Hunger" by Richard Knaak.

In "Product Given for Service Rendered" Don Perrin tells the story of two deserters from the army of the Dark Knights, who plot to rob and murder an old man they meet on the trail.

Kender make a perilous journey to the Gimmenthal Glacier in search of treasure in "Dragon's Throat" by Donald J. Bingle.

ALL FOR A PINT

BRIAN MURPHY

Light from the tavern window illuminated the faces of the two wizards as they peered inside. Stynmar's chubby cheeks rested against the pane of cracked glass and Grantheous's beard tickled the adjacent frame. Fetlin, their apprentice, stood between them, staring into the tavern. All anxiously awaited the results.

Fetlin ran his fingers through his bright red hair and looked around. His masters shouldn't be wandering around the docks of Palanthas, but they had to test the market and both had insisted on coming. Fetlin fingered the butcher's knife he had thrust into his belt in case of trouble.

The Two-Handed Mug, like every other tavern located on the docks, smelled of salt and fish and sweat. The wood floors, made from slats of yellow pine, were discolored by blood and beer, reminding the patrons fondly of bar fights of old.

Inside, the raucous laughter of the sailors changed to cheers as two minotaurs kicked their chairs back and tossed a table aside. The minotaurs growled and snorted. Patrons jumped over the bar, where they could watch in relative safety, or ran out the front door, taking the fight as an opportunity to leave without paying.

The two minotaurs gave deafening roars and locked horns and arms. The mages looked at each other, worried. Stynmar shook his head disconsolately. Fetlin, who was supposed to be taking notes, had trouble telling the minotaurs apart. He saw that one had a scarred lip and the other a nose ring, and he wrote this down in case it later turned out to be important.

The minotaurs grunted and heaved, each testing the other's strength and balance. With a sudden heave, Lip Scar flipped Nose Ring onto his back. The minotaurs rolled this way and that, knocking over chairs and tables and sailors, then Lip Scar gained the upper hand. Sitting on top of his opponent, Lip Scar raised his hands, fingers outstretched, and paused. Excitement hung heavy in the air. Sailors called out bets. Money changed hands. Lip Scar scanned the crowd, daring anyone to say anything. He sneered and, reaching down, began to tickle Nose Ring in the ribs.

Nose Ring started to laugh, and soon he was screaming from laughing so hard. He tickled Lip Scar, who snorted and guffawed. The two minotaurs were having a wonderful time. The sailors looked on, first in astonishment, then in disgust. They went back to their drinking.

Outside the tavern, Grantheous and Stynmar stared at each other in disbelief.

"Minotaurs tickling each other?" Stynmar gasped.

Grantheous frowned. "I didn't even know minotaurs *could* be tickled. I don't think anyone's ever tried."

"Or lived to tell about it," said Fetlin.

The mages nodded and said, in unison, "Much too potent!"

The two walked off, heading for their next test.

Fetlin wrote the comment "too potent" on his piece of parchment and then fell in step behind his masters, constantly looking over his shoulder to make sure no one followed them.

———◆———

The mages saw many strange things that night. Their second test was an old man, known to all Palanthas as Dour Dave because no one had seen him smile in the last fifty years. To their astonishment, Dour Dave dashed out of the tavern called the Seventh Lance, wiping foam from his mouth and laughing merrily.

Spying the mages, he called out, "Hey! You're wizards! Can you get any magic from *this* moon?"

Dropping his pants, Dour Dave gave the shocked mages a good view of his backside, shining in the moonlight. He giggled, yanked up his pants and ran off around the corner, just as a Palanthian guard appeared.

"Still too much," said Grantheous, stroking his beard.

Fetlin noted the determination on his parchment and followed the mages to the Crow's Nest. Here they found the group of dwarves they'd been watching. In previous weeks, the dwarves groused and complained about the woes of the world, what with the gods departed and evil dragons lording it over the people of Ansalon. This night, however, the dwarves were cheerful.

"Dragons and Dark Knights and all the misery they

bring cannot last forever, my brothers," one was saying. "Nothing evil lasts forever! Lads, we must hold on. We will do our part to bring about change. Every little bit helps, eh?"

The other dwarves shouted in agreement. They raised their mugs to better times.

Grantheous and Stynmar looked at each other. They smiled. Stynmar wiped away a tear.

"Just right," Grantheous told Fetlin, who made a note.

Late that night, the two mages and their young apprentice sat around the table in their snug home in the presumably safe part of Palanthas, watching while Fetlin wrote out the spell neatly on a clean scroll. They had finally discovered the delicate combination of magic and beer that delivered the desired results. Grantheous was all for celebrating, but Stynmar looked a bit pensive.

Fetlin put on the teakettle then, seeing that the two wanted to be alone, went off to bed.

Grantheous poured out the hot water. "So, what is wrong, my friend?"

Stynmar wiped sweat from his chubby face and sighed. "I'm not sure we are doing the right thing."

"Not doing the right thing?" Grantheous was shocked. "You bring this up now? On the eve of our success?"

"Now is the best time to bring up any doubts," Stynmar replied. "This is our last moment, our final out. Once we cast the spell, there will be no going back."

"So what's wrong?" Grantheous asked.

"They have a right to know," said Stynmar, gesturing to the window.

"What are you talking about?" asked Grantheous, understandably confused.

"The people have a right to know what they are purchasing," said Stynmar. "If I were a customer and I found that a pair of mages were magicking my beer, I would be upset."

"Yes," said Grantheous, "and you would have every right to be upset *if*—and please mind that if—we were doing something ugly and nasty and evil to their beer. But Stynmar, we are helping these people." He poked at his knobby knuckles, voice lowering. "You heard those dwarves. We're doing good."

"Do you realize how many evil things have been done in the name of good?" Stynmar argued. "The Kingpriest, for example."

"Now, don't get started on the Kingpriest again. Listen, Stynmar," said Grantheous sternly, "since magic has started fading, some wizards have curled up their toes and died. Others are obsessed with scouring all of Ansalon for artifacts from previous ages, hoping to suck the magic from them. Stynmar, you are the only one who came up with this brilliant idea—take whatever magic we have left in these old bones and give it to the people. 'A pint of hope' you called it."

" 'A pint for hope, a pint for love, a pint for faith,' " said Stynmar wistfully. "Yes. I know that's what I said, but—"

"No buts!" said Grantheous. "After Dour Dave, I've seen enough butts for one night. You and I created this spell. With your knowledge of the arcane and my knowledge of spell components and herb lore, we have

7

created that pint of hope. Perhaps I should say gallons of hope."

"I still think that the customers should know," Stynmar protested.

"Why?" Grantheous slammed his fist on the table. "Why should they know?"

"Did you see the minotaurs?" Stynmar shuddered.

"Bah!" Grantheous dismissed the tickling with a wave of his hand. "A minor setback. It was an experiment. Much too much briarroot. Incredibly binding, that stuff. That was a test. We had to know the exact effect of extreme potency. The final batch will not be that strong."

"I know, it's just that—"

"Haven't you done something good for someone and kept it secret?" said Grantheous.

Stynmar nodded. "All the time. That's why I chose the White Robes." He sighed. "Back in the old days when colors had meaning."

"And you're still doing it," Grantheous stated. "What would happen if they did find out that we have injected the hope and exuberance of youth into their beer? You know laymen. They would be suspicious of the magic. The brew might quickly sour in their mouths, leaving them upset and angry, mistrustful of everyone."

Stynmar pondered this for a while, then conceded the point. Despite the deception, he was doing good. Surely that must outweigh everything else. Grantheous was right.

Grantheous winked at Stynmar. "And if we make a bit of steel on the deal, so much the better."

Stynmar blanched. Magic for money? That might be

all well and good for Grantheous, who had chosen the Red Robes of practicality, but White Robes were supposed to be charitable. Or did it matter anymore? Wasn't it now a question of survival?

"Stynmar, the end is inevitable," said Grantheous gently. "Perhaps a week from now, or a month from now, or a year from now. We have seen all the signs. The magic will die, and as it dies, we mages will be left naked and vulnerable to our enemies. We must do something!"

"I know. I know." Stynmar sipped his tea unhappily. "You are right. I just wanted to clear this up before we start on the new batch of beer."

Grantheous nodded. "Your dilemma is understandable, my friend, but perhaps, by spreading a little bit of magic into people's daily lives it may help. Somehow."

Even though the magic brew had been Stynmar's idea, Grantheous had been the one to make it happen. He pushed Stynmar into working to find the correct combination of ingredients and spell components and rituals to perform on the beer casks. Grantheous truly hoped that good would come of it, and if that good had a solid form and a steely ring and would tide them over in their waning years, he saw nothing wrong in that.

"Won't you miss it?" Stynmar asked.

"Yes," said Grantheous. "The day magic dies will be the day I die. Oh, not physically, but part of me will be laid to rest. I will never be the same. None of us will." He gazed into the distance, far beyond the walls of their humble kitchen, and lifted his teacup. "Here's to a ripe old age."

Stynmar raised his cup, then chuckled. "I was just thinking what our old mentor and master would say about our beer recipe."

Grantheous snorted in derision. "Master Gerald? That old coot. Always talking about the sanctity of magic and how we must treat it with reverence. Hogwash, I say. Magic is a tool. That is my motto. No need to pester the gods about it. You would never hear a smith praying over his hammer, would you?"

Stynmar shook his head. "No. I suppose not. Still . . ."

"Still," said Grantheous, glad to end the conversation, "it is a shame about Gerald's death."

"Quite so. Forced to work in the mines of Blöde. No magic to save him."

"May he rest in peace. And so should we."

Stynmar nodded. Tomorrow they would take their scroll, which young Fetlin had so expertly written out, and go to the warehouse where the rest of the barrels were stored. Once there, they would finish casting the spell that will help people view with hope.

Grantheous rubbed his hands. "Our future starts tomorrow."

The two finished their tea and went to their well-deserved rest.

As it turned out, their future started somewhere around midnight.

"We've been robbed!" Fetlin shouted. "We've been robbed!" He held a candle high with one hand and banged on Grantheous's door with the other. "Master Grantheous! Please wake! Master Stynmar! Wake up! We've been robbed!"

"What is this about, then?" Grantheous demanded,

emerging from his room, his beard done up in a fine meshed net.

"Robbed?" Stynmar said as he struggled into his robes. "Who would rob us? We haven't anything of value."

"The laboratory," cried Fetlin. "Come, quickly!"

The three raced down the stairs to the room Stynmar called the "laboratory," which consisted of a battered table and a couple of bookcases filled with dusty books. Fetlin pointed to a broken window. A soft breeze blew the curtain in, then sucked it outside and then, as if changing its mind, blew it back in again.

Fetlin pointed to a casket that stood open on the table. A broken lock lay on the floor.

"I'm sorry, Masters. There were more than fifty pieces of steel in there. Your life savings."

The two mages stared into the empty chest, then looked at each other. Stynmar went white. Grantheous staggered and had to hold onto the chair.

"I was getting up for a drink of water when I noticed the window. I remember quite clearly shutting it. I'm so sorry about the money—"

"It's not the money!" Grantheous cried, his voice shaking.

"The scroll," said Stynmar, quivering all over. "The scroll was in that casket!"

"Oh, is that all?" Fetlin relaxed. "I know that it will be a bit more work for me to rewrite it, but you and Grantheous have that spell memorized forward and backward, right?"

"True, Fetlin," said Stynmar slowly. "We do know that recipe *forward and backward.*" He laid emphasis on the words. "That is the problem. Read forward, the spell bestows the positive energy of youth on the recipient.

Makes him feel as if he were young again, with the whole world before him. Read backward—" He gulped.

Grantheous groaned. "Read backward, it allows the caster to snuff out joy, weaken hearts, destroy hope. And if the caster is strong enough, the spell could even cause premature aging! Turn a hopeful young man into an old, embittered one."

"An unfortunate byproduct," said Stynmar. "It was unavoidable."

"But," Grantheous added, "we never worried about it, because the scroll was always kept locked under a magic ward when not in use."

He pointed to the broken lock, decorated with silvery runes.

"But, Masters, the thief would have to be a wizard to break that—" Fetlin understood at last. "Oh! Oh, dear."

"We have to get that scroll back," said Grantheous.

———◆◆◆———

The two mages were all for running out into the night in pursuit of the thief. Fetlin convinced them to allow him to investigate, suggesting that they might want to use their magic to find out more about the theft. Stynmar brightened at this and, digging into the drawer, brought forth an amulet. He held it to the light.

"This is a bloodhound," he stated.

"I don't see how your birthstone is going to help us," said Grantheous irritably.

"I didn't say bloodstone. I said blood*hound*. It hunts magic. This will help us to track the scroll.

"It's glowing red. What does that mean?"

"Red means the scroll isn't here."

"I can see that for myself," said Grantheous, his lip curled in scorn.

"When we get close to the scroll, the amulet will glow green," Stynmar said.

"So all we have to do is walk the length and breadth of Ansalon and wait for the amulet to turn green? Wonderful," said Grantheous, turning back to patching the broken window.

"I guess I should have thought this out further," said Stynmar, peering thoughtfully at the amulet.

"Masters!" Fetlin shouted, running inside the laboratory. "I may have something! I discovered a most suspicious character lurking in our alley. At first, he claimed he hadn't seen anything, but after a bit of persuasion"—Fetlin blushed self-consciously—"he admitted that he did see someone tumbling out our window. The person hurt himself in the fall, apparently, for he limped as he ran away."

"Where did he go?" Grantheous demanded.

"Into the sewers, Masters," said Fetlin.

"Of course," said Stynmar sourly. "Where else would he go?"

The Palanthian sewer system was an excellent one, its tunnels leading to all parts of the city. They provided not only excellent drainage, but also an excellent highway for the local Thieves Guild.

"Well, there's nothing for it," said Grantheous, girding up his robes. "We must go after him."

"Sirs!" said Fetlin, alarmed. "I think the man is a plant. He was placed there to lure you into following. He could be leading you into terrible danger!"

"Then we don't want to disappoint him, do we?" said Stynmar.

Fetlin argued, but the two mages refused to listen to him. The sky was starting to lighten when they stalked out of their house, bent on recovering their scroll, armed with nothing but their waning magic, righteous indignation, and the glowing amulet. Fetlin was, himself, slightly better armed with a small crossbow.

The stranger still lurked in the alley. The moment the man sighted the two wizards, he took to his heels.

"Thank the gods he didn't go into the sewer!" said Stynmar, wiping sweat from his face.

"Hurry, Masters," said Fetlin, "if you want your scroll back, we must follow him!"

Not long ago, Fetlin had been known to the Palanthian authorities as Fetlin the Felon, which was, in a roundabout way, how he had made the acquaintance of the two mages, who were now his masters and friends. Fetlin knew all the streets, corridors, and alleyways of Palanthas. He had skulked, slinked, and sneaked through every one of them. Although he now walked the straight and narrow path of honesty, he was pleased to find that he had not lost his touch for fast and fleeting furtive movements.

Unfortunately, he could not say the same for his masters.

Grantheous and Stynmar had not a sneaky bone in their bodies. They zigged when they should have zagged. They ran into carts, fell over garbage piles, small children, and their own feet. So inept were they that the stranger was forced on more than one occasion to halt so they could catch up. Deeply embarrassed, Fetlin hoped none of his old gang saw him.

The chase, such as it was, led up a lane and down several alleys, a left turn, a right turn, and then forward in the direction of the warehouse district and the docks.

The sinister man paused at the end of a street. He looked to make sure that the three saw him, then dashed across the street to a warehouse, where stood a man in flowing black robes. The man walked up to the black-robed figure. The two conferred, then both of them entered the warehouse, closing the door behind them. The one in the black robe walked with a decided limp.

"That's . . . it," said Stynmar, coming thankfully to a halt. He was gasping for breath, puffing and wheezing. "That . . . Black Robe . . . stole . . . our scroll."

"Yes," said Grantheous, gulping air. "We should go . . . get it back."

The two looked at each other.

"When . . . we've rested," said Stynmar, brightening. "Look! A tavern!"

"The very place," said Grantheous. "We'll come up with a plan, Fetlin. You stay here and keep watch. Let us know if he leaves."

The two mages bolted for the tavern. They were in such a hurry that they did not notice the faded wood sign hanging above the entrance, nor did they notice the yellow pine floor stained with beer and blood.

Fetlin noticed. He would have warned them, but he'd been told to stand guard. He could only hope his masters figured it out before it was too late.

───◆───

The two found a table near the back, as far from the windows as possible.

"What do we do now?" Grantheous asked.

"Have a drink," said Stynmar. "I can't think when

I'm thirsty. My dear?'" he sang, summoning the serving wench.

"I'm not your dear, old man. What do you two want?" she demanded, placing one hand on her hip. "Prune juice?"

"Beer," said Grantheous with dignity. "Your best brew." He pulled out a steel coin, one of the few they had left.

She eyed it suspiciously, then flounced off. She brought back two tall, almost-clean flagons. Chasing and sneaking and intrigue was thirsty work. The mages drank deeply.

"Wonderful stuff," said Stynmar, chugging his flagon.

"Tastes vaguely familiar," said Grantheous, wiping the foam from his beard.

"We'll have another!" both called out.

"So what is our plan of action?" asked Grantheous.

Stynmar polished off his second beer. "We go in after him!"

Grantheous stared down into his own pint, as if the solution to the riddle lay somewhere in its bubbly, amber depths. "But we don't know for certain that the Black Robe stole it."

"He fits the description. I say we confront this mystery man and his sinister minion. See what they know."

"Threaten them, you mean?" said Grantheous.

"He stole from our home," said Stynmar. "We know he did. We go into the warehouse—"

"The warehouse across yonder?" asked the barmaid, plunking down two more beers.

"Yes," said Stynmar, looking at the barmaid in

adoration. "You are the loveliest thing I've seen in years, my dear."

"Bah! They all say that." But she looked flattered.

"Have you seen a black-robed man sneak into that building?" asked Grantheous.

"Have I seen him? The ugly bastard's been in here the past three nights." She twirled a string of hair, coaxing it to curl, and leered at Stynmar.

"What's he like?" Stynmar asked hesitantly. "Strong? Powerful? Fiery eyes? A dark smile?"

"Hah! He's older than you two, skinny and bony. I could wring his neck like a chicken."

"Many thanks, m'lady," Stynmar said as he slid forth the last of his steel coins.

She grinned, bit on it to make sure it was good, then returned to the bar.

"He is ancient!" said Stynmar.

"And he is weak," said Grantheous.

"We go in the front!" the two said together.

They raised their glasses and tossed back the remnants of their third pint.

"One more round before we take on the evil man who has stolen from us," said Grantheous.

"One more round before we take back that which is ours," said Stynmar.

"Masters!' cried a voice. "What are you doing?"

"It's Fetlin," said Grantheous. "Our trusted apprentice."

"Have a drink, lad," said Stynmar. "Great stuff. Almost as good as our own."

"Masters!" Fetlin groaned. "It *is* your own!"

The two looked down, looked up, and looked down again. Looked into their empty flagons.

Grantheous raised a ghastly face. "We have just

17

drunk three pints of our own enhanced brew."

"The strongest of the batch," Stynmar whispered in horror. "The Minotaur Tickler!"

"What do we do now?" Grantheous asked.

Stynmar rose. He reached out, grabbed the barmaid, and kissed her. "We go in the front!" he said.

Grantheous rose. He, too, kissed the barmaid. "We go in the front!"

"The gods help us," said Fetlin.

------◆◆◆------

Grantheous and Stynmar walked straight toward the warehouse. Fetlin did his best to stop them, but they were in no mood to listen.

"We will be neither diverted nor discouraged," said Grantheous.

"With or without magic, we will fight the good fight to the end," said Stynmar. "We must not allow our recipe to be used for evil."

"Damn right," said Grantheous, and hiccuped.

Fetlin checked the small crossbow and loaded his only bolt. Stynmar adjusted his white robes and then aided Grantheous in tucking away his chest-length beard.

"Best not to allow the enemy any advantage," he said solemnly.

Grantheous and Stynmar stopped in the middle of the street to do a few stretches, limbering up their calves, thighs, and chests.

"Nothing worse than getting a leg cramp in the midst of chasing down evil and pummeling it," said Grantheous.

Fetlin could have sat down and wept.

Exercises completed, the two strolled, with strides of importance and purpose, the final distance to the warehouse.

"Nothing can overcome the stuff our courage is made of," announced Stynmar.

"Hops and barley," Fetlin muttered.

The two stopped outside the warehouse door. They turned to one another and shook hands.

"We will win today," said Grantheous, exuding confidence.

Cool and levelheaded, Stynmar agreed. "Even if we die, we will win, for this day we fight Evil."

"Evil that is the bane of the existence of mankind—"

"Oh, get on with it, sirs!" Fetlin pleaded.

Stynmar took a few steps back and then, putting his shoulder into it, charged the door at ramming speed, just as the sinister man opened it.

———◆———

Stynmar was almost halfway across the warehouse before he could stop himself. Turning, regaining his dignity, he looked about to see that he was standing in a dusty warehouse confronting a black-cloaked old man who was laughing at him.

The old man had a face that hadn't laughed at much, seemingly—a face that was so wrinkled that his wide open, laughing mouth broke the face into mismatched laughing pieces. Stynmar closed his eyes, hoping that if he opened them again, the old man would turn out to be an illusion.

That didn't happen.

"Gerald!" Stynmar gasped. He sidled over to stand beside Grantheous.

Grantheous didn't say anything at all. He simply stared, his mouth open.

"Since when do you call your superiors by their first name?" growled Gerald, scowling. "You will call me Archmagus, as you used to do."

"Yes, Archmagus," said the two mages, cringing.

"We heard your were dead, Archmagus," Stynmar added.

"You sound disappointed," replied Gerald.

"Well, maybe a little," Grantheous admitted.

"No, no," Stynmar babbled, stepping on his friend's foot. "We're glad you weren't eaten by ogres—"

"Oh, shut up," snapped the Archmagus. He waggled a bony finger at them. "You two have been disobedient. Broken all the rules. Using magic to sell beer!" He snorted. "Come now. Speak up and be quick about it. I am not getting any younger."

"*You* stole our scroll!" Grantheous cried.

Gerald scowled. "Of course."

"But why?" Stynmar wailed. "We worked over a year on that recipe."

Gerald shook his head. "I don't care if you worked a hundred years on it. It was foolish, and I will not abide by such behavior." He adjusted his robes and, almost as if it were an afterthought, said, "And tell that scrawny apprentice to come out from his hiding place."

Fetlin crawled through a side window and stood there, crossbow in hand, feeling foolish.

Grantheous twisted his beard and shuffled his feet. His voice rose an octave. He might have been the young student again. "Master, begging your pardon, but what we do with our magic does not concern you."

"We want our scroll back. Now," said Stynmar with

a blustering attempt at defiance that was spoiled by the fact that he kept trying to suck in his sagging gut.

"Please," Grantheous added.

"You must give them back the scroll, sir," said Fetlin sternly, and he raised the crossbow.

Archmagus Gerald laughed. He hacked and wheezed until he nearly fell over. "Apprentice," he said to Fetlin, "the scroll is gone."

"What?" Simultaneous gasps of horror and shock.

Gerald wagged his finger again. "I tried to instill certain lessons into these two over-grown children, but all my teachings seem to have fallen on deaf ears. I should have held them back, to be honest."

Grantheous and Stynmar bowed their heads and shuffled their feet.

"That scroll was their work and my work," said Fetlin. "You have no right to it, Black Robe!"

"Black robe?" Gerald glanced down at his cloak. "Oh, this. Nonsense." He whipped off the black cloak to reveal dingy white robes. "I have every right to the scroll, Apprentice. I taught Grantheous and Stynmar everything they knew when they were no older than you."

"But that doesn't make you responsible for everything they do!" Fetlin protested.

"You'd think so," said Gerald with a sigh. "But life doesn't work that way. If they were to slay a dragon or solve the riddle of the dying magic, they would be proclaimed heroes. Would anyone say of them, 'Heroes taught by the great Archmagus Gerald himself'? No. Not a word. But if they had gone through with this dunderheaded plan, all you would hear would be: 'What do you expect? They were taught by that supreme idiot, Archmagus Gerald.' "

Grantheous and Stynmar both protested, but a cold look from Master Gerald sealed their lips.

"I told them this Immortal Truth many years ago, and I will repeat it again, for apparently these two are slow at learning. Apprentice," he said to Fetlin, "you listen, too, and remember. Magic is serious business to be pursued by serious-minded people. The last thing a proper wizard should do is go about magicking beer. And as for you"—he pointed a bony finger at Stynmar—"keep to the courage of your convictions. You knew this was wrong, yet you let yourself be persuaded by a mixture of self-righteous claptrap and filthy lucre.

"And you." The bony finger went to Grantheous. " 'I'll die when the magic dies,' he whines. Bosh! You've other talents, inner resources. I can't think what they are, right now, but you must have something."

Grantheous and Stynmar hung their heads.

"Wh-what did you do with our scroll, Archmagus?" Stynmar asked meekly. "Did you rip it up or burn it?"

Gerald shook his head. "No, no. I told you that I wanted to teach you a lesson." He folded his arms across his chest. "I cast the spell."

"Where? On what?" The two gasped.

"The Palanthian City well, of course," said Archmagus Gerald. He pointed to the window. "And it seems to be having quite an interesting effect."

That day, in the city of Palanthas, something strange and wonderful began to happen. It was as if the gods had cast down a fiery mountain of revelry, a Cataclysm of Hope, directly on the city of Palanthas.

And none could escape its effects.

Children ran through the streets, giggling and playing. Adults ran through the streets, laughing and cavorting with the children. The rich decided that they owned too much for their own good and opened their doors to the poor. Gnomes made sense. Kender emptied their pouches. Innkeepers erased debts. Politicians spoke the truth. Dark Knights of Neraka played hopscotch. Everyone began dancing in the streets. Mages forgot that their beloved Art was dying and joined in the celebration. With what little power they had left, they tossed magical fireworks into the air to mark the festivities with a shower of blue and gold sparks and images of water lilies and lilacs.

And while everyone was in the streets having the time of their lives, the members of the Thieves Guild sneaked into the empty houses—but only to return items they'd stolen in the past with little notes of apology.

------◆◆◆------

The two mages and their apprentice wended their way through the mob and finally, after much hugging and kissing and pounding on the back, Grantheous, Stynmar, and Fetlin reached their house. Racing inside, they bolted the door and, then and there, took a solemn vow to destroy their notes for their recipe for hope, distilled into the perfect pint.

The frenzied celebration ended at dawn. People rubbed their eyes and went to their beds. When they awoke, a day and a night later, they went back to doing what they had been doing, but each knew in his

23

or her heart, that for a brief moment in time there had been true peace in their world. It had left them with heartburn and sore feet, but also a more kindly feeling toward their fellow men, though no one could remember a thing about what had happened.

No one except for two aging mages and their apprentice, who, after witnessing the effects of their best intentions, resolutely refused to drink anything other than plain milk from then on.

Just in case.

THE END

Nancy Varian Berberick

Be careful, Jai," said the librarian, Annalisse Elmgrace.

Jai Windwild bent low over the worktable to see the parchment sheets better. Three were stuck together. He suspected they were held fast by the beginnings of mildew.

With great difficulty he bent to one knee so his eye was level with the table, but he held his position only for a moment. Gripping the edge of the table and gritting his teeth, he quickly levered himself up again. His shattered left kneecap had long since healed, or at least the bones had grown together again, though they had never knitted well. Sometimes, Jai felt the bones grinding against each other, the pain like lightning shooting through him. It had been his bad luck to break his kneecap in the dark years after the gods had left and taken magic with them. There had been no one to heal him, mage or cleric or sorcerer.

"Be careful, Jai," Annalisse murmured.

He said, "Yes, madam," but didn't look around. The

librarian cared only about her books, scrolls, and manuscripts. Fond though she might be of him, her best apprentice, her true love was for the Library of Qualinost. This Jai knew, and he didn't resent it.

"Ah, excellent," she said, as he slipped one page from atop another. "These pages are among our most precious treasures."

Jai waited, hiding a smile, for he knew what she'd say next. He'd heard those words a hundred times.

"We can't forget who we were, Jai. It's how we know who we are, and how we can guess who we will be."

He said, "Yes, madam," as he had a hundred times. Hearing her dictum over and again did not lessen his belief in the truth of it.

Head bent, Jai returned to his work, for another thing the librarian liked to say was this: "Results. I care about results, and the only result that matters to me, or should ever matter to you, is that we preserve our Library in the best order."

They did that, the Lady and all her scribes and catalogers and recorders and preservationists. Their devotion was to the Library of Qualinost, heart and soul, and each had sworn the quiet vow required upon entering the service of the Lady Librarian: There will always be a Library; there will always be History's Hoard in Qualinost.

There would always be, Jai thought, his fingers teasing the edges of the parchments, looking for a way between. Yet the collection was not growing. Few new books came to the library these days. Annalisse and her staff tended what books they had in their collection. They repaired old manuscripts, brightened faded illuminations, deepened the ink of an ancient script, tried to maintain the various rooms at the proper temperature and level of humidity to keep safe manuscripts that were penned as long ago as the Age of Dreams. In the days before the Dragon Purge that had been easier to do. Then there had been elven mages to weave spells to keep the climate of the great Library of Qualinost at perfect balance.

No matter the difficulty, this was the dearest work of Jai's heart, this careful preservation of a race's history in the face of war and a dragon's oppression. Most especially because of those things. Some elves stood against the dragon's overlord—some with their bodies armed in secret or, as Jai's own parents, standing as small links in a slender chain of shadowy resistance. Jai served in his own way, safeguarding the records of ancient elven heritage, the history to stand forever as a light against the darkness. In these days after gods, in these dragon days when House Cleric did not send its sons and daughters to temples but to libraries, Jai did holy work.

Beneath his hand now lay the Histories of Kings, the tales of all the rulers of the Qualinesti elves since fabled Kith Kanan himself had separated their race and led the people out of Silvanesti and into the forest. The thin page felt like silk. So did the breeze slipping in through the high window. Out that window the towers of Qualinost rose golden—lovely structures round which a great span of bridgework ran. Upon the bridge used to walk proud elven warriors who kept the kingdom and its gleaming capital safe.

But those were older times. Jai had been but an infant in his mother's arms, and the king had been

Solostaran. In these days of the dragon Beryl, all the Qualinesti had for leadership was Gilthas, the misbred son of the old king's daughter, Princess Laurana, and her half-elven husband, but he was little more than a puppet on the Dark Knights' strings. A marshal ran the kingdom now, a human named Medan, and no one doubted it was he who pulled the strings that made the weakling king dance.

At the Marshal's order, the Qualinesti warriors had been disbanded. The young king did not make any significant protest. Troubled with ill health, when he roused, it was to dance the nights away with pretty women and then lull himself to sleep with his own— by all accounts turgid—poetry. While Gilthas danced, Medan's black-armored Knights patrolled the silvery span round the elven city and sat in their squat, ugly barracks drinking, gambling, and making certain no elf doubted the ruthlessness of the green dragon's minions.

The conflicted dragon balanced between her hatred of elves and her love of the tribute Medan squeezed out of them.

Jai's hand shook, and his breath caught ragged in his throat. Very carefully, he slipped one thin sheet of parchment from atop the other, like brushing a shadow from a shadow.

Behind him, Annalisse said, "Don't work too late, Jai."

"I won't," he said, but they both knew he'd been long at his work and would be longer still.

She laughed. "Well, at least take time for your supper, will you?"

He said he would try, and the librarian said nothing more to discourage him from returning to his work.

Those sheets needed separating before more damage occurred, and Jai Windwild had the patience for the work.

In the purpling twilight, Jai lurched down the garden path and home to his supper. He owned no crutch or cane. He owned only a slanting gait. It was his, and if he did not run on sun-dappled forest paths anymore, he'd taught himself not to regret that too much. He went each day to better places, into the lands of legend and the proud realms of elven history. There, he would have been happy to spend all his days.

The first golden fireflies danced ahead of him into the darker shadows beneath the arbor at the front of his parents' little house. The heady scent of wisteria filled the twilight. Thick bunches of the amethyst flowers brushed Jai's shoulders as he passed. He caught the door latch, balancing a little against the jamb, and the door opened under his hand.

Face white as the lone pale moon, his father gestured him inside.

"Father, what—?"

Emeth Windwild shook his head and closed the door behind his son. "Come in," he said. "We must talk."

Jai saw his mother beyond his father's shoulder. She sat still as stone in a cushioned nook near the window that overlooked the little stream beside the house. Marise Windwild loved no place in her home better than this. She did not look out though. Her eyes darted from her husband to Jai, then to Emeth again.

Someone has died, Jai thought. The house had that

kind of stillness, the breath-held quiet when sorry news
has come. He thought of his father's uncle who lived
down in Mianost, a man so old it had been a wonder
for the last ten years that he'd wakened each morning.
When he turned to his father again, words of sympathy on his lips, he saw Emeth's hand trembling. That
trembling quieted every word Jai would have spoken.
He had never seen fear in his father. Not during the terrible Chaos War, when all the world seemed to run
mad, nor afterward when the dragon came. Not even
when his son had shattered his knee, nor when he
watched Jai struggle to walk again as healers warned he
would not win that battle.

"What's happened?" he asked.

Marise Windwild drew a breath, as though her son's
question freed her. She shuddered, and her eyes welled.
"Your father . . . he has been . . ."

She choked, tears spilled down her cheeks as Emeth
finished her sentence. "We have to go, Jai. We have to
leave the city. A message to one of the agents of the
resistance went astray."

Jai's heart slammed hard against his ribs. "Father . . ."
he said, whispering as though agents of Marshal Medan
crouched in the shadows. "Father, something that
implicates you?"

Emeth shook his head. "I don't know. A spy was
found in Medan's household, and right after, someone
disappeared—someone along the chain I work with."

Cold understanding chilled Jai's blood. His father
was like a number of others who aided the resistance:
only a small link in a chain. He would, now and then,
hand a note to a tailor, information disguised as an
order for clothing. He'd speak a word to one of the

bakers in the household of a woman known for her shy and retiring ways, something that only seemed to be about bread or the price of wheat. Intercepted, these seemingly innocent messages and others like them would appear to be nothing more than the daily business of an ordinary man. But in the right ears, they were more. No man or woman passing a word understood the whole of the message, but all the words together became news when they reached their destination. Somewhere, perhaps in a dark and deep forest glen, the leader of the resistance, that fierce warrior known as the Lioness, would see to it that a plan of the Marshal's would turn suddenly sour. Black-breasted Knights would die with elven arrows in their necks, and the elven warriors would vanish.

Simple men and women made this work, risking their lives and the lives of their families every day in the cause. Now a link in the secret chain had been broken and the delicate trust betrayed to the enemy.

"The damage has been done, Jai," his mother said. "One by one, those who had to do with this matter will leave the city. You, your father, and I will go at dawn, for we have a plausible excuse for leaving and will arouse no suspicion."

They would go to Mianost, the three of them. They would leave before first light, making sure that messages were left behind to say that Emeth's uncle was failing fast, that the family wanted to gather one last time to be with their venerable relative. Passes would be secured to take them safely out of the city and past the checkpoints manned by the Dark Knights. In an occupied city, not every elf was trustworthy, not everyone a partisan. The whole of the plan to escape was not revealed to everyone who had part in it. Each knew only what he must.

"This much your mother and I know," Emeth said, "for the rest, we will do what we're told when we arrive in Mianost. We are confident that once we reach Mianost there will be a way to true safety."

Stunned, Jai spoke without thinking. "Leave . . ." He shook his head. "I just got to the last page of the histories of the kings—"

"Damn the kings!" Emeth cried. "Jai, listen to me. We have no choice. If we don't leave tomorrow, we must take our chances here. I forbid that." His hard expression softened. He was not unaware of his son's love for his work. Indeed, he had fostered it. "I'm sorry, son. Events give us no choice. We must leave. I know very little, but if I were ever made to tell even that, others would be found out."

Jai heard that as though hearing his father's death sentence, for there was a place in Qualinost not so old as the lovely houses and homes of the elves. It dated only to the time of the dragon's conquest—a crouching, ugly building of sandstone, hard planes, and biting corners. Narrow windows, like suspicious eyes, glared round the square structure. Ironbound doors opened only at the order of one of Marshal Medan's soldiers. There the Knights were barracked, and below that place was an unlit hole of a room. In that chamber, no man or woman had ever survived the torturer's attentions with all secrets intact. The telling was the fee paid for death at last.

Quietly, steadily, Jai said, "You don't have to stay, father, but I don't have to leave."

Marise rose, turning her back on the window. "You do, Jai."

"But I don't know anything! I don't know who you talk to, when or where or what you say. You've always made sure of that, so there's no need for me to flee. I couldn't tell anyone anything if I wanted to. Go to Mianost and leave me behind—"

"No," said Emeth, and now his face wasn't so pale. His hands didn't tremble. "No, Jai. If Medan ever came to suspect us, he would take you to torture."

The Knights would break him bone by bone in that terrible place beneath the barracks. Jai's blood went cold. "But I would never— Father, you know I would *never*—"

Emeth held up a hand, a gesture Jai knew well. "No more, Jai. You would never tell, but you would be killed for your silence. That won't happen. You will come with us. No more will be said."

Jai took in a long, difficult breath. In his mind he heard the words of the Lady Librarian, spoken only today: *We can't forget who we were, Jai. It's how we know who we are, and how we can guess who we will be.* How could he abandon the holy work? Breathing again, he understood he could not, and he knew it would gain him nothing to continue to press his case with his parents.

"Jai," Marise said. "Son, go back to the Library."

He shook his head, not understanding.

"Have your supper and then go back. You always do at this time. It would seem strange to anyone who might be watching if you didn't tonight."

Jai looked to his father, who nodded slowly. "Yes, but be back before the moon is highest. Say nothing to anyone about our plans."

Jai did as he was bidden, and when he left his

parents' home, his were the usual lurching steps, his hitching gait well-known to his neighbors and to any minion of the Marshal who might be watching.

———————✦✦✦✦———————

Jai sat in silence among the histories of the kings. He had no plan for staying behind. He had not even the smallest thought or idea to turn into a plan. He had only his work, and this he did, trusting that some idea would spring to mind. So sunk in concentration was he that the sound of a footfall startled him. His heart jumped, and he looked up to see Annalisse standing in the doorway.

"Here you are," she said, entering the room. "I'm not surprised." She slipped a finger around the edge of the first page of *The History of Kith Kanan*. "You are the best of my students and the most faithful of my apprentices. Any of the others would have left this work for tomorrow." She fell silent a long moment, her silence like shadows creeping. "And yet, I don't know how many tomorrows there are."

Jai looked up. "Lady?"

"Don't you hear it, Jai?" She looked at the manuscripts and books, at the sturdy tables and high stools. She turned, looking out the door, and Jai knew she saw what he did: gracefully spiraling staircases leading down into winding corridors, reading rooms, the silent nooks where once scholars came to study, and the vast, high arched chamber in the middle of all, where the most prized pieces of the library's collection were displayed. There, in older days, elven kings had entertained poets and philosophers.

"Jai," she said, "This place has been a temple, in its time as sacred as any raised to gods. Treaties were signed here, laws enshrined here. All that we are is contained in the towers of this place. In the march of Medan's Knights I hear an ending coming."

The scent of ancient ink and venerable parchment filled the room. Jai looked around at the folios, the books, the tightly rolled scrolls all here for repair. Sometimes in quiet hours, when there were only these for company, Jai thought he heard the scratch of ancient quills, the voices of elves many long years dead as they spoke the words of an age-old ballad or tale. And yes, he could feel an end coming.

"Do you think the dragon will fall upon us, lady? Do you think . . . ?"

Annalisse shook her head. "Who can know? But I *feel* . . . something. Like the future knocking on the door of the present. I have spent so much time among the histories and the long tales that I often think I can see the pattern of how things work out. You feel it, too, don't you Jai?"

He admitted that he did. An end was coming. To a kingdom, to a long and many-leafed branch of a shining history . . .

Annalisse's eyes went soft and sad. "I feel something else, a closer ending. Are you leaving, Jai?"

Shock ran like lightning along Jai's nerves.

Annalisse shrugged, a melancholy smile tugging at the corners of her mouth. "Well, I see how you look around tonight, how your fingers linger on everything—table, pen, page. You look like a man who has another road to take."

Fear made him shiver even as he scrambled to think

of something to say. In the end, he reached for a portion of the truth, hoping his voice didn't shake.

"Madam, I'm sorry. I would have told you in time. My father has had word that his uncle who lives in Mianost is calling the family to gather."

A cloud chased across her brow, then vanished. "Ah, that's a shame, but it has been a long time coming, hasn't it?"

Jai nodded. "It has."

"Well"—she sighed—"I'm going to miss you. How long will you be gone?"

Jai said he wasn't certain. "There is the gathering of the family, and then . . ."

And then they must wait for his father's ancient uncle to die. After that, the funeral rites, a period of mourning, and the settling of the will. All this, his pause asked Annalisse to understand, and she nodded gravely as though she did.

"When do you leave?"

For the barest moment, Jai hesitated, feeling he'd said too much already, not knowing how he could have said less.

"I'm not sure," he lied. "Mother said something about making an early start. Father said he had some small matters to tend to."

His lie sat like truth. He knew it because Annalisse's grave expression never changed. With his next breath, however, Jai spoke sudden words unplanned, and these were not lies.

"And," he said, glancing causally away as if this were a minor detail, "I don't know that I'll stay in Mianost as long as my parents will. After my uncle's death, that is. The business of his will and the disposition of his home . . . well, that's best handled by my father. I might well come back here."

He said this, and it was all he could do not to smile. He'd found his plan. He had, for he'd said aloud that he would return, and if he did not . . . why, that would look suspicious indeed.

Briskly Annalisse clapped her hands, as one does who doesn't like to dwell on sadness anymore. "Well! Let's make use of you while you're still here. There's no reason we can't at least begin to catalog the repair needed on the first page of the Histories tonight."

Jai agreed there was no reason, and they spoke of his departing no more.

When he returned home, Jai let his parents know he'd been obliged to say something to Annalisse about their leaving Qualinost, and he told them what other thing he'd said. About Annalisse, they seemed to understand that he'd had no choice. They agreed that he'd handled the matter well. About his decision to return to Qualinost after sufficient time had passed, his parents were not pleased. His father looked like a man being blackmailed. His mother quietly wept. Neither could change what he'd done.

———◆●◆———

The Windwild family left Qualinost as planned. The night's darkness was just going to gray, the sky yet possessed a few stars, and the moon had only an hour before sinking into the west. Like people who had nothing to hide, the Windwilds left the city riding—Marise upon a pretty roan mare, Emeth on a tall black gelding, and Jai astride a docile little gray that followed his mother's mare peacefully. At Marise's suggestion, they made the most of their pretense, taking care to greet those few who saw them and to say they were going to Mianost prepared to mourn a kinsman. At the black-breasted guards who walked the four spans of the silver bridge that girded Qualinost they did not look.

One of those who stopped them on their way was Annalisse, the Lady Librarian. Outside her home, which was not far from her beloved library, she looked up from a bench in the garden at the sound of bridles ringing. She went out from the garden and took Emeth's hand in hers, speaking quietly of her wish that his uncle pass peacefully from the world. "But not," she said, "until he experiences the joy of seeing all his kin come to gather around him, the old and the young. Travel in peace, Emeth, and keep well."

"You, too, old friend," Emeth replied quietly. "And we will meet again."

Her sapphire eyes luminous in the fragile light, the smallest of smiles tugging at the corners of her mouth, Annalisse agreed that they would.

Hearing her say so, seeing her smile, Jai suspected what he had not before: the Lady Librarian was part of the resistance.

"Mother," he whispered, his voice a little tinged with surprise.

"Hush," Marise murmured, and that one soft word was all the confirmation Jail needed.

———◆◆◆———

The small shady path at the head of a winding forest trail was known best to the folk of Mianost who liked to slip away from parents or spouses to keep a lover's tryst. There, in the late afternoon, Jai and his parents met a tall, lithe woman with flashing eyes so palely blue as to look like diamonds. She wore her golden hair in a thick braid. Her clothing was of gray and green and butternut, so that, seeing her move, one had the impression of sun-dapple and shade and fern. Jai's heart rose to see her, for she was lovely like a wild thing, quick and canny and dangerous.

She stepped toward Emeth, and though he was surprised by her sudden appearance, he greeted her courteously. Jai noticed that she did not offer her name, and his father did not offer theirs.

"Greetings, traveler," she said to Emeth.

"Warrior, I greet you," Emeth replied.

Warrior!

"Father . . ." Jai said, suddenly uneasy.

Emeth hushed him with a gesture. To the newcomer, he said, "I hadn't expected to see you so soon."

"Nor I you. There's no going on to Mianost, Emeth. A Dark Knight has been seen farther up the trail."

Jai's heart lurched. Like his parents, he darted frightened glances into the forest shadows.

"It's all right," said the woman. She put a calming hand on the neck of Emeth's horse, which had begun dancing uneasily, scenting his rider's fear. "I don't know if he's looking for you, Emeth, but we can't take the chance he is, or even that he's alone."

Emeth nodded, as though he understood something his wife and son did not. Marise voiced the very question in Jai's mind. "How will we get past the Knight?"

The lady warrior hooked her finger through a golden chain hung round her neck. From her blouse she lifted something bright green. Jai had the swift impression of a talisman of flashing emerald, the stone shaped like a leaf half furled. She dropped the talisman so that it hung outside her blouse, the stone sitting at the V of her rough gray shirt, the place where her breasts rose.

"Magic," she said. "If we're lucky."

"Father?" Jai said again, but he didn't give voice to his doubts. The newcomer looked up at him, right into his eyes. She raised a brow and smiled, and Jai found himself not looking into her eyes but at the emerald nestled on the woman's breasts.

The wind changed, shifting so that it was at the woman's back. Jai caught her scent and could think of nothing else. His mind filled with images of the forest, of oaks and elms and trees less tame than those in the orchards of Qualinost. Clinging to her hair and skin and clothing was the perfume that comes from beyond the bridges of Qualinost, from outside the city and deep in the forest where the glens are shrouded in shadow and the streams run nameless into rivers long secret.

"Let me assist you," she said to Jai, holding the gray horse still and reaching a hand to him.

Words of protest rose in Jai's heart at the thought of this tall, lovely woman handing him down from the horse as if he were a child. He said nothing, however, for he found himself foot to ground before he remembered moving. Indeed, his parents stood each on one side of him, his mother's face a little paler than it had been, his father's settling into lines of peace. Jai's heart kicked hard against his ribs. He gasped for breath. Once, twice, and then the woman put a hand on his shoulder.

"Easy," she whispered. "It's like a dream." She came very close, and his eye fell on the emerald again. She laughed, a low, soft chuckle. "Just like a dream."

And it was, the kind of dream where people did not move but suddenly found themselves in other places with no understanding of how they got there.

Jai drew breath to speak, but she warned him to silence. With that warning he realized she hadn't really spoken to him at all, not with lips and tongue. She spoke into his mind.

The magic is unstable, she said, *keep still and trust. Concentrate on being still.*

Trust! That trembled in him just as his heart did, and he wondered if that quaking heart would be enough to cause the magic to collapse or worse, to change into something the woman couldn't control. Again, she laughed. Her voice sounded like jays in the trees, raucous and challenging. Suddenly, it had nothing to do with jays at all, but became the voice of a storm. Wind and rain and driven leaves whirled along the ground.

Jai cried out—or tried to. He had no breath, no words, and no sight. The last sense to fail was his hearing, and the last thing he heard was his mother's voice, frail and thin in the storm-wind of magic, crying, "Jai! Emeth! Hold on to—!"

"Hey," said a voice, low and very deep.

Jai groaned, and then he shut his mouth. He simply lay still, in pain. He must have fallen hard. His chest hurt as if all the air had been blasted out of his lungs and only recently returned. His head hurt. Worse, pain screamed through his knee. The joint felt as if it were on fire. The ruined muscles that once supported him twitched feebly.

"Hey." A finger poked him, once and then again. "Hey! Can you hear me?"

Jai opened his eyes to see a dwarf crouching near, a glowing lantern on the ground beside his knee.

A dwarf. *How?*

The lantern light flickered and moved, but not like a candle's flame. It pulsed. The dwarf leaned closer, his bearded face so near Jai could see the blue flecks in the irises of his dark eyes. "I said can you hear me?"

Jai closed his eyes again. "I'm not deaf."

The dwarf grunted. "That's good." He kept silent for a heart's beat, then, "Your ears work. How about the rest of you?

Jai's belly clenched, but he refused to groan as he moved his leg. Pain lanced through the knee, shooting up his leg to his hip, yet in that pain he found a measure of comfort. Even all these years later, he remembered what broken bones felt like, he remembered how ripped muscle screamed and burned. His breath eased through clenched teeth. He had broken or torn nothing.

He opened his eyes again. "I'm all right."

"If you say so." The dwarf shrugged, sitting back on his heels, deeper into the shadows beyond the lantern light. In his muscular left hand he gripped the haft of a throwing axe. "I'm Stanach Hammerfell. You're Jai Windwild, I take it."

Jai frowned. "How did you know . . . ?"

Relaxing his grip on the axe, Stanach nodded toward Jai's knee. "I've been told to keep an eye out for you—a lame elf named Jai."

For a long silent moment, the dwarf looked at the

ruin of Jai's knee, the poorly knitted bones, the swelling of new bruises. He gave Jai a sidelong glance as to say, *Well, that'd be you, wouldn't it?*

But aloud, he only said, "You might like to know your mam and your da are all right."

"My what?"

Stanach looked at him as if he'd had a few wits jogged loose by the fall. "Your mother and father," he said with exaggerated care. A sly smile tugged at his lips. "You were concentrating on something when the lady did her magic, eh? That pretty emerald in its pretty nest. Not concentrating on keeping still and trusting, which is what you were supposed to do. Damn magic. I hate it when they have to use it. It's always me got to go searching miles of tunnel for the ones who fall out of it too soon or too late."

"Where am I?"

"Underground." Stanach sat back again, and this time Jai noticed that his strange eyes changed, as a dwarf's will when the light recedes. The irises opened wide, all black now, no blue flecks to be seen. "Underground, and nearer to Qualinost than Thorbardin."

Thorbardin?

At Jai's puzzled expression, the dwarf nodded. "Thorbardin, which is where you're headed. Didn't they tell you that?"

Flatly, Jai said, "No one tells anyone all of anything about escape plans."

"All right, then, I'll tell you. I suppose you or your parents did something to catch the eye of the dragon's underlings, yes?" Jai let his silence be the answer. "Thought so. Well, you're near the route you elves take when you're leaving Qualinost in the dark of night.

43

Dwarves have been delving a tunnel between Thor-bardin and Qualinost —"

"Delving? Why?"

Stanach shrugged. "Kings don't tell me why they do things. The elf-king and our thane put their heads together one day and said, 'Delve!' and off we went, digging a road between Qualinesti and Thorbardin."

Plainly disbelieving, Jai said he doubted Gilthas would look up from his poetry long enough to make such a plan.

"Really? Well, likely you know him better than I do."

Jai, who knew the king not at all, said no more.

"This place is a work-tunnel. We stashed gear and tools here when we were digging out this part of the main tunnel. The work began at Thorbardin, and once the job is done, there'll be a dark-road that starts about five miles from Qualinost and ends right at Thorbardin's cellar door. Till then there are ways into the finished part. Magic's one of them, and hunting you lostlings who fall out of the spell the gods know where gives me a way to pass my days. But the easier way is through one of the secret entrances." Stanach looked up, no sign of humor in his blue-flecked dark eyes. "Why did the lady warrior not lead your party to the Mianost entrance?"

Bitterly, Jai told him what had happened, and how it ruined his plans.

"Your plans? Promising as you say you are, there's got to be more scribes than you in Qualinost. I suppose they can find someone else to patch up the parchments now that you're gone."

"It's not about patching, it's about keeping." Jai put his palms flat to the stony floor and pushed himself up to sit. "I have to get back to Qualinost."

Stanach's left hand dropped to the haft of his axe. He looked right into Jai's eyes. "No. You're here now—"

"You don't have to take me. You don't have to do anything but point me in the right direction. I'll get there myself."

"No, you won't. Even if you could manage it, I can't let you. No one roams the tunnels alone. You're coming with me, and you're going to Thorbardin."

The hair prickled on the back of Jai's neck. A cold bleakness lay behind the dwarf's eyes, like the far stretch of a winter plain.

"And besides, what's to keep, back there in your Qualinost? A few books and papers, some old songs . . . ? For how long? Might be your homeland is still in one piece tonight. Maybe it will be tomorrow, but the end is coming, and no one's thinking it'll be a long time happening."

In his low deep voice, Stanach Hammerfell said much the same thing Annalisse had. The echo chilled Jai to the heart. Was there nothing, then, but ending? Was there nothing but the road away from the golden kingdom and all the long years of elven glory?

There had to be more!

A sound, like far-off thunder, rumbled in the stone beneath him, vibrating through his spine and painfully in his knee. Jai looked around, seeing the strange pulsing lantern-light shining on a high ceiling of stone, roughly hewn, and piles of rocks shoved up against the glistening walls.

"What's that noise?"

"Worms." Stanach said.

"Worms? How could worms—?"

Stanach waved the question away. "Better showing

than telling." He peered closely at Jai, then stood and offered his hand. "You reckon you can get up and walk?"

Jai grasped Stanach's hand. The dwarf had a surprising strength. He stepped back and pulled Jai right up to his feet. He bore Jai's weight while he found his balance and didn't seem to feel it at all. When Jai was steady again, Stanach handed him the lantern. Jai almost dropped it. The light moved like it was alive—and then he saw something living did reside in the little lantern cage.

"Grubs," Stanach said. "Well, larvae. Hold steady. You drop it, you'll likely kill it."

Jai held the lantern at arm's length, watching the fat, eyeless larva pulse, its glowing body casting as much light as an oil lamp would.

Stanach picked up his axe and slid the haft into his belt. He settled the broad belt round his waist, checking to see that all was there: knife, fat leather waterbottle, and a coil of rope. When he took the lantern back, Jai had a good look at him. He was a dwarf in his middle age, not more than two hundred years, likely a decade or so less. He stood as high as Jai's chest. His beard was black, his hair silvering at the temples and long enough to fall over the collar of his shirt. Thick in the neck, thick in the shoulders, he looked like one who knew his way around a hammer and anvil.

"You're a forgeman," Jai said.

"Used to be."

Even as he said so, Jai realized that Stanach had done everything with his left hand, holding the axe, lifting the lantern, hauling Jai himself to his feet. His right hand hung at his side, the fingers twisted and withered. The dwarf stood braced, as though waiting for the inevitable, for Jai to mumble an apology for noticing. When Jai said nothing, he relaxed.

"All right, elf," he said, "we have some traveling to do, and it's going to be a hard old walk. You up to it?"

"Walking to where?"

"We'll catch up with the work detail. That's a good two miles out. They can send a runner back along the tunnel to Thorbardin and let your mam—" He cocked his head, and offered a lean smile—"your mother and father, know all's well with you."

"Thorbardin. How far are we from there?"

"Farther than I like to be. We're standing about halfway between there and Qualinost. There's a crossway up ahead. Once we get there it's north to Qualinost, or as near to Qualinost as we get till we hit stone. From there, it's clear south to Thorbardin. You came in—or *tried* to come in—about a mile north of where we are now, near Mianost. We'll pass it on the way, but you won't see much. We hide those ways in and out pretty well.

"Come on, now. We'll make the camp, and then you can rest."

Bleak dwarf, rough as stone. His strange eyes seemed to see only winterscapes, only lifelessness and ending. But there are endings, and there are beginnings, Jai thought. Out from winter, spring. He didn't know where he'd find his beginning, that spring again. With all the world seeming to want to end around him, he couldn't imagine. He did know, though, that he would not find it in Thorbardin. His heart told him that.

No, he decided. He wasn't going to Thorbardin. He was going back to Qualinost, and the first thing he could do about that was get rid of the dwarf.

It was, as Stanach had said, a hard old walk through the tunnel. Once they turned south the going became rougher, rising and falling in ways a man able to stride out and not worry about his footing wouldn't notice. Jai felt every rise and dip, every rock on the underground road. He had a sense of walls rising high, curving to a rough ceiling, but he didn't look around much. He couldn't take his eyes from the ground. Stanach kept the light near, for the farther they went the rougher the road became.

"They haven't made the second pass yet. It's going to be hard going. Hold on to me if you want, elf."

Jai didn't, and didn't even thank him for the offer. He concentrated on the way ahead, lurching along unassisted. He was looking for something, an opportunity.

They went that way for a time. Jai looked at the walls when they stopped to rest. Stanach called them the ribs of the tunnel, and he said the ceiling was the spine, the floor the belly. Like we've been swallowed by some horrible beast, Jai thought. At these ribs, spine, and belly he looked, trying to find some sign of the Mianost entrance. He saw nothing but stone. All the while the earth vibrated beneath them, the rumbling growing stronger the farther they went. The vibrations rattled Jai's knee, sending fiery lightning lances shooting through the joint.

"That *can't* be worms," he said, his words coming through gritted teeth as he leaned up against a damp wall, again forced to rest.

"If you say so."

Lanterns hung at intervals on the walls, settled snugly in iron brackets. By their glowing light Jai saw the tunnel here was strewn with debris, boulders half as high as Jai stood, many looking like they'd been flung to the ground by some giant hand and shattered.

To balance, he put his hand on one of the piles. His fingers closed round a stone the size of his fist. His belly clenched suddenly. That might be one way to get rid of the dwarf.

"Larvae?" Jai said, speaking of the lanterns, getting a good grip on the stone.

"Lots. We're almost there." Stanach untied the leather water bottle from his belt and held it out. Jai let go the stone and took what he offered. "It's not water. Go easy."

Jai would have known what the bottle held the moment he unstopped the mouth. The pungent odor of dwarf spirits stung his nose. He took a sip, the liquor burning past his lips and down his throat, finally sitting like fire in his belly. Standing there, the spirits afire inside him, he imagined he felt pain ease. He took a step, his knee wobbled beneath him, but for the moment it didn't hurt.

"Just the lying spirits," Stanach said. In the light and the shadow, he looked like he knew those lies and maybe had believed them for a while. He took a swig, then wiped his mouth with the back of his hand and returned the leather bottle to his belt. "Rest. It isn't far to the work camp now—just beyond the bend. There'll probably be a healer there to slap some poultice or something on your knee. It won't help the pain, but if anything's inflamed, it might help that."

Again, Jai felt the stone beneath his hand. Again, he closed his fingers around the roughness of it. "You don't sound like you have a lot of faith in healers."

Stanach grunted. "Magic was better, but gods come and gods go, and this latest going of theirs isn't the first. I had the bad luck to get my fingers broken the time before, during the War of the Lance, while the crowd of them was shuffling around on the doorstep, trying to decide whether to

49

stop by again. Friends tried to help . . ." Again, he shrugged. "Healer-craft is good for cuts and boils and colds, but you probably notice it doesn't do much for the big things."

The ground beneath their feet shook again. Stanach braced with his feet planted wide. Jai caught his balance against the wall. From behind came voices, several shouting in Dwarvish. A great rumbling filled the tunnel, sounding like thunder. With gestures and words Jai couldn't hear, Stanach made him understand that he should get right up against the wall.

"Second pass!" he shouted, his words sounding small and distant. He pointed back the way they had come, and Jai's blood ran cold. He gripped the stone now.

Something huge lumbered through the tunnel from the direction he and Stanach had just come, something nearly six feet thick through the middle, and so long Jai couldn't see the end of it. It came hungry, eating all the stone and rubble in its path, chewing boulders with the same placidity as a cow chewing grass in her green pasture.

"Worm!" Stanach shouted.

His heart pounding, Jai thought the last thing you could name that creature was *worm*. And yet it did look like an out-sized worm, its hide glistening with slime in the light of lanterns, advancing as worms do, slithering in a gigantic sort of way. It had horns, and atop its back a basket sat, maybe where the neck was if, indeed, it had a neck. In that basket a dwarf stood, thick leather reins in his hands.

"Attached to the horns!" Stanach roared as the worm came nearer and the sound of the earth rumbling beneath it grew even louder. "See!"

Jai saw, and he understood that this was how the handler in the basket directed the creature, even as other dwarves jogged along beside it, poking it with long sticks when it paused in its journey or lumbered off and threatened to eat its way through the wall. Stanach warned Jai to keep still, not for fear that the worm would harm him. The thing had no eyes and no interest in anything but eating its way to some dwarf-directed destination, but it would be easy to slip in the slime of the worm's passing and fall beneath the beast.

"Then," he said, "we'd be sending to Thorbardin for sponges to sop up your remains."

The worm passed to the shouting of a parade of dwarves, hooting and poking to keep the worm in a more or less straight line. None of them looked to the side or even seemed to be aware they passed one of their fellows and an elf. It was worth the life of each of them to keep their eyes on the worm and keep the worm itself moving. It was a slow passing, like a mountain strolling by. Stanach stood a moment looking after it.

Jai pushed away from the wall, getting a better grip on the stone in his hand. Somewhere along the way he'd find the Mianost entrance. It wouldn't be an easy thing alone in the tunnel, trying to find his own way. Adrenaline shot through him in the instant he made his decision. In a brilliant moment of clarity he saw just where he would bring the stone down on Stanach's skull—there, in the center.

He cocked his arm and the dwarf turned, his own arm coming up with arrow swiftness. Stanach grasped his wrist so hard that Jai's fingers went numb.

"Now why," the dwarf said, his words edged with ice, *"why* would you want to do that, elf?"

Stanach's grip tightened. Pain shot through Jai's wrist to his elbow, to his shoulder.

"Drop the stone," the dwarf whispered, "or I'll break your wrist."

The stone fell, but not by an act of will. Jai's fingers had no feeling in them to hold. Stanach eased his grip, a little, but didn't release Jai's wrist. "Answer me. Why?"

In the pulsing light and the shifting shadows, Jai took a long breath against the pain in his arm. "I'm not going to Thorbardin. I'm going back to Qualinost."

Stanach laughed, a hard, harsh bark. "You are, are you?" He looked pointedly at Jai's knee. "And how do you reckon you're going to get there?"

Jai hated him in that moment. His blood burned with hate. "I'll get there walking."

"By Winter Night, maybe." The dwarf's eyes darkened. "You're a fool to go back up there now. Your people are running these tunnels as fast as we can build them, as fast as we can bring them in. Soon there'll be nothing for you to go back to. Nothing."

"You're wrong! Up there is all there ever was of us. Every tale of who we are, every song, every story, all the history of us. It's up there, and—" Jai stopped, shivering. "And if all that were lost, Stanach, here is one more tale that needs telling. The tale of the end. Someone needs to know how it ends, so they will know how to begin again."

Stanach let go his wrist. Jai looked at the flesh there, already bruising, then he looked away.

"Please, let me go. What's it to you, Stanach? Nothing, so just . . . let me go."

As swiftly as he'd turned before, that swiftly did Stanach turn again. His eyes took Jai's and held them. "I *hate* being here. I hate being out of Thorbardin. I was too long away in older days." He glanced at his ruined right hand, then away. "I came home broken and saw the city and the kinship broken after that. I hate being out of Thorbardin."

"Why? If you leave the city, will it fall apart without you?"

"No. No, if I leave the city, I fall apart without it."

He looked away. Jai saw nothing of his face, his blue-flecked dark eyes. He saw no sign of what the dwarf was thinking or feeling, only one small twitch of his thick shoulders.

"All right," Stanach said, his eyes still on some point south, some point in the direction of Thorbardin. "All right. It's all falling apart, elf, but if you want to stand in the ruin, off you go."

You, he said. He bent and picked up something from the shadows: a broken stick one of the worm-handlers had discarded. With one swift stomp of his booted foot, he sheared off the splintered end. The stick he handed to Jai, with two words of advice. "Use it."

Then he walked away, back south toward Thorbardin. Jai smiled, following. Before Thorbardin, or even the crossway, they would come to the way out of the tunnel, the way through and up to Mianost. It was all right. He could manage the walk. He'd come this far.

He was bleeding by the time he got there—cuts from falls, scraped hands, torn knees, his cheek ripped raw by a rock. He was bruised, and the muscles and bones of his knee screamed. He fell again, he didn't think he could get up again, but Stanach said, not gently, "Come on, elf. You said you could do it. So do it."

"Shut up," Jai snarled, and he wasn't sure it was

only sweat running down his cheeks. "Shut up and give me your hand."

Stanach did, gripping hard, laying bruises on top of bruises as he hauled Jai to his feet. Wordless, he put the stick back into Jai's hand, and he pointed to the stone wall, the rocky ribcage of the tunnel. "There," he said, but Jai saw nothing other than worm-chewed stone and moisture running down in rivulets made golden by the lantern light.

Stanach touched the wall, just a gentle nudge, and the stone swung inward—a slab as long as an elf is tall, and as wide. It moved silently, smoothly, and there was no magic attached to it, just good dwarven engineering. When Stanach held the lantern close to the entrance, he illuminated rough stone stairs winding upward. He did not, however, illuminate anything that might remotely resemble guards or any kind of watch.

"Not at this end," Stanach said. "The guards are above, and they're your folk. We delve; they ward."

They stood quiet a moment and then Stanach said, "That's your last climb up. Just hang around looking suspicious and some elf or another will find you and fetch you home."

Jai drew breath to speak, then held it. Thin light slipped suddenly down the stairs, pale and silvery. A whiff of rain drifted in on a vagrant breeze. A woman's voice wafted softly down from above, speaking in Elvish. The voice sounded familiar, distant whisper though it was. When it came closer, Jai knew it. Annalisse!

Another party of refugees was coming through, but why was Annalisse with them? His heart sank. Had she fallen foul of the Dark Knights? Had the Marshal learned of her connection to the resistance?

Annalisse's footfalls came closer. Another followed her, this one's tread heavier. A dwarf, Jai thought, and then he heard the chime of ring mail, the clank of armor.

"I told you the Marshal would want to know about this," Annalisse said coolly. "This is no cave. This is a way down into the earth."

The next voice Jai heard was human, and he knew the clanking armor was black, the wearer a man whose soul was owned by the green dragon. "Damn. That's dwarf craft."

Whistling, something dark and swift flew past Jai's face. Stanach's throwing axe made a terrible sound as it bit deeply into the throat of the Knight. The man made no sound at all but for that of his body clanking down the stairs. Shoving Jai back, tumbling him to the stony floor, Stanach leaped for the corpse and kicked his axe free of the Knight's neck.

Shouts and cursing erupted in the stairwell as three more Knights ran down the steps.

Jai got the stone wall behind his back, the cold damp rock biting into his flesh as he pressed close, levering himself to his feet. Stanach's voice swore in the name of a god years gone away.

"By Reorx! Close the door, elf!"

Close it? Close him in with the Knights and the traitor? And what? Howl for help? Beneath him, the earth vibrated. No matter how loudly he shouted, no one would hear him above the thunder of worms eating through stone. Jai kicked the door open wider and got a good grip on his stick. The first Knight to come through got his feet tangled in the stick and, while he was struggling to rise, his skull shattered by a two-handed blow with a rock.

Bone shards flew up from the broken skull, brains

and blood seeped through. Jai's stomach turned, his gorge rose.

"Close the damned door!"

A second Knight came through, staggering. Blood poured from his mouth and nose. He tripped over his fellow and Stanach's axe stuck quivering in his neck above his mail shirt.

Jai dropped his stick and planted his hands on the pile of corpses, ignoring the stench of blood and death. Balanced on one leg, he yanked the axe out of the Knight's neck and hobbled for the doorway. From the shadow within the doorway, he trembled to see Stanach standing on lower ground, three steps below a burly Knight—undefendable ground—and the glinting tip of a keen edged sword was dipped to touch his neck. Above the Knight, Annalisse stood. Her face was cold as the white moon on an icy night.

"Kill him," she said.

Icy fear washed through Jai. In his scribe's hand was a weapon that would do Stanach no good. Neither could he charge up the stairs to the dwarf's rescue. He grinned suddenly, and he moved, flinging himself into three lurching steps, the stick in his hand. With a cry to distract the Knight, Jai hit Stanach hard behind the knees.

Roaring curses, Stanach fell backwards. The Knight, just thrusting his sword, lost his balance and pitched headlong down the stairs. Annalisse cried out as Stanach staggered to his feet and took the axe Jai thrust into his hand. He finished the Knight in the space of a breath and turned toward Annalisse, arm cocked to throw the axe.

"No!" Jai cried.

For one furious instant, Stanach didn't understand.

Jai put a hand on his arm, holding his throw. "She's betrayed the resistance, Stanach. We have to know if there are others."

His words hung between the dwarf and the Lady Librarian, the question unanswered.

"Lady," he said, and he hadn't meant to speak gently, yet he did. "Why?"

She closed her eyes, as one in pain. "I did it for the library."

"The library? I don't understand."

Eyes shut, she drew a tight, pained breath. "I went to Medan and made a bargain. I told him I had something he wanted, if only he would promise to preserve the library. Through all that's to come, he must keep it safe."

On the evening of his last night in Qualinost, she'd done that. For a fleeting moment, Jai saw in her icy expression what he'd seen then—that longing look, that sense of loss's shadow as she looked around at her precious hoard of manuscripts and books, songs and fables and legends, all the golden history of the Qualinesti. She'd bargained her soul for the Library of Qualinost, and into the bargain thrown elven and dwarven lives.

"You knew before I did that our family was leaving Qualinost."

"Yes. I didn't know where you were going, but you told me that."

She'd set a Knight to linger around Mianost. When the refugees didn't arrive, the Knight had no way to follow farther. Annalisse, however, didn't give up so easily. She had more patience than Knights. She had, she believed, much more at stake.

Tonight there were, she said, with the first dawning of

shame in her voice, four Qualinesti warriors dead in the forest, not far from the entrance to the tunnel. "But we took a vow, Jai, you and I. There will always be a library. There will always be history's hoard in Qualinost."

"We did, lady," he said, the words like dust in his mouth. "But we took it to serve a truth, not a building." Softly, he gave her back her own words, often spoken in the quiet precincts of her library. "We can't forget who we were. It's how we know who we are, and how we can guess who we will be. My lady, with your bargain, you risked making us cowards before all who would look back at us. You risked ending our history in shame.

"It isn't the collection that matters. It is the *history* that matters."

He turned his back on her. He didn't look when Stanach asked if he should kill the traitor.

"No," he said. "Your folk and mine are going to want to deal with her."

The dwarf grunted and said he could save them all the time and trouble now, but he didn't insist. He ordered Annalisse down the stairs. When she passed Jai, she paused. "It's over Jai, or it soon will be. We can only try to live."

Jai said nothing, but didn't look at her.

Stanach gestured with his axe. Annalisse walked past, the hem of her sleeve brushing against Jai's hand. It felt like ice, like winter coming

---

Dwarves dragged away the corpses of the Knights, eight strong fellows come back with Stanach from the work detail. Sitting on the bottom step of his way home,

Jai heard them talking and the scrape of mail on stone as the heavy bodies were hauled away. No one came to wash away the blood.

"Stone will remember that forever," Stanach said.

Jai nodded. He had nothing to say—or nothing that would pass the grief thickening his throat. Annalisse, his mentor . . . she'd given up. In fear or despair she'd chosen betrayal and found a way to convince herself it was an option.

Stanach, a grub-light in hand, took a seat on the step above. After a long moment of silence, he said, "They're closing this entrance tonight. There's a party of you Qualinesti above getting ready, and we'll close it down here too. By morning no one will know it was here."

Jai nodded.

"Are you sure you want to go? What about your mam and your da? Will y'not want to see 'em one time?"

Jai shook his head. "Send them word. Just tell them . . . tell them I have to do this."

Stanach's voice softened, a little. "Jai."

Jai turned, startled to hear the dwarf speak his name. He'd been "elf" all along, just that— someone to move through the tunnels and then forget.

"Jai, it won't be long before it all falls apart up there. The end is told. You heard it tonight. People are giving up."

Breeze smelling like rain slipped down the stairs. A woman's voice called softly, urging Jai to come up now, or stay. Qualinesti! Secret soldiers of a king who danced, it seemed, to a tune of his own calling, one his people didn't truly understand. It wasn't over yet, not while these strove.

Jai rose, balancing with a hand on the dwarf's shoulder. "Walk up with me, will you?"

Wordless, they went. It was a long way up, a hard road, all those dozen winding stairs. At the top, Jai turned. A pit of blackness yawned below. Stanach stood in a pool of yellow lantern light on the top step. His face was like stone, no muscle moving.

"Stanach, the story isn't all told yet, because I haven't told it. I'm going back to do that. I'll send the histories and stories out of Qualinost a little at a time. I'll find a way to get them through to Thorbardin, and . . . and all the rest of the tale. How it ends."

Stanach looked down into the darkness and then back. "Just get them out. Put them in any hand coming into the tunnel. I'll see them the rest of the way home. And when the last one . . . Well, don't stay too long, eh? Come bring the last one to me yourself."

"Stanach, I don't know if . . ."

A small muscle twitched in Stanach's cheek. He took a breath; it sounded ragged. "That's right. You don't know. But you do know this: I'll be here, right here in the tunnel, trawling for lostlings." He offered his hand, his left, and Jai took it in his own left, grasping it the way Qualinesti warriors did, the hard comrade's clasp. "I'll wait."

Jai nodded. He said no more about his chance of coming back. He turned, and he left, going out into the night and the end.

THE LOST SEA

LINDA P. BAKER

Effram saw the first splatters of rain hit the window only because the neighborhood children were throwing rocks at his windows again. And they were doing it standing inside his boat.

Glass tinkled, soft as wind chimes, onto the floor in one of the second floor rooms he rarely used. Little feet thudded on the deck in imitation of a sailor's jog as the children laughed and cheered, celebrating the particularly well aimed throw. The four children, their faces dirty and their hair wild and uncombed, were all from one family. The littlest one was being newly initiated in the fine art of harassing crazy Captain Effram.

He stormed onto the back porch, reaching for the sling he kept hanging on a post for just such visits. The stones he kept beside it weren't big or heavy enough to really hurt. They were just enough to give the little brats a smart pop for trespassing again. Just enough to leave a sting in exchange for the hurled insults that still had a sting of their own, even after twenty years.

Effram stepped into the yard and drew back on the

sling. The children gave him ample opportunity for a very good shot, but just as he was about to fire, a big raindrop plopped right into the middle of his forehead. He missed his shot. With a loud thunk, the stone bounced carelessly off the hull of the boat, and the children cackled with glee.

With high pitched shouts of "Ahoy, mate!" "Where you gonna sail today, Captain—on the Sand Sea?" the children ran away, leaping directly from the deck of the boat onto what had long ago been the breakwater for the harbor, then down into the dry bed that had once been the Sea of Tarsis.

Effram ignored them. Sniffing the air, he scanned the sky to the south of the city, following the wet scent of rain to the pewter sight of rain. Boiling, silver-gray clouds stretched away to the horizon. The sky was barely recognizable as the same sky under which he'd lived for almost thirty years. Gone was the interminable, unwavering, blazing new sun, painted over with the dull, slate gray of an approaching storm—a fat, ungainly storm with a belly full of water. He hadn't seen a real storm, a wet storm, since he was a boy in Ankatavaka.

There were no storms in Tarsis, not nasty ones anyway. Sometimes there were gentle rains. In the winter there were snows, but usually the blue sky was obliterated by a wall of white, stinging sand that could peel the paint off the leeward side of a building or the skin from an unwary traveler. The old books, the ones he'd found in the ruins of the city, spoke of sea storms, of walls of gray water pounding down on the city, but there was no one alive on Krynn who remembered those days. The First Cataclysm had taken the sea, and with it gray storms and the white, flapping sails of hundreds of sailing vessels.

Now, after hundreds of lifetimes, there was a storm coming. A wet, cool, gray storm. And there was his seaworthy vessel, with a white sail, ready to catch the wind.

Effram climbed down into the pit in which his boat rested on its nest of scaffolding. He'd dug the pit himself, with his own hands, into the now useless breakwater that had once protected the harbor. In a fit of faith, he'd angled the deep ditch in such a way that his ship could be floated out to sea where there was no sea.

But, faith or no, what good was a boat built in landlocked Tarsis? Effram ran his hands over the smoothly joined planks of the hull and down to the polished keel, checking the stability of the scaffold that held the boat in drydock. The sturdy, silken heart of oak had no answers. No more than he had answers.

He didn't know why he'd spent the majority of his adult life building a boat in the middle of the desert, laying himself bare to insults and jeers. He didn't know how he'd become the crazy eccentric who lived down near the breakwater. He only knew that he had looked up one day, and the boat had been almost finished, and he had become daft Captain Effram. He had faith that one day he, as well as those who called him crazy, would understand.

As he slid his hands across the oiled hinges that held the rudder to the ship, he gazed up at the sky. The furtive spitting of rain threatened at any moment to become a deluge. The boat, a miniaturized, bastardized version of a schooner, with its wide, low deck and a sail made of tarred canvas, was as seaworthy as he could make it. He had known, for some months, that his work was done, that he was only waiting. Waiting for truth and vindication. Now, gazing at the gray line of water approaching from the south, smelling the storm in the air, he knew his waiting was over.

He tested the hinges on the rudder, which he had scavenged off the huge doors of some long-dead lord's stable and refitted to his smaller vessel, and checked the last of the waterproofing he'd done on the hull. The feel of storm in the air, the twisting wind and the spitting rain demanded action. It demanded he be ready when the time came.

He went inside his hulking, old house and made sure the shutters were closed and fastened. He stuffed a piece of leftover sailcloth in the window the children had broken. Having stalled more than he could bear, savoring the anticipation, he changed into his sailing clothes. His arms and legs felt like a stranger's inside his skin, moving jerkily and without coordination, not at all like the well oiled shifting of muscle to which he was accustomed—until he put on the heavy breeches and tunic, the cloak with its heavily waterproofed seams, the boots with soles scuffed with sand so that he wouldn't slip on a wet deck.

In his finery—sticky and smelling of tar—he walked down the street to one of the neighborhood markets. It was swarming with people, and he *had* to be among them. To see their faces as they saw him in his rain gear.

The rain was falling softly now, big fat drops that splashed onto the cobbles and bounced back up from shining puddles. The air was cool, prickly, strange compared to the heat which normally beat down upon their heads. People hurried, heads bent, zigzagging from stall to stall, as if they could wend their way amongst the raindrops.

The tarps erected over the stalls to keep out the broiling sun flapped in the unusual breeze and shielded the melons, vegetables, and apples from the rain. Children ran squealing, jumping from puddle to puddle. Old women scurried from stall to stall, gathering food into their baskets as if they thought the rain would wash it away.

The air was wild and tumultuous, alive and energetic, just like the beating of his heart, and the people responded in kind, taking up the feel of it—the blowing wind and the dancing raindrops and the peculiar coolness. Effram couldn't help but be caught up in it. Elation wavering with fear at the approaching storm. He bought a thick loaf of black bread, just in case there *was* no market tomorrow, and tucked it safely under his cloak.

Despite his elation and enthusiasm at the wind and rain that was pattering ever harder onto the tarps, he saw no difference in the faces of his neighbors as they looked at him. No appreciation that he alone wore clothes that could stave off the rain and sea. He saw no realization of what the approaching storm meant.

The baker, a man his age but with more hair and much more girth, looked him up and down, and though he said nothing, his disdain was evident. The man who sold milk and cheese and butter snickered to his wife about the Captain's "crazy get-up" before Effram was out of range. The fruit seller refused to let him touch her, but made him put his coins down on the table instead of into her hand.

Children darted about him, their voices sharper than the stinging drops of rain, lingering in the air despite the worsening gusts of wind. "Captain! Hey, Captain! Here's a puddle for you to sail your boat in!" They tugged at the tail of his cloak and stomped in the rapidly swelling puddles of water, splashed him to test the worthiness of his rain gear. But at least they noticed how the drops splattered against the knees of his oiled trousers, bounced on the back of his cloak, and slithered away.

The adults laughed and shrugged. After all, they were "just children," and what did he expect, always acting so crazy? Only Lydia, the carpet maker, chased them away, chiding them in her lovely voice for teasing him. Effram was as surprised to be championed as the children were to be scolded. She had never noticed him before, never spoken softly to him. Beautiful women like Lydia did not notice men like him.

He gaped at her, unable to stop himself, though pride dictated he turn his back. Her long, black hair swirled about her as she rolled up her carpets, putting them away. She was closing shop, as were many of the other merchants. The rug that disappeared into a tidy, tight cylinder was a thing of magic and beauty, so colorful it looked more like life than wool, more like a painting than woven threads.

A dwarf went past, carrying a chair and a jug of wine and squinting as lightning flashed overhead. Effram followed the dwarf out to the street and watched, chuckling, as the fellow sloshed toward the center of town. Water was already ankle deep in the gutters, calf deep for the dwarf. To the south, more rain was coming. Much more. The sky had gone from light gray to deadly dull, and squalls with their peculiar perpendicular streaks filled the southern horizon. Water was returning to Tarsis, this time from the sky.

Effram shivered. Fear, anticipation, chill, all swirled about him like a cyclone. No longer interested in the chaos of the market, he hurried home. He dumped his purchases on the kitchen table and went out back to check on his boat. The water in the pit was already knee deep, swirling and cloudy with sand.

Fast. It had happened so fast. There was water in the seabed, as far as he could see! Gray ripples flecked with silver and black, like a badly tarnished mirror, stretching away to the horizon. Far too much water for the simple rain. The water must be coming from the ocean to the south, being blown by a horrendous wind.

It was going to be a glorious storm, this strange unnatural tempest that was unlike any that had ever ravaged over Krynn! Perhaps crazy Captain Effram would be vindicated.

He rushed back into the house and searched frantically for the coils of rope he'd bought only last spring, when he knew that he had only a few more finishing touches to put on the boat. Their use seemed so unlikely that he'd almost forgotten where he put them. He finally found them in one of the unused front rooms under a pile of canvas. Maybe . . . maybe this storm . . .

He hardly dared hope that the water would flow high enough to float his boat. Not even as he jumped down into the pit and found that the water sloshed around his thighs did he allow himself to dream the impossible. Rain splattered on his bald head and dripped from the fringe of hair onto the back of his neck. Rain ran under the cloak, beneath his collar, and down his spine. It blew into his eyes and dripped off his nose. It tasted salty, of the sea, and not like rain at all. But the rain was a minor nuisance, barely noticed as he scuttled amidst the strong wooden beams of scaffolding, looping the rope through strategic points, sloshing back to tie the ends to a post up in the yard.

As he worked, the water rose. So fast. Too fast. He'd never seen such water, a rain that came so fast and furious it filled the vast seabed like a huge pitcher being tipped over to fill a tiny glass. The water rushed into the pit, swirling so that he could barely stand. He tied the last length of rope around his waist, just to free his hands. He pulled himself from beam to beam, dragging himself up onto land.

He was soaked through to the skin, his boots full of water that chilled his feet. Only the tops of his shoulders were dry, as if he'd stepped into a lake up to his armpits. The rainproof cloak was no deterrent to this miraculous storm. It weighed twice what it should, just from the weight of water streaming off it, and it was of no use anyway, considering he was already soaked. He tossed it aside and stood in the downpour, shivering with cold and anticipation.

Only then, standing on the edge of the pit, holding the bundled ends of rope, did he dare pray that the storm would not stop. Not until the water was lapping at his toes. Not until the ditch was full and the seabed was deep enough to bear up the weight of his boat.

He could feel the storm strumming in the rope, tugging at the thick lines, and he closed his eyes. He dared not watch for fear that in the boiling clouds of gray approaching from the south, he would see sunlight and clear blue sky. He didn't want to smell heat and sun. He wanted water. And thunder. And the chance to hear the hull of his boat splash into the sea.

In answer to his prayer, no blue sky came. No sun or smell of warm sand. Only the metallic scent of storm, more water, and stronger wind. Somewhere nearby, a shutter banged against a house, loud and insistent. Air trilled across a chimney, squealing like an out-of-tune whistle in the hands of a demented kender. Water pounded on the tin roof of his equipment shed, slapped against the breakwater, and gurgled from the ancient gutter on the eaves of his house.

The music of the storm grew ever more relentless and obstinate until one breathtaking moment he heard none of it. The sounds and the cold and the taste went away, driven out by the scraping of the boat. The most beautiful sound of all: the scratch and screech of wood against wood.

The boat, his boat, the only boat in Tarsis, tried to lift free of the arms of scaffolding. Like a child struggling to be free of its mother's arms, the boat rocked and kicked, trying to take its first baby steps. Trying to float.

With a last small prayer to gods he did not believe in, Effram twisted the ropes around his arms, doubling them then doubling them again for fear of losing the ends. He braced himself against the lone post driven deep into the ground, and he yanked, putting all his body weight into it. The muscles in his shoulders cramped, bunched. His feet slipped in the wet grass. The blades of green—waterlogged down to their hairlike roots—gave way and tore free of the mud.

Effram fell hard against the post. Air grunted out of

69

his lungs and skin peeled away from the flesh over his ribs, but the scaffolding folded in slow motion, cracking and crying out in protest. The boat slipped sideways, threatening to crash into the side of the pit, then righted, slid down the last remaining section of scaffolding, and plopped into the water.

The sound was a tiny, insignificant sound for so momentous an occasion. His boat bobbed, dipped, and floated, gracefully bobbing in the water, the bow nodding to him as if urging him to board.

For a moment, Effram was too flabbergasted to accept the invitation. She was beautiful, this clumsy, pieced together, jigsaw puzzle of a boat. Pieced together of scavenged things—mostly old wood from the wrecks of Tarsis. Long and svelte at the prow, wide and square and ugly at the stern, she was beautiful just the same. Beautiful because . . . she floated.

She was a boat. A real boat, not "that piece of junk in crazy Effram's yard." Until that moment, he had not realized how much he feared that the people who jeered at him were right—all of them, the adults who looked at him askance and the children who threw rocks and words.

He scrambled on board, slipping on the wet planks despite the work he'd done on the soles of his boots. On his knees, he walked awkwardly to the mast and clung to it. He savored the gentle rocking as he waited for his knees to stop trembling. He waited for his heart to quiet, so that he might hear the storm again.

There was a voice in that storm. A voice speaking to him.

Slowly, he pulled himself to his feet, still clinging to the thick, round trunk of wood upon which he'd hung his sail. As he came upright, the first crack of thunder boomed overhead. Lightning, so blue it looked like sky, rent the clouds. For a moment, he could see nothing but jagged streaks on the backs of his eyelids. Another boom and flash followed closely, and it seemed his pounding heart had taken home in the storm, had leaped from his throat and sailed away in joy at his finally being afloat. At being only moments from actually sailing.

Effram freed the large lateen sail from the boom and clumsily ran the rigging that hauled it up the mast. He'd practiced the maneuver hundreds of times since he set the mast into the keel, but it had been much simpler in practice, with the boat land-docked instead of rolling gently under his feet, with the sail hanging loose instead of fighting with the wind.

The sail flapped in the strong, whirling winds, snatching the boom free of his grip. The boom swung wide and then reversed back toward him, smacking his fingers sharply for his lack of agility in subduing it, but there was joy even in pain.

He tied off the boom, still allowing it to swing in the wind while he cast off the lines, forward and aft, that held him captive to the land. Then he used a pole to guide the boat toward the swirling sea. The boat bumped from side to side in the narrow pit, and his heart thumped as loudly in his chest as the thunder boomed overhead, for fear that the boat would beach itself before it had ever sailed.

The churning waters caught the stern, and the boat jerked underfoot. The starboard side slammed into the rocky edge of the breakwater, crashing him to his knees, and then the boat bobbed forward and twisted in a stomach-curdling semi-circle. It scraped the breakwater on the other side, wood screeching on stone. The sail snapped, fluttered, snapped, then caught the wind. The sail popped, as if every thread in it shouted as one, and then Effram and his boat were into the Sea of Tarsis, caught by the strong current, washed away from the jagged breakwater. He was sailing!

The boom jerked in his hand with such force it felt as if it would tear his arm from the socket. The steering oar yanked from the other direction, fighting the boom for possession of his body. The prow of his boat turned to the open sea as if guided by the hands of the long forgotten gods. With a tug that threatened to topple him over the rail and into the water, the wind and the water took his boat.

He fought with the oar, bringing the nose around so that he was parallel to the breakwater that, like a mother's arm, encircled the southern side of what had once been the harbor of Tarsis.

The round-bellied, clumsy boat skimmed across the ragged white tops of the waves with as much ease as a sleek, high-masted schooner at full sail. The prow of the boat cut through the water, the sail snapped in the wind, lines moaned against the blocks, and the mast overhead creaked with the pressure. But she held together, and she floated. She swam. She flew! Effram, captain of the only sailing vessel to sail the Sea of Tarsis for centuries, stood proudly in the stern and whooped his joy into the wind.

Cries, like the screams of seagulls, called to him from the direction of the city. Effram darted a glance at Tarsis. Children, a whole swarm of them, ran along the ridge of the breakwater, waving their arms and shouting at him. Their little faces were washed clean, streaming with rain, and they looked as exultant at seeing his sail filled with wind as he was to feel it snapping and tugging. They flapped their arms, screeched like shorebirds, and leaped as if they, too, would catch the wind and fly. The cries now were, "Hey, Captain! You're sailing! Ahoy, Captain, take me for a ride!"

He waved to them, his face stretched in a grin. He'd never thought hearing that title would sound so sweet. He wished that every child who'd so sneeringly called him "Captain" and every adult who'd smiled indulgently or snickered at his passing could see him now, like this handful of children. He wished they all could see him sailing!

Then he had no further thoughts for them, as he used the sail to turn his boat at an angle to the arm of the breakwater. The boat wallowed and groaned as it turned with all the sluggishness of a fat, sun-warmed grub, but he loved even her clumsiness. He'd expected it. With the midship and the stern built so wide, there was no way she'd be a fast vessel, but what he'd sacrificed in speed, he regained in balance. She rode low, strong, and stable, even in the churning storm.

The wind fought him as he pulled in the sail until it was close-hauled, almost parallel to the lines of the boat itself. The wind tore at the sail as if it would rip it from its fastenings, but the strong cloth held, and the boat leaped away from the wind.

All before him was darkness. Roiling clouds and sheeting water and lightning flashed like fire in the sky. The wind was solid as stone. It battered him, the wood beneath his feet, and tried to snatch the boom from his hands. It drove the salty rain into the side of his face so that it felt like stinging sand on his skin. It

LinDA P. BAKER

was madness to sail toward that black wall of storm, but that was just what he did.

Effram understood the maneuvers necessary for sailing into the wind, even though he'd never had occasion to attempt them. In order to go forward, toward that unnatural blackness, he knew he had to zigzag, back and forth so that he tricked the wind into taking him into it. It seemed only another test of his will, like all the past years had been tests, leading up to this moment.

He sailed leeward for a short while, never taking his gaze from the black horizon. As he shifted, knowing that now he must change course and sail at an opposite angle, he lost his hold on the boom. The boat careened wildly and he fell as the sail went flat. Effram flailed about and finally caught the lines that trailed from the boom. He yanked it into position, the wind grabbed the sail, and the clumsy boat turned and shot away into the storm once more.

Effram threw back his head and laughed with the joy of it all. The pure delight of accomplishment, the pleasure of the salt wind in his face, and the rushing power of the sea, singing through the planks beneath his feet.

This! This was why he'd done it all. This was why he'd spent his life building this thing that had no life except that which the sea could give it. He knew that, whatever else life brought him, he'd be a happy old man someday, to sit in the sun and remember the life of the sea beneath his feet.

As he tacked again, he noticed that the black of the storm was no longer ahead of him. It was all around him. Rain pounded steadily, unrelenting, so that he

74

could barely see through the sheets. The rain tasted of cold blood, salty, coppery, and alive. The only light came from the harsh streaks of fire that zigzagged across the sky, guiding his course through the storm—as if the lightning reached earthward, fighting against the clouds.

Was Effram the only soul left in the world? Alone, isolated in a storm that he realized could not be natural. Could not be real. This was no hearty downpour of water from over-laden clouds, no swirling of wind from the struggle between the cold air of heaven and the hot air of desert sand. This was . . . magic? Punishment sent from the gods? Except there were no gods, or if there were, they no longer cared about the pitiful races of Krynn. But someone, *something*, was surely angry. To pound the sky with thunder as heavy as boulders. To drown the smells of sun and sand. To leach the colors from the land.

For the first time since he'd shouted his exuberance at being afloat, Effram feared.

It was not safe to be so far out to sea, not safe to be surrounded by the roiling black silk of a magical storm. For the first time since he'd set his feet upon the deck, he felt the cold as something clammy and unwelcome. His shirt clung to his back like a worm clings to the stone under which it hides. His shoulders hurt from fighting the wind, his ribs still burned where he'd fallen against the post, and his legs ached from straining to stay upright. His feet were numb with cold, his fingers pruned and old from the wet.

For one heart-stopping moment, he did not know from which direction he had come. All about him was the same. Black and gray, unrelieved except for flashes of yellow, orange, and sometimes blue. Thunder groaned so loudly that he could feel it in his numbed feet. It vibrated into his clenched hands, overshouting even the song of the sail.

He closed his eyes and let the boom line slide through his fingers until it swung free. The sail flogged in the wind, a crunching angry sound of threads being beaten and abused, of a sail hungry to be filled. He was lost at sea in the middle of a dark and supernatural storm. Now he would die, unvindicated, and all those who had called him crazy would be proven correct.

The solution came to him as quickly as the despair had, gusting over him like the bursts of aberrant wind. The fear made him feel stupid and slow. To even have felt it for a moment was to deny all the years he'd spent believing in himself.

He'd been tacking into the wind. All he had to do was turn about and let the wind take him home, or if not home, then to shore. For surely that feeling that he alone lived upon the sea was purest fantasy? The raging sea could not have covered the whole of the continent. Surely there was land somewhere to the north or east of Tarsis. All he had to do was let the wind push him to safety.

He worked the sail and the tiller. The boat wallowed, a great clumsy beast fighting the stronger monster of storm. The pressure of the sea against the keel threatened to swamp him, but then the stern caught the current and the nose swung around. The sail billowed in the strong wind and snapped loud as a blow, skin on skin. For a moment, Effram thought he wouldn't be able to manage the boom—that either he would give way, the sail would snap free of the mast, or maybe even that the mast would crack at the base like a young tree snapping in the wind.

The strain on his fingers was almost unbearable, the pull on the sail even stronger, but all held. His fingers did not break, the sail did not give way, and the mast creaked and groaned but held. The sailing was as different as the gait of a swift steed was from that of an oxcart.

To run before the wind was like flying! Like being given wings and a great span of free sky in which to try them. The sail whispered and ballooned out, pregnant with storm, with the strong southerly wind that was blowing the sea of Tarsis home. The clumsy boat flew with Effram astride it, faster than any bastard sloop with a tallship's bow and a carrack's heavy stern should. It flew so fast the wind dried the water from his face, so fast it felt as if the wind would just lift him up and carry him over the sea.

Only the lightning saved him from smashing head-long into the city. One moment, he was flying across the frothing water, surrounded by the gray-black of the storm. The next he saw, in a flash of white light, the seawall that formed the other protective arm around the harbor of Tarsis arrowing toward him.

Lightning blind, he barely had time to yank the boom in, bleed the sail of some of the wind, and slow the forward slice of the boat. It turned and in the next flash of lightning, he saw the blunt end of the seawall on the starboard side. The boat slid past into the calmer water of the harbor.

The wind was still strong, swirling in angry gusts, as was the water, but it was less choppy. It was an advantage that he appreciated only now. This protected haven had been what made Tarsis the great seaport it had once been. The harbor was a circular refuge backed by the city and enclosed by a semi-circle of breakwater on one side and seawall on the other.

He shortened the sail, giving the wind less yardage on which to tug. Despite the slightly calmer water, the wind still shoved him along at a satisfying clip. There was still plenty of water rushing against the keel and rudder to send the boat skidding forward.

Across the sullen gray light in the harbor, Effram could make out the looming shapes of the waterfront buildings. So Tarsis was still there, still above water, though if the storm continued, he wasn't sure it would remain so. There was no way to tell time, no way for him to even estimate how long he'd been out on the sea. No way to tell how long it had been since he'd walked in the market and bought butter and peaches, but it felt like a long time.

His muscles, aching and tired, said it had been hours, though he suspected minutes. But if the sea had risen this far in only minutes, how long would it be before it encroached upon the city, and would there still be anyone left alive to see him sail past in all his glory?

The water in the harbor was as gray as the sky, dismal as the clouds, so dark that it appeared depthless. The outlines of what had once been tall, proud sailing ships were dark, hulking shapes in the gray curtain of storm. When the Sea of Tarsis had been taken away by the gods, the ships had been trapped, listing at odd angles on dry sand. Over the centuries, people had used the hulks as homes, an even more ignominious fate in Effram's mind than if their carcasses had been allowed to rot away.

He steered closer, a little fearful, and more than a little hopeful that one of the ships had bobbed to the surface of the new sea, but it was a wasted wish. The once proud vessels still lay upon their sides, almost drowned by the raging storm, as landlocked as he had once been.

There were people aboard the nearest one. Scurrying humans who clung to the uppermost deck and waved and shouted frantically, hoping he would see them. Effram could barely hear their cries above the cracks of thunder and sloshing water. He steered closer, standing up proud and tall in the stern of his sailing vessel. Let them call him crazy now!

As he sailed closer, wanting to be near enough to see their faces, he was horrified to see them jump into the sea, one by one, like fleas abandoning a dog. They swam toward him, flailing and shouting as they came.

A heavy smack on the side of the boat startled him as he leaned into the tiller, turning the boat before it collided with the swimmers. He wheeled to find a man hanging on the railing of the boat by one arm. Beneath the sheeting rain, the man's face was familiar.

"Are you gonna just stare or actually be of some use?" the man shouted.

It had been so long since Effram had spoken to anyone that his tongue felt numb. His tongue flopped and twisted around the unfamiliar words, and when the words finally slipped past it, his voice was rusty and unused. "Be of use?"

The man thrust his free hand toward Effram as far as he could. When Effram didn't take his hand,

LiNDA P. BAKER

the man gave out a loud sound of disgust, then he
grunted and wriggled himself clumsily up over the
side and into the boat. He brought a wave of water
with him, and he squished as he struggled to right
himself.

Effram stared at him, not sure what to do. Never once
in all the years of cutting and sawing and shaping and
tarring had he ever pictured anyone else aboard his boat.
It didn't seem quite right. In fact, it seemed sacrilege.
The sodden heap of the man's colorful clothing against
the shining wet of the deck was too bright. Garish. As
incongruous as a harlot in a temple or a cowled priest
bellied up to a raucous bar. It made the boat seem lop-
sided, weighted down. But that was crazy, for while
his boat was not huge, it was not so small that the
weight of one wet, squishing man could be felt.

The man rolled to his feet and swayed clumsily to
stay upright. "You could'a lent a hand to help me in,"
he growled.

Still shocked to have feet other than his own on the
deck of the boat, Effram stared as the man stumbled
toward him, awkward but menacing. In a flash of lightning and daydream, he saw himself tossing the man
back overboard like so much unwanted driftwood.
Effram shook his head, dispelling the image as unwor-
thy, but he thought he should at least protest the alien
presence on his deck.

The man couldn't possibly stand up to him, for
Effram was tall, strong and broad shouldered from
years of cutting down trees and carting them home,
from sawing planks and working them into place
single-handedly.

The top of the man's head barely came up to

Effram's chin. The man's arms looked spindly and easily breakable, but the man's fear was huge. His terror, as he glanced over his shoulder at the encroaching sea, was larger than both men.

The man lurched the last few steps toward Effram, grabbing his arm at the last moment to stay upright. "Turn the boat!" he shouted. "You're going the wrong way."

As shocking as it had been to see someone upon his deck, it was even more shocking to be touched, to feel the man's weight and the clammy, hot press of his hands.

As Effram backed away, the man grabbed for the tiller.

"No!" Effram pushed the man's hand off. "Don't touch my boat!"

"Then turn it around!" The man grappled with him, trying to grab the tiller through Effram's longer reach. "There are people over there—children who aren't strong enough to swim!"

The boat rocked as another man dragged himself over the rail. The movement was slight, but enough for Effram to feel it. This man was bigger than the one who had managed to get one hand on the end of the tiller.

"Trouble, Blaies?" he rumbled.

"This fellow don't want to go back for the others."

Effram opened his mouth to protest, but still his tongue felt rusty, tarred to the roof of his mouth.

"Sure he does," the bigger man said easily, fixing Effram with a glare every bit as sharp as a flash of lightning. "You just gotta explain it to him right. If he don't wanta swim, he can turn this tub around."

Then the man turned away from the shocked Effram

and fished a bedraggled child from the sea. Then another. He slapped a boy, who was coughing and crying at the same time, on the back. "You're all right, boy. Stop yer sniveling and sit down." He thrust the child to the middle of the deck.

Blaies tugged, then pushed on the tiller, trying to break Effram's hold on it, but he was pushing the wrong way and the boat turned even more toward the dock. The man swore softly. He pointed toward the closest of the beached ships. "That way. There's more in the water. And more on that house." He paused to swipe water from his face. "Unless you want to swim?"

"All right. Just . . ." Effram shoved his hand away from the tiller. "Just move away."

Blaies released his hold and moved away to give Effram room to work.

Effram thrust the tiller away. It was not that he feared going into the water, but he would do anything, *anything,* to keep another's hands from controlling his boat. The boat slipped across the water in the direction Blaies indicated.

As the boat slipped past some of the people who had taken to the water upon seeing Effram, the bigger man scurried along the rail to help the stragglers over the stern. Blaies stumbled forward to help them move to the center of the deck. Coughing and gagging, they fell onto the deck and lay where they'd landed until pushed amidship.

Effram stared at the soaked, half-drowned people littering his deck. He did not register Blaies's demand that he sail further among the old shipwrecks until he said it a second time. Even then, it didn't register as words. Only as annoyance and a buzzing sound of fear that cut through the rage of the storm.

"Here." One of the men on the deck crawled to his feet. "I have money, if that's what you want." He took two ungainly, rolling steps towards Effram and thrust a small bag of coins into his hand. "Go that way. That house right over there. The smaller one. In the middle. That's where my family is."

Effram stared at the leather bag in his palm. It had a heavy, rich feel to it. He didn't even have to jiggle it to know it was full of steel coins—more money, in just the one small moment, than he'd ever made in a month of selling carved bits of wood and old books.

Effram looked up to find Blaies and the bigger man watching him intently, knowingly. As if it was just what they'd expected. As if they'd thought, all along, that behind his façade of craziness had roiled greed and any number of other unsavory motivations.

"I don't want money," Effram said, and he handed the small, weighty bag back to the man. He tugged on the tiller until the boat moved in the direction the man had pointed. The man had the grace to look away, to flush and mumble, "Thanks."

Blaies rolled his eyes, obviously thinking this was just more evidence of craziness. He braced himself against the rail, looking down into the water for more survivors.

The water was already up past the door that had been cut into the side of the small merchant vessel. The man's wife and a passel of dark-haired children hung out the windows. Effram maneuvered alongside, and the man held up his arms to receive the first child. They came out the window one by one and huddled, wet and miserable, amidst the clutter of people already in the boat.

Effram peered at them through the rain, wondering if any of these were the brats who had yelled into his windows, thrown rocks at his porch, and climbed over his piles of freshly cut wood. All children looked alike to him, save for the differing colors of their hair.

He looked down at one of the children the man had handed into the boat, a little boy who was probably blond but whose hair was so wet and plastered to his skull that it looked as dark as Effram's own. The child stuck out his tongue at him, than clambered to his feet and jumped up to grab onto the boom. He swung from it like a monkey.

Effram gave it a vicious twitch and jerked the child off. The child thumped in a heap to the deck and sent up a wail to rival the thunder. A woman crawled over, cuddled him, and looked in fear at Effram.

"Hush, now, you're not hurt," she said to the child. "You musn't play on Captain Effram's boat. Not after he's saved us."

Effram turned away, more uncomfortable with the kind words than he had been with the child's playing. At least the child's transgression was straightforward devilment. These adult's words were something else. He'd seen her fear. He'd heard it.

By the time the last child had been dragged onboard, shouts could be heard from the ship-house next door. The man who had offered to pay him pushed the boat away from his house with his hands and pointed at the next one.

The boat was more sluggish, weighed down, and difficult to steer amongst the ships where there was less current.

There was another husband and wife and three soaked children clinging to the next ship. "I can't believe this damned boat actually floats," this new addition said, as soon as his feet touched the deck of Effram's boat. He smiled sheepishly to ease the sting of his words.

Effram knew this face, too, and the grating tone. The man was a merchant in the main market, one of those who smiled nicely to his face then snickered and snorted when he went on his way. Effram's anger must have shown in his eyes, because the man flushed and turned his head away.

A few feet away was another ship-house, crawling with bodies trying to avoid drowning. Effram directed the boat to them without being told and stood bracing the tiller, fighting the current's attempt to push them onward, while those who could stand in the rocking boat helped these new ones climb aboard.

"All this time," a man gasped, "I thought this thing was a waste of trees."

Someone snickered in response and a woman shushed him, reprimanding him as if he was a naughty child. "Captain Effram saved us. He's the only one who could."

That silenced the snickers, but not the other voices. Where before there had been only the lonely, lovely voice of the storm, the crash and crack of thunder and lightning, there was now coughing and crying and gasping and moaning, screams for help and demands to be saved. Watery voices thanked the long-gone gods and the hands that reached over the railing and fished them from the sea to lie like gasping, floundering fish upon his deck. Some even touched the sanded and waxed deck beneath them with reverence and joy. Most of them thanked Effram. A few even took up the woman's words and praised him as the "only one" who could have saved them.

Effram stared at those collapsed on the deck of his boat at his feet, sodden and pale as fish. They mouthed the right words, the words that should rightfully have come to him from the moment the first rain drop splashed down.

But they were too late. Too little.

"Should have said that to begin with," he mumbled softly under his breath. "Should have said that all along." He stiffened his spine and turned his boat towards the docks even though there were more waving, shouting people farther into the clump of prostituted ships. He could not bear to load more of that noise onto his boat.

"Hey!" Blaies waved to larboard as Effram turned the boat. "There's more over there."

Effram ignored him. He ignored the scowl of Blaies's big friend. They would have to kill him to make him let go of the tiller. They would have to break his fingers to uncurl them from around it.

Effram looped his fingers through the rigging that controlled the sail. Ignoring the sharp pain of the lines, cutting into his flesh, he yanked on it. It gave, barely, the blocks squealing in protest as he put his weight on the line and on his hand. The sail edged up. Up the mast, reaching greedily for the wind.

The boat leaped forward, bringing shocked gasps from his passengers. He could almost hear their nails dig into the planks of the deck. His fingers felt as if they might fall off his hand, but he didn't care. He didn't care if the passengers all washed off the deck and back into the water from which they'd been fished so long as he got them off his boat. Quickly.

It was difficult steering the boat with one hand wrapped in rope and the other clamped around the tiller. The wind tearing at the sail was as strong and angry as he was. The current inside the harbor was stronger—strange, almost as if a whirlpool was building at its center, the water starting to froth and show little white-capped waves out across its gray, mottled surface.

Two passengers, a man and a woman, joined Blaies, protesting that there were still more people out amongst the wrecks. They all went silent at one glance from Effram. He growled, "If you don't like it, you can swim." It felt good to see them shrink back and shiver and clutch at their chests. It felt good to see even the big man stagger as Effram put his considerable muscle on the rigging.

His skin broke under the rough rope, and slick drops of blood dripped down his wrist like warm rain. The sail inched higher, catching even more of the mad wind. The boat rushed inland, toward the waterfront that was visible now through the gray air. Effram could make out the different buildings, the white stone of the main dock, the muted yellow of lanterns trying to shine through the storm.

The dock sped toward them at an alarming rate, approaching even faster as he hauled up more of the sail. A woman squeaked in fear, threw her arm over her eyes, then changed her mind and clutched at the person nearest her. Blaies staggered toward him, fists balled, then stopped. A flush of power ran down Effram's

spine, hot and spangled and sweet as wine. They
wanted to stop him. They all wanted to stop him, but
none of them knew how to sail his boat. None of them
knew how to stop it from smacking into the wall of
stone.

At the last moment, just before he'd gone too far, just
before he committed his boat into slamming her elegant
bowsprit into the dock, he shoved the tiller viciously to
larboard and swung the boom in. It barely missed cracking the head of the little monkey child, but it did send
Blaies sprawling across the deck.

The boat turned, faster than Effram thought it
could, with such elegance it made his heart swell. The
boat swooped in a graceful circle before the waterfront.
Effram could see faces pressed to the cloudy windows
of the nearest tavern. Some of the more hardy patrons
ran out into the wind and rain to watch them sail past.
Effram wondered if they could hear the shocked, gull-
like cries of his passengers, the shrill pleas for rescue.

For good measure, he sailed along the dock, just so
they could all see him. Then he took his ungrateful
passengers for a great looping ride across the waterfront. Maneuvering the boom, the tiller, and the twisted ropes around his hand, he slid the boat into place
alongside the dock with the expertise of the only sailor
in Tarsis.

Blaies and his big bully of a friend grabbed hold of
the dock. They clung to it with all their strength,
though the rough stone must surely be cutting their
hands to ribbons.

"All ashore that's going ashore!" Effram called
heartily. He'd read that in storybooks. He suspected
that it was something made up, something no sailor had

ever really said, but these fools didn't know the difference, and it felt good to shout it, to see them all slip and trip and fall over each other in their rush to exit the rocking boat.

His passengers greeted the stone dock with glad cries and much scrambling. He gave them one last chance to look at him the way they should. He stared at them, at their mewling little children as they climbed to safety. In none of those wet faces did he see the respect or the grudging admiration he was due. All he saw was fear. They dragged their belongings or their children up onto the docks and even further up into the town, all the while glancing fearfully over their shoulders at the sea and the storm.

At him.

There was reason to fear. In just the few moments while he'd been at the dock, the storm had darkened more than seemed possible. Water shrieked past, so fierce it stung his ears, blowing rain almost parallel to the deck. The rain looked like streaks of gray satin ribbon, whirling and twisting in the wind. The blackness he'd likened to night was a pearly gray compared to the encroaching darkness on the horizon.

At least, right now, he could still see the waterfront buildings, the gawking tavern patrons who stood against the front of the building as if it could shield them. In the flashes of lightning, he could still see the jumble of ships-become-homes, but the coming darkness threatened even midnight.

What would that velvet darkness be like? How black would darker than night be? Would he even be able to see the lightning? He raised his arms up to the rain, as if it could wrap itself around him and trail behind, like the ribbons on a girl's hat. Would the rain follow him the way it followed the wind?

"You are to be commended!" he screamed into the sky. "Whoever you are, it's a glorious storm!"

The last quaking passenger, Blaies, who had also been his first, pulled himself up the wet, slick stone and wobbled a few steps. From the safety of still land, he paused to look back at Effram. "You're mad," he hissed. "Mad."

Effram laughed at him. Inside, in that dark place where dreams slept, darker even than the storm, his hope of vindication warbled, shivered, and died. Shriveled, it dropped back down to silence, another dream that would never come true.

Effram wrenched at the boom and tiller in unison. It was automatic to him now, the way these two moved opposite each other, but to the same effect. His boat slipped away from the dock with practiced, expert ease. He turned back into the harbor.

To starboard, the tall, abandoned ships were suddenly more menacing than the blackness of the sky. They'd only been shorn up to bear the weight of occupancy, not completely clipped of their wings, and now the water reached that one inch more of height that was enough to bear their dead, beached weight. The storm lifted them, those ghost ships. They shifted and groaned with each slosh of water and threatened to break free of the land that locked them.

He barely heard the scream, followed by an unmistakable splash, over the roar of the wind. He looked back in time to see a whirl of white cloth and frothing foam sucked underwater. A moment later, a woman—really only a mass of black hair—popped to the surface.

She screamed for him to come back, motioning toward the abandoned ships.

For a moment, he stared at her, at the mass of black hair that floated about her like wriggling seaweed. He could see the air between them darkening, visibly, second by second. The yellow lantern light from the tavern was a mere pinprick in a dark curtain now, like a firefly seen across an evening field. Choking and coughing, slipping down into the water then fighting back to the surface, the woman waved for him to return. He turned from her, from the mass of black hair to a blacker sky. To the sea. The storm over it.

He sailed away from her and the waterfront buildings and the warm, yellow light, in a great loop that would take him around the harbor, back along the docks. Perhaps up and down through a few of the old ships.

Even in the darkness, they could not fail to see him. The lightning would light him up like a spotlight upon a stage. Those who clung to the ships they had defiled, those who clung to the land would see him. They could not fail to see him. To know that of them all, only he sailed.

Only crazy Captain Effram sailed the storm and the lost Sea of Tarsis.

And perhaps the ghost ships would follow in his wake.

SOME ASSEMBLY REQUIRED

Nick O'Donohoe

The stone floor shivered with the hum of a nearby high-speed axle that was gradually spinning faster and faster.

An accompanying crescendo of thuds sent puffs of dust rising up off the age-darkened wood floor. The thuds grew stronger and came closer together.

The resulting explosion shook the shelving until it rocked on its springs, throwing the topmost book out of the shelves.

Sorter, the gnome seated behind the desk that stood in front of the shelves, caught the book in his left hand seconds before it could smash his head and knock him senseless. He opened the volume and leafed through it, scanning the drawings and bills for materials.

"Self-winding," he muttered to himself. "Self-propelled walker. Transport Section, East Outer Upper Right. Agricultural propulsion."

He closed the book and looked wistfully out a side window, where he could see thick black smoke and the occasional teetering Multi-Story Fire Suppressor chasing a thoroughly soaked gnome.

"Nothing ever happens in here." He sighed.

Beyond the smoke he could see the usual hammering, sawing, fastening, and soldering that was Mount Nevermind. Only inside the Great Repository was there quiet. Far too much of the stuff, to Sorter's way of thinking.

He dropped the walker plans into one of the wicker baskets on the Flying Cata-Shelver, then laboriously cranked the windlass until the trigger on the basket arm caught in its latch. He dropped a few more dislodged portfolios in the labeled baskets and cocked each of the arms. Stepping well back, he gave the multi-trigger cord a single, quick tug.

The Cata-Shelver flew down the aisle, throwing books with unerring accuracy at the wrong shelves. Sorter followed the Cata-Shelver, picking up the strewn volumes and putting them in place.

At the end of the aisle he nearly bumped into a stocky older gnome, who was reading one of the thrown volumes and cautiously feeling a bump on the back of his bald head.

Sorter winced in sympathy. "I'm sorry, Blastmaster. Did it hurt?"

"Double-reciprocating action," Blastmaster murmured as he read, oblivious to Sorter. "Who thinks of these things?" He looked up. "What was that? Oh, not much." He rubbed his head again, blinking as his fingers touched the bump. "I think that shelver's stronger than it used to be."

Sorter nodded vigorously. "I added a second windlass. You should see it whip books into the Upper Stacks." He gestured to the high shelves, where gnomes on ladders and the odd trapeze read the books they were supposed to be shelving.

Sorter added shyly, "The same principle would apply to a larger machine—"

Blastmaster was already shaking his head. "Sorter, Sorter, we have discussed this before. You may not design or build. You are a *librarian*—a sorter, chosen and named from birth."

Blastmaster patted the younger gnome's shoulder. "It is a noble role, and you fill it well. Stacker has nothing but praise for you."

"He does?" Sorter asked, astounded. Stacker had always seemed exasperated by Sorter.

"Well, he says you work his crews hard, and that's all to the good." Blastmaster smiled at Sorter. "Take joy in your work, son, for you will never leave it."

Sorter tugged glumly at the lever beside an empty stack of shelves and didn't even smile when it slammed into the floor with a loud *thunk*.

"I'll try to find some joy," he said, sighing. "Even if it kills me."

Before returning to his desk, he felt obligated to ask, "Blastmaster, there was an explosion a few moments ago . . . ?"

Blastmaster beamed. "That was mine." He pulled a scroll from one of his many pockets and unrolled it. "There is a very old legend that with the right detonating device, you can detonate water. I was testing a new device this morning." He shrugged and laughed proudly. "What a marvelous detonator! Blew itself into more pieces than you can imagine. Completely destroyed the work of thirty years. I'll have to start over."

Sorter nodded and returned to his desk, muttering bitterly, "Some gnomes have all the luck."

———◆•◆———

Sorter had been at his work long enough to accumulate a few stray volumes and stack them on a corner of the desk when a voice from the stack said, "Excuse me."

Sorter blinked. "Excuse me?"

"That's what I said." The voice said reproachfully. "You have to say something different."

"Ah." Sorter looked this way and that, but saw nothing but the books. "Excuse me—I mean, sorry." He opened the topmost book cautiously, peered inside. "Hello?"

"Down here." A hand waved above the edge of his desk.

Sorter leaned forward and saw a small face with large eyes staring back at him. At first he thought the face belonged to a child, but children weren't usually allowed to go around carrying dangerous-looking sticks like that.

"A kender," Sorter said with certainty and some wonder. "You're a kender."

"I know I'm a kender, but how did you know?" the kender asked, sounding impressed.

"From reading," Sorter said, though he hadn't read very much about kender at all.

"That's what I wanted to ask you about." The kender looked up at the gnome earnestly. "Have you actually read all those books?"

Delighted, Sorter smiled down at him. "Nobody

reads these books. They review parts of them and then come to revise them. What is your name?" Sorter's right hand picked up a steam-powered quill pen that had all its feathers singed off and hovered over the Visitors Log.

"Franni," the small visitor said, but he wasn't paying attention. His gaze took him through the shelves, the aisles, all the myriad books. "If nobody reads them, what good are they?"

Sorter was shocked. "What good? Why, they're history. They're the history of the progress of gnome engineering down through the ages. Did you really think anyone could read all these books?"

"Well, I wasn't sure," the kender said cautiously. "Do you at least know what's in them?"

"By category at least," Sorter said. "Is Franni your full name?"

Sorter marveled. A short name for a short being. He was thoroughly charmed.

Franni kicked at the desk, watching with interest as his kicks drove the top book bit by bit off the corner stack. "It's all the name I've ever had. What's your name?"

Sorter beamed and took in a deep breath and launched into his name, which took several hours and a large jug of ale to tell in full.

When he paused a good while later, Franni broke in, "Can't we pretend I asked your nickname?"

Sorter stopped himself before launching into the second part of his full name. "Actually, it's just that first bit—Sorter."

The kender's repeated kicking caused the book to slide off the corner stack. Sorter caught it nimbly.

"Careful, Franni. I wouldn't want you to get hurt."

Franni's eyes went round with interest and his ears twitched. "Is it dangerous here?"

"Oh, my, yes." Sorter looked around proudly. "There is nothing more dangerous than the knowledge in any library." He waved an arm at the shelves. "And this isn't just any library. This is the Great Repository." He saw the blank look in Franni's face and explained, "A copy of every design a gnome has conceived is stored here."

"And they're all dangerous?" Franni repeated. He stared, fascinated, at the shelves. "Can I read one?"

"Of course you can. And no, they're not all dangerous." Sorter shook his finger with mock severity. "But just you watch yourself in North Central Lower Left. That's the Large War Machines section. Killers, every book."

Franni nodded vigorously. "I'll remember," he said solemnly, and walked away whispering, "North Central Lower Left, North Central Lower Left, North Central . . ."

Sorter chuckled and returned to his work. As stated, he had not read much about kender, or he might not have been so complacent.

Several hours later, Sorter was standing in the central portion of the Repository, confirming the shelving of a rarity in the Grinders and Meta-Rasps section, when he heard the *thump* of a bookshelf snapping back into the floor.

"Busy morning," he said under his breath.

Then he heard another *thump*, and another, and another—

Then he heard a sound that began softly and grew until it was louder than the thumps: the thud of book after book being flung out of their shelves, slamming into the floor like gigantic hailstones.

The concussion of the books and the thumping of the shelves grew so severe that the vibrations caused the floor to shake. Sorter stood staring as if in a dream while the lever holding up the nearest shelf jarred free of its holding loop. He looked down a line of shelves to see row on row of levers coming unhinged.

An older gnome, hanging by his legs from one of the shelves, cupped his hands around his mouth and bellowed over the growing din, "Threshold effect! *Book avalanche!*"

Sorter sprinted into the stacks. Diving underneath a thundering cascade of books, he slid to safety beneath a reading table.

Like many disasters, the book avalanche seemed to take forever but was actually over in moments. Sorter crawled uncertainly out from under the table and stared around the Repository, aghast.

He could see from wall to wall. Every last shelf section on the lower level had slammed into the floor. A veritable snowdrift of books lay on the floor, some almost the height of a tall gnome.

Teams of gnomes swung or dropped out of the upper-level rafters to examine the chaos.

"There hasn't been a shelf avalanche of this magnitude in four generations," said one, awed.

Another turned and bawled, "Stacker!"

"Stacker!" The others began shouting as well. "Stacker! Stacker!"

Sorter cringed. He was going to be blamed for this. He was certain.

A remarkably tall, thin, and long-armed gnome appeared from nowhere. Standing in the middle of the chaos, he judiciously surveyed the drift of books that extended from one end of the Great Repository to the other and said, "Congratulations, Sorter. You've given all of us job security for some time."

"It wasn't him," said one of the stacking gnomes defensively. "It was that little person with the funny ears. I saw him in the epicenter."

"Franni? Oh, no!" Sorter cried with heartfelt grief. He immediately began throwing books to either side of a pile. "The poor kender! Is he under there?"

"I don't know," said the stacking gnome dubiously. "The last I saw him, he was running from to stack to stack, pulling levers."

"He did this on purpose?" Stacker had also not read much about kender.

"I'm sure the little fellow just panicked. Probably trying to find a way out," Sorter said firmly. "Let's keep looking for him."

Stacker put two of his fingers in his mouth and gave a series of piercing whistles. The standing crew began methodically stacking books to either side of the avalanche. Sorter ran to and fro, moving books from the piles back to the drift and generally getting in the way. He was sick with worry over the kender.

It was sunset before the gnomes finally removed all the books from the floor. Miraculously, they found no bodies.

"We didn't lose a single gnome," Stacker said dryly.

"We should put up a shrine to someone."

Sorter sighed with relief. "We didn't lose any kender either. The little fellow is all right. Or at least he was all right enough to leave."

"Not without taking something with him." Stacker pointed to one of the piles of books.

"What do you mean?" Sorter asked.

"I mean," Stacker said, scanning a scroll of parchment on which he had been making hatch marks, "that this morning's shelf-census showed a grand total—counting the new entries—of one hundred and twenty thousand, five hundred, and fifty-seven books."

He flipped the scroll over. "This evening's count, taken as we stacked the books, totaled one hundred and twenty thousand, five hundred, and fifty-four."

"The count's wrong," Sorter said, and he was instantly drowned out by a furious chorus.

"The count is never wrong!"

Stacker's brushy eyebrows furrowed with righteous anger.

"You're right, of course," Sorter said meekly. "We must find out what's missing."

The gnomes set to work. Checking off books, sleeping in shifts, the gnomes had an answer by dawn. Stacker handed a sheet of foolscap to Sorter, who read off the titles with horror.

Walking Sledgehammer—for smashing small battlement walls. Complete plans, bill of materials. Additional plans for miscellaneous machines of destruction included, no extra charge.

Rolling Ram, for opening fortress gates. Complete plan, bill of materials.

Automated Siege Engine for demolishing cities. Complete plans, bill of materials. Addional plans for strike-while-launching fire arrows, no extra charge.

Sorter clutched the foolscap in his fist and wailed, "I warned him of the dangers of that section!"

Stacker rubbed his tired eyes. "Well, he didn't listen. What are you going to do now?"

"What a good librarian does," Sorter said firmly.

"File a report?" Stacker said, sneering. "Two things every gnome thinks he can do: draw plans and file a report."

"And manage a library," Sorter said with diginity. "And no, I'm *not* filing a report. I'm going to go recover those books."

He should have definitely read more about kender.

II

Sorter packed quickly, throwing everything into a bundle-cloth. He put in a change of clothes, a compass, a lamp, food for three days, water for six, a seed planter and a cloud-seeder for after that, and a wonderful multi-purpose machine that was designed to part oceans and make crop circles.

After he tried to lift it, he began to unpack, leaving only a change of clothes, a day's food and water, and some parchment and pens. He tied up the bundle and left Mount Nevermind quietly. In a few hours, the Great Repository would open for the day, and Blastmaster would realize that Sorter was gone.

Sorter shook his head. Stacker and his crew had many months of work to do before the library could re-open. For a while, at least, no one would miss Sorter at all.

Sorter had no sooner left Mount Nevermind than he found himself at the first fork in the road beyond the mountains. He looked about, confused. He knew little geography and even less about the inhabitants of these strange lands. He knew that the island of Sancrist was not large, but at the moment, it seemed as immense as all of Ansalon with a few other unknown continents thrown in. He knew that one of these roads was an important trade route, leading through several small villages and finally into the great city of Gunthar. He knew that the other road was inconsequential and led into a swamp, but which was which?

Peering down the right-hand fork, Sorter thought he could see a wisp of smoke in the distance.

That decided him. If Franni had gone that way, he might be in need of help. Sorter tightened the knots on his sack, grasped his walking stick, and strode determinedly toward the smoke.

By the time he arrived at the village of Gormar, the wisp of smoke was a thick, dark, black cloud. A bucket brigade of men and women extended from a nearby stream to the center of town, where flames shot from the roof of a huge warehouse. Smoke poured from the front double doors and an upper window with a hoist above it. Men and women dashed through the doors of the warehouse, emptied their buckets, and dashed back out, coughing.

Just behind the bucket-wielding adults stood a knot of dirty children dressed in tattered clothes. The adults looked harried and worried. The children looked extemely happy as they toasted bread and cheese over the conflagration and watched gleefully as the fire consumed the building.

"Shouldn't you be in school?" Sorter asked the children.

"School?" said one. "What's that?"

"We don't go to school," said another. "The adults made us work there." He pointed to the blazing building. "That is—they used to."

The children laughed and munched toasted cheese.

"Guess we won't be working there anymore," said another. "Maybe we'll have time to play."

"Play," said a small child. "What's that?"

Sorter naturally wanted to do his part to help the poor people of Gormar. Sitting down on a rock, he pulled a scrap of parchment from his bundle and began designing a bucket conveyor with a flow-and-direction control trough at the upper end.

He worked feverishly and was able to complete the entire schematic by late afternoon. He hastened over to an old man, who was standing beside a vast expanse of smoldering ashes, chewing his beard. The children were long gone. They had gone off to play.

Sorter handed the man the schematic drawing. "This will save your building," he said earnestly.

The man blinked at the drawings, then blinked at Sorter. "Oh." Rolling the plans up, he tucked them under one arm. "Thanks," he said with a nasty tone.

"What was in the building?" Sorter asked.

"Trade goods. Cloth, furs, some jewelry and worked

metals. The metal and jewelry, at least, will be likely unharmed. And I suppose the children won't grow too spoiled by their time off from work."

"I'm sure they'll have a wonderful time," Sorter agreed. He felt about children the way he felt about Franni. "Ten years from now, they'll remember this day as something special, roasting cheese and dancing by firelight."

"I suppose." The old man chewed on his beard again. "I am Elder Ammion. I lead the village of Gormar. Who are you?"

"I am Sorter." To clear up any confusion, he added, "A gnome."

Elder Ammion eyed him suspiciously. "You are the second stranger to stop here this day. And the coming of the first was not a sign of good fortune."

"Was he a kender?" Sorter burst out.

Ammion raised an eyebrow. "Indeed. A friend of yours?" He gestured to a young man and woman who both wore swords. Fingering their weapons, they walked up to stand beside the elder.

"I barely knew him," Sorter replied.

The two holding the swords put them away.

"I'm following him," Sorter continued. "It's my duty."

"Someone should," Elder Ammion agreed, glancing back at the ashes of warehouse. "What else has he done?"

Sorter raised his index finger in the air for emphasis. "By accident, and I'm sure through no fault of his own, Franni—this kender—departed from Mount Nevermind carrying on his person instructions for building some of the most dangerous machines that gnomes have ever designed."

He paused for emphasis, then went on solemnly, "Can you imagine the disaster that could befall a kender in possession of the Fire-Breathing Calliope? Can you understand how important it is that we come between him and danger?"

Elder Ammion, chewing on his beard even more slowly, looked at Sorter in a sort of pitying way. "Tell me, gnome, what do you know about kender?"

"Not much, really. Just what they look like." Sorter added earnestly, "But I've met this kender, and he is friendly, he loves books, and I'd hate to see him come to any harm because of the gnomes." He added, sadly, "Because of me. It was my fault, you see."

"Then you must leave here at once if you're going to catch him." Ammion led Sorter out to the road. The elder had a thoughtful expression on his face. "This road leads to the village of Dormar, our rival— That is to say, our sister village. If you find your kender before you reach Dormar, be sure to take him to Dormar. It's a trading town, like ourselves." He stared hard at the gnome. "Trade competition is fierce. Yes, I would think Dormar would be a good place for a kender to stop and rest."

Sorter was touched by the human's concern for the kender.

The third-to-last thing Elder Ammion said, as Sorter was starting off, was, "Will you be coming back this way?"

Sorter looked at the twisting road ahead. "I hope to."

The second-to-last thing Elder Ammion said was, "And will you be bringing your kender back with you?"

"Oh, no." Sorter shook his head vigorously. "Only

the books he mistakenly took with him. The village of Gormar is obviously much too dangerous a place for a kender."

The last thing Elder Ammion said was, "In that case, I bid you safe journey. Travel far, good gnome. *Really* far."

The village of Dormar was a day's journey away, but the trip took Sorter far longer, due to the poor conditions of the highway. The road was extremely muddy. Entire parts of it had been washed out. Sorter walked carefully, leaping over the gullies, slogging through the mud, and climbing around the potholes. Finally, he left the road and walked alongside it. The grass and brush were soaking wet, but at least they didn't stick to his boots.

The village of Dormar looked odd to him upon arrival. It was all roofs with no houses. When he got closer, he realized that there were houses, but they had all been covered with mud.

Upon entering the mud-clogged village, Sorter noticed children having a wonderful time, stomping in the puddles, wrestling in the mud, sailing small stick-boats in the streams of water that ran down the streets. He smiled, and stopped a moment to help a child create a three-masted schooner that sailed upstream until it grounded itself on a cobblestone.

Next Sorter noticed a group of adults moving through the village. The men had sopping wet hair and clothes and were covered in mud. They carried shovels, rakes, and threshers and looked extremely menacing.

Leading them was an old man, who chewed menacingly on his beard. Glaring at Sorter, the man stopped and brought his troops to a halt behind him.

"I am Elder Bammion. Who are you, and what brings you to Dormar?"

"My name is Sorter," said Sorter. "I'm looking for a kender."

"So are we!" the men growled.

"He was here, then?" Sorter looked around, appalled. He couldn't believe the kender's bad luck in village-visiting. "Did he survive?"

"We haven't found him yet," said one of the men darkly, "if that's what you mean."

Elder Bammion looked uphill, where Sorter could see what remained of a dam. "I suspect he was on high ground when it happened."

"That's a relief," Sorter said. He explained briefly about the missing books. "So I must find him before he hurts himself. Can you imagine how dangerous it would be for him to be roaming around with a Perambulating Hole-Puncher?"

The men stared at Sorter in a silence he took to be fraught with concern for the kender.

"And what will you do with him when you find him?" asked the Elder. "Will you be bringing him back here?"

"Thanks for your care and generosity," Sorter said politely, "but clearly, the village of Dormar is much too dangerous a place for the little fellow." He gestured at the wreckage of a warehouse. "What was this place anyway?"

"Our goods warehouse. Cloth, fur, jewelry, metals . . . The jewels can be washed, but I fear the metals will rust and the cloth is ruined. And the children are now without any place to work."

"But now they can play," said Sorter.

The elder grunted.

"What was in here? Trade goods?" Sorter asked.

"Exactly. We are on a trade route." The elder's eyes narrowed as he chewed his beard. "And trade is very competitive."

Sorter nodded. "So Elder Ammion said."

Elder Bammion stiffened. "Ammion from Gormar sent you?" He gestured. The men with the farm implements moved closer. "He didn't happen to send the kender, too, did he?"

"Oh, no," Sorter said. "But he did say that if I saw the kender, I was to bring him here to this lovely village. And he wished me a safe journey, and a long one."

"Did he now?" The Elder seemed thoughtful. "Then we can do no less. Take our blessing, and food for the journey. Do not stop until you have reached the next village on the road. The village of Mormar. If you find your kender friend, I trust he will be comfortable in Mormar. I can't help but feel our competit— I mean, our sister village would benefit by his presence."

Sorter, touched, shook the elder's hand. "You say competition is fierce, but you can't keep yourself from thinking of others."

"I can't," the elder admitted, chewing on his beard. "It is a habit born of trading."

Noon of the third day found Sorter walking down a non-muddy road with no more damage to it than wheel ruts. The gnome was highly gratified to arrive in the village of Mormar without seeing any signs of disaster. The dam on the hill above the city looked strong. No buildings were going up in flames. The marketplace was free of firefighting equipment and sandbags. The central warehouse stood as solid as if it had been erected yesterday. Through its windows, Sorter could see bundles and crates piled from the floor to the ceiling.

Ragged children worked carrying bundles and crates from the market into the warehouse.

"Hello," said Sorter, thinking that he'd never seen children look so very tired or unhappy.

One of the children, a girl with golden hair, wearily dropped her wooden box before she spoke to him.

"Are you people?" she asked.

Sorter smiled and bowed to her. "I'm people, but not mankind. Have you seen a gnome before?"

She stared at him wide-eyed. "An inventor! This is wonderful—" She stopped and looked back at a frowning adult. "I'm sorry. I have to stay in line." She hoisted the wooden box over her small shoulders that bent beneath the weight.

"Wait!" Sorter said. "What's your name?"

"Lila. I'm sorry, but I can't wait." The child turned and shuffled into the warehouse.

Sorter peered through the window, watching her as Lila climbed carefully to the top of a stack of crates. He was startled by a hand on his shoulder.

"May I ask your business here?" said an old man, chewing his beard.

"I'm looking for a kender named Franni," said Sorter.

"And what would your business be with a kender?" asked the elder.

"I just want to make sure that he is safe."

"Safety is our first priority. After profit." The old man bowed. "I am Elder Cammion."

Sorter looked at him curiously. "Do you come from a large family?"

"Large," he said, nodding, "and, like trade, competitive. Are you a friend of the kender?"

A number of humans carrying sickles and scythes came up behind Elder Cammion.

"I'm an acquaintance," Sorter said, "but I'm working in his best interest. Is he safe here?"

"Oh, yes." Elder Cammion said. "We act in his best interest because he acts in ours. He has offered us the help of wonderful technology."

"Technology?" Sorter gasped. A chill traveled up and down him before settling near his heart.

Elder Cammion nodded. "The plans he carried were quite interesting."

"But they are plans for war machines! Machines for killing! Machines for war!"

"Just so. We are, after all, one of three trading villages. Competition," the elder said slowly and solemnly, "is fierce."

Sorter looked about in all directions, but saw no kender. "Will you tell me where he is?"

Elder Cammion looked as he chewed his beard. "Franni the kender is working at our technology a good distance from the village. I thought that was for the best."

Sorter was relieved. "It seems to me that villages like this are dangerous places for a kender."

———•◆•———

Sorter followed the elder's directions that led to a cleared field outside the village. He saw that someone was raising a wood frame for a house in the field.

As he drew closer, he saw that he had been mistaken. The frame had three sides, not four, as would be required for a house, or at least so Sorter supposed. Three upright poles connected with what must be roof beams. The beams in turn connected at the apex, above a platform.

Sorter moved closer. Why a platform? Why did the platform have a rocker arm on it, with a huge pole extending, and a mallet head on the pole.

"That's the Automated Siege Engine with the remarkable Gatling Ballista Attachment!" exclaimed Sorter.

Sorter walked under it, staring up. Strange noises came from above, but he couldn't see anyone.

"Franni?" he called.

An iron chain with links as long as his forearms dropped almost on top of him. He dived for the ground as a cast-iron hook came to a stop so close to him that it ruffled the hair on the back of his neck.

An oil-soaked and thoroughly delighted kender slid down the chain, stopping with one foot in the hook.

"Mr. Sorter?"

"Just Sorter." The gnome crawled out from under the hook. The kender had so much grease, oil, glue, and other substances on him that he was barely recognizable. "Franni?"

"It's good to see you!" The kender hopped off the chain. "What are you doing here?"

Sorter said with a stern glare, "I'm looking for library books."

Franni stared innocently back. "Then you should have stayed where you were, Mr. Sorter. There were lots of books there."

"I'm looking for three books that *aren't* there," Sorter said.

"Three books? Now there's a coincidence." Franni pointed to his duffel, which lay alongside one wooden leg of the Walking Sledgehammer. "I happen to have *exactly* three books. Do you think they're the ones you're looking for?"

Sorter rubbed his eyes. "That depends. Where did you get them?"

"Oh, around," Franni said vaguely. "Nobody was reading them, and that seemed a shame. They're really interesting. Do you know the best part? The people of the village of Mormar are supplying parts for me to build the machines in the books. I'm nearly done with this one."

He slapped one of the tripod legs affectionately. An unattached beam slid off from the drive mechanism and slammed into the earth beside him, nearly knocking him senseless.

"Are you all right?" Sorter gasped. "Are you hurt?"

"Not yet," Franni said, poking unhappily at the beam. "I don't think it was supposed to do that. Do you know how these things are supposed to work?"

Sorter spoke with absolute faith. "I could build them off the plans."

"Good! Then you can stay and help me build these machines! I'm having a bit of trouble with this one," Franni admitted.

Sorter said flatly, "I can't. I must take the books back to the Repository immediately. It's my duty."

Franni looked disappointed. Sorter stood staring up at the machine. His palms itched. Before he quite knew what he was doing, his palms had taken hold of one of the books and opened it to the plans of the Walking Sledgehammer.

"Can you tell what's wrong?" Franni asked innocently. "The others worked fine, but this one—" He caught himself, shut his mouth tight, and kept his eyes on the gnome.

Sorter looked at mallet hanging over them, its handle as long as a mature tree trunk.

"Franni," said Sorter uncomfortably, not wanting to hurt the kender's feelings, "is there any chance that you've . . . er . . . exaggerated some of the machine's dimensions?"

Franni stared blankly. "Dimensions? Dimensions . . ." He glanced at one of the books. "Oh. Right. Those little numbers beside each the sketches." He shrugged. "I didn't know what they meant, so I ignored them."

"You *what?*" Sorter said. "Franni, you can't ignore the numbers! Gnome designs are very complicated. They have to be executed to every specification, or they may not work. Even then," he conceded, "sometimes there are a few problems. But if you change the dimensions, you don't have any idea what the machine will do when you start it up."

"But we'll know now, won't we, Mr. Sorter? Because you know what the numbers mean, and you can help me fix it. Toss me that thing with the propeller on the end, will you? I think it fits up here."

Sorter thought of the Great Repository. He thought of Blastmaster, of thirty years of work going up in a moment's spectacular explosion. Sorter picked up the propeller thing and handed it to the kender.

III

Construction took a month. During that time, Sorter dodged falling bricks, ducked swinging beams, and fled varying sizes of rolling objects—not always successfully. He was covered in welts, bruises, calluses, and one extremely interesting scar that ran the length of his left arm. He lost a fifth of his body weight, and his skin grew dark and weather-beaten. He was happier than he had ever been in his life.

He peered up at the Automated Siege Engine with the remarkable Gatling Ballista Attachment. In just thirty days, he and the kender had raised a tower ten times the gnome's height and seventeen times the kender's. They had equipped the tower with three tiers of enormous bows and more than a dozen racks of pitch-dipped fire arrows. In a burst of inspiration, they had added on the Rolling Ram and the Walking Sledgehammer.

Surprisingly, it was the battering ram portion of the Siege Engine that gave them the most trouble. The governor on the engine spun out of control three times, leaving Franni and Sorter to dance frantically around trying to shut the engine down by throwing rocks at it or poking at it cautiously with sticks. Then, once that was fixed, the wheel blocks slid mysteriously out from under the undercarriage, sending the entire structure rolling downhill while they chased it. Franni enjoyed that part a lot more than Sorter did.

Now the ram stood shining in the starlight, the mallet's steel plated head gleaming.

"Tomorrow's the big day," said Franni.

"It is," Sorter said, trying to imagine it. "The whole village of Mormar is turning out to watch."

"Think the test will go well?"

Sorter fell back on the old gnome maxim. "I can't think of a single reason why it shouldn't work."

Franni said solemnly, "Then you'll take your books and go back to the library."

"Of course," Sorter said slowly. "That's my duty. I'll miss the children, though."

Every few days, Lila and some of the other children would run out from the town with loaves of fresh-baked bread and food. She and the children stayed as long as they dared, asking questions about the machines and climbing over them with a reckless courage that even Franni admired. Then they would run back, late for work. After the children left, Franni was always very sad—an odd thing for a kender, or so Sorter had read.

Franni rolled over on his pallet. "It's all right that you want to go back. It was really fun at the Repository, just not as interesting as what we've been doing. To me, anyway," he finished tactfully.

"To you," Sorter echoed. "Well, our work *has* been interesting. To tell you the truth, I've enjoyed myself."

"I'm glad," Franni said. "I'd hate to think that I'd completely wasted your time."

"Not a bit." Sorter looked around with awe at the machinery the two of them had assembled. "I'll remember this all my life."

Franni was delighted. "You really think so?"

"I swear it. Listen, we'd better get some sleep."

"For the big day, and for your journey home."

"For the big day," Sorter agreed.

Franni rolled over and fell asleep. Sorter stared into the stars, saying nothing more out loud.

———◆———

The day dawned clear and warm, with next to no breeze. Sorter scanned the sky and saw no clouds at all. They couldn't have asked for a better day.

The test was going to be conducted on a city wall and a warehouse that the people of the village of Mormar had built in the field near the machine. Flags flew atop the warehouse and battlements— the flags of Dormar and Gormar. The people of Mormar told the gnome that the flags had been placed there for a joke.

The festivities began the moment the sun rose. A band consisting of a flaternette, a floozle, a rebec, a citterne, a serpent, a tabor, a tambour, and three large brass instruments that sounded like extremely unhappy livestock marched into the field. The people of the village of Mormar gathered near the band but not too near. Elder Cammion stood with his people, wincing occasionally at the music.

There was a rustle of motion in the grass and Lila appeared, carrying a bouquet of wildflowers in her hands. She was scrubbed clean of work-dirt and wore a linen dress. Sorter barely recognized her. She handed him the flowers.

"Good luck!" she said.

Sorter put the flowers in an open-ended canister used for injecting grease onto axles, making a mental note as he did so: *Automated Siege Machine with the remarkable Gatling Ballista* and *Flower Vase*.

"Thank you, Lila."

"This is fun," Lila said. "Today I don't have to haul boxes or check inventory." She ran back across the field.

Sorter noticed that Franni was once again sad about something.

Sorter put his hand on the kender's shoulder. Hoping to cheer him up, he said, "We'd better start the pre-test checklist."

They climbed up and down each part of the machines, inspecting bolt tightness, wheel lubrication, gear mesh, and worm-gear travel distance.

When they dropped to the ground, Franni asked, "Is that everything?"

"You have a grease smudge on your nose," Sorter told him.

"Yes," Franni said impatiently, "but is that every-thing?"

"Are you nervous?" Sorter asked. "I didn't think kender were ever nervous."

"I don't know what you mean," Franni said, and he clearly didn't. "I'm just excited by all these people watching."

"Me, too." Sorter confessed, and added shyly, "It's the best day of my life." To cover his embarrassment, he said quickly, "Isn't that Elder Cammion in the center of the townspeople?"

Franni squinted and shrugged. "I never could tell them all apart. You don't suppose he's going to make a speech, do you?" Now he sounded nervous.

"Why don't you engage the Siege Engine?" Sorter suggested hastily.

Franni clambered up the lashed timbers of the Siege Engine. On the topmost platform, fastened in place with a panoply of rivets, grommets, staples and tabs, was a huge blood-red button. The plans called for manual controls.

Franni looked at the breathless crowd. He waved his hand at Sorter, who stood off to one side and prepared to take notes. The kender raised his fist and punched the button.

There came a strong smell of hot metal. A motor whined. Seconds later, the siege engine, its bows bending and its arrows loading, rolled and rumbled toward the test fortifications. According to the plan, the engine would stop in front of the walls, fire its arrows and strew about a few flowers.

Franni leaped clear of the platform, landed on the rolling ram, and pulled back on the stick that freed the flywheel.

Now Sorter was nervous. The siege engine was supposed to be rolling to a stop about now. Instead it was picking up speed, rumbling toward the fortress. Something was very wrong.

Sorter ran alongside. "Did you override the safety cutouts?" he hollered.

"Who needs 'em?" Franni shouted back happily, and spun a crank. The air filled with a high-pitched whine, and the rolling ram rolled on.

"Yaaaah!" Franni screeched, as he leaped to the dangling starter pull of the mallet.

The sledgehammer engine turned over with a roar. As the great tripod legs strode forward, the mighty hammer swung down with a threatening whoosh. The crowd sighed expectantly.

At that point, the starter-pull tried to rewind, swinging the kender to one side. He dropped down to land on one foot of the walking sledgehammer tripod. Off balance, he steadied himself using his hoopak, which, unfortunately, happened to jam in between the toes of the tripod foot.

The tripod turned on the stuck foot. The mallet, slicing down, knocked the rolling ram sideways. The rolling ram hit a corner of the siege engine, which spun around one hundred and eighty degrees.

The Automated Siege Engine with the remarkable Gatling Ballista and Flower Vase shifted away from the fake village of Gormar and Dormar and rolled, walked, and crawled inexorably toward the real village of Mormar.

The assembled villagers stared, stunned, at the technology that was headed straight for them. They scattered for the high ground, leaving behind a few musical instruments and the elder's notes for a speech. The children, shouting gleefully, cheered the machine.

Suddenly Sorter saw that one of the children, Lila,

had fallen down. The siege engine was headed straight for her.

"No!" Sorter cried, and dashed toward her as fast as he could.

A shadow fell on Lila. She looked up, frozen, at the mallet head swinging forward, prepared to crush her against the city wall.

Sorter threw himself on top of her. His last thought was, "It's been fun—"

"Hop on!" cried a voice.

Sorter looked up, saw that Franni had managed to regain control of the machine. It jumped over both of them, as the whizzing mallet head smashed a chunk out of the city wall.

Sorter and Lila jumped onto the machine. Sorter shouted over the sound of falling stone, "So you've got the manual controls working again?"

"Yes. Sort of. Well, no," Franni answered, hunched over the ropes. "I can't untie them." He tugged at a loop and a tiller spun to the left. The ram swung toward the city wall. "I think we all better hop back off now."

The three of them hopped. The ram smashed into the wall and kept going. The walking sledgehammer, with monumental unconcern, stepped over the wall and began hammering public buildings. The siege engine rolled through the new gap in the wall, firing flaming arrows into thatch and wood, but it was clear that the machine was winding down. The great warehouse stood unharmed.

Sorter breathed a sigh of relief.

Franni chewed his lip. "You know, I thought that all of this would go better."

"We need to put out the fires," said Sorter. "Before they reach the warehouse." He pointed to the dam above the city. "If we can send some of that water down here—"

"What a wonderful idea!" Franni cried, and leaped to his feet. "Come with me."

He scampered toward the rolling ram. Sorter and Lila followed.

The ram hit a cobblestone and spun toward them. Franni used his hoopak to vault onto the ram. He leaned down, hand extended, and hauled Sorter and the excited Lila onboard the ram. Franni pulled at the half-tied rope on the manual controls, and the rolling ram changed direction, careened madly uphill.

"We're here!" shouted Franni, adding gleefully, "I can't stop it!"

Sorter grabbed Franni with one hand and Lila with the other and jumped for their lives.

The rolling ram plowed straight into the center of the earthen dam. A few drops of water leaked through the dirt. The drops became a trickle. The trickle became a stream, then two streams.

Sorter grabbed Lila's hand and Franni's hand and said briefly and succinctly, "Run. For the high ground."

"And miss this?" cried Franni.

Before Sorter could stop him, the kender was gone, dashing downhill and keeping three steps ahead of the mud.

Sorter and Lila sprinted uphill. Franni and the mal-functioning siege engine thundered down.

Turning around, Sorter was astonished to see how quickly the dirt had mixed with the mud, forming a slurry that bore down on the village like the blade of a shovel. The streets backed up with water, as if a sewer had overflowed. Sorter tried to keep sight of Franni. Water rose to the kender's knees, then his waist, then Franni vanished altogether, as did the warehouse.

The villagers stood on top of the hill and watched, dumbfounded.

The mudslide ceased. The water level stablized. Furniture and crates filled with trade goods floated past.

"What a mess," said Lila, awed.

Sorter paid no attention. "Franni?" He cupped his hands and bellowed. "Franni!"

"Over here!" Franni shouted, climbing on the tottering remains of the siege engine that was still staggering about the village, thumping and malleting whatever was still standing.

At that moment, the siege engine, its joints popping bolts right and left, collapsed with a groan and a crash directly on top of the kender.

"No!" Sorter cried and ran forward, heedless of the water that was knee deep. "Please, no."

Arriving at the twisted wreck of the tower, he heaved at broken beams and joists.

"Franni!" he cried desperately.

A hoopak rose to meet him.

Sorter grabbed it. His hand was muddy and the hoopak slid out of his grasp. The hoopak was braced against a cog and a beam, working as a lever and fulcrum.

This was technology. Sorter understood it. He seized a disconnected drive rod and braced against the beam, pushing to dislodge it. Lila came running up to join him, helping him lift with all the strength given to her by years of toting trade.

The beam shifted. Franni popped out, muddy but unharmed, and tugged his hoopak free. He glanced around at the wrecked machinery.

"Isn't this great?" he said happily. "We did it." He gestured at the ruined walls and warehouses.

Lila looked back at the town and said again with frank disapproval, "It's a mess."

"It sure is," Franni said, and added with a grin, "but I'll bet you don't have to work for weeks. Months maybe." He looked around at the destruction, thoroughly satisfied. "Fire *and* water. This is even better than the other two."

"Other two *what?*" Sorter asked, a horrible suspicion forming in his mind. "You don't mean—"

Franni shrugged and looked Sorter in the eye. "Children should have time to play."

"What's 'play?' " Lila asked.

"You'll get the hang of it," said Franni, patting her shoulder.

She smiled suddenly and radiantly, then ran off to where a group of her friends were splashing around in the muddy puddles.

Franni looked at the ruined town, then at the villagers who had been on the hill but who weren't anymore. Indeed, they were coming toward the gnome and the kender, and they didn't appear particularly pleased.

"I think our work here is done," said Franni. "I know that the grateful populace will probably want to give some sort of reward, but we didn't do this for the money, did we?"

"No, we didn't," said Sorter.

"So I think we should leave," Franni hinted. The villagers were getting up speed. "Now."

It is an unfortunate fact, however, that the legs of gnomes and the legs of kender are shorter than the legs of humans.

Elder Cammion caught both of them before they'd taken much more than twenty steps.

Cammion stood in front of the wreckage and chewed his beard. "I see your machinery works."

"Indeed it does," said Sorter. He looked at the faces of the crowd and would have chewed his own beard if he'd had one. "I grieve for the destruction of your town."

Elder Cammion waved a hand dismissively. "The knowledge you brought us is cheap at any price. In fact, we owe you money."

"You do?" Sorter was astounded.

The elder poured steel coins into a bag and added more, coin by coin. "Plus, we are prepared to augment this payment with a construction grant."

"A grant?" Sorter repeated, stunned. "But we haven't filed the proper paperwork with the Committee on GrantsLoansHereTodayGoneTomorrow—"

"You were the only applicant we considered," said Elder Cammion hastily. "Your construction talents are unique. We want you to continue to exercise them. Besides," he added, "there are still the villages of Bomar, Comar, and Formar, guided by the Elders Nammion, Pammion, Tammion . . ." He passed the kender the bag of coins. "We owe it to my brothers— to *our* brothers in trade to share your technical expertise."

"You want me to do for these villages what I've done for yours?" Franni asked.

"Indubitably," said the elder. "We are on a trade route. Competition—"

"Is fierce," Sorter agreed. "Yes, I've heard."

Elder Cammion raised his palm in warning. "This grant has two conditions. One is that you visit only villages other than ours."

Franni nodded.

The Elder pointed at Sorter. "The other is that you take the gnome with you."

Franni glanced unhappily at Sorter and shrugged. "Well, that's that, then. He has to go back to his library. Overdue books. Thanks anyway." The kender muttered to himself, "All those kids . . ."

Sorter looked at the kender, then at the ruined town, then at the wrecked machinery on the plain.

He turned to Elder Cammion and handed him the books. "The next time you leave on your trading, will you take these to Mount Nevermind? Mention that Sorter will not be coming back."

The gnome took a few of Franni's coins and dropped them into the man's hand. On impulse, he added two more. "Thank Stacker for his kindness, and tell him I will send a design or two his way."

Sorter turned to Franni. "Time to go. Have we forgotten anything?"

"But how are we going to build anything?" Franni wailed. "You sent away our plans!"

Sorter took a sketch out of his pack. "Bear in mind that this is a preliminary."

Franni looked reverently at the sketch. "That's wonderful, Mr. Sorter. All those sharp blades going every which way."

Sorter nodded, pleased. "I call it the Solamnic Army Knife."

"I'd make it ten times bigger," Franni suggested.

"And add wheels. And a motor."

"Perfect," Sorter said fervently.

"Then we'll add a rotary saw with sharp teeth on a swinging arm at the front."

"Great." Sorter unrolled a blank piece of parchment and began sketching. "Now we're getting somewhere."

A few moments later, walking southward, they surely were.

GO WITH
THE FLOE

PAUL B. THOMPSON

Sea, sky, and Raegel's face were almost the same color, a flat green-gray, relieved only by white-caps, pale shredded clouds, and, in Raegel's case, a shock of carrot-colored hair. Raegel mumbled something to Mixun about being seasick, but Mixun knew better. They'd been at sea long enough to get over being seasick. Raegel was just plain scared.

He had reason to be afraid. Both young men lay on their sides, facing each other. The deck rolled gently beneath them. They were twenty-two days out of Port o' Call, twenty-two days as prisoners of a man they had sought to cheat of five hundred steel pieces. Most of the voyage had been spent in the ship's rope locker, unable to see where they were going. Last night, after eating their once-daily ration of beans, the pair had fallen into a deep sleep. Some soporific had been added to the meal. When they woke, it was gray, cold morning, and they found themselves on deck, with their hands and feet tightly tied.

Balic Persayer, captain of the caravel *Seahorse,* emerged from his cabin. He was heavily swathed with scarves and wore a thick woolen coat and peaked hat. Very little of his face showed save for his piggish eyes, red-rimmed and veined with blood, the broad tip of his nose, and his ruddy cheeks, all of which glowed in the raw wind like a trio of ripe crabapples.

"Let's have them up," Balic said. Sailors in rough cloaks and fleece jackets hauled the two men to their feet. Only then did Mixun get a clear view of where they were. His previously stubborn spirits sank.

Lying off *Seahorse*'s starboard rail was a high, rugged coastline, sheathed in ice and snow. Wind, steady as a flowing river, blew off the ice and over the bobbing ship, chilling everything it touched.

Icewall. Captain Persayer had brought them to the frozen end of the world.

"Well, gents, I hope you had a pleasant voyage," the captain said genially. Mixun told him what he could do with his pleasant voyage. Balic promptly boxed the young man's ear. He had a fist like a tackle block, and the blow drove Mixun to the deck. Laughing, the sailors dragged him upright again.

"What's this about?" quavered Raegel. "Do you mean to kill us?"

Balic chuckled unpleasantly. "By my beard, no! If that's all I wanted, I could have cut your throats back in Port o'Call."

"Yeah, but murder's a crime there," Mixun said.

"So it is, and I am a respectable ship's master." Balic gestured, and the sailors behind Raegel and Mixun cut the bonds around their ankles. Their hands were left tied.

Instinctively the two men moved apart. "What are you doing, then?" Raegel asked anxiously.

"Dispensing justice," said Balic. "Prepare the longboat."

"What does he mean?" murmured Raegel.

"We're being marooned," answered Mixun. "The good captain is putting us ashore on the worst land in the world."

Two sailors with drawn cutlasses prodded Raegel and Mixun to the rail. As they watched, the ship's longboat was rigged and lowered over the side.

"Call it what you will, you're murdering us," Mixun said as he watched the preparations.

"No sir, I am not," said Balic, sounding quite cheerful. "You shall leave this vessel alive and breathing. What happens to you afterward is between you and the gods who still live."

"No!" cried Raegel. "Please, good captain, don't do this! It's all a misunderstanding! We never meant to cheat you—"

Balic crossed the deck in two strides and took hold of Raegel's flimsy shirt. "Of course not! You didn't know the casks of fine pearls you sold me were filled with old oyster shells, eh?"

"No, we didn't! Our supplier from Schallsea duped us!"

"Enough lies!" Balic backhanded the frightened man. "Get this scum off my ship!"

Struggling and protesting, Mixun and Raegel were herded to the gap in the rail at swordpoint. With their hands tied in front of them, they were able to hold a rope as they descended the hull cleats to the longboat. Six oarsmen and the bo'sun, a quarter-elf named

Tamaro, were waiting for them. Mixun missed a step near the bottom and fell into the boat. Raegel made his last step, then toppled over as a vigorous wave dashed the longboat against the caravel's hull.

"Wear away!" Balic roared. "Look to your oars!"

"Aye, Captain!" Tamaro shouted back. He took his place at the tiller and ordered the sailors to dig in. Slowly, the longboat worked its way toward shore. Rowing into the wind made the bow leap and plunge, but Tamaro kept them on course for the flat, rocky beach beneath a frowning glacier. Mixun struggled upright as his tall companion slid down among the boat ribs.

Raegel's lips were already turning blue. "I'm cold."

"We're going to be a lot colder," Mixun said. He was glad now he hadn't cut his hair in Port o' Call. It was well below shoulder length and gathered in a thick hank. At least it warmed his neck a little.

There were no shallows near the beach. The dark water never lightened, never gave way to curling breakers as they rowed in. Tamaro ran the bow right on the stony shore, and the sailors shipped oars.

Drawing his cutlass, Tamaro said, "All right you two, out!"

"You're murdering us! You know that, don't you?" Mixun said.

"Captain's orders," replied the bo'sun. "If I didn't obey, he'd have me put ashore with you."

Sullenly, Mixun stood up and worked his way forward. He swung his leg over the bow post and dropped to the gravel. With much cursing, bumping, and thumping, Raegel staggered through the waiting rowers and joined his companion on the stark shore.

"Are you leaving us any food or clothing?" Mixun gasped, clutching his arms against the knife-sharp wind.

"I've none to give you," Tamaro said. The quarter-elf's features were not without sympathy. He came to the longboat's prow and opened his coat, revealing the hilt of a sturdy iron dagger. Concealing his movement from the sailors behind him, Tamaro flipped the weapon over the side. Mixun caught it before it clanked on the rocks.

"And now we're done," said Tamaro. "May you find the fate you deserve."

He resumed his place at the rudder and ordered the sailors to backwater. The longboat grated off the gravel beach, spun around, and rowed briskly away. As it receded, Mixun saw Tamaro's face, white against his dark wool cloak, as he looked back at them several times.

"Wretch!" said Mixun. "He should've used his dagger on Captain Persayer!"

Raegel took the weapon and began sawing through the cords around his wrists. "But it was very decent of him to help us," he said. Lengths of cord fell at his feet. Free, he set to work on Mixun's bonds. "I always had hope for Tamaro."

Mixun raised a single eyebrow. His partner had the habit of making puns at the worst possible moment, like the time in Ergoth they were caught selling painted lead bars as real gold, and were thrown into a dank, rat-infested dungeon in Gwynned. Mixun remarked about having been in worse jails, to which Raegel said, "As prisons go, this wasn't so bad, barring the windows."

"Don't start," Mixun said. He shivered hard. His

flimsy city finery, intended to impress the gullible, was no help against the climate. Already the brass buckles on his knee breeches were conducting blistering cold into his legs. His thin velvet boots offered little resistance to the insistent chill.

It began to snow.

"We've got to find shelter," he said. "We'll be dead in an hour if we don't."

Raegel stamped his feet, trying to warm them. "Maybe there are caves in the cliffs?"

There was nothing better to try, so they set off for the towering glacier. Before the snow completely closed them in, Mixun cast a last look. *Seahorse*, topsails set, was driving out to sea. Someday, he fumed, someday he and Captain Persayer would cross paths again, and the result would be much different.

"Come on," Raegel was calling. He'd found a path to the glacier. Different layers of ice had fractured and fallen, creating a broad, slippery set of steps leading to the summit. Mixun untied the ribbon holding his hair in place and combed the long strands forward to protect his dark, frowning face from the raw wind.

Raegel, Rafe's son, was a country boy from Throt. At twenty-four, he'd been on the run for seven years. While hoeing onions on his family's farm one day, he was taken by a press gang from the Knights of Neraka. The Knights needed men to fill out the depleted ranks of their army, and lately they'd begun impressing free men rather than hiring expensive mercenaries. Raegel went along without a fight, and the press gang sergeant was the first of many to take him for a simpleton. He didn't look like he had two thoughts to rub together. Tall, gangling, with a shock of red hair that had the habit of standing up on his head like a worn-out broom, Raegel learned at an early age to let people think what they wanted about him. While everyone discounted his wits, Raegel went about life with a peculiar grace, unhindered by conscience.

He escaped the unwary Nerakans, and after various adventures, made his way to Sanction, where he found work as a footman to the seer Gashini. Old Gashini did a lucrative trade in fortune-telling and dispensing advice to the high and low in Sanction, but his powers were not derived from magic. Gashini was a snoop, and he employed an army of lesser snoops to ferret out gossip and private news which he later dispensed as supernatural revelations. Raegel learned pick-pocketing and eavesdropping from Gashini, among other vices.

While working waterfront grog shops for his master, Raegel met a kindred spirit—a tough, sullen young fellow named Mixun, "short for Mixundantalus," as he often said. Mixun was down on his luck. He wouldn't speak of his origins, but he'd come to Sanction as the bodyguard of a steel merchant named Wendelsee. Wendelsee had died—poisoned by a jealous rival—and Mixun was left without gainful employ. It was hard for a bodyguard to find a new job when it was commonly known his last master had perished violently.

The two men hit it off, although a more disparate

pair would be hard to imagine. The tall, seemingly guileless Raegel and the dark, dangerous-looking Mixun began running small capers of their own, like rigged dice games, or liberating high-value goods from warehouses. They did well at petty larceny for a while, until the lord governor of Sanction, Hogan Bight, announced his intention to clean up the waterfront and drive out the criminal gangs hiding there. Less than a week after Bight's decree, Raegel and Mixun found themselves invited to leave town, which they did, taking ship to the west before the leaves changed that fall.

Ironically, the duo did very well in honest, upright Solamnia. Posing as refugees from Nerakan oppression, they worked a number of successful capers in Port o' Call, including the pearl scam. They salted oysters with seed pearls and convinced their marks they could grow pearls of any size by using a magical powder (which was just black sand from Sanction). They worked this scam successfully three times. On the fourth try, they ran afoul of Captain Persayer, who was not fooled. Instead of a handsome payoff, the farm boy from Throt and the sullen bodyguard found themselves taken by the vindictive captain and left to die on the frozen shore.

By the time they reached the top of the glacier, the snow was pelting down in great feathery globs. It was very wet, sticky snow, and they quickly found themselves soaked through to the skin.

Raegel gazed across the featureless plateau of ice. His

scarecrow hair was laden with handfuls of fluffy white snow. "I don't see any place to go."

Mixun replied, "Inland is just ice. We must stay close to the ocean, where the glaciers break off. Maybe we'll find a cave or something."

They trudged on, the taller Raegel breaking a trail. Every footfall broke through the crust of ice over the last layer of snow, and lifting his heavy feet reminded Mixun of trying to free himself from a bear trap. They blundered on like this for almost a mile, getting colder and wetter with every faltering step, then Raegel broke through an extra deep drift and sank into the snow up to his chest. He struggled for a moment, lost his balance, and fell face down in the snow. Mixun halted. His friend tried to stand, but another shell of ice cracked beneath him, and he disappeared below the surface.

"Raegel! Ho, Raegel!"

Mixun moved forward carefully, but not carefully enough. The ice gave way under him too, and he slid feet first into the depths.

He slid quite a ways—more than twice his own height—before coming to rest against a pile of loose snow. Mixun sat up and saw Raegel lying on his stomach a few feet away.

"Ho!" he said. "Are you alive?"

"So far," was the whispered reply. "Don't talk so loud, if you want to keep living."

Mixun looked around and saw the reason for Raegel's concern. They had fallen into a large hollow in the ice, ten feet or more below the surface, and if the rest of the roof gave way, they'd be buried alive under tons of ice and snow.

With great deliberation, Raegel sat up. His face and hands were chalk-white with cold, leaving only the tips of his ears and his nose with any color in them. Mixun was shocked, but knew he was at least as far gone.

"Well, we're out of the storm," Mixun said in a very low voice.

His lanky friend remarked, "Snow news is good news."

Mixun was too cold to groan. He drew his knees up to his chest and rested his square chin on them.

"Never thought I'd go like this," he muttered. "I always thought I'd die with a sword in my hand, fighting to the end."

Raegel imitated Mixun's fetal posture and said, "I always wanted to die in the arms of a beautiful lady. A rich, beautiful lady."

They said little more. Breath froze on their lips, sealing their mouth with ice. After shivering apart for a while, Raegel crawled to his friend's side and huddled close to him.

Last post, Mixun thought. He would never see home again, never complete the task he'd dedicated his life to. Everything had ended in this white desert, forever frozen and dead.

He closed his eyes. With his last bit of strength, he found Raegel's hand and clasped it. His friend returned the gesture with a slight squeeze, just to let Mixun know he was there.

Shut off from the sensations of his body by the encroaching cold, Mixun fell into a twilight of dreams, images, and lost desires. He saw again the wide sandy wastes of home, the burning sun overhead, and the wind stirring the dust into whirlpools around him.

Strangely, he felt no heat from the sun, which should have been beating down on his exposed face like a torch. He felt nothing at all.

The landscape shimmered, though not with heat. It trembled with a rapid, rhythmic pulse that he first thought was his own heart beating, but it was too fast, too even. The pulsation grew stronger. The darkness around Mixun lightened a bit as he struggled to rise to consciousness.

"Stop kicking me." Raegel sounded slurred, like a drunken man.

"I'm not kicking you, you idiot." Mixun did kick Raegel then, and was delighted to feel his leg respond to his mental command.

A roaring filled the ice chamber, and snow cascaded down. The cold skin of Mixun's face was still warm enough to melt it, and he opened his eyes, breaking the lacy crust of ice on his lashes. He sat up. Raegel was lying on his side, curled up in a ball. The noise wasn't in Mixun's head, it was real.

"Raegel! Raegel, wake up!"

"Scratch my back, will you?" the drowsy man replied.

"Get up, jackass! The hole's coming down around us!" Mixun said hoarsely. He drew back his foot and planted a sharp kick on his friend's backside. Raegel flinched hard and rolled over, rubbing the spot.

Dragging his benumbed friend by the collar, Mixun scrambled up the ramp of snow created when he and Raegel had tumbled down into the ice cave. The tremors were very rapid now, almost continuous, and the roaring, grinding sound was deafening.

Mixun glimpsed the chill gray sky and burst through the last few inches of loose snow. Once in the open, he thrust both hands into the hole and hauled Raegel out.

Towering above them was the source of the noise and shaking—an enormous wheel, fully thirty paces high, made of heavy timbers and strapped with black iron bands. The wheel stood upright and was turning at a goodly rate, digging plow-like teeth into the ice. Snow and ice sprayed out behind the wheel in two high arcs, creating artificial drifts on either side of the deep trench the device was carving. The axle on which the wheel turned was as broad as a man was tall, and protruded some distance from the center of the wheel. Rising from the ends of the axle were two tall wooden masts, topped with windmill vanes, spinning briskly.

"What is it? What in the name of the four winds is it?" Mixun shouted, backing away on his feet and hands, sliding on the seat of his pants across the ice.

"Some kind of machine," Raegel said.

"I can see that! But what kind of machine?"

As if in answer, the churning wheel sounded a shrill blast on a brass horn. The windmill vanes canted, presenting their edges to the breeze, slowed, and stopped. At once the vast device slowed. The plow blades no longer tore smoothly through the ice crust, but bit and bounced on the stone-hard surface. Lethally large chunks of ice flew, and for some moments the two men were kept busy dodging them.

Without high rotational speed to steady it, the great wheel wobbled. Finally the long axle touched the snowy ground, and the amazing contrivance ground to a halt, leaning on its side like a monstrous child's top.

A hatch opened on the axle's upper surface and a head covered by a puffy black hat emerged. Mixun, though stiff and reeling from the cold, stood up and tried to look dangerous. Raegel didn't bother. He sat crossed legged in the snow, awaiting whatever fate lay ahead.

The puffy black hat was attached to a puffy black suit. The person in the suit climbed out and dropped to the ground, staggered, and fell down. Another round, padded hat appeared in the hatch.

Mixun started toward the strange visitor. Raegel grasped his leg as he passed.

"You don't know who they are," he warned.

"They have warm clothes, and probably have food and drink," Mixun said. "And I want some!"

By the time he reached the axle, four black-suited figures had come out. They all wobbled in circles, as if drunk. Mixun grabbed the closest one. He was small, shorter by half than Mixun, who was not a tall man. Mixun snatched at the lacing on the front of the puffy hat and shoved it back. Out came a mass of silver-white hair and an ageless pink face.

Gnomes. He should have guessed. The strange giant wheel had all the earmarks of a gnomish mechanism.

"Greetings!" cried the gnome. When Mixun did not promptly reply, he repeated his salutation in Elvish, Old High Dwarvish, Ogrespeak, then whinnied like a centaur.

"Common tongue will do," Mixun said, setting the little fellow back on his feet. "Who are you?"

Eight minutes later the gnome concluded his name.

PAUL B. THOMPSON

Three-quarters frozen, the only part Mixun remembered was the first bit: "Master maker of wheels, wheelrims, spokes, hubs, axles, cotter-pins, bearings (roller and ball), fabricated in wood, bronze, brass, iron, and steel . . ." In lieu of all that, Mixun thought of him as "Wheeler" from then on.

The other gnomes gradually recovered their equilibrium and surrounded the freezing pair. They chattered volubly about the weather, thickness of the ice beneath their feet, the formation and texture of snowflakes—on and on without pause, as Raegel slumped to his knees and Mixun's eyelashes grew heavy with frost.

"We're dying!" he managed to gasp. "Can you help us?"

"What's the matter with you?" asked Wheeler.

The near-identical gnome on his right said, "Overactive glands. Gets 'em every time, these big people."

"Maybe they have the Wingerish Fever?" said another.

"*You* have the Wingerish Fever," said Wheeler severely. The gnome in question put a hand to his neighbor's forehead.

"How can you say that?" he replied. "My blood pressure feels normal!"

"The c-c-cold," Raegel chattered. His eyes fluttered and closed, and he fell backward in the snow.

"Dear, dear," said Wheeler. "They aren't dressed for the climate, are they? Come, let us repair to the Improved Self-Propelled Ice Engraver and warm these poor men."

"Did I hear you say the ISPIE needs repair?" asked the gnome with the Wingerish Fever.

"No!" said the other four gnomes.

Wheeler took Mixun by the hand and led him to the hollow axle of the stupendous wheel. The rest of the gnomes took hold of Raegel's hands and feet and dragged him to the open hatch.

The interior of the axle was very tight, sized as it was for beings of gnomish height and bulk. Mixun crawled through a thorny hedge of levers, rods, and pulleys, finally falling exhausted between two brackets of the axle frame. At least it was warm.

The gnomes put Raegel in the niche across from Mixun. One gnome gave him a steaming mug of liquid, and Mixun took it gratefully. He raised the cup to his lips, but the smallest of the gnomes stopped him.

"That's not a beverage," he said.

Mixun looked over the mug rim at the round, pink-faced creature, framed by a wreath of silver-white hair. The gnome's wide, round eyes were filled with concern.

"What's it for?" he asked.

"It's Supreme Cold Weather Foot Wash. You pour it on your feet."

Mixun stared at his boots—encrusted in snow, which was rapidly melting. The littlest gnome took the mug from his hand and poured the steaming green liquid over his feet. The snow disappeared, and a strong sensation of warmth flooded Mixun's feet. Unfortunately, the most appalling stench also arose. Mixun covered his nose with his hand and said, "Faw! What's that stink?"

"A side effect of the compound," said the gnome. "I'm still working on it. But your feet are warmer, are they not?"

He had to admit they were. Pleased despite the smell, he asked the gnome his name.

Seven and a half minutes later (for he was younger than Wheeler, and therefore had a shorter name), the little gnome finished his proud epithet. From it, Mixun understood the gnome was a maker of oils and unguents, a mixer of soaps, greases, and anything slippery. Because of his expertise, Mixun dubbed him "Slipper."

"Take start positions!" Wheeler shouted. Slipper thrust a second mug of footwarmer upon Mixun.

"For your friend," he said, and dashed away.

"Flywheel to neutral! Spring tension sixty percent! Wind velocity, twenty-two!"

"Blood pressure one hundred seventeen over fifty-five," said the gnome with Wingerish Fever.

"Shut up!" said the rest.

Huddled between the axle ribs, Mixun could see the gnomes hopping about, working their mysterious apparatus and happily shouting numbers and figures at each other. The center of the axle was a cage-like structure made of wire and rattan, and inside this stood Wheeler, his feet planted on a narrow board studded with four small wheels. That puzzled Mixun. Why was the gnome standing on a wheeled platform?

"Make secure all loose securables!" Wheeler cried.

The gnomes took turns strapping each other into bags of rope netting hanging from rings on the axle wall. When one gnome was fully laced into his bag, his neighbor would climb into his own hammock and wait for the secure gnome to wriggle out and lace him. Mixun thought this would go on forever, as one gnome would always be left free by such an absurd process, but after several go-rounds, the last free gnome was tied in place by Wheeler, who left his rattan cage just long enough to finish the job. He climbed back onto his wheeled plank, threw a big lever, and the giant wheel began to shake.

All at once Mixun realized he and Raegel weren't tied down at all. "Ho!" he called. "What about us?"

"No time for tea or hotcakes now," said Wheeler, setting a pair of leather-framed goggles over his eyes.

Mixun was about to protest when the gnomes threw several levers at once. The windmill vanes outside caught the wind, and their motion was transferred by crown gears to a huge stone flywheel inside the rim of the great wheel itself. As the ponderous disk of granite gained speed, ropes wound tight, sandbag counterweights rose and fell, and the entire device shivered with building power. The tip of the axle lying on the ice rose a bit, then fell back with a bump. Mixun braced his arms against the hull and looked on wildly.

His feet warmed and stinking, Raegel came to. Rubbing the melted frost from his eyes, he saw his friend facing him, gulped, and said, "Hullo, Mix. What's happening?"

"Gnomes!" That said it all.

The axle rose again, higher this time, wobbled in a circle and dropped back once more. Both men were thrown in the air and settled back in their former places with a heavy thump.

Wheeler picked up a mallet and used it to whack a large, red-painted peg outside his cage. With a shriek of tortured tackle and straining leather straps, the full force of the flywheel was applied to the outer wheel structure. The axle leaped into the air, shaking violently. Pounding blows rattled Mixun's teeth and made Raegel's head bang painfully against the wooden axle wall. Mixun knew what was causing the bone-jarring vibration—the sharp iron plows were chewing up the ice again.

The noise was deafening. Vision blurred by the heavy pounding, Mixun could see his friend's mouth move, but he could not hear what was being said. Then the gnomes launched the great wheel forward.

Raegel and Mixun tumbled over each other as the cabin turned a full revolution with each rotation of the wheel. During his wild flight, Mixun saw Wheeler standing upright and unconcerned in his rattan cage, his wheeled board canceling out the motion of the manic machine under him. The other gnomes twisted and tumbled in their rope bags, allowed to turn head over heels, but held in place.

The two men were thrown together like dry peas in a cup. Raegel's suede boots, no doubt toasty warm on his feet now but smelling like all the sewers of Sanction, kept colliding with Mixun's nose. His own noxious footwear were curled beneath him, but he managed to straighten them out so he could return the favor to Raegel.

"Try . . . to . . . get a . . . grip!" Mixun cried as they whirled.

"On what?" Raegel retorted.

Mixun braced his feet and hands against the axle ribbing, and that stopped his dizzy tumbling—or it did until Raegel fell on top of him and broke his hold. They rattled around a few more revolutions, then Raegel managed to loop his arms around a wooden bracket. He ran in place as the great wheel turned, then planted his feet against the ribs as Mixun had done. Soon they were both stable, though rotating with the axle. Raegel found himself staring at Mixun's kneecaps, and Mixun's view of the world was framed by his friend's long, bony legs.

The gnomes thundered along in this fashion for some time, the massive wheel chewing through layer upon layer of packed snow and ice. The machine bore right and picked up speed. Suddenly there was an extra hard jolt, and the wheel bounced into the air. For a second the noise and shaking stopped. There followed a resounding splash as the wheel struck the water.

"See! See!" Wheeler was crowing. "Thus it is proven! The ISPIE works as well in the water as it does on land!"

"Nonsense! Preposterous!" his fellow gnomes responded. "The efficiency of the plows as paddles cannot exceed thirty percent!"

"Fifty!" Wheeler shouted back.

"Thirty!"

"One hundred twenty-six over forty-nine," announced the gnome with the Wingerish Fever.

"Shut up!" the gnomes chorused.

"Excuse me," Mixun said in the brief moment of silence that followed. "Not that my friend and I aren't grateful, but where are we going?"

"Nevermind South," said Slipper, turning in his rope bag to see their guests. "Our base of operations for the Excellent Continental Ice Project."

"And what, pray, is the Excellent Continental Ice Project?" asked Raegel.

"Our purpose here," Wheeler said. "We've come to harvest the abundant natural concretion of solidified sub-freezing water."

"The what?"

"The ice," said all five gnomes in unison.

The giant wheel, which the gnomes informed Mixun and Raegel was named *Snow Biter*, paddled down the coastline, making good time in the choppy gray sea. When the wind dropped, the vanes outside slowed and *Snow Biter* lost speed. When the wind kicked up again, the strange contrivance churned ahead. The axle, as tightly caulked against wind and water as a well-made ship, kept everyone inside dry and warm.

Well past midday, Wheeler announced they were going inland again. Everyone braced themselves. Angling ashore, *Snow Biter* climbed the beach and tore at the crusty, rock filled snow. Amid a barrage of nonsensical orders, the giant wheel turned sharply to the left and halted. The sudden cessation of motion and noise was startling. Raegel neglected to lower his voice and kept shouting everything he said, while Mixun seemed to want to keep on turning of his own accord. Men and gnomes tumbled outside, weaving and spinning like dandelion seeds caught in a zephyr.

Gradually the world stopped turning, and Mixun was able to survey their surroundings. The gnomes had created a fantastic miniature town. It lined the shore of a shallow bay like a toy village wrought in snow by children. Everything was gnome-sized, and hundreds of the little people were about, coated in all

manner of strange garb. The men saw gnomes dressed
in waxed cotton coveralls smeared with grease, leather
capes with seagull feathers glued all over, and furs of
every shade. A pair of busy-looking fellows rolled past,
sealed inside globes of glass four feet in diameter.
Oddest of all were the gnomes who wore only a breech-
cloth and stockings, yet stood about in the frigid air as
calm and comfortable as they pleased. Raegel was about
to inquire about their state of warmth when the wind
changed.

"Awk!" he said, gasping. "That smell!"

"Slipper's foot-warming lotion," Mixun said, nodding. "They must use it all over."

He and Raegel were freezing, so they loudly demanded some protection from the cold for themselves.
Wheeler was in a hurry to report to his colleagues, and
he dashed off, leaving little Slipper to assist the humans.

"I'm doubtful there's any clothing in camp that will
fit you," he said, stroking his beardless chin.

"Anything you have—blankets will do. Anything!"

"Very well. Follow me."

They followed Slipper to a low structure made of
driftwood and blocks of ice, cut and fitted with all the
care of traditional masonry. Both men had to duck to
enter the icehouse. It was surprisingly warm inside,
which accounted for the walls running rivulets of water
and the ceiling yielding a constant supply of shockingly
cold drops.

The building was a warren of corridors and rooms,
all sized to gnomish standards. Slipper led them a merry
route through the bustling halls, and more than once
Mixun lost sight of their guide as he passed through a
crowd of fellow gnomes.

"Little mites all look alike!" he declared under his breath. Raegel chided him for his ignorance.

"They're as different as you and me," he said. "See? There's Slipper, over there."

"All right, hawkeye, you lead!"

Graciously, Raegel did just that. Before long, Slipper led them to a supply room. Furs and yard goods lay in heaps everywhere. "Help yourselves," said the gnome. He turned to leave.

"Wait!" said Mixun. "These aren't clothes. They're just piles of cloth!"

"Can't you make your own clothes? I can show you how to make your own, using the Improved Squirm-Proof Full Body Stitcher. You lie down on a table, see, with cloth beneath you and on top, and the machine sews around you, creating perfectly fitting clothes—"

"Never mind, friend Slipper," Raegel said. "We'll manage." He found a brown woolen blanket and cut it into strips with Tamaro's dagger, winding the strips around his legs as puttees. Mixun draped a gray linsey-woolsey blanket around his shoulders like a mantle.

Slipper sniffed. "If you want to be crude about it!" He tried to leave again.

"Wait," Mixun said. "What about food? Where can we get something to eat?"

"Follow your nose. It will lead you to the Nevermind South Efficient Eatery and Experimental Food Shop."

Raegel tied his leggings in place. "Now *that* sounds like fine dining to me."

More warmly dressed and their hunger assuaged by a visit to the Efficient Eatery ("Just our luck—it's experimental food day," Raegel said when he saw the strange victuals offered), the men wandered around the gnome camp, trying to figure out what the little men were doing.

Former farmer Raegel, who developed an eye for counting free-roaming chickens as a child, estimated there were a thousand gnomes in Nevermind South. Other giant wheels, like *Snow Biter*, came and went via the sea. Since gnomes were always shouting their business for all to hear, Mixun heard every returning wheel master declare things like "The cut is sixty-nine percent complete," or "the cut is seventy-seven percent complete." At one point he snagged a busy gnome and asked, "What is this 'cut' I keep hearing about?"

"The cut that will make the Excellent Continental Ice Project," said the gnome.

"You're cutting out blocks of ice?" said Raegel.

"No, just one block." The full-bearded gnome, clad in the cut-down pelt of a polar bear, slipped out of the puzzled Mixun's grasp and hurried on.

"These little men are mad," he declared.

"That's been said before," Raegel agreed. "Still, they do have lots of energy."

Just then a shrill metallic whistle screamed, causing the two friends to leap, ready to run from whatever danger had just been announced. Instead of an attack, the gnomes poured out of their huts and houses and formed themselves into a disorganized mass, all facing northwest.

Even then, they couldn't stop talking. A quartet of senior gnomes (recognizable by their knee-length

beards) climbed atop a platform of ice bricks and waited
for the mob to calm. It never did, so one of the elders
put a large, elaborate-looking horn in his mouth and
blew. The same piercing shriek emerged, overpower-
ing all conversation.

"Comrades! Fellow inventors! Lend me your aural
and ocular attention!" cried the longest-bearded gnome
on the platform.

"Lend him what?" asked Raegel.

"I don't know, but I'm not giving them any money,"
Mixun warned.

"Shh!" said six gnomes in front of them. "The Chief
Designer speaks!"

"Fellow technocrats! As of three o' clock and ten
minutes past this afternoon, the cut has reached eighty
percent of our goal. At this rate it will take just two
more days to reach the next phase of the Excellent Continental Ice Project!"

The gnomes on either side of the Chief Designer
did some rapid calculating with nubs of chalk on
slates.

"Uh, Chief, it will take two days and eight and half
hours," said one.

"Ha! You forgot to carry the one! It's three days, two
hours—"

"*You* forgot to allow for wind resistance!"

"Colleagues, colleagues! What about the Wingerish
Fever?"

"Enough!" bellowed the Chief Designer. "Culmina-
tion is nigh, whatever the exact hour! At the Splitting
minus one day, the hammer towers will begin opera-
tion. At Splitting minus six hours, all colleagues will
secure their work and await the Splash."

"Do you have any notion what he's talking about?" Mixun asked.

"Not a whit," Raegel said. "Seems to me they're digging trenches in the ice with those wheel-machines—maybe to roof 'em over and make tunnels out of them. That way they can get around no matter how much it snows."

Mixun was impressed by his friend's analytical powers. He had only one objection. "What could the gnomes be getting around to? There's nothing here but snow, ice, and rocks."

In answer, Raegel only shrugged.

The men passed the night and all the following day in idleness, eating, sleeping, or wandering around the camp and observing inexplicable gnome behavior. The snowy scene was littered with their odd machines, often highly complicated devices to do the simplest jobs—like the pendulum powered potato masher in the Efficient Eatery, or the snow whisk operated by the increasing weight of seagull droppings collecting on a teetering platform overlooking the sea.

Their second night at Nevermind South, Mixun and Raegel bedded down in the storeroom of the main ice-building. They were alive and well, which was a great improvement over their prospects since leaving Port o' Call, but Mixun was already restless.

"We've got to find a way off this snowpile," he whispered in the dark. "I'll go mad if I have to stay here too long! How're we going to get back to the real world?"

"If we had a boat, we could sail across Ice Mountain Bay to the Plains of Dust," Raegel said.

Mixun said, "That won't do."

"What's wrong with that? The gnomes must have

gotten here by boat. We could borrow one of theirs, I'm certain."

"I'm not against taking a boat. I just can't go to the desert country."

"Eh? Why's that?"

"Because I can't, that's why. Why don't you want to return to Throt?"

Raegel cleared his throat. "I get your meaning. Hmm. Ergoth is a possibility."

"Are we still wanted in Silvamori?" Mixun said.

"Um, dead or alive. I told you we shouldn't have gulled Lady Riva's factotum out of all that steel."

Mixun snorted. "Fool. He deserved what he got."

"Tdarnk still rules in Daltigoth," Raegel said. "Plenty of opportunity there for men of wit and daring."

Yes, opportunity to get drawn and quartered, Mixun thought. Raegel went on, listing cities and lands of the west, weighing the possible pickings they might find. Mixun stopped listening in the midst of his companion's dissection of Zhea Harbor and lapsed into a deep, untroubled sleep.

Somewhere far away, a great bell tolled. The pealing was dirge-like and vastly deep. Mixun, who could sleep through most disturbances, opened his eyes. He and Raegel had rigged a hide tarp over their pallets to keep water from dripping on them as they slept. With each toll of the bell, a cascade of chill droplets ran off each corner of the tarp.

"Raegel? You awake?"

"Uh-huh."

"What's that sound?"

"Gnomes." Raegel turned over, away from his friend. "Just gnomes."

That wasn't good enough for Mixun. He threw back his fur blanket and made his way out of the storehouse. It was an oddly warm morning for Icewall—still below freezing, but just barely. Heavy, low clouds reached down from the sky, gripping the stark landscape.

Bong.

The note was held a very long time. It seemed to come from all directions at once. Mixun would have asked the nearest gnome what was going on, but there were none in sight. Nevermind South was empty.

Bong.

The wind was still for the first time since their arrival at Icewall, and the sound carried with great clarity. It seemed to be coming from both east and west. Mixun drew his cloak tight and made his way through the snowdrifts toward a ridge of ice that ringed the landward side of Nevermind South. As he topped the rise, he heard the ringing sound again, followed by high, cheering voices. The gnomes were excited about something.

Mixun walked toward the cheering, and gradually he saw a tall tower in the clouds. It was a spindly construction of logs, with long ropes attached to it. As Mixun watched, a huge, wedge-shaped object rose inside the tower, drawn up by ropes. The gleam of metal meant it was sheathed in steel, and the iron box above it was filled with loose gravel. When the wedge reached the top of the tower, the tackle released, and it fell heavily to the ground.

Bong.

"So that's it," Mixun mused aloud. The gray sky echoed the massed cheers of the gnomes.

On closer inspection, he found the little people had carved out an amphitheater in the ice facing the tower, and they sat raptly watching as the great weighted blade rose and fell. The tower straddled a deep trench that ran as far as the eye could see east and west. From the piles of frozen slush on either side of the pit, Mixun guessed this was the cut plowed into the ice by the gnomes' digging machines. The trench was so deep he couldn't see the bottom, just glassy blue ice as far down as the eye could see.

He spotted Slipper in the crowd and hailed him. The tiny gnome waved back, never taking his eyes off the rising weight.

"Slipper—"

"Shh!" hissed two hundred gnomes at once. Mixun snapped his jaw shut, quelled by their unanimity. With a screech, the shackle opened, and the wedge plunged into the ravine. The gnomes cheered wildly.

"Slipper," he said again, once the noise died down.

"What is it?"

"What are you doing?"

"Watching."

"No. I mean, what are you doing there, with that tower?"

"This is the Splitting," said the gnome beside Slipper. He had a fantastic snowsuit on, all covered with small, mirrored glass panels. Mixun asked what the Splitting was.

"The next phase of the Excellent Continental Ice Project," said Slipper. Mixun had to wait until the wedge dropped again, then with strained patience he asked what the Excellent Continental Ice Project really was.

"We are separating a quantity of ice from the glacier, to take back home to Sancrist," said the mirror-clad gnome.

"What for?" asked the amused human.

"Fresh water," said Slipper.

"No, for our Low Temperature Laboratory!" said Mirror Suit.

A tubby gnome seated behind these two thrust his head between theirs and boomed, "Yer both wrong! The ice will be used to fight the red dragon, Pyrothraxus, who occupies our ancestral home, Mt. Nevermind! We'll freeze 'im in his lair!'"

Bong.

This time the blow sounded different. A prolonged cracking sound rose, like cloth being torn asunder. Every gnome in the theater rose on stubby legs and gazed rapturously at the tower.

"Slipper?" The little gnome did not answer Mixun until he tugged on the gnome's down-stuffed sleeve. "How much ice are you taking?"

"One point six-eight cubic miles."

"Miles?"

"Hurrah!" cried the gnomes. "Now the Splitting! Next the Splash!"

The ground heaved beneath Mixun's feet. Before he could question or exclaim, the tower over the ravine snapped apart with a loud crack. Rope and timbers whipped into the deep gap, and the gnomes began spilling off their icy seats with commendable rapidity. Mixun found himself being borne along with the flow of white-haired folk. The glacier canted, first a little, then more and more. Gnomes went down like leaves in a fall wind, skidding into hummocks of snow or into

157

Mixun's legs. As little men piled up around him, Mixun lost his balance and fell too.

"Eight degrees! Fifteen degrees! Twenty-one degrees!" shouted a gnome gripping a surveyor's quadrant. Mixun had the horrifying thought that "the Splash" would come when he and all the gnomes were dumped into the frigid sea.

The glacier shivered like a living thing, wracked from end to end by powerful forces. What was left of the derrick vanished into the widening ravine. Mixun rolled over, clawing at the snow for support. To his amazement, green seawater gushed skyward from the gap the gnomes had cut in the ice. So it was true. The little men had carved off a massive piece of the Icewall glacier!

For a fleeting, thrilling moment, Mixun felt himself falling. The ice dropped away from him and, in the next heartbeat, slammed into the yielding sea. Mixun flattened on the ice, spun around, and found himself buried under a squirming mass of frantic, excited gnomes.

By the time he extricated himself, Mixun felt a very slight rolling motion in the ice. He stood easily and surveyed the scene. Where once had been an expanse of ice all the way to the horizon, there was now a widening channel of swirling green water. Mixun dashed to the edge and looked left and right. There was nothing but ocean between them and shore. Cold wind was driving them out to sea at a notable pace.

The gnomes had sorted themselves out and were busily scribbling notes on any surface available—thick pads of paper, scraps of parchment, even their sleeves and the backs of their colleagues.

"What have you done?" Mixun asked, incredulous.

"Splash successfully survived," noted Slipper on his foolscap. "The Splitting was more extreme than calculated."

"Not so," said another gnome. "My figures, posted three days ago on the wall of the Efficient Eatery, clearly indicate a maximum angle of twenty-six degrees before the Splash."

"How many degrees was it?"

The quadrant-bearing gnome had marked his instrument at the most extreme angle. "Twenty-six degrees, two minutes, forty-four seconds!"

Slipper and the other gnomes bowed to the successful predictor. "Excellent calculations, my dear chap! Simply excellent!"

Mixun scratched his sprouting beard and said, "Excuse me, but what happens now?"

"Now we return to Sancrist Isle," said the calculator.

"But how? Won't we just drift with the wind?"

The assembled gnomes laughed in explosive chirps and soprano guffaws. "Not this iceberg!" Slipper declared. "We have propulsion!"

Mixun picked up a handful of snow. It melted quickly in the warm palm of his hand.

"Sancrist is a long way from here. Will the ice last, or will it all melt before we get there?"

This time the gnomes didn't laugh. They deferred to the successful calculator, who made a rapid computation on his neighbor's pants leg. When he was done, he smiled broadly.

"We can lose sixty percent of our total ice and still stay afloat," he said. "The maximum amount we can expect to melt between here and Sancrist is no more than thirty-two percent."

Mixun didn't understand the percentages, but he was soothed by the gnome's bland confidence. He had no reason to complain. Raegel had wanted to get off Icewall, and now they were—in a way.

Raegel! He was still in the storehouse! Without a word, Mixun leaped over the gnomes, scrambling over the ridge toward Nevermind South. As he skidded down the slick hill to the camp (now teeming with gnomes again), he saw the great wheel machines being partially dismantled. One wheel was already being pegged into place at the edge of the iceberg so that the heavy plow blades dipped into the sea. Once in motion, the machines would act like giant waterwheels, paddling the floating island of ice to its ultimate destination.

Mixun burst into the storehouse, expecting to find a frantic Raegel stricken with fear. He did not.

"Raegel?" he called gently. The only reply was a soft and steady snoring.

Once he was wakened, Raegel didn't believe Mixun's story. The gnomes had sawn off a giant raft of ice, three miles long and a mile wide? It was ridiculous, and damned impossible!

"Come see for yourself," Mixun said, rising from the iceblock table in the Efficient Eatery.

From the snow village, the only view was out to sea anyway, so Mixun and Raegel climbed the ridge above the town to see water all around them. Raegel opened his mouth a few times, but no words came out. He sat down on the mound of ice and gazed at the endless ocean.

Mixun held a finger to the wind, then squinted at the sun. "North by west," he said sagely. "Dead on for Sancrist Isle." He sat down by his bemused companion. "It's too much to believe. If these little folk can do something this grand, why don't they command the world?"

"Don't let the size of the deed fool you," Raegel said. "Gnomes are smart, but they're also more than a little loony. It took a thousand of them to carve out this island of ice, but in another time and place the same thousand might devote themselves to something totally useless, like . . ." He struggled for an example. "Counting the ants in an anthill or trying to catch clouds in a jar."

"There's gotta be something in this for us!" Mixun said, rising suddenly. "Some way to turn this to our advantage!"

"I'll think on it. All this ice must be worth something. After all, it's a chill wind that blows us no good."

Mixun frowned and slapped Raegel on the back of the head.

———————◆———————

The ridge above Nevermind South was the highest point on the floe. From there they could see for miles to all points of the compass. On their second day at sea, Mixun spotted the white sails of a ship bearing down on them from the northeast. It was running before the wind, while the ponderous ice island was paddling steadily against the prevailing zephyr. He interrupted Raegel's plotting and pointed to the oncoming vessel.

"What do you think they're thinking right now?" he said.

Raegel grinned. "They're likely wondering what a big berg like this is doing so far from Icewall!"

The ship, a tubby two-master flying the colors of Solamnia, closed rapidly. It crossed the narrow "bow" of the island and drove down the length of the iceberg, barely a cable's length away. Mixun and Raegel waved cheerfully to the astonished sailors working the rigging of the merchant ship.

The two-master sailed on, and so did the floe. The vast, bulky berg could not manage much speed, but the gnomish machines were tireless, and drove them at a tireless pace. Within three days, they were passing through the Sirrion Straits into the southern sea. The farther north they went, the more shipping they encountered. Five days after the Splash, the iceberg entered the major trading route between the western islands and the mainland. An hour did not pass without some vessel in sight—fat argosies with scarlet sails, trim sloops with brightly striped hulls, and dull gray fishing smacks from the coast of Kharolis. Their reaction to the mighty floe was the same: all put their helms over and steered wide of the glistening apparition.

All but one ship, that is. At sunset on the fifth day, a lugger appeared astern, loafing in the wake created by the iceberg's paddles. Its green hull and dark blue sails made the craft hard to see against the water or evening sky. Mixun spotted the lugger and hunted up Raegel to get his opinion. The gangling redhead, munching a frozen fish fritter from the Efficient Eatery (every day was experimental food day, it seemed), climbed the ridge and followed his friend's pointing finger until he spied the small ship.

"Pirates," he said flatly.

"My thought too!" Mixun said. He dodged to and fro, nervously flexing his hands. "I wish I had a sword!"

"Why?"

"Why? Why? Pirates, that's why!"

"I don't think they'll bother us," said Raegel, pulling an uneaten fish tail out of his mouth and tossing it aside. "We're not exactly a rich merchant ship."

Mixun insisted on warning the gnomes, and Raegel agreed. They slipped and slid down the hill to camp. It was much warmer in the Sirrion Sea, and the iceberg was melting noticeably. Every surface was covered with a thin sheen of water, rendering everything slicker than an old gnome's bald pate. Raegel and Mixun got used to falling down, but the gnomes embarked on an orgy of invention, trying to come up with devices to provide sure and steady walking. As the two men made their way to the Chief Designer's house, they passed through a mob of bizarrely equipped gnomes. Some were on stilts. Others had fastened various spiky protuberances to their feet, while some merely sought to lessen the damage of frequent falling by covering their bottoms with pads and pillows.

Upon reaching the Chief Designer's door, they saw a hand-lettered sign that read PULL STRING. There was no string in sight.

"Now what?" asked Mixun.

Raegel pointed to another, smaller sign over the doorknob: IN CASE OF STRING FAILURE, RING BELL.

"What bell?" Mixun demanded, voice rising.

As if in answer, a young gnome appeared through a swinging flap cut in the bottom of the door. He handed

Mixun a brass hand bell, bowed, and crawled back through the door flap. The stocky fighter looked to his friend for guidance.

"Ring it," said Raegel.

Mixun tried. He swung the bell hard, but instead of "ding-ding" or "clang," the bell made a sweetly musical sound, like a songbird. It contrasted so sharply to the expected sound of a bell Mixun almost dropped it. He tried again, and the bell again went "tweet-tweet."

"Even their bells are crazy!" he said.

The young gnome reappeared, opening the door this time. He did not admit the men but emerged with a step ladder and a ball of twine. Without a word, he set up the ladder and used it to replace the broken cord on a bracket beside the door. Once more he bowed and went back inside.

"Oh no," said Mixun. "I'm not pulling any string. It's your turn!"

With much affected dignity, Raegel grasped the string. "Twine waits for no man," he said, giving the line a yank. No bell rang. There was a flat, flatulent sound, and a strange, unnatural voice boomed, "Come in!"

Mixun opened the door. Inside, he saw the string was attached to a bellows. When pulled, it forced air through a series of carved, flute-like tubes. Wind passing through the holes made the device speak two understandable words. Muttering, Mixun and Raegel went inside.

The Chief Designer, whose beard was longer than its owner was tall, was perched on a tall stool in the center of a round table. He was drawing furiously on a long roll of parchment, and when he finished what he was doing, he tore off that portion of the roll and handed it to a waiting assistant. This room, and the room beyond, was filled with young gnomes seated at long communal tables, busily scratching away with long quill pens.

"Ah, hmm," Raegel said, clearing his throat.

"Yes, what is it?" said the Chief Designer, not looking up from his frantic scribbling.

Raegel stopped. He didn't know how to address the gnome properly. While he dithered, Mixun burst out, "There's a pirate ship following us!"

"Is there?"

The gnome's mild response surprised both men. "Yes, I'm quite sure," said Mixun.

"That's interesting. Of course, we are passing within ten nautical miles of Cape Enstar. I understand the region is infested with maritime malefactors."

"What?"

"Pirates," said Raegel. "Cape Enstar crawls with pirates like flies on horse dung. Can we change course, steer wide of the cape?"

The Chief Designer finally looked up. "Change course? No." He resumed drawing.

"But why? There may be danger if we stay on this heading!"

"Give me the rate figures for surface alluviation," he commanded. Six gnomes slid off their benches and came running with sheaves of paper covered in close columns of figures. The Chief Designer ran through four sheets, tossing the unwanted pages in the air, until he came to the one he sought.

"Can't change course," he said. "We'll lose too much ice if we do. Must get home with the maximum amount of ice."

"What if the pirates attack?" asked Mixun.

The head gnome shrugged. "The ice must be defended."

"How? Do you have weapons?"

"No, but we will invent some. I will appoint an Emergency Committee for Iceberg Defense."

Both men were about to protest, but the Chief Designer turned his back on them and resumed work. The other gnomes ignored them too, so they left.

"Little fools," Mixun said when they were outside. "I could take this berg with fifty good men."

"No doubt, but what would you do with this gnome-man's land?" Raegel said. Mixun winced and changed the subject.

By night, lights appeared to the north—colored and, in some cases, blinking. Mixun was sure the Enstar pirates were signaling the lugger on their tail. He hunted through the gnomes' trash heap, looking for a suitable weapon. He found a staff of seasoned wood and lashed Tamaro's dagger to it, making a workable spear. It seemed mighty inadequate for defending an island three miles long from an unknown number of pirates.

Dawn came with slate gray clouds towering in the southwest, and the low green coast of Enstar was in sight. It was warm enough now for Mixun to discard his mantle and go about in his shirt. He sat atop the slowly melting ridge, watching the sea. There were now two luggers tailing them. The wind had died when the sun rose, but the luggers had run out oars and were rowing to keep up with the iceberg.

The sun broke through the thick clouds a while later, filling the translucent ice with fiery brilliance. Glowing like a diamond, the ice began to melt more rapidly.

Streams of water ran off the upper surfaces into the sea. Mixun cupped his hands under one stream and drank the runoff. It was good water.

With the warming, the gnomes' devices suffered. Ice-block houses collapsed, and the paddling machines began to work loose from their mountings. One by one they had to be shut down and the axles reburied in firmer ice. The berg's forward momentum was great, but it soon slowed down. Currents around the cape started pushing the berg toward land.

While the gnomes were busy repairing their paddle machines, more ships appeared out of Enstar. Mixun counted twenty vessels, luggers, galleons, even a captured caravel or two. They all wore dark blue sails, which marked them as pirates as surely as any formal ensign.

Raegel scrambled up the slippery slope and saw the flotilla coming. "This ought to be something," he said.

"You seem mighty calm."

"I don't think we're in much danger."

"How can you say that? Look!"

Raegel smiled. "Relax, will you, Mix? Have faith in our little hosts."

Scowling, Mixun slid down the north slope of the ridge and hurried east, to the stern of the iceberg. The pirate fleet was massing there. The largest ship, a caravel with a gilded figurehead, took the lead. Sunlight glinted from the caravel's tops and forecastle. The pirates were inspecting them with spyglasses.

Mixun kept low, creeping along crevices and cracks in the ice. All were full of water, which made his progress uncomfortable. A few hundred paces from the end of the floe, he settled into a niche between two streaming ice boulders and watched the pirates close cautiously. Before long they were near enough for him to hear the thump of oarlocks, and the shouted commands of individual ship's masters.

Where were the gnomes? They were about to be invaded, and not one of them was in sight!

Mixun watched anxiously as a single lugger under oars approached the tail of the iceberg. The mighty island of ice was riding easily in the waves, bobbing far less than the small ship coming up to it. The edge of the floe stood well above the lugger's rail, a good seven feet above the surface of the ocean. At once Mixun saw the pirates' dilemma—how would they get on the berg?

After some deliberation, the pirates resorted to ropes and grappling hooks. Mixun crept out from his hiding place, spear ready. Crouched low, he couldn't see the pirates, but from the grunting he reckoned some of them were climbing the ropes. He used the dagger to chip out the tines of the imbedded hooks. Both ropes whipped free, and with loud cries, the pirates tumbled into the water.

Grinning, Mixun waited to see if they tried again. Sure enough, three hooks clattered onto the ice shelf and bit into the gleaming surface. He hurried to the first one. The three hooks were widely spaced. Mixun was hard pressed to dig out all three. The first pulled free and fell, then the second. Before he could reach the third, a pirate gained the top of the iceberg. Their eyes met.

"Ai!" the fork-bearded buccaneer cried. "There's someone here!"

Mixun whacked the man on the chin with the shaft of his spear, sending him plummeting to the deck of the lugger below. In response, archers loosed arrows at

Mixun. None hit, but they flicked disturbingly close. He dodged away, arrows splintering on the ice at his heels.

"Alarm! Alarm!" he shouted. "Pirates! Pirates on the iceberg!"

He didn't think there was anyone to hear him, but he hoped to make the brigands wary to follow him. Back in his hidden vantage point, he saw more lines thrown up. In minutes, fifteen well-armed pirates were on the ice. Since they had bows, it was foolish for Mixun to try and fight them, so he beat a retreat over the slick, melting hillocks for help.

He hadn't gone half a mile before he ran into Raegel and a band of gnomes laden with mysterious (and probably pointless) equipment.

"Pirates!" Mixun exclaimed, grasping his friend by the arms. "They're here!"

"Hear that, boys? Go get 'em," Raegel said.

The gnomes broke ranks and streamed around the stationary men.

"You're sending them to their deaths," Mixun protested. "They aren't even armed!"

"What do you mean? That's the Emergency Committee for Iceberg Defense. They're armed enough." Raegel's blue-gray eyes danced with inner laughter. "Come and see."

On a plateau above the end of the berg, the gnomes deployed their strange hardware. Mixun saw canvas hoses and bright metal tubing, windlasses and bags of salt.

Gnomes circled the flattened area, tapping the ice with small brass hammers. Now and then one would crow, "Found one!" and another gnome would mark the spot with a colored stake hammered into place.

Looking beyond them, Raegel and Mixun saw the pirates, now more than thirty strong, massing at the eastern tip of the berg.

"Better get ready," Raegel said. The boss of the Committee—their old savior Wheeler—waved and shouted orders to his helpers.

Augers bit into the ice where the colored stakes had been driven. The drills were withdrawn and bronze pipes six inches wide were shoved into the holes. Bags of salt were cut open and the contents dumped into the tubes. When that was done, hoses were clamped to the tube and attached to the windlass powered machines. More hoses protruded from the other side of the devices, and teams of gnomes grabbed onto them, pointing them at the oncoming foe.

"Begin!" cried Wheeler.

Gangs of small, sturdy arms turned the cranks. The machines wheezed and burped. Wheeler called for more speed, and the gnomes raced around the crankshafts. Gradually, the hoses bellied. Mixun looked to Raegel for an explanation. Raegel just pointed.

The center team fired first. A jet of water burst from the open end of their hose, arcing off the plateau and striking the ice ahead of the pirates. The men withdrew a few steps, unsure what they were facing. Then one pirate doffed his hat and caught some of the stream in it.

He tasted it and laughed. "It's just seawater!"

It wasn't seawater, but salted fresh water. Raegel explained the gnomes' plan as Wheeler had explained it to him. The many hollows in the ice had, over the past few days, filled with melted water. By adding salt, the gnomes made sure the water stayed liquid while pumping it out.

"What good will spraying water at them do?" Mixun said, despairing. He didn't have long to find out.

Laughing, the pirates advanced. More gnome pumps spewed forth, and they focused on the front rank of pirates. The flow was hard, but not hard enough to knock the men down. It didn't have to. The pirates came on a few paces and began to fall. They couldn't walk on ice doused with salt water. They fell, got up, fell again, and kept falling. The archers tried to pick off the gnomes with arrows, but once they were drenched, their weapons were useless. Mixun let out a whoop.

"You've not seen anything yet!" declared Wheeler. "Special Super Pumps, on!"

Levers were thrown and the machines almost leaped off the ground. Hoses bulged, and the gnomes holding them down danced madly to keep their feet. Water roared out at many times the previous pressure. Now the pirates were washed away. A pair of streams hit one man and carried him several yards. He hit the ice sitting down and continued to slide until he shot off the end of the berg, into the sea. He soon had plenty of company. A dozen more pirates were sluiced into the ocean. Wheeler and the gnomes cheered.

Then things went wrong. The pump on the far right burst apart under the pressure, soaking everyone in the vicinity and sending fragments of jagged metal whizzing dangerously through the air. The gnomes on the third hose lost their grip, and the tube began thrashing about wildly, like a living thing. A portion of its powerful stream hit Mixun in the chest and knocked him down bereft of breath. Raegel helped him stand.

A second pump exploded, and the gnomes abandoned the rest. They ran for their lives, shouting

"Hydrodynamics! Hydrodynamics!" over and over as they fled. Mixun decided Hydrodynamics must be the patron deity of the gnomes.

Sodden and shaking, the remaining pirates managed to stand. Seeing only Raegel and Mixun opposing them, they uttered fearsome oaths and vowed revenge. They slopped their way back to their ropes and climbed down to their ship. Signal flags fluttered from the lugger's mast. More pennants appeared on the pirate flagship's yards, and the fleet cracked on sail. At first the men hoped the pirates were departing, but this was not so. The blue-sheeted ships crossed behind the drifting iceberg and forged ahead.

"They're making for Nevermind South," Mixun said.

"How do you know?"

"It's the only place on the floe with a beach. Their scouts must have seen it. They tried to surprise us by landing on the tail here, but since that's failed, they're going for the jugular."

Mixun's grim metaphor seemed apt. He gripped his makeshift spear, hands tingling for a fight. How he missed the clash and clang of deathly combat!

He stood up to strike a martial pose, slipped on the watery ice, and fell flat on his face.

The sky was heavy and darkening, threatening to storm, but the wind favored the Enstar pirates, and by the time Mixun and Raegel managed to stumble back to the village, it was all over. Scores of longboats were in the water, each deeply laden with fierce buccaneers. The gnomes had no defense to offer.

Raegel was all for hiding in the ice, but Mixun took his comrade by the ear and dragged him forward to help defend the gnomes. Here was his chance to perish gloriously in action.

All that really happened was his spear was taken away from him while he was picking himself up off the ice. Raegel sat down, crossed his legs, and waited what would be. Pirates forced the angry Mixun to kneel in a puddle of cold water, a brace of sharp swords at his back.

A stout, gorgeously dressed fellow wearing a gilded breastplate and a stolen Solamnic helm clumped ashore. As the most grandly dressed buccaneer in sight, they took him to be the pirate chieftain. He looked over the assembled mass of gnomes and scowled.

"Is this all?" he boomed. No one answered. "Who commands here?"

The Chief Designer elbowed his way to the forefront, hands still full of drawings and computations. He began his stupendously long name, but the master pirate snarled and cut him short. Mixun, for one, was grateful.

"I am Artagor, son of Artavash," the pirate said. "Consider yourselves taken. What loot have you?"

"Loot?" said the Chief Designer.

"Gold, steel, gems, silks, furs, strong drink! Where is it?"

"We have no gold or gems, O Son of Artavash. We have some steel tools, which we need, but we do have some furs about somewhere. If you're cold, we do have a special warming lotion—"

"Silence!" He drew a long, curved cutlass and laid the blade on the Chief Designer's shoulder. "Rile me, and I'll have your head."

"If you need a head, mine has a larger cranial

capacity," said the gnome on the Chief Designer's left.

"Rubbish and rot!" said the gnome behind him. "My cranial dimensions are much greater than yours, plus I have the Wingerish Fever!"

Like a match to tinder, the claim to having the biggest head spread through the gnomes until all one thousand of them were shouting and waving calipers, trying to prove that they had the largest skull around. Artagor roared impotently for quiet. He might as well have shouted at a waterfall.

He raised his ugly blade to strike down the Chief Designer. Before he could do so, Mixun evaded his distracted guards and caught the pirate chief's wrist.

"Don't do that," he said mildly.

Artagor glared and tried to free his hand. To his surprise, the smaller man's grip was hard to break. When a trio of sailors closed in to aid their chief, Mixun released him.

For all his previous bluster, Artagor held his temper in check and said, "Who are you, sirrah? I take you for a man of arms. You're not with these mad tinkers, are you?"

"No indeed," said Mixun. "They're with me."

Raegel gnawed his lip and said nothing. He'd worked with Mixun long enough to know when his partner had a scheme working.

Artagor laid the dull side of his cutlass on his shoulder. "Explain yourself, and be quick."

"I am Mixundantalus of Sanction, and this is my colleague, Count Raegel." The redhead gave the pirate chief a jaunty nod. "We hired these gnomes. They work for us."

"Doin' what?"

"Harvesting ice, of course."

Artagor looked from Mixun to the mob of gnomes arrayed around them. The little folk were quieter than they ever had been, standing and watching the humans with clear, unblinking eyes—a thousand pairs. Artagor tugged at his beard.

"It changes nothing," the pirate declared, unnerved by the gnomes sudden, quiet attention. "You're all my prisoners. I want all your valuables gathered here"—he stabbed the ice with the point of his blade— "within the hour. You two will be my guarantees. I want no gnomish nonsense!"

"Of course not," said Raegel, standing at last. "Take what you will, excellent Artagor."

The pirates ransacked Nevermind South with brisk, professional thoroughness. The results were disappointing. A small heap of metal trinkets, mostly steel, grew in front of the impatient chief. As time passed and the pile did not progress, he began to roar again.

"What's this?" he bellowed, gesturing to the modest haul of swag. "All you tinkers, and this is all the metal you've got? And you, from Sanction—if you're the pay-master, where's your pay chest?"

"The gnomes are working on account," Raegel said smoothly. "They're to be paid off when we reach our destination."

"Which is where?"

Mixun opened his mouth, so Raegel let him answer. "Sancrist Isle, of course."

A pirate wearing a mate's cap ran up. "That's all, captain. There's no more to find."

Artagor shoved the young buccaneer away roughly.

"They've hidden their loot!" he declared. "I'll have it out of them, one way or t'other!"

Torture on his mind, he ordered a fire laid. The pirates tried, but there was no dry wood or tinder on the iceberg, and the ice beneath their feet was too cold and wet to allow a flame anyway. As Artagor consulted his mental repertoire of brutality, lightning flashed overhead.

Slipper sidled up to Mixun. "Sir," he whispered. Mixun discreetly waved the gnome aside. "Sir," said Slipper, more insistently.

"What is it? Can't you see we're all in peril?"

"It's going to storm, sir."

"I can see that!"

More lightning crackled overhead. The wind shifted direction, died, then started again from the opposite side of the compass.

"There's going to be a cyclone," Slipper muttered.

Mixun shot a look at the smallest of the gnomes. "Are you sure?"

"Barometric readings do not lie."

As usual, Mixun had no idea what Slipper was talking about, but he believed him. The wind was increasing in strength out of the southwest. It was so balmy the ice around them began to visibly soften and lose its shape. Artagor was shouting for wood to build a pair of frames. Mixun understood he intended to hang him and Raegel by their feet and question them about hidden treasure.

Thunder boomed. The first fat drops of rain landed, followed quickly by an almost sideways sheet of wind-driven rain.

Signal flags whipped from the masts of every pirate

ship. The lesser captains pleaded with Artagor to allow them to withdraw, lest the storm drive them into the ice island.

"I'll not be cheated of my booty!" Artagor cried. "Not by the likes of them!"

"You already have been!" Mixun shouted back. "This is no natural storm! The gnomes have ways, devices, to influence the weather! Go now, Captain, before your fleet is destroyed!"

At his words, the pirates bolted for their boats. Artagor dithered a moment, then raised his sword. "I'll not leave you to boast how you bested Artagor!"

He cut and slashed at Mixun and Raegel, who promptly leaped apart, dodging each other and the pirate's savage swings. Rain and wind tore at them, making the ice impossible to stand on. Down went Artagor, heavily. Mixun would have leaped on the fallen foe, but he fell too. Raegel managed a strange pirouette and collapsed onto the crowd of gnomes.

The Chief Designer was shouting orders. Mixun heard something like "engage the propulsion units," but the wind made hearing difficult. He got up on his knees just as Artagor did. The pirate thrust at him. Mixun felt the rake of cold iron, and a cut three inches long opened on his left cheek. He threw himself at Artagor's swordhand and both men spun away, sluicing down the ice hill toward the water's edge.

All the pirates had fled except Artagor's boat crew, who stood by their gig anxiously waiting for their master. When he appeared, sliding down the ice on his back, grappling with the short, muscular Mixun, they broke ranks and ran to help. Not one made it two steps before falling. Several went right into the tossing sea.

Mixun was strong, but Artagor outweighed him by sixty pounds. He threw the smaller man off and rose warily. Mixun floundered helplessly at his feet. Grinning through his beard, Artagor raised his cutlass high.

There was a thump, a loud twang, and something struck the pirate chief in the face. He yelled and flung his arms wide, losing his sword. When he came down again, he was in the sea. Artagor surfaced once, spouting water and terrifying curses. It was obvious he couldn't swim in his heavy breastplate and boots, and he went down again.

From his knees, Mixun saw the tall, gaunt figure of Raegel and the tiny beardless Slipper standing a few paces away. Raegel held some kind of fork-shaped device in his hand. With great effort, Mixun climbed the slippery slope on hands and knees until he reached his friends. Raegel was grinning widely.

"What happened?" asked Mixun.

"Friend Slipper loaned me his hand catapult," said Raegel. With great ceremony, Raegel returned the device to the gnome, who shoved it in one of the many pockets on the back of his coveralls.

The pirates were gone. Artagor's gig, rowed by just four sailors, was pulling for his ship. Of the pirate chief there was no sign. The rest of the fleet had scattered before the tempest and were trying to beat their way back to Enstar.

"We must take shelter!" Slipper piped. Most of his comrades had already done so. With the wind and rain

pelting their backs, both men and the gnome slowly
climbed the hill to camp.

———◆◆◆———

What paddle machines there were still working rapidly collapsed in the storm. Their mountings in the ice
had melted loose, and the fierce wind smashed them
down. Powerless, the great iceberg turned in the wind,
plowing sideways through the heaving sea. Raegel got
seasick again.

In the storehouse, the gnomes were furiously working—sewing hides together, painting hot pitch on
wicker baskets, and other nonsensical doings. Mixun
and Raegel shut the driftwood door and slid to the floor,
their backs against the flimsy, quivering panel.

"It's a cyclone all right," Raegel said, wiping his face.
"We'll soon be aground at this rate."

"I estimate we will reach Enstar in ninety-two minutes," said the gnome who calculated the Splitting so
accurately. Despite his earlier success, he instantly had
fifty other gnomes disputing his estimate. Mixun
ground his teeth.

"Time waits for gnome one," Raegel said, leaning his
head back.

"Shut up! Are we in danger?" asked Mixun.

"Danger enough, even if this floe isn't a ship. It may
be ice, but it's solid. We'll go aground and that'll be
that."

The gnomes were not about to see their great project end so ignominiously. They sewed their store of
hides into a gigantic sail, which they announced they
would spread between the peaks atop the iceberg. Using

179

the wind, they would sail the floe away from Enstar.

"And what," Mixun asked, "are the baskets for?"

The explanation was lengthy, but the crux of the matter was that they were gnomish lifeboats, for use in case the iceberg broke apart.

Tied together by an endless rope, the gnomes ventured forth in the storm. Small as they were, they were carried hither and thither by the tempest, hopelessly snarling the makeshift sail. Driven to help by sheer exasperation, Mixun and Raegel climbed the ridge, dragging the heavy sail behind them. At the top, Mixun threw one leg over and surveyed the scene. His heart climbed into his mouth.

The coast of Enstar seemed close enough to touch. Above a white sand beach, a dark headland loomed. Trees tossed in the scouring wind. Under him, Mixun felt the huge floe roll and pitch as it drove relentlessly toward land. Raegel arrived a few seconds later, still dragging the gnomes' useless sail.

"Forget it!" Mixun shouted. "Look!"

The deep underbelly of the berg struck sand, and the island heeled sharply, throwing the men over the ridge. They skittered down the melting face of the ridge, jolting to a stop in a ravine full of rain and meltwater. Soaked, Mixun tossed the wet hair out of his eyes. They were still a good fifty paces from dry land.

With amazing delicacy, the ponderous floe pivoted on its natural keel. The 'bow' of the island was pushed ashore by the thundering wind. A monstrous grinding filled the air. The ice quivered.

"Here we go!" Raegel shouted.

With a crack as loud as the Splitting, the fore-end of

the iceberg, fully half a mile long, broke off. Fragments
of ice the size of houses crashed into the raging ocean.
Out of balance, the broken segment heeled over on its
end and piled ashore amid heavy waves. Now the rear
of the iceberg was unsupported, and the floe swung in
the other direction, grinding hard onto the sand. The
vast crystalline mountain of ice, formerly clear as diamond, seamed with a million cracks.

Mixun got up and ran, ice disintegrating under his
feet. Raegel overtook him, long legs pumping. Both men
would have bet anything it was impossible to run on a
slanting sheet of ice, but panic put spurs on their heels.
Passing Mixun, Raegel was a dozen steps from the edge
of the berg when the whole section shivered and fell
apart. His startled cry was lost in the wind and the
grinding of the ice.

Mixun went down on all fours and scrambled to the
new edge of the berg. He looked down and saw the
surf was dotted with ice—small chunks, large slabs—
and Raegel's head as he tried to keep afloat. The floe
was still pushing against the shore, forced by the roaring storm. Mixun's shouts to his friend could not be
heard. When Raegel went under and did not immediately surface, Mixun slid feet first into the foaming
water.

He was promptly brained by a piece of floating ice
the size of a horse. Driven underwater, he shook off the
blow and opened his eyes. He saw Raegel, stuck
beneath a large slab of ice, arms and legs swinging back
and forth limply with the tide. Mixun sank down until
his toes found sand, then sprang forward and upward,
catching Raegel around the waist. He pushed the ice
aside and broke the surface, gasping.

With a noise like the end of the world, the center of
the iceberg, two miles long and still almost a mile wide,
heaved ashore. The ridge that ran down the center of
the floe exploded into fragments, peppering the water
as Mixun dragged his unconscious friend onto drier
land. He hauled Raegel up the beach above the high tide
line and fell breathless on the sand.

The great floe disintegrated before his eyes. To his
right, the bow segment rolled ashore upside down,
waves breaking over it. To Mixun's left, the stern section was still at sea, caught in an eddy. It spun madly,
half a mile of ice whirling like a soap bubble in a wash
basin. Between these two spectacles, the main portion
of the iceberg was breaking up. Each fresh wave helped
pound the floe against the unyielding island, and the
cyclonic wind threatened to roll the monstrous mountain of ice onto land. Mixun tried to stand and pull
Raegel to safety, but he was too drained. He turned
Raegel over on his stomach to protect him from flying
shards of ice and threw his arm over his face to await
what would be.

He heard voices—many voices, high-pitched like
children. Peeking out from under his arm, he saw the
surf was full of gnomes. Some were bobbing in water-
tight baskets, other were dog-paddling around with
inflated pigskins tied to their waists. They seemed
not the least concerned by the tempest or the crumbling iceberg. Indeed, upon sitting up, Mixun realized
the gnomes were shouting theories and calculations
at each other even as the catastrophe thundered about
them.

Mixun began to laugh. Waterlogged, beset by pirates,
storm, and mountains of ice, he laughed and laughed.

Shaking Raegel's shoulder until he revived, Mixun laughed in his comrade's half-drowned face.

"We're alive!" he said between guffaws. "Rejoice, son of Rafe! We are *alive!*"

<hr>

By the time the storm was done, there wasn't a piece of ice in sight bigger than a gnomish house. The coastline of Enstar was covered with melting blocks of ice for miles, and all the flotsam of Nevermind South came ashore, too. Not one gnome was lost in the wreck of the iceberg, but there were many broken bones and bruises.

The Chief Designer got his people organized. (Disorganized is more like it, Mixun thought privately.) Teams of gnomes combed the sand for lost equipment. Mixun and Raegel scrounged as well—Mixun for valuables and Raegel for food. They found little of either.

At dawn the following day the gnomes gathered to hear long-winded reports on their situation from a series of designated committees. Mixun let them wrangle a while, then asked, "Now what? How will we all get home?"

"I'll appoint a committee to study the problem," said the Chief Designer.

"I'm sure you will. What about the ice?"

The gnome wrung seawater from his long beard and shrugged. "The Excellent Continental Ice Project will have to be repeated," he said.

Before noon, the first islanders came down from the cliffs above to investigate the strange castaways. They were tough looking folk, darkly tanned and chapped from

183

the wind. They weren't pirates, but they had dealt with Artagor and his kind before and probably weren't above wrecking and looting if the opportunity presented itself. The Enstarians looked over the gnomes' wreckage and scratched their heads. Where was the ship? Where was the cargo?

Raegel watched the hard-eyed men and women poking among the melting ice. He had an idea—a surprising idea. He whispered part of it to Mixun, who grinned when he got the gist of it.

"I'll ask," he said, hurrying away.

"Wait, Mix, there's more to it—"

Mixun did not wait for the full explanation, but sought out the Chief Designer, the calculator, Wheeler, and other important gnomes. With expressive gestures, he pointed to the growing crowd of islanders picking over the remains of the gnomes' experiment. The gnomes all regarded him blankly.

"Just say yes," Mixun said tersely.

"What you say is not scientific, so it does not concern us," said the Chief Designer. "Do as you will."

Mixun clapped his hands together and waved to Raegel. Together they approached a likely mark—a lean, hungry-looking Enstarian who wore the rod and chains of a moneychanger on his belt.

"Hail, friend!" Raegel said. "Fine morning, is it not?"

" 'Tis always fair after a great storm," the man replied warily. "You're in good spirits for a shipwrecked man."

"Oh, we're not shipwrecked, friend! We were blown off course by the storm, but we meant to land here all along."

The moneychanger narrowed his already close eyes. "What brings you to Enstar?"

Mixun gestured broadly. "Ice!"

"Ice?"

"Ice. Tons of ice, made from the sweet, pure snows of Icewall and brought to you by the enterprise of my colleague and I, and by the skill of our gnome friends," said Mixun. He introduced himself as Mixundantalus and Raegel as a count again. In glowing terms, he described their expedition to Icewall to retrieve an iceberg and sail it to Enstar.

"Why here?" said the woman on the moneychanger's left. "Why bring your ice to us?"

"As a test, dear lady," Raegel said. "Being close to Icewall, yet surrounded by temperate seas, we wanted to see if we could bring our ice to you without losing too much to meltage. I think we did all right. Don't you, friend Mixundantalus?"

"We did, Count Raegel."

"You mean to *sell* that ice?" said another islander.

"We do," Raegel said. "One steel piece per hundredweight."

The moneychanger laughed harshly. "One steel piece! What's to stop us from picking up your ice from the beach?"

"Why, nothing but the loss of future fortunes to come," said the bogus count.

"What's your meaning, stranger?"

Mixun picked up two fist-sized chunks and banged them together. He passed out the resulting slivers to the growing crowd of islanders. They put them in their mouths, chewed on them, or held them in their hands until they melted to pure water.

"You hold the finest fresh water in the world, and the coldest," Raegel said grandly. "Our company intends to sell Icewall ice in every port between here and Sanction—for drinking water, chilling beverages on hot days, preserving meats, and many other uses! We need a friendly port where we can store the ice before we ship it off to its ultimate destination. Enstar could be that place."

"Are you selling this ice for one steel per hundred-weight to others?" asked the moneychanger. He sucked noisily on a sliver of ice while Raegel answered.

"Not at all!" he said. "As a luxury item, we plan to sell ice in port cities for one steel *per pound.*"

The islanders murmured to each other, trying to calculate the wealth in sight if the ice could be sold at that price.

"It's good ice," said one man. "I have a plot of land on Kraken Bay. You could build your warehouse there."

"Not so fast, Jericas!" the woman interjected. "I saw the strangers first!"

"I *spoke* to them first," the moneychanger shouted.

"Friends, friends!" Raegel said. "There's ice and profit enough for all. Since our stock is currently melting on the beach, why don't those of you interested in our proposition leave us your names and a small deposit? Once our fortunes are restored, we'll mount another expedition to Icewall for more ice."

Like gnomes arguing over an obscure point of mathematics, the Enstarians crowded around the two men, thrusting handfuls of coins at them while shouting their names. Mixun made a great show of writing down everyone's name and the amount of their payment. He then urged them to help themselves to all the ice they could carry. Whooping like children, the hard-bitten islanders swooped down on the rapidly melting ice and hauled it away in buckets, jackets, even women's skirts.

Away from the mob of islanders, Raegel and Mixun counted their money. "There must be two hundred steel pieces here," Mixun chortled. "Who'd have thought? We can sell anything to anyone!"

"We must share the money with the gnomes," Raegel said.

"What! Why?"

Raegel looked at Mixun, but said nothing.

"All right," Mixun said. "They did save our lives back on Icewall. We'll give them something." He mused. "Twenty percent?"

"Fifty percent. They'll need it."

"For what?" said Mixun, raising his voice.

"To equip our next trip to Icewall."

Mixun jerked his comrade farther away from scavenging islanders and the gnomes. "Are you crazy?" he hissed. "We're not going back to Icewall! That was a song for the marks, that stuff about selling ice in every port—"

"I'm going to do it," Raegel said simply.

Mixun stared. "You're not serious, are you?"

"I am. The figures I gave the island people weren't lies. We can get a steel piece per pound in any port, mark my words. And how many pounds do you think was in that ice floe? A million? Two million? Twenty? That's serious coinage, Mix, my friend."

Twenty *million* steel pieces? All the scams for the rest of his life wouldn't net Mixun so much money. Was this scheme of Raegel's the real thing? On far less than twenty million he could redeem his inheritance and fulfill his destiny in his homeland.

He studied Raegel's face. The former farm boy from Throt was lost in a waking dream—no doubt surveying some distant vista of ice. If they could sell it, they could turn an island of ice into an island of money. In that moment, Mixun caught the dream too.

"Hey, Slipper!" he called. The little gnome, seated on a broken barrelhead, turned to face him. "How much ice was in that berg, anyway?"

The calculations took only minutes, but the resulting argument lasted the rest of the day.

THE GREAT GULLY DWARF CLIMACTERIC OF 40 S.C.

JEFF CROOK

At the corner of Globe and Market Streets, in the City of Seven Circles, Palanthas the Ancient, two kender skidded around the corner of the Military and Medical Guild of the Gnomes of Mount Nevermind—Local 458, Palanthian Division, the MMGGMN (mmggmn for short). Farther up Globe Street, from whence an angry mob surged, stood the ancient and revered Cartographer's Guild, and it was no surprise that many in the mob brandished an assortment of compasses (the pointy kind), long metal rules, and T-squares. Even a few surveyor's sticks bobbed in their midst, like pikemen in a ragtag army.

Neither was it surprising that, from the voluminous pouches of the elder kender, there protruded a shock of newly acquired rolls of parchment bound with green ribbons and bearing the great seal of the Cartographer's Guild impressed in an official-looking red wax. The two kender were not aware that it was they who were the object of the chase. They were simply trying to get out of the mob's way, while at the

189

same time clambering for a glimpse of the two thieves who had so earned the mob's ire.

The two kender ducked behind a stone staircase and watched the mob roll by, cross Market Street, and sweep onward along Poulter's Lane, chickens rising before them like dust before a cavalry charge. The elder kender stepped into the street to watch the tail of the mob dwindle away, a grin on his face that seemed to continue all the way up to the tips of his pointy ears. His companion, however, remained seated in the shade of the steps, for it was an uncommonly hot day, and he looked miserable. His hair (if one could call it that) was a veritable rat's nest, with an honest-to-goodness rat living in it. His clothes, leggings, vest, and even his pouches appeared to be held together by force of will alone (or maybe it was the dried mud). Likely, they had not seen a tailor's shop, even from a distance, since the Second Cataclysm. Were the companion kender to sneeze, in all probability he would have emerged from the resultant cloud of dust naked as the day he was born. Contrary to popular belief, kender are not born fully clothed, their pouches already stuffed with other people's belongings.

The elder kender was as unsurprising in appearance as his companion was exceptional. He was the living epitome of a kender, from his hoopak to his lime green leggings to his orange-furred vest, all the way up to a topknot that had grown beyond preposterous and was dangling over the edge of absurd. He'd been meticulously growing it every day of his eighty-odd years, and it was now as long as the tail of a beer-wagon horse. In winter, he wore it as both a hat and a scarf at the same time. He could also tie it under his nose and pretend to be a dwarf. If the kender race could be bothered with writing books about themselves, they might have put his picture on the cover.

Now that the fun was over, the elder kender looked around for something new to do. In Palanthas, there was always something new to do. But as his gray eyes fell upon his miserable companion, a spasm of sadness passed over his wrinkled brown face. Blinking back a tear and almost reaching for a handkerchief, his eyes strayed up the side of the imposing marble building looming over them. Suddenly, his face brightened, the wrinkles around his eyes writhed with glee, and he stuffed the hanky away before he'd finished drawing it out.

"Whort, my boy," he said, "we're here."

———◆·◆·◆———

Hearing the riot outside, Dr. Palaver set aside his delicate alchemical experiment for a moment, exited his office, and crossed the lobby to the front door. It being late in the day, all of the other members of the Military and Medical Guild of the Gnomes of Mount Nevermind, Local 458, Palanthian Division, had already gone home, and the doors were locked.

As he approached the door, he searched his pockets for the keys, found them, then dropped them. He bent to pick them up, heard a loud bang, and the next thing he knew, two kender were sitting beside him, patting his cheeks and waving various bottles of ointments, esters, and tinctures under his long bulbous nose, while going through his pockets as though they were their own. His keys had vanished altogether. He was flat on his back on the floor, with a large knot swelling on his enormous bald head. He slapped away their hands, sat up, swooned, and awoke again just in time to keep them from pouring some concoction of their own mixing down his throat.

"What's all this?" the gnome managed to bluster.

"What's wrong with your voice?" the elder kender asked, his jaw falling open.

"My voice? My voice? Does it sound confabulated? Oh, dear. I hope you didn't pour anything unmaturated down my throat while I was napping. Say, what happened? The lastthingIrememberisbendingovertopick-upthekeysandhearingaloudbang . . ."

"Someone hit you on the head with the door," the elder kender answered, interrupting him. "We found you here. I thought for a moment that you weren't a gnome. You looked like a gnome, but you were talking much too slowly. It is very important that we see a gnome, but now I see that you are one after all, and so it is much better." He helped the gnome to rise.

"By the way, my name is Morgrify Pinchpocket," the kender said, extending his small brown hand.

The gnome placed a pair of spectacles on the end of his nose and examined the kender's hand. "Whatappearstobethetrouble?" he asked, while removing a small rubber mallet from one of the two-dozen pockets in his long white coat.

"Nothing's wrong with my *hand!*" Morg responded, snatching back his hand and stuffing it safely into one of his own pockets (as opposed to someone else's). "It's my nephew here, Whortleberry Pinchpocket. Show your manners to the doctor, Whort."

The younger kender stepped forward and dragged

his foot across the floor, his head bowed. "Erngh," he said, or something very like that.

"Remarkable! I've never seen a case like it. What-doyoucallit?" The gnome dropped his hammer and pulled a rather large book from a rather small pocket in his coat, opened it, and began flipping through the pages. "Manners, do you say? Let me see . . . mumps, mouth-and-foot disease, melancholy measles, mealy mouth malthasia . . . Nope, no manners. Is it a partic-ulated kender confliction?"

"A what?"

"Is it peculiar, to your knowledge?" the gnome attempted to elaborate.

"Most peculiar," the kender answered. "You see, he's broken, and I'd like to get him fixed." He leaned closer and whispered, "I think he's been afflicted."

"Anafflictedkenderohhowmarvelous!" Dr. Palaver exclaimed as he led them through his alchemical labo-ratory.

Several large pots galloped atop a small stove, which caused the whole contraption to rock and scoot slowly around the room. Morg stood on his toes to see what was cooking and very nearly set his topknot on fire. Meanwhile, the doctor led Whort through a door that opened into an examination chamber.

"I've never had the opportunity to study an afflicted kender before. How did he come by it? I have heard that it is caused by expostulation to some source of vaporous fear, like that induced by dragons or other . . . do you mind if I measure his skull?"

He took down from the wall a device that looked like a giant nutcracker and approached the younger kender. Whort backed away, shaking his head and moaning "Erngh!" most emphatically.

"What is he afraid of?" the gnome asked.

"Everything!" Morg groaned.

"Everything?"

"Everything."

"Mostpeculiarindeed!" the gnome squeaked with a little gleeful spring. "Kenderareafraidofnothingbuthe-isafriadofeverythinghowmarvelous!"

He began opening cupboards, of which there were perhaps three score, and drawers numbering in the hundreds. In the middle of the room stood a squat white marble examination table covered with what looked to be the same paper a butcher uses to wrap pork chops or whatnot. The large drain in the floor also did not bode well.

Dr. Palaver rattled about the room, gathering his instruments onto a large wooden tray and spilling various gleaming metal contraptions in his wake. Morg dutifully followed behind him, picking them up, but most of them somehow ended up in his own pockets rather than atop the doctor's tray. The gnome did not seem to notice, so intent was he on his "unprecedented opportunity maybe even an article in the MMGGMN semi-quarterly annual," and with running about, snapping his fingers and exclaiming, "Yes, I shall need that too!"

Whort crawled onto the examination table and curled up into a ball of dirt. His rat poked its head out of his hair and watched the doctor with growing alarm.

Finally, Dr. Palaver stood beside his patient and fingered through the instruments on the wooden tray. He picked up a small yellow card and held it at arm's length from his face, peered down his nose and through his spectacles at it, reading aloud, "Now then, what seems to be the problem?" He dropped the card, lifted a device that looked like a flat piece of wood, and shoved it into Whort's mouth. "Say ah."

"Erngh."

"He can't speak," Morg said.

"Cannot speak? Tch-tch. What a shame." The doctor sympathized while trying to maneuver the beam of a bullseye lantern into the kender's gaping mouth.

"It's a tragedy!" Morg exclaimed.

"Erngh," Whort agreed, choking on the stick.

The doctor removed the stick from Whort's mouth and snapped the lid on the lantern. "Repeat after me. Big brown bugbear biting blue bottleflies."

"Erngh."

"You have been living with gully dwarves," Dr. Palaver noted.

"Erngh."

"That's remarkable!" Morg said in awe. "I found him in the sewers in the company of about forty gully dwarves. You see, his mother sent me to look for him—"

"Elementary. The smell alone testifies to his modus homunculus," the doctor said.

"Yes, I had noticed that. You see, his mother sent me—"

"The prognosis is obfuscated," Dr. Palaver announced.

"She sent me— It's what?"

"I know what is wrong with him."

"You do?" Morg asked excitedly. "Can you fix him?"

"I am not a surgeon, and even if I were this boy's cure is not to be found at the point of a knife," Dr. Palaver said, as he dumped the tray of instruments on the examination table. He lifted a long butcher's blade from the mass of metal and held it up to the light. "Not this one, anyway."

"Erngh."

"Whortleberry is suffering from acute panic psoriasis," the doctor pronounced.

"It sounds horrible!" Morg cried. "Is it catching? Does it itch? Will he live? What is it?"

"It means that he is afraid."

The elder kender's face hardened. "We already know that! Are you sure you are a doctor?" he asked. "Don't you fellows carry a badge or something?"

"There is the name on the door if you care to look," the gnome answered, somewhat miffed. "In any case you did not allow me to complete my diagonal, concerning the gully dwarves. You see, the laborious odor of these creatures has permutated into his speaking glands, interrupting their normal effluvia of sound, while his fear—whatever its cause—has conscripted the muscles around his talk bone, preventing its ability to swing freely."

"So what is to be done?" Morg asked.

"There is only one cure, and of course I have only just invented it today. That is why I was so late leaving, or you might not have found me on the floor," the gnome said as he helped Whort from the table. The rat retreated back into Whort's hair.

"The cure," Dr. Palaver said as he led Morg and Whort down a low, dark, odiferous tunnel, "is to face the fear that produced the affectation, while at the same time indigesting a special formula—of which I am the inventor and which should evacuate the speak glands.

Since I speculum that the source of the fear originates down here in the sewers, where you first found your nephew, the cure for the fear must also lie in the sewers."

"If you only just invented it today, how can you be sure it will work?" Morg asked.

"There is an old gnomish axiom which states that something will work until it doesn't," Dr. Palaver explained. "And since we don't know that it doesn't work we must assume that it does. It really is elementary if you think about."

"I see," Morg sighed, though he really didn't see.

When they had reached a certain section of the tunnel that seemed significant to the gnome, but which was no different than any other they had passed along the way—except perhaps that there was a particularly vile smell wafting from a nearby passageway—the gnome paused and removed a strange-looking device from one of his coat pockets.

"This inflatable sleeve monitors the thickness of the vines in the arm," the gnome said, as he wrapped a thing around the kender's arm that looked like the air bladder of a large fish. A long tube ending in an onion-shaped bulb of similar material depended from one end of the device, while from the other hung three tiny brass bells of varying sizes and tones. "It is believed that the thickness of the vines in the arm is directly provisional to the state of health. Any sudden changes could indicate a converse reaction to the potion, but we will be alerted to such changes by the ringing of the smallest bell. This middle bell indicates that there is a problem with the first bell, and this largest bell indicates that there is a problem not associated with either bell."

Next, the doctor removed a strange set of spectacles from the upper-middle breast pocket of his white coat. They were not ordinary reading spectacles like the ones perched on the tip of his own very large, bulbous nose. Instead, they seemed made of some kind of thick, dark, opaque material through which no light could possibly pass, and which wrapped completely around the face.

"How marvelously hideous!" Morg exclaimed, as the doctor slipped them onto his nephew's nose and wrapped the arms behind his pointy ears. Once on his face, the lenses magnified to grotesque proportions the size of his eyes behind them. He blinked, and it was like someone quickly opening and closing the shutters of a pair of dark windows.

"These spectacles measure the pupae reactions of the eyes for any changes which could indicate possible side effects such as a sudden onset of death-like symptoms. The lenses also prevent any outside influx of proprietary confluences which might construe the results obtained from the measurement of the potion's benefits. Do you understand?"

"Not really."

"Erngh."

"Excellent! Shall we begin?"

The gnome snapped open the cover of his bullseye lantern. Pointing a long narrow beam of light ahead of him, he led the two kender into a smaller passage of the sewer. He splashed heedlessly through the muck, while Whort trudged behind and Morg brought up the rear, leaping nimbly or pole-vaulting with his hoopak from dry spot to dry spot in a vain attempt to keep his bright green leggings clean.

Few but the most esoteric of scholars and thieves

knew this, but the sewers of Palanthas weren't really sewers at all. They were an ancient dwarven city, carved into the bedrock centuries before the first humans sailed into the Bay of Branchala, even before the wizards raised the Tower of High Sorcery with their magic. But the city was abandoned by the dwarves long before the humans took over the land above it. Those who first discovered it found it empty and desolate. Some say it was once part of the great dwarven empire of Kal-Thax, which vanished without a trace before Thorbardin was even a dream in the mind of Reorx.

As they rounded a bend in the sewer, the trio entered a much larger passage than any they had encountered so far. It was also by far the most pungent. Before them lay a small lake of sewage, in which floated as varied a collection of garbage as any city could boast—everything from a toy boat with a broken mast to a dead and very bloated pig to a whole wagon bobbing belly up with its wheels in the air. Large brown globs of thick and apparently solid foam bumped about among the more common rotting rinds of vegetables, slicks of oil, and shingles of congealed fat.

"We call this place the Gully Dwarf Stew Pot," the gnome shouted over the smell, as he tied a bit of white cloth across the front of his face. "This section of the tunnel invertabrately clogs up during the rainless summer months, and gully dwarves find this place irrefutable. The Civil Engineering Guild Local 1101 is currently discussing a hundred and forty-three possible solutions, but in the meantime I can think of no better place to begin to effect a revolution of the patient's melody."

"I've never smelled anything quite so extraordinary," Morg said, while pinching his nose. A burning and curiously itchy curiosity to explore every inch of this place and see what might be found floating in the water competed with a very real concern for the future state of his clothing.

The gnome hitched up his coat and jumped in, promptly sinking up to his white beard. Being a kender and thus somewhat taller than his gnomish companion, the sewage only came up to Whort's pouches, but his uncle, being much weighted by his more recent acquirements, slipped upon landing and vanished below the surface. He came up spluttering and thrashing, while his maps spread around him like a jam of small logs. They quickly began to sink, many vanishing into the dark mucky water before he could recover his wits and grab them.

"Come along, this way. Follow me!" the gnome ordered as he started off, flailing the water to aid his progress. Morg stuffed his remaining maps into a shoulder pouch, making sure to tie it securely shut before continuing.

Though this section of the sewer was illuminated at irregular intervals by iron grates set in the roof, there was very little light to see by, and the water was so thick with muck that no light could pierce its depths. At each step, there was a danger of dropping into some deep hole. The three explorers felt their way along the slimy bottom as they slogged through the water, wary of sudden drops, or worse.

As the sewer merged with the Market Street tunnel, the grates in the roof gradually grew more frequent, providing more light and helping to speed their

progress. Because this section of the sewer opened
directly into Market Street, one of the busiest streets in
all Palanthas, it was no wonder that citizens of Palanthas desired some means of preventing it from clogging,
or to clear the clog once it was, well, clogged. To this
end, the local gnomes had been diligently working for
a number of years, with varying degrees of success. One
of their most promising devices, the very large SNAKE
(Self Navigating Auto-Keyhole Eviscerator—the original design was much smaller and was intended to clean
keyholes clogged with rust) proved unreliable and was
last reported still burrowing away somewhere near the
town of Lemish.

Their most recent design was originally thought too
simple to work, but to date it had passed every test. It
consisted of a large wooden ball only slightly smaller in
diameter than the passage it was meant to unstop. The
ball was deployed upstream from the clog, then carried
to the clog by the flow of water, where it punched
through by the force of its own weight combined with
the mass of water that had built up behind it. Down-
stream, it would be caught and wrestled back up an
access passage to the street, for redeployment or stor-
age, as needed. For explorers of the Palanthian sewer
system, often the only warning of this bowling disaster
came when the sewer suddenly drained away, rather
like the surf before an oncoming tidal wave. So it was
with no small alarm that Dr. Palaver realized he was
crawling along the bottom of the sewer rather than
swimming through its sludge. He looked back and
found his companions standing only knee deep in the
water, with the level swiftly receding.

Whort, who had spent some time, years perhaps,

living in the sewers of Palanthas, knew immediately that danger loomed. The bells on his sleeve commenced to tinkle quite vigorously in his agitation. He grabbed his uncle's arm and pulled, but Morg was much too intent on what was, by the sound of it, bowling from behind them.

The thing filled all the passage, blotting out the light streaming from above and casting the passage into ever deepening darkness. It was constructed of circular layers of wood bolted together and coated by a hard slick varnish to keep out the water and maintain buoyancy. It ground along the passageway, pushed from behind by what appeared to be a wall of water reaching all the way to the roof.

"We'll be crushed!" Morg remarked gleefully.

Dr. Palaver had already fled, abandoning his patient, before Whort got his uncle turned around and headed in the right direction. But there was nowhere to run. They quickly caught up to the puffing old physician as he stood before the tunnel blockage—a massive dam of sticks, treelimbs, bones, bits of furniture and cloth, a wheel, the bodies of more rats than they cared to count, even a bathtub, all cemented together by the thick black sewer sludge.

"Trapped like gully dwarves!" the doctor cried, pulling at his beard.

But Whort had no desire to be flattened, crunch or no crunch. Turning his uncle once more, he shoved the elder kender into a hole in the wall barely wide enough to admit his pouches and hoopak. Complaining volubly of missing all the fun, Morg climbed inside. Dr. Palaver followed, with Whort dragging his feet to safety a bare heartbeat before the sewer ball cast the tiny upward-sloping pipe into pitchy darkness.

Of course, a moment later, raw sewage roared in behind them, blasting the two kender and their gnomish companion up the length of the pipe, disgorging them into a small, round chamber dimly lit by a grate in the low roof above.

"Ah. We have reached a safe room. Good show," the gnome said as he wrung out the sleeves of his no-longer white coat. "We should be quite safe here. You see, the safe rooms lie above the highest level of the sewer. Even at flood time, we will have to wait a bit for the level to subsist, but then I think we may then continue our search for gully dwarves."

"Won't those do?" Morg asked while pinching his nostrils. With his free hand, he pointed into a dark corner, where a half dozen pairs of beady black eyes gleamed back at them.

"They will do admiralty," the gnome answered. He rushed to Whort's side. "I will minotaur your reactions as you approach the gully dwarves. Are you afraid?"

Whort shook his head that he wasn't, almost dislodging the strange spectacles still clinging to his pointy ears.

"Approach them now," the doctor ordered. "When I tell you, you must drink the potion. Do you have it?"

Whort shook his head that he didn't. Dr. Palaver frantically searched his own pockets, until Morg produced it from one of his own. "You left it on the table back at the office," he explained.

Whort took the potion, then stepped toward the gully dwarves, moving into a thin beam of light descending through a tiny grate in the roof. Perhaps it was his eyes, hugely magnified through the glasses, which frightened them, for the gully dwarves began to scream and bite each other. Whort backed away, hiding his features in the shadows opposite the room. "Erngh," he groaned miserably.

The gully dwarves screamed again at the sound, and continued to chew one anothers' ears, fingers, noses, and whatever was handy. Soon, the cries turned from fright to anger, and a fight broke out which threatened to engulf them all. The two kender and the gnome backed up against the wall, wary of flashing yellow teeth or grubby nails.

"Inflections! Inflections!" the gnome cried. "Do not let them bite you or you'll get an inflection!"

Finally, the disagreement subsided, with only a few missing ears and one gnawed pinky finger. Like a shark-haunted bank of herring, in the blink of an eye the gully dwarves had turned, swirled, then collected back in their shadowy corner, all facing in the same direction again.

"I suppose I may have misdirected you," Dr. Palaver said as he examined Whort's sleeve and protective goggles. "I had hypostacized that agharaphobia might be the cause of your fears, but obviously you aren't afraid of gully dwarves as I first surmounted. Say ah." He whipped out another wooden plank (this one much begrimed and hardly very sanitary) and shoved it into the kender's mouth.

"Erngh," Whort gagged.

"As I suspected! The talk bone is still constricted. Well then, we shall just have to find the true source of your fear. As my tormentor used to say, when all other probabilities have been exploded, whatever remains, no matter how smelly, must be the truth." Dr Palaver tossed aside his dipstick. "One of you wouldn't have anything of interest to a gully dwarf?"

"Would a rat do?" Morg asked, wrinkling his nose in disgust as he withdrew the dead rat he had just discovered in one his pouches.

In answer, the gully dwarves began to slaver and creep forward, eyeing the limp, wet morsel dangling from the kender's fingertips. Dr. Palaver took the rat from Morg and shook it temptingly before the gully dwarves, drawing them even farther from their shadowy nook.

Taking great care to speak slowly so that they could understand him (gnomes were notoriously rapid speakers), the doctor said in sweet tones, "Whoever shows me the scariest place in the whole sewer gets this rat. Do any of you know where the scariest place in the whole sewer is?"

At this point, some kind of conference commenced among the gully dwarves. There was many a loud meaty smack, for like most of their race, they spoke more eloquently with the back of the hand than the mouth. They also tended to repeat the same two-word argument endlessly—"No! Yes! No! Yes! No! Yes!"— like a shutter banging back and forth in the wind.

Finally, one of them seemed to have gained the upper backhand, so to speak, for as he turned and the others started to protest, he raised one grubby fist and silenced them all. "Me know!" he said. "Give rat." He held out his hand, black palm upward.

"What is the most scariest place?" the gnome asked.

"Don't say, Grod," one of the other gully dwarves begged.

"Place called . . . The Hole!" the head gully dwarf

said with the best dramatic flair he could muster. The other gully dwarves screamed and bit each other anew.

"What is the Hole?" Dr. Palaver asked. The gully dwarves screamed again.

"The Hole"—again with the screams—"is deep, dark place where no aghar ever come back from."

"Take us to it," Morg said, leaping into the conversation. The head gully dwarf backed away a step and shook his head until his yellow teeth clattered.

"No get rat until you take us to the Hole!" the doctor demanded as he hid the dead rodent behind his back.

The gully dwarves screamed.

◆━◆◆◆━◆

"That Hole," the gully dwarf leader said, pointing to a small, collapsed section of the wall in another part of the massive Palanthian sewer system. The other gully dwarves, too terrified by the sight of it, still managed to scream, even if it was a whisper.

"Doesn't seem much to me," Morg said as he approached the hole in the wall. He stuck his head into the dark aperture and shouted, "Tally-ho and view halloo!"

As he removed his head (still attached to his neck), and his bright kender voice came chirruping back to him by way of a magnificent echo, the gully dwarves breathed an awed sigh to kender bravery. "Do again," one whispered, but he was promptly attacked by his fellows for even suggesting anything so frightening.

Dr. Palaver approached and tilted his ear toward the opening. "I hear something," he said. "Some sort of deep rumbling. Could be the snore of a sleeping beast."

He sniffed. "And a smell like stale beer and dead rats. Definitely something in there," he concluded.

"Something, yes!" the gully dwarf leader agreed.

"Then go in there and find out what it is," the gnome retorted.

The gully dwarves backed away in horror, until Morg (who had gotten hold of the dead rat again) dangled the morsel before them. They stopped, and a few even managed a step forward, filthy bearded jaws slobbering hungrily.

Morg swung the bait before them, back and forth, back and forth, hypnotically, watching their eyes watch the movement of the rat, watching their bodies begin to lean side to side with each sway. Suddenly, he flung the rat into the hole, and the lot of them dived after it before they knew what they were doing. One managed to actually get through the hole. The others merely piled up against the wall, clawing and scratching at each other angrily until they realized where they were. Then, with a horrific yell, they pelted away, leaving the gnome and the two kender alone beside the hole.

They waited a bit for the victim of the rat toss to emerge, then waited in growing alarm as he failed to make his anticipated appearance and exit.

"Perhaps they were right," Morg suggested. His eyes were almost as large as his nephew's, but without the benefit of magnification. "Let's go and see," he added, in a tone that seasoned travelers had learned to dread when spoken by a kender.

They crawled into the hole, Morg leading the way, the gnome bringing up a reluctant rear. They had only gone a short distance before they realized that they were no longer in the sewer. They had come through into a cellar somewhere, a place filled with casks and barrels. Judging from the ancient stone pillars supporting the roof, it appeared to have once been a catacomb.

The deeper into the hole that they went, the louder the contented purring snore became. It sounded like the enormous rumbling of a snoozing dragon—a thing Morg had actually heard, once upon a time. But the reek of stale beer and wet rat and, they now noticed, gully dwarf, grew stronger with each step forward. Finally, rounding a corner, they came to a section of the catacomb illuminated by torchlight shining through a grate in a large iron door. The flickering beam of light that slanted through the grate fell directly on a pile of gully dwarves. They were not dead, though they smelled like they might be. Instead, they were sleeping off a marvelous drunk. Nearby, a cask had been broached, and it was but one of many other empty ones. The owner of the cellar obviously had not been in this section for many days—weeks perhaps, or even months.

Morg saw a large iron door nearby, and his kender-curiosity got the best of him. Straining at the massive ring, he pulled the door open. An even larger cellar, this one lit by numerous torches, lay beyond it.

However, his opening of the heavy iron door had caused it to groan on its rusty hinges. The noise awoke the gully dwarves and sent them bolting in all directions. One gully dwarf bowled into Morg, almost knocking him off his feet. It was a good thing that he kept his balance, or the gully dwarf would surely have devoured him in its fright. Yellow teeth flashed and champed inches from his face. Finally, he had to whack the grimy creature with his hoopak just to settle him down. It worked. The gully dwarf settled down on the floor with a thump.

"Oh dear," Morg grimaced while gnawing on his top-knot.

———◆◆◆———

Dr. Palaver brought the gully dwarf around by applying something he called "smelly salts, or bicarbonate of ammonia" to a kerchief and waving it below the gully dwarf's nose. The miserable little creature came fully awake in an instant, teeth already snapping together in defense. Morg gripped his hoopak in case he needed to reapply the anesthetic.

But the gnome managed to mollify the creature enough to talk to it. "What is your name?" he asked slowly, so the gully dwarf could follow his words.

"Rulf," the creature belched.

"He sounds like he is about to be sick," Morg said.

"Rulf, we have rescued you from the Hole. Doesn't that make you happy?" the gnome asked.

The gully dwarf shook his head. "No. Me happy here. Plenty good beer, stinky cheese . . . this heaven. You rescue me from heaven. Go away." He crossed his arms sullenly and chewed a remnant of cheese still stuck in his beard.

"Come now, Rulf. We have rescued you, so you must come with us. You must do us a little favor, and if you do, I will catch you a nice, big, fat rat with one of my mousetraps," the gnome offered.

"How big?" Rulf queried.

The gnome held up two fingers (he had dealt with

gully dwarves before). "This big," he said, wriggling his stubby digits for emphasis.

Rulf sucked in his breath, which caused him to choke on the bit of beard he had been chewing. He spat it out. "That big, huh? Who Rulf gotta kill?"

"Rulf kill no one. All Rulf gotta do . . . er, ahem," the gnome cleared his throat and blushed. "All we desire of you is to show us the scariest place you know."

"Scarier than this?" Rulf asked, indicating with a wave the catacomb cellar around him.

"The scariest you know," the gnome said.

"It better be big hog rat," Rulf said as he rose wearily to his feet, rubbing his hoopak-knocked noggin with a grimace.

———◆———

Deep beneath the city of Palanthas, below its sewers and deepest dungeons, lay a system of sea caves known only to a few scholars of Palanthian lore. The caves had not been explored by the surface-dwelling citizens of that city in many a century, but they were well known to those who inhabited them.

The denizens of the caves were, of course, the gully dwarves. Those who knew of the gully dwarves living in the city's sewers knew only the tip of the dwarf's beard, as the saying goes. There is often a whole dwarf behind it. In this case, there were several thousand of the generally mistreated and wisely disliked race of aghar dwarves, all living out their private lives in their private desolation, deep beneath a city of a hundred thousand blissfully ignorant souls.

Rulf picked a silent way through these caverns, warily avoiding any large groups and generally keeping to the shadows. When Morg asked him why he was hiding from his people, their guide turned on him with a snarl.

"This not my people," he spat in disgust. "These nasty stinky Gulps. Rulf is a Bulp, the highest Bulp. These lazy Gulps live like kings while we prince Bulps eat bugs. Good bugs!" he added. "But not so good as here."

Indeed, the Gulps of Under Palanthas had been living as good a life as any gully dwarves in all of Krynn for many generations. There was plenty of room, for the caves were most extensive, and plenty of nice, slimy, glowing fungus grew on the walls and floors. Whenever the aghar were hungry, all they had to do was chew on a wall. Most of them could be seen even in the dark by the weirdly glowing streaks of phosphorescent fungus-impregnated saliva drying in their beards.

But the good life here had come to a screeching halt some thirty years ago. Rulf laughed as he recounted the tale.

"That when big boss come. Big boss tell Gulps make plenty torches, smoky torches, torches day, noon, and night, torches all the time. Big boss eat smoke, they say. They say he love smoke like you and me love rat."

"Speak for yourself," Morg said.

"That where me take you: to see big boss. They say he scarier than the Hole. They say he make the Hole look like just a regular old hole in the wall."

At the mention of the Big Boss, Whort began to back away. Morg caught sight of his nephew just as he was about to round a corner. Despite his advanced age, he was easily able to run his younger nephew to ground and drag him back to the gully dwarf and the gnome. He arrived just as Rulf was explaining to Dr. Palaver how the gully dwarves made torches.

"They take sticks and bones—nice bones, waste of good bones—and dip them in pool of black goo. Black goo burns, makes lots of black smoke. Big boss happy. When torches burn out, Gulps take stubs and dip them in black goo again to make new torches. Big boss happy. He eat smoke and leave Gulps alone, but when he mad, he eat Gulps, too. Nasty, stinky Gulps," he ended with a snarl.

Dr. Palaver turned to his patient. "This is the source of your fear," he commented, seeing the way Whort's eyes bugged even more grotesquely behind the spectacles. "You must face it and drink the potion of mighty heroes that I invented today. Now what have I done with it?" He frantically patted his pockets, then turned them inside out.

Finally, Morg produced the bottle from one of his own pouches. "You left it in the office!" he replied to the gnome's angry remark about the kender race in general. "I thought it might be important. Lucky for you, you have got me with you."

The doctor pressed the bottle into Whort's hands. "When I say so, you must drink it down no matter what happens, do you understand?"

The younger kender nodded, swallowing a lump the size of a dragon egg in his throat.

Rulf led them along a series of winding passages and empty, torchlit chambers. The smoky torches provided an excellent cover for their secret entry into the lair of the Gulps and their Big Boss. Finally, they slipped around a corner and entered the largest cavern of all, a cave so big they could have parked a three-masted Palanthian galley in it and still had room for an Ergothian river cog. One half of the chamber was brightly lit by at least a hundred torches, all smoking to high heaven. The other half of the cavern was as dark as a minotaur's heart. The darkness was so thick and smoky that it seemed to be a substance in and of itself, like fog, only much thicker and blacker than even the sulfurous night fogs of Sanction.

Upon seeing this chamber, the first half of Whort's cure was effected. His voice returned in the form of a wail, long and quavering like that of a banshee, and only ending with his head knocking against the floor. Morg tried to clap a hand over his nephew's mouth, but it was too late. Dr. Palaver checked the inflatable sleeve and bug-eye goggles to see if Whort was experiencing any adverse reactions. The gully dwarf bit through the meat of his own thumb in his anguish.

Of course, all of this woke the dragon. At the horrendous noise, the big boss dragon unwound its great smoky coils and crawled from its niche in the far wall of the chamber. Its body seemed made of living darkness, smoke, and fog. It was a shadow dragon, one of the rarest and most temperamental of all dragons. Its body was made of the essence of shadow itself, a creature born of the substance between the waking and sleeping worlds.

"Kender, gully dwarves, and gnomes!" the beast roared when it spotted the intruders. It spread its great black wings, trails and tatters of shadow swirling from their edges.

Rulf cast himself on the ground and gnawed the

floor, trying desperately to fill his belly before he died. Dr. Palaver held his smelly salts beneath Whort's nose, while Morg edged closer to have a better look. Never had he seen such a magnificent creature. The red dragons and blue dragons of the world paled beside this being of shadow. Only a death knight could possibly have been more frightening, and though Morg's mind still wanted to get a closer look, his feet wisely took another course and began to run the opposite direction. He swooped up his nephew as he passed, dragging Dr. Palaver after him.

But not even kender feet could outrun the dragon. It breathed its black despair-inducing breath in a cloud that quickly overtook the fleeing intruders. Rulf, who had remained prostrate on the floor, felt it first. They heard him cry out in his sudden blindness, and then his cry was cut short by a sickening crunch. Before they could begin to feel sorry for the miserable creature, the breath caught up to them as well.

Dr. Palaver, who was behind the two kender, stumbled and fell, struck blind by the darkness of the dragon's breath. Then it overtook Morg. He dropped his nephew, then fell over him and caught himself against the wall. As he felt the will to live drain from his body like water from a leaky bucket, leaving him in a most uncomfortable black despair, he slid to the floor.

For the first time in his life, Morgrify Pinchpocket didn't really care about anything. He didn't look forward to anything. He didn't anticipate the next moment with all the gusto of his diminutive race. He was blind, but the blindness was more than the physical inability to see. He was blind to the future, blind to all hope of what lay in store for him tomorrow or the next day or the next. With sudden insight, he realized that this was indeed fear, the selfsame fear that had stolen his nephew's voice and every aspect of his kenderness.

With that realization, he resolved not to lose his own particular kenderness, even if he had but a few more moments to live. Death, as his old Uncle Dropkick used to say, was the grandest adventure of them all, and Morgrify Pinchpocket determined then and there not to miss his own death, no matter how horrible it promised to be. Privately, he had always hoped for a horrible death—the more horrible the better. Dying in his sleep didn't appeal to him at all, not even now.

Morg roused himself. Since he was blind, he turned his attention to his other senses. He smelled his nephew. The boy seemed near at hand, well within spitting distance, while the gnome, by his groans and moans, was a bit farther down the passage. Also within the range of his hearing was the sound of the dragon as it finished its meal of Bulp gully dwarf. The crunching of the bones and the way the dragon purred as it fed was particularly unnerving, but Morgrify was no longer afraid.

He crawled to his knees and felt around for his nephew, found him, and lifted the boy onto his old shoulder. Staggering away from the sound of the dragon, he paused only to grab a handful of the gnome's coat and drag him along. He bumped and thumped his way down the passage until he thought they might be beyond the area of the dragon's black breath. He was still blind, but the air here did not seem so close and smoky. He gently lowered Whort to the floor and tried to rouse him.

Slowly, the young kender came to his senses, then

all at once he stood up with a shout. Although he was now able to put together a string of noises that sounded rather like the bellowing of a yearling calf with its foot stuck in the fence, he still had not freed his talk bone from its restriction.

Morg tried his best to calm his nephew, knowing that the boy's continued noises would only draw the dragon to them. By the tightening feeling in the air, he knew that the beast was not far behind.

"You must drink the gnome's potion, boy," he urged his nephew. "Have you still got it? No? Why, I've got it in my pouch here. Now how did that get there?"

He pressed the bottle into Whort's hands. Whort took it and looked at it with his goggle eyes as though he had no idea how it had got there.

Morg had been right. This area of the tunnel was beyond the range of the dragon's breath. A few torches smoked on the wall, providing a thick, yellow light. Morg lay on the floor, staring around as blindly as a newborn kitten. The gnomish doctor writhed nearby, a stream of incomprehensible babble pouring from his bearded lips as he banged his bald head on the floor in the blinding despair wrought by the dragon's breath.

However, Whort, who had been unconscious when the dragon breathed its black breath upon them, was not blinded by it, nor did he experience the despair now torturing his uncle and the gnome. His fear and affliction remained. He was almost paralyzed by it, but he was used to it, and the sight of his blind and helpless uncle projected new courage in his vines (as Dr. Palaver might say).

Whort looked again at the bottle and knew what he had to do. He had to drink it before the dragon appeared. Only the potion of mighty heroes, as Dr. Palaver had named it, might give him the courage to rescue his uncle and the good doctor from their predicament.

He uncorked the bottle, loosing a pleasant smell not unlike popcorn popping over a winter blaze. Encouraged, he tilted the bottle to his lips, but at that moment, the shadow dragon loomed around the corner. Whort's nerve almost abandoned him altogether, but his uncle's pleading cries to hurry, cries tinged with a fear he had never known in his redoubtable uncle, roused Whort enough to pour the contents of the bottle into his mouth and swallow.

It tasted like licorice, and when he had drunk it all, Whort tossed aside the bottle and tried his voice. To his horror, nothing happened, except that he hiccupped. But from this hiccup there fluttered a black butterfly with yellow bands on its wings. Whort opened his mouth in surprise at this strange occurrence, only to experience something quite beyond the pale.

Sunlight streamed from his open jaws, poured from his nostrils, and waterfalled from his pointed kender ears. It spread like a pool of melting ice cream across the floor in an ever-widening circle. As it flowed over the gnome, he ceased his babbling and sat up, wiping his runny nose with a filthy sleeve and blinking blindly. On the other hand, Morgrify fell immediately into a deep and contented sleep, a heroic snore ripping across the chamber. The dragon paused, unsure of what this portended.

The magical sunlight reached his shadowy scales, searing their fleshless substance like white-hot iron. The scent of a warm spring morning in a rose garden assaulted his nostrils, driving him back into the comfortable gloom of his lair.

Seeing the dragon retreat, Whort's talk bone was set free, erupting in a storm of expletives worthy of the crustiest sailor to scrape a barnacle from the belly of a ship.

Meanwhile, the sunlight from his mouth continued to swell across the floor. The dragon retreated before it, hissing and thrashing its mighty tail. Whort stepped toward it, assaulting it with such a plethora of kender taunts as few before him had ever strung together in one sunny breath. Wherever he stepped, green grass sprang up in his footsteps. The dragon writhed with anger, but it dared not move into the kender-born sunlight. Finally, it retreated into its lair, belching up what it hoped would prove a protective wall of darkness to block the passage behind it.

Whort returned to his uncle, who smiled up at him, the wrinkles around his blind eyes just a shade more pronounced than Whort remembered them. Taking the elderly kender in one hand and the strangely silent gnome in the other, he led them from the sewers of Palanthas.

———◆◆◆———

Many well remember that day. On the surface, the sun had set and people were just settling down to their dinners, when swarms of gully dwarves poured up from below the streets. Driven mad by the sweet scent of spring roses that streamed from Whort's every orifice, every Bulp and Gulp beneath Palanthas fled upward, the only direction of escape. Never in all its centuries had the city faced such an unexpected danger, and not since Lord Soth stood at the gates and the flying citadel floated over the walls had it been in greater danger.

The Knights of Neraka, ever prepared for almost any eventuality, were quickly overwhelmed, forced to retreat into their gate towers, palaces, and barracks, as the gully dwarf horde swarmed through the streets like a storm surge from the sea. Many later speculated that, had the Great Gully Dwarf Climacteric of 40 SC begun earlier in the day, the casualties would have been much higher. As it was, only one old beggar lost his life that night. They found his well-gnawed bones lying where he had fallen. Many folks mourned the loss of beloved family pets that had been left out of doors for the warm summer's night, but most counted themselves extremely lucky.

Everyone, that is, but the owners of twelve ships, and the fishermen who made their living plying the waters of the Bay of Branchala.

For as quickly as the invasion began, it ended. In mass, the gully dwarves swept down to the sea. Many were drowned outright. A few were rescued by the brave and the foolish, and twelve ships were sunk as the creatures gnawed through their hulls. However, perhaps the worst tragedy was revealed when hundreds of thousands of dead fish washed up along Palanthas's pebbly shore.

———◆◆◆———

The next morning back at the Military and Medical Guild of the Gnomes, the first gnome to arrive—none other than the famous EET (Ears, Toes, and Throat)

Doctor Whizbang—found a young, bedraggled kender sitting on the floor of the lobby beside an old, bedraggled kender and something resembling a gnome in a doctor's coat.

"My friend and my uncle are broken," the young kender announced loudly. "They are blind, and I would like to get them fixed, if I could."

BOND

KEVIN T. STEIN

Damn wolf!"

Karn dragged the leash, threatened with the rod. The wolf bared his teeth, head jerking against the leather rope. Karn wrapped another loop of leash in his palm and dragged the wolf inches closer. The animal barked, snarled, pawed the ground, and pulled back. His teeth were dirty yellow and brown.

Karn sweated, raised the stick, gathered another loop in his palm. The wolf jumped forward, jaws wide, and Karn kicked the wolf. Blood flowed from a shallow gash. The wolf yelped, turning from the attack, saliva spraying from his muzzle as he dragged himself sideways. The wolf thrashed his head, patches of fur missing, showing scars.

The braided leather of the leash dug deep against the calluses of Karn's hand. Dirt ran free, loosened by sweat into streams of grime. Arms and bare legs shone in the firelight. The wolf stopped thrashing and turned his head toward Karn. Karn bared his canine teeth— sharp and pointed like the wolf's, filed. He cracked the

KEViN STEiN

lash against the wolf's scarred flank. The wolf snarled
and Karn snarled. Karn propped his elbow against his
waist and pulled hard, dragging the wolf a few inches
closer.

"Give in, damn you!"

Karn let the leash slacken, sat crosslegged, and beckoned the wolf forward. The wolf lowered himself to the
ground, head in Karn's lap. Karn braced a rod end in
the crook of a leg, the crook of an elbow, pressed the
rod against the wolf's throat. The wolf growled.

"Shut up." Karn smoothed the fur between the
wolf's ears and scratched the wolf's muzzle. The wolf
nuzzled Karn's hands. Karn pressed the heels of his
hands into the pinion of the wolf's jaws, prying them
open. His fingers exposed the wolf's yellowed teeth.
The wolf pushed with his rear legs. Karn's rod pressed
into the wolf's neck, prevented the wolf from moving.
Choked off his howl.

Karn scraped his fingers along the jawline of the
wolf's mouth. The wolf tried to bite his fingers, and
Karn pressed his palms harder, continued to scrape.
The underside of his long nails were caked black. The
wolf moaned. Karn pulled a flower from the ground,
flicked the yellow head off with his thumb and pressed
the moist green stem into the wolf's mouth. The wolf
moaned again.

"Shut up," Karn muttered. "Your own fault."

Karn pressed harder. Blood flowed around the
flower-stem where the wolf's gums had swollen around
old food. Karn dragged the animal higher into his lap
when the wolf tried to pull away. Karn lifted himself
to one knee, leaned against the rod, and wrapped his
other leg around the wolf's flanks. Worked hard at a

piece of old food. The wolf moaned loudly. Blood flowed, the food finally worked out.

Karn released his hands and the rod, pushed himself back. He sat in front of the wolf and stared into his brown eyes. From a pocket, Karn took out a piece of salted beef, held it between his lips and lowered his head. The wolf's eyes flicked between Karn's and the food. The wolf lowered his head. Chin touching the ground, Karn pushed his face forward. The wolf shuffled forward. Carefully taking the beef from between Karn's lips, the wolf raised his head and chewed loudly.

Karn sat up and grabbed the animal around the neck. He ruffled the wolf's fur between the ears. The wolf plodded into Karn's lap, still chewing loudly. Karn smoothed out the animal's fur with his hands, laid down the rod next to him.

"Not so bad, eh, Blood? *Wülfbunde?*" Karn asked. The wolf finished chewing and swallowed the beef. Karn checked the gash in the wolf's side, blood still flowing from the kick. He wiped his bloodied fingers on the grass.

"Who said a wülfbunde needs his teeth cleaned?" Brek asked. His wülfbunde lay on its stomach, eyes on Blood. Brek ran a hand over his wolf's back.

Karn picked another flower, flicked off its head, cleaned his own teeth. "Idiot," Karn said.

"Idiot I may be, but why have you have beaten the fur from your wülfbunde?" Brek asked.

"My discipline is harsh," Karn said. He cleaned the underside of his fingernails.

"Your wülfbunde can't take care of himself."

Karn leaped over Blood, past Brek's wülfbunde, a knife in each hand. Brek drew his own knives. Karn knocked the first one aside and the second fell from Brek's left hand. Karn straddled Brek, knee against the man's throat, outstretched leg pinning Brek's left arm. Brek's wülfbunde jumped near to Blood, who sat up and watched.

"Speak against my wülfbunde, and I'll kill you," Karn said.

"Stand down, scout," Arana ordered, hand scratching her wülfbunde's ear. "Another time to settle. Tonight is for a sacred mission."

Karn bared his teeth. Brek bared his own canines. Arana said a wordless command. Karn jumped off Brek, returned to Blood's side. Blood panted. Arana's wolf stood at her side, watched the other two.

Each of the five scouts straightened their uniforms, faced the fire. The wülfbunde sat next to their masters—black, brown, mottled fur. Blood's fur was patched and uneven, revealing old scars and lashes.

"Report," Arana said.

"We entered the village," Brek said. "The Dark had been there. We did the killing."

"And that was where it happened?" Arana asked.

"The Dark took his spirit, yes," Brek said. "He is Forsaken."

"How did you know?" Arana asked.

"The Forsaken killed his own wülfbunde," Karn said. He ran his hand over Blood's forehead.

"Yes, that is proof," Arana agreed. "Now the Forsaken runs wild. He must be stopped."

The scouts bowed their heads to the fire, its burning and cracking the only sound. Arana spoke to the fire, to each of the scouts and to their wülfbunde.

"In the Age of Might, the Dark Queen brought us the

word of Canus. Canus is the faithful. Canus is the
guard. Canus is the hunter. Canus brought the Bond
between wolf and man, wülfbunde and master. We
become like the wolf, and the wolf like us."

The ears of the wolves twitched. A howl echoed in
the high, surrounding hills—the howl of a wolf from
the throat of a man.

Arana heard the howl, said, "By accepting the Bond,
we accept the sacred mission of Canus. Canus is the
hunter. Once we hunted the enemies of our Queen.
Now that she is gone, our mission is to hunt the Dark.
Canus is the guard. We guard life. Canus is the faithful. We give our lives to our service."

Blood yawned and sat. Karn batted the wolf's ear.
Blood stood.

Arana said, "The Dark are threads escaped from the
mantle of Father Chaos. The threads drive a man to
madness. The Dark causes father to murder child, comrade to kill comrade. In the Knighthood, the Dark
destroys discipline. With us, the Dark breaks the Bond.
The Dark must end with death."

Arana stopped, listened to the howl in the high hills.
She closed her eyes. "The Bond is dagger and fang
against the Dark. The Bond can be proof against its
power. Thus, we fight the Dark."

The wolves around the fire were still, like their masters. Arana drew a crescent-bladed dagger, cut a line
into her palm. Drops fell into the dirt at her feet.

"The Dark has taken one of our patrol. The Forsaken is mad. He will try to kill us as he killed his wülfbunde. He sees comrades as enemies. We know. We
know what happens to those who fall victim to the
Dark."

Arana let her blood fall into a line. Each of the scouts drew their daggers, did the same.

Arana said, "As the Bond is proof against the Dark, the broken Bond is the scent of weakness. If the Dark remains alive in him, he will become a force for Chaos. Shall we suffer him to live?"

Each of the scouts dripped another line in the dirt, forming a cross with the original. Jaren first, then Syllany, then Brek, each touching their wülfbunde on the neck, turning them. Karn made another line, turned, touched Blood's neck. Blood turned.

They all sheathed their daggers.

Arana made a line through her first line, formed the cross. She turned her back to the fire, wülfbunde following. "We have all agreed to the judgment of Canus. By dagger and fang we have agreed. The decision is death."

Each scout walked into the darkness. The scouts were silent on bare feet. The four wolves turned toward Blood. Blood turned back to face them. Each wolf's dark eyes fixed in anger and question on Karn, then each turned and followed their masters.

Blood did not move. Karn grabbed Blood by the remaining fur around his neck, urged the wolf toward the forest. Blood growled and bit. Karn slapped the wolf. He slapped the rod against his thigh. Blood crouched back.

"We have turned our backs and accepted the judgment of Canus. By dagger and fang, we have agreed. I know you understand this well, Blood, because you are the best of all wülfbunde."

Karn pointed the rod into the dark. Blood stood straight, proud, walked into the forest. Karn followed.

The firelight caught the pattern of leaves, branches, threw them large and dark against the ground. The howl of the Forsaken filled the forest. Karn slipped the rod into its loop on his belt. He drew his twin daggers, cutting edges away from his body, curved blades down. Their metal was old, nicked, sharpened with new whetstones.

The hills and mountains of Neraka penetrated the night sky, walled off the stars and Krynn's new moon. Karn found prints within a hundred paces. The Forsaken had passed several times, circling the campfire, the scouts, and their wülfbunde. The prints were hidden with corps technique. Karn pointed at the prints. Blood bobbed his head, sniffed, stared into the forest.

"What do you see?" Karn asked.

Blood coughed.

"Take me."

The two wove through the trees and underbrush. The air was clear and warm. The forest floor was covered with leaves fallen from recent storms, tracks from smaller animals. There was an occasional low rumbling the two felt in their feet—the distant power of the volcanic Lords of Doom. Karn listened, but he did not hear the voice of the Forsaken. Blood kept his nose close to the ground, walking easily.

Karn and Blood found a small clearing, similar to the area around the scouts' campfire. In the center of the clearing was a cairn made of rocks, covered with dried blood. A pair of corps knives formed a crescent, handles stuck in the ground, tips touching. Drawn into the dirt between the handles of the blades was the glyph of the Forsaken's wülfbunde. His grave.

Karn touched his upper canines to his lower lip. Blood sniffed around the stones, poked his muzzle toward the glyph, jerked away when Karn slapped him with the rod.

"You know not to touch the sacred mark," Karn said. Blood growled low. Karn raised the rod, let the lash dangle. Blood sidestepped away. The two glared at each other. Karn replaced the rod at his side.

Karn bowed to the small monument. "Masters and wülfbunde have turned our backs and accepted the judgment of Canus," he said.

Karn studied the clearing and the empty forest, sloped his shoulders, walked into the brush.

Blood bobbed his head as Karn walked past, brown eyes on the scout. Karn stopped, slapped his side for Blood to follow. The wolf stood, did as commanded, sniffing the trail. He quickly found the trail leading away from the blooded monument.

The covered tracks, in wider circles, continued to lead around the patrol's campsite. Karn again heard the howl of the Forsaken. The night was half gone. Karn slapped his hand against his thigh, walked faster, then loped, like Blood, through the forest along the trail.

The howl was closer, with the rustling of leaves and branches the only other sound. Karn increased the pace, right hand knuckles down on Blood's back, knife still in his grip. The uniform of the corps stuck to his sweaty body. Karn kept his eyes wide, his body loose. He tightened the grip on his knives.

Blood followed the trail. Karn followed Blood. The ground was more firm. The Forsaken was better able to hide his circling tracks. Blood stopped, sniffed the air, peered into the darkness. Karn stopped a pace ahead of his wülfbunde, searching the night forest. Blood turned around, sniffing the air, turned back. He coughed.

"What do you—?"

The Forsaken howled in Karn's ears, bare hands clawing his chest, canines tearing at Karn's throat. Karn fell to the ground, brought his knees up, pushed the Forsaken away, howling in return. The Forsaken fell on his back, growl cut short. Karn sprung to a crouch as the Forsaken turned on his belly and launched himself forward. The Forsaken drove Karn stumbling backward into a tree.

The black wolf was the first to arrive, standing at the edge of the clearing. The brown wolf was second, then the mottle-furred. The last was Arana's wülfbunde.

Blood moved toward his master, was cut off by the sudden circle of other wolves. Blood dodged, but was blocked again.

Arana's wülfbunde licked at the fresh wounds from Karn's lashes. Blood shied away, tried to dodge around the circle again, finally sat, watched the fight.

Karn tried to drive his daggers into the Forsaken's back. The Forsaken opened his arms wide, preventing the curved blades from reaching his flesh, and bit Karn with his filed canines. Karn dropped to his knees, bodyweight forcing the Forsaken's arms down. The Forsaken spat and snarled, drove a knee into Karn's face, knocking the scout's head back against the tree. Karn dropped his knives.

Karn growled, swayed. The Forsaken pulled Karn to his feet, bit deep into the man's shoulder. Karn howled, shook his body, but could not free himself from the Forsaken's teeth. He beat the Forsaken with his fists. Blood ran from his wound into the Forsaken's mouth.

"Wülfbunde!" Karn called, desperate.

Karn brought his fists against the Forsaken's ears, struck again, and again. The Forsaken's bite loosened. Karn kicked and pushed the Forsaken back. Karn tried to raise his hands in defense, but his left arm wouldn't work. He kept his right hand up, left dangling, helpless. The Forsaken shook his head, fixed his eyes on Karn, charged, and knocked Karn to the ground.

"Wülfbunde!"

Blood looked to each of the other wülfbunde, toward Karn. Arana's wülfbunde bit his paw, dragged a line of blood in the dirt. The black wolf bit her paw, did the same, then the brown, then the mottle-furred. They each crossed the lines with another, forming crosses of blood.

"Wülfbunde!" Karn cried. He held the Forsaken off with his right arm, slowly losing strength against the other man's weight and insane rage.

The Forsaken's jaws opened wide over Karn's throat. Karn's own blood dripped from the Forsaken's canines. The Forsaken's jaws closed, canines puncturing Karn's neck. Karn raked stiff fingers and sharp nails across the Forsaken's eyes.

The Forsaken yelped, threw himself backward, twisted to his feet, and ran into the forest.

Blood moved toward his master, but was blocked by the other wolves. He growled at the other wülfbunde. They bowed their heads, backing away from the crosses. Blood watched them lope off into the cover of the forest.

Karn's eyes opened, hand lowered to his throat. His

life seeped around his fingers. He tore a strip of cloth from his shirt, pressed it to the wound. He rolled on his side.

"Get help." Blood licked his muzzle. Karn patted his hip, where the rod dangled from its loop. "Go."

Blood stood and stepped toward Karn. He coughed, yelped. Turned to go, turned back. Karn raised himself up, holding the bandage with his right, left arm dangling. One-handed, he wrapped the loose ends of the bandage around his neck, brought them around, binding.

"Go," he said. Blood yelped, sat, did not move, eyes on Karn's wound. "Fine, wülfbunde. Help me up."

Blood forced his muzzle under Karn's arm. The scout pushed himself up, braced by Blood's strength. Karn stood. He turned his head. The bandage held, the outer roll still white. He touched his left arm, pinched his bicep, the back of his hand. He moved his left shoulder. The wound there had stopped bleeding. With his right, he tucked his left arm into his shirt.

Blood turned away, picked up Karn's dropped daggers. The wolf sat in front of his master, dropped the daggers at the scout's feet. Karn retrieved the daggers, sheathed them at his belt. Blood licked his muzzle, groaned. Karn removed the rod from the loop at his side, let the lash fall, raised it, struck Blood.

The wülfbunde yelped, shied. Karn struck again with the lash, grabbed the leather, struck the wolf with the rod. Blood crouched, pressed himself down, away. Karn followed, lashing, striking with the rod.

Blood leaped up, catching Karn between strikes, paws on the scout's shoulders, teeth bared. Karn kept his balance with a step backward. He forced the rod up into Blood's lower jaw, knocking the wolf's jaws shut. He turned and pushed his right shoulder into Blood's throat and forced the wolf onto his back.

Karn pointed the rod. "You let me be attacked!" he said. "Is this the sacred bond of Canus? Why?"

Blood howled, was cut off by a kick reopening the recent wound in his side. Karn used the lash again, stripped fur from Blood's flank. The wolf moaned, crawled away on his belly. Karn lashed Blood's flank.

"Remember the oath as I do, wülfbunde. My life for yours, yours for mine."

The Forsaken howled. Karn bared his fangs at Blood. He raised the rod. The Forsaken howled. Karn growled and kicked at Blood, missed. He snarled, pointed into the forest. Blood crawled toward the howl of the Forsaken, raised himself, eyes on Karn. Karn swept the rod toward the dark. Blood loped into the undergrowth. The Forsaken howled. Karn followed Blood.

The Forsaken had run in a straight line from the fight. The forest floor was black with leaves where the trail stopped. Karn lost the trail. Blood put his nose to the ground, sniffed, walked past Karn, sniffed the leaves. He looked left, right, sniffed again. Sat and moaned.

"Found it?" Karn asked. Blood coughed. "Do it."

Blood lowered himself to the ground, crawled, put his nose into the leaves. He sat up, sneezed, shook his head, sneezed again. He tried again, walking onto the leaves, poking his muzzle toward the forest floor. He sneezed and moaned.

Karn bent down, rubbed dirt between his fingers. He sniffed, sneezed, stood and wiped the dirt onto his shirt. "*Bänscent.* He's trying to throw us off the scent. Don't put your nose in it."

Blood paced back into the undergrowth, kept his nose higher, sniffed, moaned, sniffed again. Picked a direction, waited for Karn to follow. Karn readjusted his useless left arm, drew a knife.

The new moon set behind the mountains. Stars and the distant red halo from the Lords of Doom lit the forest. Karn and Blood walked carefully, quickly across the floor. Blood stopped, sniffed the ground, almost sneezed, tried again. Headed east, continued until he reached a small pond.

Karn knelt, brushed his knuckles over the grass at the water's edge. He sheathed the knife, put his hand into the water, rubbed it over his face and into his nose to clear the bänscent. He did the same for Blood. Scratched the wolf between the ears. Blood lowered his head, lapped from the pond. The Forsaken howled nearby. The two dashed away from the pond. Karn drew his knife.

The forest grew lush where the Lords of Doom lightly spread their ash. Blood followed the howl of the Forsaken, the howl sounding again around the far side of the pond. Karn ran behind, checked his strides to avoid fallen tree limbs, short brush. His left arm jogged loose. He tucked it back.

Blood ran straight. The wolves of the patrol appeared to Blood's right, hidden from Karn by trees, matched Blood's pace, Arana's wülfbunde in front. Karn watched his feet and Blood's trail. The Forsaken howled. Blood increased his pace. Arana's wülfbunde coughed. Blood leaped right.

Following, Karn slipped, fell, undergrowth cracking with his weight. He slid down the hillside, struck the knife into the dirt, lost his grip, clawed. His right leg struck an outgrowth of roots, buckled. He tumbled to the bottom, landing hard on his back. Blood stopped, wheeled, returned to where he had leaped. Looked down at his master.

Karn did not move.

The wolves of the patrol walked to the hillside edge, peered down the hill at Karn, then at Blood. Arana's wülfbunde bit his paw, reopened the wound, and dragged a red line in the dirt. Blood shied away, paced near the edge, finally sat. He looked down at Karn, moaned.

Arana's wülfbunde licked at the newest wounds of Karn's lashes, where the gash had been reopened, fur had been stripped. Arana's wülfbunde bared teeth, growled at Karn. The black wolf drew a line in the dirt, then the brown, then the mottle-furred. Arana's wülf-bunde put a paw near the line in the dirt, started to drag another line to form a cross.

Blood snarled, clenched his jaws over the wolf's paw before the cross could be finished, pushed the other wolf away. Blood barked at the other wolves, then carefully edged over the edge of the hillside, inched his way to the bottom. Blood poked his muzzle under Karn's chin, took hold of the scout's uniform shirt in his teeth, and shook.

Karn lifted his head. He breathed deeply, tried to raise himself. Blood forced his body behind the man's back and lifted. Karn raised himself to a sitting position. Waited, then stood. His right leg was weak but supported his weight.

"The Dark is not in me, Blood. The others don't understand. You do. You know. The Bond between us is strong."

Blood circled his master, yelped. Karn put his left arm back into his shirt, fastened his shirt over his arm to ensure it would not slip out. He checked himself for new abrasions, found the wound in his shoulder was bleeding again. The bandage around his throat was damp on the outside. Blood sat, panting. Karn touched his canines to his lip, stared at his wülfbunde, removed the rod from his belt.

"Never have you failed me twice," Karn said. "You are the best of all wülfbunde. By dagger and fang, you are the best. With you, I have long been blessed by Canus. I will remind you."

Karn raised the rod and struck Blood once. Blood howled, the other wülfbunde howled. The Forsaken heard and howled in return. Blood stumbled away, ran in a circle, bit, and licked his flank where the rod had struck. The wolf spat, barked fury at his master, moaned, crawled and leaped up, barked again. Karn replaced the rod at his side, checked the bandage at his throat, securing the end.

"I am off to find the Forsaken," Karn said. He left Blood standing.

The wolves of the patrol made their way down the hillside wall after Karn was gone. Blood limped. Arana's wülfbunde drew a red line in the dirt. Blood bit his own paw, crossed the line, judgment on his master made.

———◆———

Karn followed the howl of the Forsaken. He put weight on his left leg, dragged and hopped on his right. His left arm was still secure in his shirt. He held his

last dagger in his right hand. The Lords of Doom shook
the leaves. Their light faded with the dawn.

The undergrowth was constant and not high. The
path Karn found was clear—crushed leaves, snapped
branches, curving around north, west. The hillside's
base sloped back up toward Neraka. Karn was forced
to work harder.

His uniform shirt was dark with his sweat and
blood. The bandage around his neck was wet near the
wound, dry where the cloth had once been soaked. The
end of the bandage was loose. Karn kept his pace
steady. He used the trees to support himself. He didn't
stop moving. He bared his canines and breathed
quickly. The forest was quiet.

The Forsaken's path led back to the original encampment. The fire was still lit. The cross in the dirt made
by Arana had not been blown away by the wind. Karn
did not enter the encampment. He hunched by a tree,
scouted. He held his dagger to his chest, waited, stood.

From behind, the Forsaken leaped on Karn, forcing
him into the encampment.

Karn twisted, brought the dagger around as he fell
on his back. The edge of the blade caught the Forsak-
en on the bridge of the nose, bone cracking, skin shorn.
The Forsaken howled, dropped on top of Karn with a
knee, breaking ribs.

The Forsaken pinned Karn's arm with a knee, bared
bloody canines, and struggled to reach Karn's throat. Karn
struck with his left leg, tumbled the Forsaken up and
over. The Forsaken rolled, twisted, jumped to his feet.

The wolves of the patrol stood behind the Forsaken.
Blood stood behind the cross in the dirt, Karn's lash-
ings still fresh on the wolf's body.

Karn turned, got to his feet, dagger ready. He looked past the Forsaken into Blood's eyes, at the cross in the dirt. Karn understood.

"I, too, have been judged," he said. "By dagger and fang."

Blood bared his canines and growled.

The Forsaken snarled, charged forward, broke Karn's wrist, dagger falling. Karn spat and howled, drove his left heel into the ground for support. The Forsaken forced Karn backward into a tree. Karn snarled, struggled, dodged as the Forsaken tore and missed, gouging bark from the tree. The Forsaken pinned Karn by the throat.

Blood leaped, breaking the Forsaken's hold on Karn. The wolf's jaws ripped, tore at the Forsaken's throat, finding arteries, finding veins and tearing them loose. The Forsaken staggered, holding the wolf upright, the two stepping sideways, backward. Blood's muzzle was covered, dripping, from the Forsaken's wounds. The Forsaken raged, slowed, stumbled, toppled backward.

Blood breathed heat into the Forsaken's face. The Forsaken growled at the wolf, did not move. Blood's chest heaved with breath. Waited.

The Forsaken wept. Growled, snarled and clawed the air.

Karn sank to the ground. "Why, wülfbunde?" he asked Blood. "Your judgment was made."

Karn heard the Forsaken laugh, choke around the blood flooding his throat. "In the Age of Might, the Dark Queen brought us the word of Canus. Canus brought us the Bond between wülfbunde and master."

KEViN **STEiN**

Blood backed away from the Forsaken, turning to Karn. The wolf walked slowly to Karn, shuffled, put his head in Karn's lap, forced his head beneath Karn's hand. Karn tried to brush his fingers against Blood's fur, but could not make his fingers move. Blood moaned, brown eyes meeting Karn's.

Blood's ears twitched. He lifted his head, coughed, lowered his head again. Karn listened. The patrol was nearby. He could hear the other wülfbunde leading their masters to where he lay.

The Forsaken tried to move, lay still. He said, "The Bond is the bond of love. The Dark cannot break the Bond. Above all things, a man loves his wolf."

Karn looked into Blood's eyes and understood. "The Dark cannot break the Bond," Karn said. "Above all things, a wolf loves his man."

A TWIST
OF THE KNIFE

JEAN RABE

The snow came at her in a blur—icy shards stinging her face and hands, turning her skin a hurtful pink and chasing her farther into the folds of a tattered woolen cloak. She had no hood or hat, and her long hair whipped about, spun silver dancing madly with the keening wind.

She didn't *have* to be out in this weather. She could have stayed in the goatherds' village, claiming a spot by a cozy hearth and eating her fill of something warm and reasonably tasty. But she was driven this night, like the snow was driven, and so she struggled to pick up the pace along a narrow path where the drifts were a foot deep in places.

It was the onset of winter in Neraka's Broken Chain Mountains. In the foothills and in the rest of the country there was likely only a dusting of snow—and perhaps no snow at all in the southern parts of the Dark Knight-held land.

But this brutal storm is not so bad, certainly not as bad as others face, she told herself, as if her thoughts might somehow soften the wind's vicious bite. People she knew in Southern Ergoth, where the white dragon Frost held sway, faced weather like this—or worse—every day of the year. Word was they had blizzards so fierce that no man could last outside for more than a few minutes, and she was lasting—*and walking*—making headway toward the next village.

She didn't see the man against the rocky outcropping. He held his breath and listened, hearing the wind. To him it sounded like a chorus of mournful ghosts. Her boots crunched on the snow as she passed by his hiding spot. He waited, silently counting, then stepped out, an inky shadow against the stark whiteness that stretched in all directions.

Shiv was taller than the woman, but only by a few inches, putting him a bit above six feet. His back was straight, his shoulders broad, and the rest of him was oddly narrow, a gaunt man whose silhouette resembled a dagger stuck into the drift growing at his feet.

He was dressed in a smoke-gray jacket and trousers made from the hide of a worg and lined for winter use. A knit cap hugged his hawkish face. Unlike the woman, Shiv did not wear a cloak; he knew it could lash about in the wind, entangling his arms and flapping noisily and perhaps giving him away. He had a pack on his back, padded so it would not rustle, and a purse at his belt—nearly empty, as it had taken practically every coin he owned to find this woman. But his purse and his pockets would be splitting at the seams soon enough, filled with steel and gems. Before the month was out he would be happily doling out some of his riches to the most exotic, perfumed ladies for hire he could find in Jelek's colorful foreign quarter.

Shiv held thin-bladed knives in each gloved hand, smeared with an oily black substance so they would not reflect any gleam off the snow. He'd bought them two years ago from an expert weaponsmith in Bloodspring. Their metal was as hard as the set of his jaw, the edges so keen he hadn't yet needed to resharpen them. Worth every coin, these tools of his trade.

He intended to kill the woman with them.

He would do it quickly, effortlessly, stepping close and slipping the right blade across her throat while plunging the left into the center of her heart. He'd done it so many times before. Afterward, he would drag her off the trail, take her body a little higher into the mountains where the wolves would catch the scent and devour the evidence.

But he wouldn't do it here. It was too close to the village she'd just left, too risky that someone following after a stray goat might—despite this damnable storm—glimpse the deed.

And he wouldn't do it tonight.

It was too soon.

He'd only just managed to find her, late this afternoon. He didn't *know* her yet, didn't have her *walk* down, hadn't looked into her eyes. He didn't know how strong she was, and, most importantly, he had no clue about her contacts in these mountain villages. This last crucial bit could take a few days to ferret out, perhaps longer.

So he followed several yards behind her, gloved hands reflexively closing on the handles of his weapons before sheathing them, dark eyes squinting against the frenetic snow as they trained on her back.

It was work to keep her in sight, his chest burning

from the exertion, his legs aching from slogging through mounds of snow. Twice he dived into a drift when she turned to check her bearings. Were it not for the whirling snow she might have spied him or his tracks. His teeth chattered, and he muttered a silent curse that perhaps he'd been a fool to take on this job *at this time*. Couldn't her assassination have waited until spring?

He guessed it took them nearly two hours to reach her destination—a ramshackle assortment of wood and stone buildings wedged into a mountain overhang. He made out on a sign partially buried by a drift: KETH'S CRADLE. More like the Abyss's Cradle, he thought.

She hurried toward the largest dwelling, a turtleshell-shaped affair that was busily belching smoke into the sky. He watched her for a moment more, then quickly began to circle the tiny community, which by the malodorous aroma that hung in the air, and the pens he barely made out, declared it another village of goatherds.

She rapped firmly on the door.

"I am Risana," she stated.

Ree-shanna. That was the name Shiv had been given, though his employers had pronounced it differently—*Ris-aye-nah*.

"Risana," she repeated, as the door finally opened. "Risana of Crossing." Her voice was musical and held no trace of the tiredness she most certainly felt. "You sent word that you needed me."

"Yes!" came the breathless reply. "The Solamnic Knight."

"I—"

"At last you're here, dear woman. Please."

Without another word she was ushered inside, and the heavy door slammed shut behind her.

Shiv worked his way behind the turtleshell dwelling, peering through the cracks of a shuttered window that couldn't close properly because the frame had warped. He could see only the main room from his vantage-point, but it was enough. The merrily burning fire-place made it appear warm, and Shiv pressed himself against the wall in the futile hope of catching some of that heat.

An old, bent man with a mustache and goatee, who Shiv idly thought parroted the village's cloven-hoofed charges, drew Risana to the center of the room, where four blanket-wrapped forms were stretched out on cots. There were a half-dozen women of various ages sitting in straight wooden chairs, their backs to the fire and sympathetic faces angled toward the forms. Their conversation stopped as Risana moved to the smallest patient. Their eyes trained on her now.

Shiv watched her, too. On initial inspection the fire-light revealed nothing untoward about Risana. She was just a tall, young woman wrapped in a tattered cloak, the rosy hue of which suggested the garment had been red at one time. She was a plain-looking woman, really, Shiv thought, a commoner who could have lost herself in the lower- or middle-class quarters of any town, someone most folks wouldn't stop to give a second look. But then he gave her a second look, a careful one, and saw that she was young, all right, very. Certainly not yet twenty, he decided, and nothing common about her. The woman was singular. One simply had to see past her tattered garments and fatigue.

Her face was well defined, angular without being sharp, the planes of it smooth and unblemished, and it looked as if she was blushing because of the cold and windburn. Her nose turned slightly upward, a hint of aristocracy, and the bearing suited her. While her hair had looked like sparkling silver outside in the snow, here, wet and flat against her head, it seemed an unusual shade of blonde, the color of cooled ashes—an almost whitish-gray that shone like silk. He imagined it must be soft to the touch.

Her eyes were charcoal, dark and large and rimmed with long black lashes. Those eyes seemed to take in everything, and measure—the women by the fire, the bundled-up people on the cots, the old, bent man who was speaking to her, and the windows, where her gaze lingered. Had she seen him? He held his breath, not blinking. Were her eyes locked with his? No, he breathed a sigh of relief. Her eyes were clearly fixed at some point far beyond this room and Neraka.

Shiv turned his face, concentrating to catch fragments of what was being said inside.

"It's not pneumonia," the bent man was telling Risana. He wrung his hands nervously. "I know pneumonia. I can treat pneumonia. Someone here gets it every year. It's something worse, this is—a plague maybe, something that spreads. Emil and his family have it, too. They're in the house across the way. And the Donners might be getting it."

"We might be next," the stoutest of the six women cut in.

"We shouldn't be sitting so close to the sick," another whispered in a high-pitched voice.

"I'll sit where I please," the stout woman returned.

Risana knelt at the cot nearest the window, tugging the blanket back to reveal a red-faced child with dozens of lesions on his arms and neck. The boy, no more than six or seven, coughed deeply, shoulders bouncing against the pine frame of the cot. The child was overly thin, there was a sheen on his skin, and his clothes were dark with sweat.

"A plague," the bent man continued. "It has to be. The runner said Graespeck and Tornhollow have sick folks, too. Just like this. Some of 'em dying. That's why we sent for you. The runner said you were fixing folks in the villages to the south of here. Said that you maybe knew how to cure this kind of illness. We're desperate."

She replaced the covers and smoothed the boy's hair. He started to offer her a smile, but began coughing again, which was echoed by one of the other blanketed forms. The stout woman loudly sucked in her breath.

"That's why our message said this was an emergency, ma'am. We're a small village. Don't want more people catching this disease, and we don't want no one dying. Our Jamie—the little one here—he's real bad."

Softer, the bent man added, "He's my youngest grandson."

Risana nodded and ran her fingers across the child's forehead.

"A very strong fever," she said. She twisted to her right so she could reach to another cot, feeling the forehead of an elderly woman.

"My wife," the bent man said.

"Mother," one of the six women added, choking back a sob. "She's not been conscious for two days."

Shiv noted that there was some resemblance between the women by the fire. Sisters. The other two patients no doubt were relatives also. The sisters had started talking again, filling the room with the sound of their buzzing. They asked Risana what she could do to help the ill. The thickset one, practically begging, made it clear Jamie was her son and should be tended to first. None argued with her.

The oldest sister politely asked what had brought Risana into Neraka, and why she was healing folks in the mountain villages when Solamnic Knights were considered the enemy around here. "Not that *we* take you for an enemy," she added, "but if the Dark Knights catch you, they'll kill you."

Risana didn't reply. She stood, taking off her voluminous cloak, which was quickly gathered by the bent man. She stretched, rolled her head to work a kink out of her neck.

A Solamnic Knight with no armor, Shiv thought, knowing his mark was now an easier one.

The firelight from the hearth played across her tall form. Her sword seemed well maintained, the pommel highly polished silver that was fashioned in the shape of a griffon's claw. The scabbard was worn and ripped in places, and the blade showed through, catching the light and reflecting motes that danced across the walls.

Risana unbuckled her sword belt, and the bent man took this too, shuffling away and hanging it and her cloak on a hook near the door. She had a big pouch tied to her waist, and she was fumbling with this now, pulling smaller pouches from it, a few tiny vials, softly issuing instructions that Shiv could not hear. He got the gist of it though, as the bent man and two of the sisters hurried to heat some water over the fire. The remaining four women resumed their buzzing talk, the thick-
• set one casting frequent concerned glances at the coughing boy.

Risana did not pause in tending to the ill until dawn threatened to take over the sky. She constantly moved between the turtleshell home and the one called "Emil's place." She had diagnosed the malady as Redlant Fever, adding that a few of the eldest Knights in the Solamnic unit she'd been assigned to were struck with it shortly after coming to Neraka well more than a year ago. A potentially deadly threat that seemed to strike the young and the old the hardest, she demonstrated that with the right medicines it was not terribly difficult to treat. She gave them details about the mixtures she was using so they could duplicate it with their own herbs, then she sat by the bed of the old woman.

Just as the small community began to wake up, Shiv stepped away from the shadows and moved around to the front of the building. He was dressed differently now, in well-worn clothes he had retrieved from his pack. He no longer stood straight. He adopted a list to his right, rounded his shoulders and turned his left foot so he appeared clubfooted. He shuffled forward and knocked on the door. Several moments later it was answered by the bent man, whose eyes were rimmed by dark circles from lack of sleep.

"Snow's filled the trail t' Graespeck," Shiv said, sounding half out of breath, his voice all craggy. "Too tough t' walk it right now. Lookin' for a place t' stay until it stops snowin'." He looked up at the sky for effect, the snow still coming down hard, though the wind had dwindled to almost nothing. He shivered, something easy to do as he was indeed cold, and he thrust his hands into his pockets. "I was wonderin' if I could . . ."

The bent man yawned wide and gestured inside.

"Thanks for your hospitality. Name's Safford," Shiv lied as he slipped past.

"Wilcher," came the reply. "Erl Wilcher. Take care, Mister Safford. We've sick folks here, though we've got someone busy healing them."

Shiv shuffled into the main room, heading straight to the fireplace and waving his hands in front of the flames. The heat felt good to his sixty-year-old frame, and he let himself bask in the sensation for several moments before he turned to study Risana.

Her shoulders were slumped. Still, she kept her vigil at the old woman's side.

The daughters moved between the other three patients—all who were remarkably improved and sitting up on the cots. There were only a few lesions remaining on the boy called Jamie. He no longer coughed, and his mother was clucking her thanks to the young healer.

"Here. Drink up!" One of the sisters thrust a bowl of soup at Risana. "It's spiced chicken broth."

Risana declined, until the three improving patients, the sisters, Wilcher, and even the newcomer had some first. Then she took a chipped bowl between her hands, closed her eyes as if in prayer, and drank.

The soft light that streamed in through the windows gave silver highlights to her hair and revealed cuts to her garments that only could have been made by a sword.

"You're a Knight," Shiv stated, trying to draw her out into conversation. "A Solamnic."

She didn't answer.

"That charm a pokin' out from your shirt," he

continued, gesturing with a finger. "That says you're a Knight of the Rose."

Risana fingers fluttered to her neck, finding a gold chain and charm that had worked itself free. She was quick to stuff it under her shirt and tabard.

"A wilted rose," he said wryly, noting that the sisters were upset at his prying. "And one without any armor. Where's the rest of your unit?" Any information about other Solamnic Knights in Neraka would be worth something to his employers.

"Dead."

He raised an eyebrow and clamped his teeth together to stifle a yawn. Shiv desperately needed some sleep.

"All of them dead. Dead and buried."

Shiv cocked his head to the side, a gesture that encouraged her to continue.

"We were directed to Neraka about a year and a half ago, twenty of us ordered to the foothills just north of the Lords of Doom. We were to meet a Dark Knight commander there, escort him safely out of the country."

"But . . . ?"

"But we learned too late that the commander didn't intend to defect. He meant merely to lure Solamnic Knights into Neraka. He must have been disappointed that the council sent only twenty. I guess he expected a small army. Still, he had some measure of triumph, as two of our number were from the council itself."

"What happened?" This came from the child Jamie. "Were you ambushed?"

A nod.

"But you escaped," Shiv said. "Obviously."

"I was the only survivor." She let out a deep breath,

the sound like sand being blown by a hot breeze.

One sister came forward and poured her more broth. "Then don't mind my asking, and don't believe we're not grateful—we are—but why are you here?"

She didn't answer, and so Shiv pressed, "Why didn't you join another Solamnic outfit? Why aren't you . . . ?"

Her doe eyes regarded the disguised assassin, cutting off his words. She ran her thumbs around the lip of the bowl and finally replied. "Elsewhere? I'm not needed elsewhere. I'm needed here."

Shiv *really* saw her then—selfless, driven, filled with a determination he had never seen before, and perhaps touched by madness. He finished his broth, his eyes never leaving hers.

"You're tired." This came from Wilcher, who hovered at Risana's shoulder.

"A bit." She smiled slightly. It was the first time Shiv had seen her smile—a smile that melted the coldness in her face.

"Rest here, in my home. As long as you like. Please."

"I will stay with your wife until . . ."

"I thank you for helping my grandchildren. I know you can't help her." There was a deep sadness in the old man's eyes. "I'll tend to her alone. You don't have to sit with her."

"Yes, I do."

Two hours later, their vigil was over, and Risana allowed herself an all-too-brief rest before getting up. "I am sorry for you loss, Erl Wilcher," she said, as she reached for her cloak.

The old man nodded, his eyes filled with tears. "Stay for a while," he said. "Have dinner. Spend the night."

She shook her head. "I must be on my way. As you said, there are ill folks in Graespeck, and I'd like to get there before nightfall."

Wilcher clasped her hands and gestured with his head toward the assassin. "This fella here—"

"Safford," Shiv stated.

"He said he's going to Graespeck, too."

"Then I shall have company."

"Her name is Risana," the Dark Knight commander told Shiv several weeks earlier. The commander and a half-dozen of his esteemed fellows met with the assassin in a closed banquet hall in Telvan.

"She is concentrating her efforts in the Broken Chain Mountains, and has been for much of the past year from what we've gleaned. She heals the sick, traveling from village to village, and she touts the glory of the Solamnic Knighthood. She relies on the witless and the grateful to keep her hidden and to feed her. The villagers will not give her up and will not reveal her contacts. Locating her could be difficult."

"Not for me."

The commander's lips edged upward in a sly grin. "That's why we sought your services."

Shiv steepled his fingers. "I am, as you've acknowledged, your most expert spy and assassin. And the most expensive. But why send me all this way for just one woman?"

The commander let out a laugh, then instantly sobered. "At first we thought her inconsequential," he said, eyes flitting to Shiv's, then finding the assassin's gaze uncomfortable and looking away. "We have done nothing about her for several months—considering her, as you said, just one woman."

"At first," Shiv mused.

"At first. But singlehandedly, she appears to be turning the villagers against us."

"One woman?"

The commander growled. "We've had reports of youths in some of the mountain towns leaving Neraka under her direction to join our enemy. Others are talking against us. She is a blight that must be stopped. Her allies and contacts must be found and eliminated."

"Why not send an army of Dark Knights to deal with this blight?"

"There can be no hint of Dark Knight involvement. The mountain villages embrace this Solamnic, and we cannot afford to make a martyr of her. That would only make matters worse. No clues can point to us."

Shiv agreed to the job. They offered him more than enough money—despite the weather.

* * *

The assassin followed Risana, glancing over his shoulder to see the people of Keth's Cradle smiling and waving good-bye. In the space of less than twenty-four hours the "blight" had been thoroughly embraced by the village.

"Graespeck isn't all that far," he told her after Keth's Cradle was out of sight, "but all of this snow makes it seem leagues away."

Shiv had straightened his back and was no longer pretending to have a clubfoot. Walking behind Risana, he didn't need to keep up the ruse. However, an hour past sunset they neared her new destination, and he adopted his crippled guise again. They plodded into

Graespeck, a place only marginally larger than the previous village. Once again, he watched her go to work.

There was a group of young men in this village who were keenly curious about the woman, tales of whom had obviously preceded her arrival. As she moved from home to home, ministering to those who were stricken with the fever and offering kind words to the elderly, the young men followed her, plying her with questions about the Order of the Rose and about life outside of Neraka. A few made it clear they wanted to be Solamnic Knights.

The blight spreads, Shiv mused, noting, however, that she encouraged no one to join her Order. At least not here. Furthermore, it was clear she had no contacts in this village and that she hadn't known a single soul here before she arrived.

They spent the night in a log home with one family. Following dinner, they helped shore up a shed that was threatening to collapse, then they slept for a few hours and headed out at first light.

For weeks Shiv accompanied Risana, and not once in that time—despite his many questions—did he hear her mention other Solamnic Knights in Neraka or name villagers who might be in league with her. In that time she never asked why, upon reaching Graespeck, he kept going along with her on her healing missions. In truth, he wasn't quite sure himself.

She simply seemed to accept his company, enjoying it at times between places where they stopped to rest. He regaled her with stories he made up about a boyhood that never happened and a family that never existed.

Gradually, she told him quite a bit about her own youth and, one night, about why she came to Neraka. They were hunkered just inside the entrance to a small cave, watching the snow fall and the evening deepen.

"I was a chirurgeon," she said, her voice and eyes soft. "The youngest and the most inexperienced of the Solamnic Knights sent here. I was brought along as an assistant, really, for the two council members, as I am not the most skilled with a sword. Councilman Crandayl suffered from gout. I was there to aid him." She paused and turned to stare at Shiv, again her eyes seeing something far beyond him and the darkening cave. "I was charging forward into the battle against the Dark Knights when I fell, slipped on the blood already thick on the ground. I struck my head and lost consciousness. When I awoke hours later I discovered that someone had fallen on top of me—Crandayl. He was dead. Everyone was dead. And the Dark Knights had taken me for dead, too. It took me three days to bury my brethren, nearly another day to bury the Dark Knights who had fallen."

"And you left your armor there?" Sanford asked.

A nod. "I left my oath there, too."

Shiv waited.

"I'm not a Solamnic Knight any longer. If I was, I wouldn't be here."

"I don't understand."

"A Solamnic Knight would have returned to the Order's nearest outpost. I would have let them assign me to another unit."

"Then why . . . ?"

"Am I here? I'd rather wander these mountains helping people live than return to the Order and ride off to kill people. I hate fighting. I hate the regime and the mandates and the notion of always following orders. And maybe I hate the Knighthood because it fosters bloodshed."

"The villagers think you're a Solamnic Knight."

She shrugged. "Better, perhaps, they think that than to know the truth—that I'm a deserter."

"Maybe you're still a Solamnic at heart. After all, the pendant . . ." Shiv gestured to where he knew the charm hung on the gold chain beneath her shirt. "You still wear a symbol of the Order of the Rose."

"I wear a symbol of my guilt," she corrected him. She paused and resumed studying the snow. "Get some sleep, Safford. Morning will come too soon."

Morning did come too soon. Shiv knew Risana well enough by now, better than any of his previous targets. He knew she worked alone, that there had never been any contacts or fellow Knights supporting her cause. She had never encouraged a soul to leave the mountains and join the Solamnic Order. He could kill her and complete his assignment. It would be simple.

They were nearing a branch in the trail that led back to Telvan. There were places nearby to hide her body. A journey of seven or eight days and he could tell the Dark Knight commander that the contract was fulfilled. He could finally collect his pay.

"Aren't you worried?" Shiv asked her, the fingers of his right hand brushing the handle of a knife. "Rish, aren't you in the least little bit worried?"

"About . . . ?"

"The Dark Knights. This is their land, after all.

Aren't you worried they'll be hunting you? If you keep this up, healing people and ending plagues, they might try to do something to stop you."

She shrugged. "Let them send someone, Safford. Let them send their very best assassins. I'll stay here until my last breath."

"Till your last breath," Shiv whispered, staring at the trail ahead. "This way," he said louder, stepping onto the trail toward Telvan and, for the moment, taking the lead.

Shiv didn't hear the boots crunch on the snow ahead, or see the shadows stretch out from a spire along the path. If the sun hadn't been shining so fiercely, he wouldn't have caught the glint from their swords, which they stupidly hadn't blackened. The glint was the only thing that alerted him.

"Rish!" he shouted as his hands tugged free the twin blades. He crouched as he heard the swoosh of steel behind him, Risana drawing her long sword.

"Safford, what is it? What—?"

Shiv darted forward just as the first assassin lunged into his path. He was a young man, full of muscle and energy and, fortunately, not terribly skilled. Shiv dropped below the swing of his short sword and drove one of his knives up into his belly. The second knife stabbed higher and punctured a lung. He twisted the blade for good measure.

Shiv stepped back and kicked the man down the mountain path. The young man struggled to stop his descent and managed to grab onto an embedded stone. Shiv turned his attention to the second figure. This one was older, well into middle age, and careful from experience. His eyes narrowed as he caught Shiv's angry expression.

"Shiv." The word was a hiss of remembrance. Then, much louder, "Shiv of Telvan!"

Shiv grimaced. He had seen this one in a Dark Knight camp last year, a mercenary who had the favor of the commander who had ordered Risana's assassination. The man opened his mouth to say something else, but Shiv cut him off, hurling one of his knives and watching as the sharp, slender blade pierced the man's throat.

So the Dark Knights have sent more assassins, Shiv thought. They are tired of waiting for me to finish her. They are in a great hurry to have this woman die.

There was a sudden clash of steel and Shiv whirled, shaken from his thoughts. Risana was battling her own foe, a third man whose weapon was blackened and whose presence Shiv had not sensed. Perhaps the two Shiv had dispatched had been sacrificial lambs, part of a ruse to distract the woman from the more dangerous killer.

"Who are you?" Risana demanded. She was trading blow for blow with the man. "What do you want with us?"

No answer.

The assassin was a professional, Shiv quickly understood, one who was merely gauging Risana's strength and skill. The man was dressed like the first two, as a shepherd with ragged clothes, but his unlined and unweathered face made it clear he wasn't native to the mountains.

"The contract is mine," Shiv hissed, as he charged up the path, drawing his remaining knife and taking aim.

The man crouched and spun, catching Risana off guard and slicing at her abdomen, then continuing on past her and hurtling toward Shiv. Risana stumbled back as Shiv threw his knife. The blade lodged in his opponent's shoulder.

"Saf—" Risana cried, as she regained her footing and darted forward.

Shiv's opponent was quick, stabbing down and catching Shiv in the chest. Before the man could deliver a second blow, however, he was speared in the back. He made a gasping sound, then crumpled.

"Safford?"

Risana pushed the corpse away and knelt at Safford's side, putting her hands over the growing blossom of red on his chest.

"There might be others," he managed to gasp. He felt himself growing weak. "Dying," he said. "Leave me, Rish."

Instead she stayed at his side all through the night and the following day, using herbs from her pouch, shielding him from the cold with her own body. When she was certain he would live, she carried him to a rocky overhang and wedged him into a crevice, using her cloak for a blanket. She then tended to burying the three assassins. The ground was so hard she had to fashion cairns.

"They were Dark Knights," Shiv told her when she finally returned.

Risana shook her head. "No. Knights, even Dark Knights, would be wearing armor, something to identify themselves. And they wouldn't be using short swords."

"Agents of the Dark Knights then," Shiv returned.

"I guess you would know." Risana's words made him aware of the chance she had taken, healing him and not leaving him for the wolves.

In Brighthollow Risana assisted with the birth of the mayor's twin daughters. In the next three villages she saw to scattered cases of fever, helped bury individuals she could not heal, mended clothing and fences, and stalked and killed a wolf that had been preying on the local herd. Shiv followed after her, rarely speaking, but intently watching.

"I'll start toward Telvan tomorrow," Risana announced one evening.

Shiv growled. "There are Dark Knights there."

"I guess you would know." Again the telling words. "But I need some clothes. These can't stand up to many more washings."

He knew he could find the Dark Knight commander there, or someone else of authority, and that he could collect his fee simply by marching her into the camp.

"I'll lead the way," he said.

It was shortly before sunset, two days later, that the tall buildings in Telvan appeared in the distance and another band of assassins struck.

This time Shiv caught their intake of breath from around a sharp bend in the trail in front of him. The assassins were using the spires and overhangs for cover. He drew his knives and spun around the bend, jamming the blades deep into the stomach of a man he knew well, one he'd trained himself years ago.

"Risana is my contract," Shiv said, half under his breath.

The man collapsed, his weight taking Shiv down with him. As Shiv struggled in a failed attempt to pull the blades free and to get out from under the corpse, he heard Risana drawing her sword behind him. She stepped around him and his fallen foe, quickly engaging her own target.

Shiv finally pushed the body off. It rolled down the side of the mountain, with his twin knives protruding from it.

"Ah, thank the vanished gods for this!" Shiv retrieved his onetime student's dropped short sword.

A few yards away, Risana was exchanging blows with a pair of Dark Knights.

"Given up on assassins, have they?"

Shiv watched her for a moment, noting with admiration that she had some skill with a blade, but her two opponents were gradually wearing her down.

"Time to share, Rish!" Shiv called, as he pressed by her and engaged the shorter but bulkier of the two men. The Knight he fought was strong, his swings forcing Shiv back. Shiv spun to his right, the Dark Knight following him, then he pivoted to the left and entangled the Knight's legs. Pressing the attack, he rained blow after blow on the man, one finally biting into the chainmail gusset of his armor between the shoulder and breastplates. The Knight dropped his sword. Shiv kicked and sent him to his knees, knowing the man was dying.

Shiv whirled to see how Risana was faring. She was parrying her foe's repeated strikes. Her wide charcoal eyes were unblinking. A corner of her mouth turned up as she shifted her weight and became the aggressor, varying her swings and forcing the Dark Knight to back up.

Shiv watched in admiration as she increased the tempo. Unarmored, she was more agile than the Knight, and within the span of several minutes she had her foe gasping for breath. She made quick work of the man now, wresting his blade from him with one fierce swing, then thrusting her sword into a gap between his plates.

She jumped back as he fell, then leaped forward and

over the dead knight, charging along the narrow trail straight toward Shiv.

"Shiv!" she cried. "Move!"

Shiv turned as she raced past, following her movements in horror as he saw the Knight he thought he'd killed back up on his feet, his arm drawn back to hurl a dagger.

The metal caught the sun as the dagger flew deep into Risana's abdomen.

"No!" Shiv stared in disbelief as she fell, sword clattering on the path.

The Dark Knight was unsteady, blood flowing down his breastplate. Still, he refused to die, drawing another dagger from a band at his waist, taking aim at Shiv this time. The master assassin stood frozen. Then he saw a bloodied dagger fly over the Knight's head. Risana had tugged the weapon free and sent it back.

The bad throw was enough to distract the Knight. Shiv plunged in, ramming his borrowed short sword into the knight's chestplate, cracking the armor and lodging it deep in the man's chest.

"Rish!" Shiv hurried to Risana's side. For an instant he considered doing nothing, waiting for her death to come and hiding her body, collecting his pay. Instead, he found himself groping for her pouch that held herbs and powders. He'd become knowledgeable at using them just by watching her, but he didn't know how to treat such a serious wound. "Tell me what to do. What do I use, Rish? Tell me! What can I do?"

She stared at him a moment, doe eyes meeting his worried and confused ones, lips faintly smiling. He bent close, turned his ear so he could hear her.

"Maybe they'll think I'm dead and stop sending assassins," she mused.

It was spring, and the snow had started to melt on the slopes. Shiv was walking behind her, listening to her cloak flutter in the breeze and enjoying the scent of the pale purple flowers that were poking through the snow here and there.

"Maybe," Shiv said after several moments. "Maybe they'll think I'm dead, too." We make quite a pair, he thought, a former Solamnic Knight and an old assassin.

"A pair of deserters," Risana said, as if she'd heard what he'd been thinking.

Shiv looked over his shoulder, studying the spires and overhangs, watching for out-of-place shadows and the glint of steel.

They were heading north, to a string of villages that were being visited by a bothersome pox. There would be herbs to gather along the way, their healing pouches to be refilled, roofs to be repaired, fences to be mended . . .

Shiv knew an old man's luck would not last forever. What mattered to him now was how long hers would hold out. He realized now he'd become undone that first night he saw her, when he peered through the crack in the shuttered window and watched the fire-light dance across her selfless, determined face. He had a new contract now, one he'd made with himself—he would protect her as long as he could.

"Till my last breath," he said as he walked.

HUNGER

RICHARD A. KNAAK

"Massster Brudasss! Massster Brudasss! May I beg of you leave to enter?"

Brudas looked up from his work, barely containing the rage that had swelled up the moment the irritating voice of the Baaz had grated on his sensitive ears. If he could have fulfilled this mission without the aid of the lowest of all draconian kind, he would have done so, but that would have meant muddying his hands himself—something the Bozak would only do for his mistress, the great black dragon Sable. Digging in swampy mud was definitely work for Baaz, and they were welcome to it.

"Enter, you fool!" Brudas snapped, eager to get on with his own responsibilities.

He and a trio of Baaz had come to the half-sunken ruins of the city of Krolus on a quest for their mistress. Sable had come across scraps of information that led her to believe that some powerful relics, including those created by a dark wizard of the Third Age known for his trafficking with the undead, still lay buried somewhere in the heart of the old kingdom. In the past, her minions had combed the devastated area for such items without success. Brudas, however, hoped to change that. He had uncovered old scrolls that hinted of places missed by his hapless predecessors and had convinced the black dragon to let him lead this latest hunt for the elusive artifacts.

Success would further the draconian's own ambitions. Of course, at the time he volunteered, he had not considered that there was no more stench-infested, waterlogged region in all the overlord's domain than this one.

Bowing as he entered, the Baaz hurried to the bench and table where his superior sat glaring at him. He quickly fell to one knee. Brudas eyed the newcomer with distaste. Baaz were the least of the draconian races, a far cry below the elegant Auraks Brudas so admired and emulated, and certainly not nearly advanced as the Bozaks, of which he himself was a sterling example. The stinking, mud-encrusted figure before him was typical of his kind.

They were a contrast, these two, whose only connection was the fact that they, like all draconians, had been created full-grown by dark magic from the stolen eggs of metallic dragons, the so-called dragons of light. Baaz sprang from the eggs of the brass leviathans and their scaled hides showed a tarnished hint of that coloring. Pathetic in so many ways, Baaz had wings that would not even let them fly. They could merely glide. Once they had been the most numerous of the draconians, but as even the Dragon Highlords had seen their uselessness, many had perished fighting in the front lines in the War of the Lance. True, Baaz were more muscular than the taller, slimmer Bozaks, but they

lacked the quick wit of the latter. Little wonder, since
Bozak sprang from the magnificent bronze dragons and
had been granted a great gift—the ability to wield magic
in a manner that all the other draconians, (save the
imposing Auraks, of course) could only dream about.

The Auraks. As much pride as Brudas felt concerning his own heritage, he dreamed of being as skilled and
advanced as the tall, wingless ones. The Auraks were
the epitome of draconian superiority, the creations of
corrupted golden dragon eggs. They could cast better
spells in swifter fashion, were taller, sleeker, and spoke
eloquently, boasting intelligence and wisdom.

Brudas tried his best to emulate Auraks, even to the
point of dressing in sorcerer's robes and practicing his
speech so he didn't sound like one of the lesser draconian races. The Bozak felt, with some justification,
that he could now number himself among the most
gifted of his kind, yet still he felt inadequate in comparison to the Auraks. To add to his frustration, his sorcery had begun to fail of late, a horrible thing to happen
to one born with the gift. He hadn't told anyone, hoping
that he might manage to find and ferret out a magical
artifact for himself in the ruins of the city of Krolus.
The expedition had to succeed. . . .

"Get up, you imbecile!" he snarled at the crouching
Baaz. Other races occasionally confused the two draconian types because of the similar coloring of their
scales, a fact that always irritated Brudas. Could not the
color-blind fools tell the difference between tarnished
bronze and knavish brass?

The Baaz rose. Brudas recognized him as Drek, the
lowliest of his lowly kind, perhaps the stupidest of the
three draconians who accompanied him on this quest.

Drek had the ambition and intelligence of a rock, perhaps even less. To Drek, the Bozak tended to delegate the most menial and disgusting labor.

"Forgive me, Massster Brudasss!" Drek hissed. "I did not mean to dissturb you."

The sibilant hiss annoyed Brudas even more than the Baaz's blunt snout. Even though sitting, he managed to stare down his own sleek, narrow snout—more akin to a true dragon's than Drek's swinish nose—and, with perfect enunciation, he retorted, "You disturb me simply by existing, Drek! If you have something to report, report it and get out of my sight! I still hope to find out if one of these artifacts—" he waved a slim, taloned hand at the table, upon which lay nearly a dozen supposedly magical items— "has any latent power, something that will please our mistress!"

At mention of Sable, the Baaz cringed. His kind feared Sable utterly. Brudas feared her, respected her, and hoped to betray her when the opportunity presented itself—which was why he had suggested this odorous and, so far, futile expedition.

Something had happened to the magic of Krynn, to all spellcasters, not simply Brudas. The sorcerers and other mortal spellcasters had noticed it first. Spells began to falter, then fail completely. Attempt after attempt left nothing but the taste of futility in the wielder's mouth. The sorcerers, of course, blamed it on the overlords.

Soon, though, the overlords too began to complain of the loss of their abilities. Brudas still recalled how Sable had for weeks blamed one rival or another for her faltering spells—until she had learned that her fellow dragons were having troubles, too. With that realization, she had turned to the same desperate remedy sought by the sorcerers—Sable sent her minions out to find whatever magical talismans and artifacts they could so she could drain the relics' power and use their ancient magic for her her own magic.

Only a handful of her most trusted servants knew the complete truth and, of them, only Brudas knew the full extent of his mistress's weakness.

"Many, many apologiesss, Massster Brudasss," Drek babbled again. "It'sss jussst I think I may have found sssomething!"

"You found something?" Quickly, Brudas's ire faded. He rose from his chair, his nearly seven-foot frame towering over the more compact Baaz. "Where is it? What is it? Bring it in, you dolt!"

"We can't! Not . . . not yet! It's in a chamber. We're still excavating the entrance, but—"

"Lead me to it immediately!"

"Yesss, Massster Brudasss!" Drek turned and darted out of the tent.

Seizing his staff, Brudas followed after him. The Bozak momentarily decided to forgive the lowly creature for not holding the tent flap open for him. If Drek and the others had found something of value, it would be the first silver lining to this black-cloud of an adventure since their arrival more than two weeks before.

Damp and gloom greeted the draconian as he stepped onto the soft, drenched soil. He had chosen the most stable patch of ground for his tent, but still the moisture tended to seep everywhere. Not for the first time Brudas wondered what fascination a dragon could have with such a muddy, bug-infested quagmire.

With great care, the two wended their way through

the hazy marsh into the heart of what had once been a thriving city. Although Sable had transformed much of her domain into swampland, Krolus had been destroyed in the Great Cataclysm centuries before. As happened with so many other cities, the people who lived here had been caught entirely offguard. In the veritable blink of an eye, their proud city had been swallowed up by the cracked earth and shifting wetlands. In the years since, the swamp had only encroached further on the ruins. Sable herself could not have created a more nightmarish place.

The spiraled tip of a watchtower jutted out of the brackish water to their left. A pair of long, emerald serpents crawled over the tiled roof of a stone building—possibly an inn once. Brudas's gaze fell upon a statue of some human warrior, its head gone, with great cracks along its body. An arachnid as large as the Bozak's hand had spun a web between the body and an upraised arm.

Although it was midday, the sulfur-ridden haze made it seem more like twilight. A dim glow up ahead marked one of the oil lamps that Brudas had commanded the Baaz to spread over the vague path leading to their latest digging site. Searching for dry wood in this soggy domain would have been fruitless and so the Bozak had commandeered numerous oil lamps for their journey. However, their supply of oil had already dwindled drastically, and Brudas suspected they had three days' of lamplight left—at best. Not good, considering how little the expedition had to show for its efforts so far. If Drek's latest find did not pan out . . .

Rubble from a massive, broken arch forced them to take a more circuitous route to their destination, but

Brudas held his impatience in check. Drek would not have disturbed him without a good reason. The Baaz knew the penalty for that.

Brudas's clawed feet sank an inch or two into the ground with every step. Nothing remained dry long here. Those buildings and structures that had not sunk entirely into the swamp were covered with mold and moss. Even though many of the citizenry had failed to escape— as evidenced by the skulls lying amid the grass—those who had some link to magic evidently had been luckier than most. The treasure trove of relics that the Bozak had hoped to find had so far proved nonexistent.

Sable would not like that. More importantly, Brudas did not like that.

One of the most intact structures was, of all things, a temple of Mishakal, the goddess of healing. As they approached on what had once been the main thoroughfare of the city, Brudas noted that the temple now listed to one side even more than on the first day he had glimpsed it. Some of the columns had begun to crack. Too soon this monument to a departed goddess would join so much else under the water and mud of the black dragon's domain.

Who was to say that, long ago, some relic had not made its way into the temple, perhaps brought there by a pious follower who feared the sinister ways of magic and sought to keep at least one artifact out of the ambitious hands of the old wizards? Some of those magical artifacts might still remain within. . . .

Yet, Drek led him past the temple, where the three Baaz were supposed to be digging, heading instead to the far quarter of Krolus that had suffered the worst destruction.

"You were supposed to finish exploring the temple!" Brudas snapped.

Drek looked even more miserable than usual. "Found nothing there, Brudasss!" he replied, forgetting to call the Bozak by his title. "We gave up yesssterday."

Yesterday? And no one had informed him? The slim draconian opened his mouth to berate his underling— only to pause as the pair came to where the palace of the local ruler had once stood.

Once, this had been a fairly elegant abode that had towered over most of Krolus. The Cataclysm, however, seemed to have taken special interest in wreaking havoc on the building, for not only had a good portion of it disappeared beneath the swamp, but over time, rising water and vegetation had conquered the rest of the structure. Fearsome trees with sickly-green vines covered the interior. On all sides, the walls had crumbled or caved in.

Suspicious, Brudas halted. He knew that the Baaz hated their leader nearly as much as they feared him. Had their days in this monstrous ruin caused them to revolt? Did they hope to do away with him?

"Where are we going? Where is this supposed artifact, Drek?"

The lowly Baaz paused, gasping for breath. "You know how we could not find any way into the palace? Any way to reach the lower depthsss? There isss one!"

"Impossible! I led the search myself. Who found it?"

Drek had the audacity to look proud. "I did, Massster Brudasss!"

"Did you now? And how did you manage that?" To think that a Baaz could do what a Bozak could not . . .

Now the other draconian looked rather embarrassed. "I fell into it, mossst high one."

Brudas laughed, despite himself. Yes, trust Drek to fall into a secret entrance. How else could this particularly useless creature succeed where more intelligent life failed? The laughter died as the Bozak considered the potential of what Drek had discovered. Surely the palace, of all places, held something.

"Lead me there—quickly!"

Drek did so, guiding Brudas along a path that circled widely until it brought them around to the back of the ruin, where a mountainous slab of wall rose at a precarious angle just above the water. Its dark but dry interior showed steps leading downward like a shaft. Small wonder that Brudas had not seen it earlier. Mud and swamp grass surrounded it on all sides.

"Hunnh," the Bozak grunted. "Where are the others?"

"Below. Digging."

"How deep does it descend?" Dare he hope?

Drek shrugged. "Four levelsss, four and a half if you count our digging."

Better and better. "Lead on." After a pause, "Good work, Drek."

The Baaz beamed at this rare compliment. He leaped down the steps of the passage, but Brudas followed more carefully. The entrance just barely allowed him to use his staff, and the angle of the passage required the Bozak to grip one wall with his free hand.

The stench of rotting vegetation and other dead matter assailed his senses, but Brudas did not care. As his eyes became accustomed to the near dark, he noted the cracks in the walls, the moisture all around. Not the safest place.

After an eternity of a journey, Drek at last brought him to his prize. The other two Baaz, Molgar and Gruun, stood knee-deep in swampy water, trying their best to dig a stone doorway out from the mud and muck. They stepped aside when they saw their superior. Above them, a single oil lamp made visible not only their efforts, but the curious symbol on the door.

Although the swamp had tried its best, the colors of the three intertwined spheres carved into the door were still evident. White, red, and black—the signs of the old moons, the moons of magic. A nostalgic emotion rippled through the Bozak as he reached to touch the spheres, feeling their solidity. Even the fact that he was ankle deep in mud did nothing to dampen Brudas's excitement. Yes, Drek had found a prize, indeed.

"Don't just stand there, you dolts!" he snapped at the Baaz. "Finish digging the door free!"

Under his baleful gaze they performed the remainder of the task. The moment they finished, Brudas reached for the handle and tugged.

Nothing happened. He inspected the handle, saw that some lock mechanism kept him from whatever was inside. The Bozak, though, would not be defeated. Ordering the others back, the draconian raised his staff.

Not much magical power remained in the staff, but Brudas could not see why he shouldn't expend some of its last precious energy on this doorway, clearly a sanctum of sorts for some great spellcaster, likely the court wizard.

Muttering the words, the draconian unleashed his spell on the lock.

The power. Give me the power.

Brudas stumbled back as the lock flashed and flamed. He spun around, glaring at the miserable trio of Baaz and looking for the one who had spoken the odd words. "Who dared interrupt me at such a crucial moment? My spell might have gone awry!"

The Baaz looked at one another confusedly, Drek finally daring to reply, "No one ssspoke, sssir! I ssswear!"

The Bozak hissed, but did not pursue the matter. He could deal out punishments later. Greedily, Brudas returned his attention to the lock.

The spell had not worked as well as it should have. Frustrated, Brudas turned and studied the lock closer. Tiny plumes of smoke still rose from the blackened section. Not destroyed, as he had hoped, but certainly weakened. A shovel or pickax would finish the job nicely.

Backing away, Brudas commanded, "Drek! Your shovel! Strike the lock!"

Drek seized the tool and stepped to the door. Raising the shovel high, he let loose with his enviable strength, smashing the lock. The lock broke with a satisfying *crack.*

Breathing heavily, Drek stepped back. Anticipation rising, Brudas glanced at the other two apprehensive Baaz. "Open it!"

Molgar and Gruun swiftly obeyed. The muscles of the draconians strained, but the two soon had the great door ajar, enough to let a single figure squeeze through at a time. Seizing the oil lantern, Brudas thrust it in and swept it over the interior.

More water and mud greeted him. Nearly three-fourths of the chamber lay submerged. He couldn't hope even to get inside more than a few yards.

A waste of time. If there were any artifacts within, the sloping floor would have sent them all deep down in the swamp, to a place not even Brudas could command the Baaz to go.

With hope fading, he swung the lamp around for one last inspection—and caught a glint of metal.

Brudas stared, at first certain he was mistaken, but, no, the tip of some metallic object was poking above the muck. The Bozak somehow sensed he had not simply found some bit of rusted tableware or old sword. No, Brudas could sense magic . . . the old magic.

"Drek! Over there! See that? Retrieve it! And be warned! If you lose it, you'd best just follow it to oblivion, understand?"

With a fearful nod, the Baaz strode into the ruined chamber. Brudas nearly held his breath, but Drek managed to pluck the relic free and return with it in only a couple of minutes.

"Give me that!" the Bozak demanded, fingers twitching in excitement.

The object that Drek anxiously passed on to him proved to be a bracelet of sorts, but of a design Brudas had never come across before. It seemed too large for either draconian or human wrists and far too bulky to be worn practically. Much of it had been fashioned out of silver that seemed to hint of moonlight, but what fascinated him most was the intricate centerpiece to the artifact, a crest with a horned, animal-skull design that hinted of the lost god Chemosh, lord of the dead.

Adding to its effect were two black stones flanking the skull design. Staring at them, the Bozak could have sworn that they flared briefly in response to his intense gaze. The stones appeared to be entities separate from the rest of the bracelet. Brudas sensed some spell attached to them, but the level of power paled in comparison to the rest of the relic.

One of the stones seemed slightly ajar, as if something had nearly knocked it free of its mounting. With great caution, Brudas brought one talon gingerly to the stone. He did not want to lose the stone by accident.

As his talon touched the ebony gem, a brief spark from the stone startled Brudas, nearly causing him to drop the entire bracelet.

The power. Give me the power!

Clutching the relic awkwardly in one hand, he glared at the three Baaz, but none of them looked as if they had spoken the peculiar words. The Bozak shook off the whispering voice. Perhaps he had imagined it. Inspecting the bracelet, Brudas decided not to risk touching the loose stone again. Still, the mild jolt he had received had been enough to encourage him.

Brudas eyed the sunken chamber. The prospects of finding anything else in this danger-laden, unstable ruin were minimal at best. He had been fortunate to find even this one artifact. Still . . .

"Continue the search. Leave nothing untouched! I will return to my tent to study this item." Ignoring the dismayed expressions of the others, the Bozak strode away, as best he could, climbing laboriously up to the surface and shaking mud off all the way back to his tent.

For the first time since coming to Krolus, Brudas had made a real find, one that might help him realize his dreams of success, of power.

Brudas had grown tired of serving Sable and receiving little in return. He had grown tired of his own failing magic, making him feel even more useless than a Baaz or a Kapak. Auraks had their fabled craftiness to serve them when magic failed, and the others were good for either battle or labor, but a Bozak without magic was worthless. He was not even of any use to himself.

However, with the forces Brudas sensed in this artifact, he might be able to depart the black dragon's domain and make his way to better climes, to some place where he, not some overgrown, fat lizard, could rule. Then Brudas would be master, not servant. . . .

Entering his tent, he stalked to the table and, with a contemptuous sweep of his arm, cleared it of the lesser relics. Hanging his oil lamp nearby, Brudas placed the bracelet on the table, then leaned toward it, reptilian orbs slitted. He cared not for what purpose its designer originally had created it. Sable would have found the artifact's background of interest, but all Brudas cared about now was how he would be able to draw the magic and use it for his own spells.

A test. It required a simple test. The Bozak would cast the easiest of spells, utilizing only the least amount of energy.

With growing eagerness, Brudas clutched the sides of the bracelet, making certain to leave both index fingers atop the skull design. Feeling the nearness to strong magic sent a chill of excitement down his spine. He could barely contain himself as he began to recite the words of the spell. If all went as planned, the Bozak hoped to create a small sphere of light that would float just above the table. A simple spell. In the old days, even a novice wizard could have cast this with ease.

As he whispered, Brudas noticed a slight movement

of the tent walls. The lamp dimmed a bit for no reason he could discern.

The final words slipped from his toothy maw.

And a pale, cadaverous hand suddenly slipped across his own, while a moaning, demanding voice like a winter wind cried out, *"Give it to me! I must have it!"*

Caught by surprise, Brudas stumbled backward, losing his grip on the relic. His gaze fell upon a ghostly form, an older, bearded man wearing tattered robes. The face had little flesh and the eyes were so hollow and hungry that for a moment Brudas, who had as a servant of the goddess Takhisis dealt before with the undead, could only stare back in astonishment.

In its skeletal hands the ghost held a glowing force, and, as both spectre and burden faded away, Brudas realized the ghoulish creature had just stolen the magic from his spell.

Hissing in both anger and consternation, Brudas rose to his feet and raced out of the tent. Outside he saw nothing but the swamp and the ruins. Both the ghost and glowing magic had vanished.

For a moment, he considered calling for the Baaz, but thought better of it. To ask them if they had heard or seen a ghost would only make him look ridiculous in their ignorant eyes.

However, one ghost would not stop him. The Bozak knew some dark spells, one that could repel the undead. Trudging back inside the tent, the draconian eyed the bracelet. Best to keep away from it for now. The creature clearly was attached to it, perhaps had even been its creator. Well, come the morrow, Brudas had an idea that would send the ghoul on its final journey.

As could be expected, the Baaz found nothing more worthwhile. Drek, while excavating, had almost been crushed by the weakening ceiling of the chamber. Brudas sent the miserable creatures to yet another site he believed worthwhile, then he began his research. That took not only the rest of what could laughingly be called the day, but also well into the night.

He had not touched the bracelet again, not wanting to accidentally summon the spirit. As Brudas lay down on his cot to sleep, he pondered his options. Should he capture the ghost, perhaps make the spirit tell him where other magical artifacts of significance might be found? A waste of power most likely. Better to be rid of the creature entirely.

Brudas drifted off to sleep, his thoughts still on spells. He dreamed of spellcasting and saw himself upon a great mountain, using his magic to drive the overlords away and, in their place, he took over the rule of all Ansalon. The draconian took special pleasure in humbling his mistress, Sable. In his dreams, he forced the ebony leviathan to cower before him, her head buried so flat against the earth it made him laugh to see it. No more would the Bozak follow anyone else's dictates. Even the Auraks would acknowledge his greatness.

In the dreams, hundreds of craven subjects crowded around him, begging his mercy, cheering his might. Brudas granted them the wonder of witnessing his spellwork, casting wondrous display after wondrous display. . . .

Then the draconian woke to find his fingers twitching. He felt magic briefly course through him . . . then out again.

He opened his eyes—

And let out a startled shout as more than a score of ghoulish, semi-transparent figures wafted close to him, surrounding him, their hollow eyes filled with an insatiable hunger.

"Get away from me!" Brudas cried, rolling off the bed. "Get away!"

The ghosts did not touch him, but neither did they move away. Wherever the Bozak went, the spectres followed.

They talked, begged, pleaded, and demanded.

"Give it to me!"

"I must have it!"

"No! It's mine!"

"Please! I *need* it. . . ."

With a wordless cry, the draconian stumbled out of the tent. From the tent shared by the three Baaz, Drek emerged with a sleepy expression, sword in one hand.

"What isss it? Are we under attack, sssir?"

Brudas seized him by the throat and spun the Baaz around so the fool faced his superior's dwelling. "What do you think, you imbecile? Look at them and ask me that idiotic question again!"

Drek did look . . . and then gave Brudas a bewildered glance. "Who do you mean, Massster Brudasss? Where? I sssee no one!"

Turning, the taller draconian found that his underling had spoken the truth. There were no ghostly figures. They had vanished. The Bozak inhaled deeply, trying to regain his composure.

The other Baaz emerged from their tents, joining them. Gruun scanned the area nervously, while Molgar was so tired he seemed to be sleepwalking. They looked at their superior.

Suddenly feeling like a fool, Brudas grew irritated. Perhaps he had dreamed it all, although surely the first ghost had existed. But a host of them . . . his subconscious must have played tricks on him.

"Go back to your tent!" the Bozak snarled at the other draconians. "Now!"

Puzzled, the Baaz wandered off. Brudas heard them muttering under their breath, no doubt discussing their superior's sanity.

———————◆———————

The morning mist made it difficult to actually know exactly when dawn arrived, but Brudas found he could not stay in bed any longer. The draconian had not slept well, for each time his eyes closed he felt as if the shadows gathered around him again. That no spectres were there whenever he finally chose to open his eyes did not ease his troubled mind a bit.

Weary but determined, Brudas rose and sought out the Baaz. He needed privacy for his project. After kicking Drek and the others out of their slumber, he sent the trio off to a distant part of the sunken city, a place it would take them hours to reach. That would afford him the quiet he needed—not to mention preventing a repeat of the previous evening's embarrassing episode.

Alone now, the Bozak gingerly took the bracelet from the table, brought it out into the open. He looked around, but saw no sign of any spectre. At last, taking a deep breath, the draconian mouthed the simple spell that had first brought him the ghastly visitor. In the back of his mind, though, he kept a second spell ready. The spectre would be in for a nasty surprise.

Come to me, the draconian thought. Come to me, you damned spirit! You'll find me ready, this time.

As his spell grew to fruition, the ghost reappeared. The same bearded man with the hollow eyes beckoned to Brudas, and the Bozak could almost hear the same words, even though the specter had not yet spoken.

Give it to me.

Brudas would give it to him. Brudas would give the ghost a taste of magic, but not the way the phantom wanted. He stopped the first spell, intending to unleash the trap—

Only to see a second, a third, then more and more ghosts rising from the earth, materializing among the trees, drifting forward from the ruins . . .

There had to be at least three dozen of them—maybe more. Each of them had that hungry, hollow look, and their voices, although different in tone, sounded as if they blended into one.

"Give it to me!"

"It's mine! It has to be mine!"

"I need it!"

Brudas whirled and saw that they approached him from all sides. He counted far more than before, possibly as many as a hundred!

"Away from me, spirits!" he snapped. "You'll get nothing from me! Nothing!"

They ignored him, though, their arms outstretched, hands grasping, clutching . . .

A shriveled claw passed through the draconian, and although he felt nothing, Brudas nonetheless shook. Then, reminding himself that the ghosts seemed unable to hurt, much less touch him, he grew defiant.

"You were warned, spirits! No one assaults Brudas! Not even the dead!"

Holding up the bracelet, he began the banishing spell. Then, to his dismay . . . the ghosts stole the magic from him again. Their fingers caressed the relic as each spectre carried off some of the power.

Still, their numbers grew. It seemed as if every citizen of Krolus who had ever died rose to haunt him, yet some of the ghosts did not seem properly placed. A few wore armor more like that used in Solamnia. Others were dressed in recent fashions. A man in full sailing gear from the southlands walked beside a Knight of Takhisis. A cadaverous minotaur with a slit gullet kept pace with a kender.

The truth suddenly stared him in the face. These were not just the spectres of the sunken city. They were phantoms from all over Ansalon.

Over and over, they chanted the same dreadful litanies. They wanted, they needed, they demanded . . . It threatened to drive the Bozak mad just listening to them!

What they wanted, needed, demanded was the magic. Brudas stared at the relic, his prize. At the moment, the Bozak desired nothing more than to be free of this monstrous horde. He held the bracelet high, waving it so that the ghosts could see it.

"You want the power? You want the magic? Here it is!"

With a tremendous effort, Brudas sent the artifact sailing through the air.

Instantly, scores of the ghosts turned and followed, still mouthing their damnable words. Yet, to the

Bozak's consternation, many more stayed where they were, even drew closer to the draconian. These ghosts had no interest in the bracelet. They wanted *his* magic.

His nerve broke. Brudas turned and fled. He did not have to glance back to know that he was pursued. Worse, even as he ran, the draconian saw still others rising from the stones, floating through the walls, even descending from the sky.

Magic. They all sought magic. He stumbled through the ruins, trying to find a place to hide, but everywhere he looked, the ghosts crowded toward him. They were legion, an endless flow of hungry souls seeking to devour his essence.

A small human, a ghost-child who should have been nothing to the once-arrogant Bozak, emerged from the wall of an inn half buried in the muck of the swamp. This ghastly urchin stared with the same hungry orbs, the same hideous look of the other ghosts, but on a child, it appeared even more strange, more monstrous.

"Get back! Get back!"

They would not listen to Brudas, though. Strong arms seized hold of him as he rounded a crumbling house. Brudas let out a gasp of surprise, wondering if the spectres, no longer satisfied with asking or demanding with words, had now found a way to take what he would not willingly give.

"Sssir! Massster Brudasss! Are you all right?"

The sibilant voice dragged him back to reality. Brudas managed to focus on the one who held him— Drek, of all creatures.

"Drek!" Never before had he been so filled with pleasure at the sight of a Baaz. Brudas clutched the other draconian tight before realizing how silly he must look. Summoning up a modicum of dignity, he glared at his subordinate. "Drek! What are you doing in this part of the city? You should be farther to the west!"

The Baaz gave him a sheepish expression, then held up a broken staff. "Cracked my shovel, sssir! Forgot to bring a ssspare."

"You—" Brudas nearly broke out in laughter. So mundane an accident, so typical of Drek. He dared not tell the Baaz how pleased he was, but surely the fool saw what was happening.

"Are you all right, sssir?" Drek repeated, eyeing his commander as one might eye a three-legged chicken. "You don't look well, if you'll pardon me for sssaying ssso, sssir!"

"Well? *Well?* How can I be well? They're surrounding us, and you dare to ask such a question?"

"Who? Who'sss around usss?" the Baaz hissed, reaching for his sword. "Ogresss? Are they hiding in the ruinsss?"

Brudas looked at the Baaz in consternation, then glanced around quickly just to be certain. Sure enough, even though the ghosts had backed away slightly at Drek's appearance, they still milled nearby, eyes hollow, hands grasping, voices calling.

But Drek neither heard nor saw any of it.

The situation struck Brudas as absurd as some of the comical plays watched by humans. Drek stood close to him, hissing and snarling at imagined foes. He even had his sword out and was waving it wildly. The ghosts, undaunted by his fearsome performance, passed effortlessly through his blade, then even through the Baaz himself. Still, Drek saw nothing.

Gritting his teeth, the Bozak muttered, "Never mind,

Drek. There's no one. There's no one for you to fight."

His companion blinked, then once more gave Brudas the three-legged chicken stare. The Bozak did not care. All that concerned him were the spectres and their ungodly hunger. No longer did Brudas dream of carving out his own realm somewhere, some day. Now all he wanted was to be left alone by the legion of undead.

Drek sheathed his weapon. "Sssir, if I may. You've been working hard, sssir. Maybe you should get a little more ressst. Yesss, maybe a little ressst would do you sssome —"

"Do not treat me like a hatchling!" Brudas pulled his arm away from Drek's reaching hand. "All I need —" He hesitated, eyeing the monstrous faces all around. He was awash in a sea of dead. "All I want," Brudas muttered, "is to be left alone."

The ghosts paid his plea no mind, but Drek, who did not realize to whom his superior actually spoke, took the words as a command. With just a slight hint of annoyance in his sharp salute, he responded, "Yesss, sssir! Asss you wish!"

The taller draconian almost called him back, but to do so would have further shamed him in the Baaz's eyes. Besides, of what use was Drek to his troubles? Drek neither heard nor saw the phantom horde and simply thought his commander had gone mad.

No! Brudas would not be so readily defeated. He had survived the loss of the gods, the coming of the overlords, and years under the tasking of his mistress. He would not let a bunch of moaning ghosts bring him to madness and ruin!

With the ghosts stalking his every footstep, Brudas forced himself back to his tent. He would be rid of these damnable spirits somehow! He must think like an Aurak! Think like the highest of all draconians! That was the way to solve it!

Yet as the day progressed, no clue dawned on him. He sat at his desk, surrounded by the death-faces, trying his best to think and be inspired and always getting distracted by the burgeoning numbers, the constant, whispering demands of the ghosts.

"Give me the magic!"

"I need it!"

"I must have it!"

And on and on and on . . .

The trio of Baaz returned to camp without Brudas even noticing. Only when Drek came up to report did the Bozak realize that the entire day had faded into darkness.

The lowly Baaz walked ignorantly through the army of ghosts, unaware of the horrors eyeing him. He saluted Brudas as always.

Brudas forced his eyes up. "Yes, Drek? What is it?"

"Giving my report, sssir."

Not really caring, the weary Bozak waved for his subordinate to continue. At least Drek's deep, sibilant voice would drown out a bit of the constant pleading and wailing.

Drek, however, did not immediately begin. Instead, he first eyed Brudas with something approaching concern. "Massster Brudasss, you don't look well. Perhapsss you should lie down."

Lie down? How could he lie down? If he slept, the ghosts wormed their way into his dreams, urging him to cast spells from which they could purloin the magic! Brudas had not forgotten the previous night, how he had woken to feel the power seeping from his twitching fingers. Lie down? Didn't the fool Baaz know anything?

"Just give your damned report!"

Cringing, Drek did so. Brudas paid him little attention, however, using the droning of the Baaz as an opportunity to focus his thoughts on his predicament. He could not sleep; he could not cast magic. The ghosts remained with him at every moment and their numbers seemed to be growing. What could he do?

". . . and that'sss all, sssir."

Defeated for the moment, Brudas waved a taloned hand in Drek's direction, dismissing him. However, as the Baaz turned to go, something Drek had said finally registered with the desperate Bozak.

"What's that you said about a magic staff?"

With another sheepish expression, Drek replied, "We found what ssseemed a wizard'sss staff, Massster Brudasss, but I tripped and fell on it. Broke it. I'm sssorry, sssir!"

Under normal circumstances, Brudas would have punished the careless Baaz for such heinous stupidity, but a thought was stirring within his head, a possible salvation from the ghouls.

"The bracelet! Find me the bracelet!"

"Sssir?" Drek glanced at Brudas's tent. "Isssn't it inssside there?"

"No, you imbecile! It's out there!" He pointed, not bothering to explain how the artifact had come to end up out in the swamp, and Drek had the good sense not to ask further questions. Instead, the Baaz called to his two comrades and, under Brudas's manic guidance, they searched for the bracelet.

Drek finally found it, half-sunken in the mud. Had the Bozak tossed it just a little farther, it would have ended up in the depths of the swamp, no doubt forever lost. Relic in one hand, Drek trotted back to Brudas, who seized the bracelet immediately and, without another word, turned away from the three Baaz.

As he headed back into his tent, Brudas inspected the bracelet. The relic remained intact, even down to the loose stone. It was the black stones that interested him now, for Brudas realized he had not seen the first ghost until he touched one of them. For some reason, the spell surrounding the stones must enable the bracelet's wearer to see the dead.

"You did this to me," Brudas muttered at the black gems. "Let us see what happens if I remove you entirely, eh?"

The Bozak drew a dagger and pried at the loosest of the pair. To his surprise, it took him far more effort than he expected to break the stone free. It seemed almost as if the stone did not want to be cut from its mounting, but at last it popped out, falling to the ground at the draconian's feet.

Glancing around, Brudas thought that the ghosts already looked less distinct. Better yet, their voices had faded to whispers. Eagerly, he went to work on the second stone.

Freeing this one proved more troublesome, but Brudas put such manic effort into it that eventually the second gem flew high into the air, landing some distance from the first. As the final stone dropped, the ghosts vanished.

Brudas listened closely, but the only sounds he heard now were those of the swamp creatures and the wind.

He slumped for a moment, exhausted. "Free . . ."

Then, pulling himself together, the Bozak tossed the bracelet on the table, roaring, "Drek! Get in here!"

A moment later, the rather disgruntled Baaz entered. Drek immediately saluted, but otherwise said nothing. Brudas realized that he had summoned the fool from his evening meal, but there were more important matters than filling a Baaz's cavernous stomach.

The tall, slim draconian pointed at the stones. "Take those and throw them into the swamp as far as you can, Drek! And be certain to follow through with my command, because if I find you've disobeyed and kept them for yourself, you know what I'll do to you."

Shuddering, the Baaz scooped up the gems and rushed from the tent. As a safety precaution, Brudas stepped out of the entrance to watch. Drek stood at the edge of the water, his feet half-sunken into the soft mud. With a throw that put Brudas's own to shame, the Baaz hurled both tiny stones far into the swamp.

The Bozak exhaled in relief. He had escaped the ghosts. An Aurak could not have been more clever, Brudas thought with some pride.

A sudden exhaustion overtook Brudas and he recalled that he had not rested much the prior night. Now, with no more dead, hungry eyes or mournful, demanding voices to haunt him, the draconian could at last get some peaceful slumber.

"Drek!"

The Baaz, only steps away from his supper, turned back to his superior. "Yesss, Massster Brudasss?"

"I'm going to sleep. See to it that I'm not disturbed by anything, understood?"

"Yesss, sssir."

Brudas reentered the tent. How appealing his cot

looked! How wonderful the thought of deep, undisturbed sleep sounded!

He dozed off almost the very moment he settled into the cot.

At first, the draconian slept well and deeply, but then something disturbed his rest. Nothing he could at first identify, but it was a gnawing, creeping feeling. Brudas tossed about, clawing his way closer and closer to consciousness, until—

With a scream, he tumbled from the cot. A shiver came over the Bozak as he glanced down at his hands, which still twitched.

"No-o-o," he whispered, reptilian eyes glancing about. "No!"

With much trepidation, he concentrated on a simple spell of levitation. For his target, he chose the bracelet, which still lay atop the table. Brudas had cast this spell a thousand times. Casting it successfully should have been child's play.

Yet, when the draconian tried to complete his spell, nothing happened.

He had been a fool! By damaging the bracelet, he had destroyed its ability to show him the dead, yet that did not mean that they had left. They still surrounded him . . . and likely in greater numbers than before. He imagined hundreds, perhaps even *thousands* at this point, numbers that chilled even the hardened Bozak to the core.

Thousands of ghosts swarming about him, hungering for his magic, silently urging him to activate it for them. . . .

The tent rippled in the night wind, causing Brudas to start. From somewhere far off, or maybe right next to him whispering in his ears, came a moaning sound. Even though he could not see them, the draconian

knew that the pleading, demanding dead encircled him
. . . and that they waited for their opportunity.

"I've got nothing for you!" he snapped at the wind.
"Nothing for you at all!" The anxious Bozak whirled
about. "Find yourself another mage from which to
leech! I'll not cassst any more ssspells! You'll sssuck no
more magic through me!"

But the wind seemed to mock him. The ever-grow-
ing legion of wraiths swirled invisibly around him,
silently watching him.

All around him. Unseen, but everywhere.

Brudas hissed. He imagined the clawing hands, the
hollow eyes. The Bozak began pawing at his elegant
robe, the one he wore in order to better emulate the
Auraks. He tried to peel away the grasping fingers.
Sharp talons ripped fabric, and yet still Brudas felt the
ghostly presence. He looked around, saw the bracelet.
Grasping it, Brudas rubbed his hand across the skull
design, trying to find some way to unlock the power.

Nothing. Brudas's gaze fixed on the two empty spaces
where the stones had been mounted. Had he, by ripping
them free, ruined any hope of using the artifact?

"Fool! I've been a fool!" Brudas swung the bracelet
about in wild anger and frustration. His hand smashed
against the oil lamp, sending it flying against the tent
wall. The oil and fire spread across the fabric, quickly
turning into an inferno. Brudas backed away, only to
discover that the hem and sleeve of his robe were
afire.

He turned, trying to douse the spreading flames. In
desperation, the draconian began to cast a spell, one
that should have been able to quell any ordinary fire.
However, as the last words left his mouth, Brudas again

experienced the unsettling sensation of feeling the magic drained away from his very lips.

In that terrible moment, dark, maddening thoughts flew into his mind. Had the ghosts planned this, too? Had they led him into this desperate situation so he would be forced to try magic—which they would then swoop upon, unseen vultures hungry for even the tiniest morsel of his power?

"No!" the Bozak shouted at the air, heedless of the fire consuming his garments. "I know what you intend! I'll not be your puppet! I'll be free of you somehow—free of all of you!"

The flames now covered his robe and burned his scaly hide. Brudas tried rolling on the ground, then, in desperation, he dashed out of the burning tent, startling Drek and the others, who had come to stop the fire.

Brudas ran past them toward the swamp. In his agonized mind, he saw only the water, and as the three Baaz watched, their superior ran headlong into the swamp, ignorant of its many perils. Brudas waded farther and farther out into the muck.

With each step he made less progress, sinking deeper. Still he pushed on. His shoulders and arms were ablaze. He took a breath and plunged underwater to kill the fire.

As his head went under, the Bozak caught sight of something in the mud—two tiny objects gleaming. Two tiny black stones.

Struggling to hold his breath, Brudas reached for the precious stones, but they were too far away. He managed another step and, his lungs straining, tried once more to grab them.

Brudas's hand plunged into the mud and seized the stones. A slight shock ran through him and suddenly, all around the Bozak, floated the legions of dead.

Terrified, Brudas opened his mouth to shout, forgetting for the moment that he, unlike the hungering spectres, needed air to breathe.

Drek, leaning over as far as he could, ceased calling his superior's name and watched with horror as the last bubbles rose to the surface . . . and the angry swamp finally calmed again.

The silence shattered as an explosion, the final mark of death for all Bozaks, sent a shower of water high into the air. Drek stepped back just enough to avoid being drenched, then eyed the swamp, still confused by what had happened.

Molgar and Gruun reluctantly joined Drek and the three Baaz stared for a time, almost as if they still expected their superior to rise out of the water and castigate them for standing around doing nothing. At last, Gruun broke the silence, turning to Drek.

"What do we do now?"

Drek shrugged. He had lived his life obeying orders, not giving them, but the other Baaz seemed even more uncertain about what to do. At last, he gave them the only answer that made any sense at all under the circumstances.

"We pack up and go back to our missstressss."

"So this is all?" the black leviathan rumbled dangerously. "This is the result of your grand expedition?"

Drek could not help but shiver before Sable. The great creature towered over the tiny draconian, her form so massive she had to bend over and contort herself to fit into this cavern, one of her many sanctums scattered around her domain.

"Yesss, missstressss! It isss all!"

Spread before the overlord were the handful of items that the three Baaz had been able to salvage from Brudas's destroyed tent. Not much to show for their work, and Drek knew it. Yet, as a lowly servant of the great dragon, he had no recourse but to bring it all to her, no matter her certain disappointment and anger.

The ebony leviathan's head swung back and forth as she surveyed their meagre findings. Drek already knew that she would find them of little interest. Brudas had mentioned time and time again how pathetic these magical relics were.

"It is fortunate for your superior," Sable announced, her malevolent gaze fixing on the Baaz again, "that he chose to die in Krolus. He wasted my time and hopes on this mission, it seems. I should have sent an Aurak to lead the expedition just as I had originally planned." Her eyes narrowed. "And as for you—"

Drek blinked, suddenly realizing that he had forgotten one item. Fool! He had wanted so much to protect it that he had forgotten to remove it from his pouch and add it the pile. "There isss one more, missstressss! One more!"

She pulled her head back, waiting.

The draconian plucked the object from the pouch, then set it down before her. Drek backed up as Sable's head dived down to scrutinize the relic.

Her eyes lit up. "Yes! I can sense the magic within! Strong magic! This has to be the work of the dark mage the scrolls spoke of." She reached down and delicately took the bracelet in her tremendous talons. "This has been damaged, though."

Under her baleful gaze, the draconian stammered, "It wasss Brudasss, missstressss! Brudasss in his madnessss! I am only a lowly Baaz and understand nothing of magic!"

"But you understand wealth and treasure, do you not?" Sable said. "Even you wouldn't be so foolish as to steal a couple of paltry gems and risk my wrath . . . would you?"

An intense blast of dragonfear overwhelmed Drek. He fell to his knees. "No, missstressss! No!"

She seemed satisfied, both with his reply and the relic. "So perhaps the mission was not a total failure." Sable held up the bracelet, admiring it. "I shall make use of this, yes! The damage means little overall. All I need is the raw magic within!"

The gargantuan dragon turned away, eyes fixed upon her prize. Even though only a lowly Baaz, Drek knew well enough to rise to his feet and hurry from her sight.

Drek did not look back as he rushed from the cavern and, even if he had, all he would have seen was the dragon studying the artifact. He would not have seen the trailing legions of ghosts who followed him, the legions that Sable herself could not see without the black gems. There were hundreds, perhaps even thousands of them, already floating around the black leviathan, eagerly awaiting her spells.

Ghosts with hungry, hungry eyes.

PRODUCT GIVEN FOR SERVICES RENDERED

DON PERRIN

I hate rain," Gnash said.

"Yeah, me too," Yarl agreed. "I hate everything right about now."

It had been raining forever. For as far back as they could remember, it had been raining.

The two brothers wore chain armor over leather jerkins, and carried kite shields. The clothes they wore under their armor were soaked through, and their boots—what was left of them—squished as they plodded through the mud. The rain fell in a steady downpour that was neither light nor heavy. The ground in the pine forest was soaked.

"Wait!" Yarl stopped, sniffed the air. "You smell that? I smell somethin' good"

"I just smell you, and it ain't good." Gnash answered flatly.

Yarl thumped his brother on the arm. "No, I mean it. It smells like food. I can't remember the last time we had a good meal."

"You always think of food. Damn it, Yarl, we're

deserters. If they catch us, they'll hang us. On top of that, we don't know where in the Abyss we are. We've been walkin' in circles"—he pointed to a rock formation that they had passed at least six times—"and all you're worried about is your empty belly! What if there are Solamnics around?" He glanced about nervously.

Yarl scowled. "I know exactly where we are. We've only got to go another fifty miles or so until we reach a port, and from there we can catch a ship that'll take us anywhere we feel like, so shut your goddamn mouth! As for that boulder, it's not the same boulder."

"Is too," Gnash muttered, but he was too cold and hungry to fight about it. "I do smell somethin' though. It smells really good. Take a whiff."

"By the Vision, you're right, Yarl!" Gnash sniffed the air like a hungry dog. The smell was faint, but suggested warm bread.

"Kinda like a home smell, ain't it, Gnash?" said his brother.

The brothers sniggered.

"Ma could sure bake bread." Yarl sounded wistful.

"Now don't get started," Gnash, the elder, said severely. "Sure we got some bread, but we had to eat it buttered with all that religious hokum. Paladine this and Mishakal that and 'Remember to say your prayers, boys,' and 'You know it looks bad for the sons of clerics to be wastin' time, hangin' out in taverns.' Well, Paladine's gone, and good riddance, I say."

"That big red dragon we sold 'em to sure did make short work of them," said Yarl, cheering up at the memory. "Chomp, chomp. Didn't even bother to cook 'em first, like I thought she might."

"Don't talk about red dragons, neither," Gnash said

nervously. "If she or the Dark Knights finds out we deserted, she'll go chomp, chomp on us!"

"Bah! She won't find out," said Yarl confidently. "As for the Knights, they were getting whupped so bad when we lit out we don't have to worry about them no more. I think the smell's coming from that direction. Someone's cooking us dinner, brother."

"I think you're right," said Gnash. He grinned. "Only they don't know it yet."

Yarl patted the broad saber hanging at his side. "Ain't no one gonna mess with us! We're sergeants from the army of the Knights of Takhisis!"

"Gentle, brother!" warned Gnash. "First let's poke around."

The two moved forward at a lope, heading toward the smell that grew stronger and more tantalizing the nearer they came. The rain grew heavier. The water poured down the center spine of Gnash's helmet, down the nose guard, then dripped off the tip of his nose. The fall storms would only get worse, then eventually turn to snow, Gnash thought, hoping they reached some seaport long before that happened. At least in this downpour, no one would hear them coming. And he couldn't get much wetter than he already was.

The pine forest ended abruptly. The brothers looked out of the woods to see a clearing of tall grass that drooped in the rain. A huge pile of freshly turned dirt rose up out of the grass.

Yarl gripped his saber. Gnash looked at his brother, shook his head, and proceeded stealthily.

"What is all that dirt?" Yarl asked in a low tone.

"I think it's a grave—one of those big ones where they dump a lot of bodies after a battle. Damn it, Yarl,"

Gnash swore, "do you know what this means? This means we're still somewhere close to the war! Too damned close." He felt for his saber. The grip was wet, but he wanted it close if a fight erupted.

"Yeah," said Yarl, and after a moment's consideration he added, "but if they're digging graves, then the battle must be over."

"I guess you got a point," he admitted, admiring his brother's sound logic. "But just be careful. We don't know *who's* diggin' the graves!"

He crouched low and crept forward. Yarl stayed right at his side. Creeping past the mound, they stopped at the far end. A stone marker stood at the head of it.

Gnash nodded to his brother. "Go see what it says."

"You want me to walk close to a grave?" Yarl asked, horrified. "What if somethin' grabs me?"

"How old are you? Ten? Nothin's going to grab you," said Gnash, disgusted. "Now go on."

Yarl did as he was told. Gnash was the older brother by a year and Yarl always did what his brother told him to do. Yarl cautiously approached the stone marker, sinking in the fresh mud with every step.

"Says THREE HUNDRED EIGHTEEN SOLAMNIC SOLDIERS, FIFTY-ONE SOLAMNIC KNIGHTS, AND TWO QUALINESTI ELVES. BATTLE OF THE SOLACE WATERSHED, CHAOS WAR, YEAR 384 AFTER CATACLYSM. THEY DIED BRAVELY. Stone's been fresh cut, Gnash." Yarl glanced about. "That means there must be Solamnics still about."

"Solamnic grave-diggers," said Gnash, relaxing. "They won't have swords, just shovels."

The clearing ended another fifty yards ahead as it led into a forest of poplar and oak and scrub pine. The brothers entered the forest warily, but saw no sign of anyone.

The smell was stronger now—the sweet smell of fresh baked bread with something else, cinnamon or nutmeg, Gnash wasn't sure. Both were so hungry they wouldn't have much cared if the whole Solamnic army had been up there waiting for them, so long as they were fed.

The trees stopped ahead, with another clearing opening out beyond it. An ancient road, overgrown with grass and weeds, crossed the clearing. The two stopped and stared into the wet landscape. The clearing opened onto several old farm fields, with an old, tumbledown farmhouse at the end. A wagon stood parked beside the ruin of the building. Smoke and the wonderful smell rose from some sort of chimney-like contraption sticking up out of the back end of the wagon. No one was in sight.

"Think we should sneak up?" Yarl asked.

Gnash shook his head. He felt braver now that he was certain there wasn't an army around. "Naw. We strut in bold as brass. Make friends with 'em first. Then later, we do what we must. Either way, we'll eat good tonight, brother!"

"You bet!" said Yarl, grinning.

The two headed across the open expanse, sabers sheathed but at the ready. They might have drawn their weapons, had they seen an enemy, but still there was no one to be seen. Gnash waved his hand toward the right side of the farmhouse. He pointed to left. The two brothers split up and circled the farmhouse, peering inside. No one there. They met up outside the wagon that had to be the strangest looking vehicle they'd ever seen. It was actually closer to a house on wheels. All sorts of pots and kettles dangled from hooks on the sides. The wagon was seemingly meant to carry heavy loads. Several large draft horses grazed nearby, glanced over their at the brothers, and went back to eating. Gnash pointed at the horses.

"No more walking," he said softly.

"Hey! Wagon!" Yarl shouted boldly.

A canvas curtain hung over the back end parted. A beard poked out. So thick and black was the beard that it took the brothers a moment to realize the beard was attached to a head. Two black beady eyes stared at them, then the head withdrew and another head—this one with a salt and pepper beard and intense brown eyes—poked out. The curtain parted. An elderly man, hale and hearty to judge by his upright bearing and quick step, walked down the stairs that led up to the wagon. Behind the old man came a short, stocky person, the owner of the full black beard.

"That little guy's a dwarf," said Gnash, showing off.

"I know a dwarf when I see one," Yarl stated indignantly. "I wasn't born yesterday."

"The old man's wearing robes. He looks like a wizard. Let's see your hands, Old Man," said Gnash, reaching toward his saber.

The human held his hands out, so that the two could see that he had no weapons. The dwarf did the same.

"Good afternoon, gentlemen," the old man greeted them.

He walked forward, his hands in plain sight, his gray robes trailing in the mud. The dwarf remained behind, near the wagon.

The two brothers each fingered their sabers nervously.

"You're cold and wet," said the old man in friendly tones. "You must be hungry, as well. Am I right?"

Gnash was taken aback. He'd expected the old man to run off screaming at the sight of two such fearsome warriors. Gnash could have drawn his sword and just sliced the old man in two at that point and taken what he wanted. But what did the old wizard have up his sleeve besides bread? He was acting so nice to them that Gnash felt obligated to talk to him.

"Uh, what's that smell?" Gnash asked.

Yarl nodded and licked his lips.

"I'm baking bread, and I've got a pot of beans on," said the old man. "You are welcome to share supper with my associate and myself. You like spicy food?"

Gnash watched the old man warily. He should be afraid of them, for he must know that they would steal his food and his horses and probably kill him in the bargain. But the man didn't appear to be afraid of them at all, and that made Gnash even more nervous.

"You got a weapon on you, Old One?" Gnash asked, motioning at the man's cloak. "Or maybe stuff for spellcastin'?"

"No weapons on me," the old man responded, shaking his head. He pulled back the cloak to show that he had no weapons or bags of bat wings attached to his belt. "I do have a lot of weapons over here near the wagon, though. Perhaps you'd like to see them?"

The old man motioned toward the wooden crates piled beside the wagon. At his gesture, the dwarf clomped down the stairs and opened the lid on one of the crates. Suspecting a trap, Gnash moved forward slowly. He kept his distance, peering inside the box.

"By the Queen! How many swords you got in there?" Gnash demanded, astonished. "Hey, Yarl. Come look at this!"

"There's gotta be a hundred swords!" Yarl added, awed. "Enough for an army."

The old man smiled. "No, only forty, with another forty daggers or dirks. They're not in very good shape though. I can still use them, however."

"Use them? You got an army we should know about, Old One?" Gnash glared at him.

The old man glanced at the dwarf. Both of them seemed amused. "An army?" the old man repeated, chuckling. "Oh, dear, no. When I say I use them . . . well, I can show you, if you're interested. You need to come into the wagon to see. There's food for you here, too."

The man turned and walked back up the three steps into the back of the wagon. He flipped up the left flap of canvas, then stepped in. After a penetrating look at the two brothers, the dwarf followed.

"Wait here and be ready for anythin'," Gnash said in low tones.

"In the rain? While you get to go inside with the food?" Yarl demanded.

"I'm the one walking into danger," Gnash returned with a swagger. "You stay outside where it's safe."

"In the rain," Yarl muttered, but under his breath.

Gnash marched up the steps and entered the back of the wagon. He maintained a grip on his blade, not knowing what to expect.

The inside of the wagon was lit by a lantern hanging from one of the spines holding up the canvas. The smoke came from a small field forge, such as the one an army blacksmith used on the battlefield to make weapons or repair armor.

"You some sort of weaponsmith, Old One?" Gnash asked. "Maybe serving with the Solamnic army?"

The old man struggled out of his cloak, hung it from another hook on the same spine as the lantern. The dwarf shook himself like a dog, raining water from his heavy beard.

"My name is Flannery. This is my associate Digger Cutterstone. We're not with the army. We're from Palanthas, and I assure you that we mean no harm to you or your friend."

"Brother. Yarl's my brother," Gnash corrected. He grinned in a nasty sort of way. "We know you don't mean us no harm, Old One. And we don't mean you any harm, although we're the ones with the swords. Swords in our *hands,*" he added quickly, thinking of all the swords in the box.

"Oh, he's your brother." Flannery said, with a significant glance at the dwarf. "We should have guessed. Should have seen the resemblance. Won't you invite your brother in? We'll eat soon. The beans are almost done."

Gnash looked around the wagon. A pot of beans bubbled onto a steel plate that had been mounted over the top of the forge. To the side of the forge were bread loaf tins and two ladles. Some sort of strange machine stood at the back of the wagon. The machine looked like a leather punch, only much bigger, with a handle that pulled down a cylinder. On the other side of the wagon were two beds that had been covered with planks so that they turned into benches. At the back of the wagon stood a large chest with a heavy iron padlock. Gnash eyed the chest.

"All right, Old One. I guess I trust you. But no funny stuff. We're sergeants with the army of the Knights of the Takhisis, so don't you mess with us. We don't take kindly to no messin' from no one from Palanthas."

Gnash backed up his warning with a threatening look. He stroked the hilt of his saber blade menacingly, then whistled to his brother.

"Come on in, Yarl. He's going to give us some food," Gnash said.

Yarl entered the wagon. He looked at Gnash, who winked. Yarl knew that wink from their childhood. It meant that there was going to be some fun later on.

The two sat down on the bench. The dwarf rolled over a large barrel for them to use as a table.

Flannery served four bowls of beans that had been flavored with a hint of cinnamon in a brown tomato sauce. He gave each of the brothers a small loaf of fresh-baked bread.

"Usually, Digger and I eat alone," Flannery explained. "Tonight we're happy to share our food with you."

"Why are you out here digging graves?" Gnash asked, eyeing the food in his bowl, but not touching it yet. "Are you sure you don't work for one of the armies?"

"No, I don't work for any army—" Flannery began.

"Did you find any valuable jewels on the bodies?" Yarl interrupted, looking greedily at the chest with the iron padlock.

Flannery smiled. "No jewels. I'm not really looking for jewels. I look for armor and weapons."

"Grave robbers, huh," said Gnash.

"Dear me, no!" Flannery was shocked. "We don't rob the dead. We make a pact with them. The standard contract." He glanced at the dwarf, who shoveled beans in his mouth and nodded his agreement.

"Contract for what?" Gnash asked, after waiting what seemed like an eternity for the old wizard to continue.

"For their armor and their weapons. In exchange, we give them a proper burial. You see, we work this way: My associate and I search for battlefields, particularly those where the dead haven't been properly buried in the afterhaste of battle—those where the bodies are just flung into a pit or maybe never buried at all. We dig up the bodies and remove their armor and weapons."

"Grave robbers," said Gnash indignantly.

"Not really," Flannery argued. "The dead aren't using their armor or their swords anymore. They don't mind giving them to us, especially when we explain that we're providing a service. Product given for services rendered."

"Service for product," said Digger, the first words the dwarf had uttered. Yarl's eyes widened suspiciously.

"In return," Flannery continued smoothly, "we bury the dead and perform the proper rituals so that they may rest in peace."

"Yeah, yeah," said Gnash, rolling his eyes. "Get to the interesting part. What do you do with the armor and the swords? Sell 'em as souvenirs?"

Flannery reached into his pocket and pulled out two shiny steel coins. He handed one to Yarl and one to Gnash. Both examined them. The coins were marked LORD CITY PALANTHAS on one side and BANK OF PALANTHAS on the other.

"Yeah, so?" Gnash said, fingering the coins. "You get a little money from selling old weapons."

"Must be about twenty copper's worth of old weapons out there," said Yarl, disgusted.

"No, no, nothing like that," Flannery said. "We don't sell the armor for coin. We melt down the armor and the swords and use the steel to *make* coins. I minted both those coins you're holding in your hand."

Yarl gasped. "You . . . you *make* your own money? Can you do that?"

"We can, and we do," said Flannery. "We work for the Bank of Palanthas."

Gnash thought this over. "Then how come everyone's not running around making their own money out of old armor?"

"Excellent question, my friend. The reason no one else does it is that steel is extremely difficult to work with. I have developed a magical powder that I add to the steel that causes it to melt at a much lower temperature than normal."

Flannery pulled out a bag and opened it. Inside was a fine, gray powder. "I use just a pinch. Can't waste any magic. Not these days. After the steel is melted, I pour the steel into sheets and then use that machine you see over there to punch out the coins. A good sword or piece of armor makes a surprising number of steel coins."

Flannery motioned at the dwarf to open the iron padlock on the chest at the rear of the wagon. Digger frowned and looked at the old man questioningly, but Flannery gave him a reassuring nod. Shrugging, Digger opened the chest for the brothers to see.

Gnash and Yarl peered inside. The chest was full to the brim with steel coin, all gleaming and freshly minted.

Gnash stared at the man in disbelief. "Are you telling me that you have a wagonload of steel coins, and you're all alone out here with nothin' but a dwarf for a bodyguard? I don't believe it."

Jumping to his feet, he grabbed his sword hilt and looked about, as if expecting a huge warrior to leap out at him at any moment.

"I assure you, we are quite alone," said Flannery.

"Then why tell us? We're really bad guys, you know." Gnash and Yarl both scowled ferociously. "You know we're gonna have to kill you now and take all your money."

"I'm afraid that's a risk I have to take," said Flannery with a hint of sadness. "You see, I tell you this because I need your help. I was trained as a cleric of Paladine—"

"We don't think much of clerics," growled Yarl, rattling his sword in its sheath.

"Oh, I'm not a cleric anymore," said Flannery hurriedly. "It's because I *was* a cleric of Paladine that I am able to bury the dead Solamnics and dead elves with the proper sacred rituals. But I'm in a bit of quandary when I come to the bodies of those who died in the name of Queen Takhisis. I can't bury them with the proper rituals so that they will sleep the sleep of the dead, which means that I can't take their armor. I've been hoping I'd run into someone who would understand the proper procedure for burying the dead of Queen Takhisis. Now you gentlemen are here, and you might be able to help me. Besides having my utmost gratitude, I'd be glad to pay you, of course."

The brothers looked at each other. They couldn't believe this old man was so foolish. But then, their parents had been the same way. Always prattling about trust and loving your neighbor and all that rot.

"You're gonna pay us all right," said Gnash tersely. "As for buryin' dead guys, we'll see to it that we bury you both nice and proper."

He yanked his sword out and pressed the point of his blade to Flannery's breast, then glanced over at Digger. "You, dwarf, start shoveling that steel into sacks. I want to know how much we're going to make for this night's work. Make it quick or you'll get to see me start cuttin' pieces off this old man."

Flannery gave a slight nod. Digger started to count out stacks of steel coins.

Flannery looked down his nose at the blade that was pressed against his chest. "Nice weapon. A little rusty, but still in good condition. How much did you pay for it?"

"It cost him forty steel up north," Yarl answered proudly. "It's a really good blade. I got one too."

Flannery touched the edge with his finger. "Sharp. Know what it's worth?"

Gnash sneered. "Yeah, it's worth forty steel."

Flannery shook his head. "I reckon I could make sixty steel coins out of that blade this very night. And I could make another sixty out of your armor."

Gnash's jaw sagged. "Sixty! I only paid twenty-five for the armor!"

"Now you see why I'm in this business," Flannery explained. "You could rob us, of course, and kill us into the bargain, but in truth you'd be cheating yourself out of a lot more money. Whereas if you help us, I'll cut you in for a share of all the armor of the Knights of Takhisis."

Outside the wagon, night had fallen. The pattering of rain stopped. Inside, the dwarf halted his money counting and turned around.

"You really mean that?" Gnash asked eagerly. "You could make our armor and blades into a lot more money than they're worth?"

"And if we help you dig up dead Knights of Takhisis, we get a share of their armor, too?"

"It's not so much the digging up we need help with," Flannery explained—a tad reluctantly it seemed. "It's the putting back into the ground that's giving us problems".

Gnash and Yarl looked at each other. The old wizard was talking riddles again.

"What do you say? The standard contract for services rendered?"

Digger reached into his shirt and drew forth a sheaf of parchment. He held it forth temptingly.

"I know what I say," Gnash said to his brother.

"It tops the reward for Mom and Pop," Yarl agreed, eyeing the steel coins in the chest. Leaning close, he whispered, "Besides, once we learn the trick of that there powder, then we can kill them both anyway."

"Smart thinking, little brother," whispered Gnash admiringly. Lowering the sword from Flannery's chest, Gnash thrust the weapon back into its sheath. He reached down to undo the buckle of his sword belt.

"Just a moment," said Flannery, raising his hand. "Remember our bargain: product given for services rendered. Tell me the ritual for burying the dead of the Knights of Takhisis."

"Some mumbo jumbo about commending the souls of the dead to Takhisis for all eternity," said Gnash, not much interested. "That's the important part. The Gray Robes say that settles 'em. There's wrapping of cloth and incense and candles as such if there's time. Spooky waste of time, if you ask me."

"Thank you!" said Flannery with a deep sigh. Lifting his hand, he held it over the heads of the two brothers. "And I commend your souls to Takhisis for all eternity."

Swords, sheathes, belts, buckles, chain mail and helmets made a sharp banging and clattering sound as they all hit the floor. For a brief instant, two skeletal figures stood staring at Flannery, a flicker of enmity in the hollow, empty eye sockets.

"Product given for services rendered," Flannery reminded them sternly.

"Standard contract," said Digger Cutterstone, exhibiting the paper.

The skeletons collapsed in a heap of tangled bones onto the pile of metal that had once, thirty years ago, been their armor.

The dwarf and the old man stood looking at the remains.

"That was a close one," said Digger.

"Indeed it was," said Flannery, wiping sweat from his face with the sleeve of his robe. "We must be more careful next time. But at least now we know that part about commending their souls to Takhisis. Seemed to work fine."

***

The wagon rolled off the next morning, heading for the site of the next battle—Chaos War, War of the Lance, it didn't matter. There were enough battlefields to keep Masters Flannery and Cutterstone busy for the rest of their lives.

They left a peaceful gravesite with two grave markers on the large mound.

The first read:

THREE HUNDRED EIGHTEEN SOLAMNIC SOLDIERS, FIFTY-ONE SOLAMNIC KNIGHTS, AND TWO QUALINESTI ELVES. BATTLE OF THE SOLACE WATERSHED, CHAOS WAR. YEAR 384 AFTER CATACLYSM. THEY DIED BRAVELY.

The second read:

TWO DEAD BROTHERS, SERGEANTS OF THE KNIGHTS OF TAKHISIS, BATTLE OF THE SOLACE WATERSHED, CHAOS WAR, YEAR 384 AFTER CATACLYSM. THEY DIED . . . FINALLY.

DRAGON'S THROAT

DONALD J. BINGLE

They say the upper reaches of Gimmen-
thal Glacier are so beautiful it's hard to think. Goodness
knows it's hard to breathe. Tumbling down from the air-
less heights of Icewall, rugged, jumbled chunks of ice
pack together to inch down onto the Plains of Dust. Ice
crystals sparkle as they sift into pristine drifts spanning
awesomely deep cobalt fissures in the massive river of
ice. In the summer, so I've heard, it's so quiet you can
hear the melt-off trickle down into the shadowy blue
depths of the broken ice to refreeze again once out of
the baleful glare of the never-setting summer sun.

'Course nobody much goes there. Even the Ice
Nomads visit the head of the glacier only sporadically,
and then in the gloom of winter to start the longest and
most challenging of their Ice Boat races.

Nope, for thousands of years, nobody much cared
about Gimmenthal Glacier at all. And then the kender
came.

It's not like the pesky little troublemakers suddenly
decided to hike up the glacier to appreciate nature. Nah.

The idiots prefer to camp in the mud, scores of miles from the heights of Icewall and about twenty miles east of Ice Mountain Bay, where Gimmenthal dies in a sprawl like the flow of dirty, molten wax from a cheap candleholder. Streaked with dirt, rock, and mud in ragged stripes, pushed into its midst as tributary glaciers join the mammoth torrent of ice in its inexorable downslope progress, Gimmenthal melts. Strange as it may seem, the kender come for the melting.

Y'see, in winter, that old glacier creeps forward onto the Plains of Dust, pushing mounds of gravel and topsoil before it. Come summer, it retreats again, leaving a pockmarked landscape of mounded earth and muddy pools of water. It's this messy melt-off that makes the glacier so popular with kender not afflicted by the destruction of Kendermore by the great dragon Malystryx.

These merry, irrepressible kender long for adventure. They want to see and "handle" baubles and gewgaws of all sorts, trade 'em, and "find" them yet again. But with the mood of Krynn these days, they find few enough places to be happy. Their afflicted cousins are no longer any fun. Every sheriff or Knight of Neraka they run into shuffles them off to jail. Magic is getting scarcer and less interesting all the time. And travelers are few and getting fewer as the Great Dragons close roads and terrified communities close their borders.

'Bout the only bright spot for curious kender is, of course, a visit to the Tomb of the Last Heroes in Solace, where they can celebrate the mighty feat of Tasslehoff Burrfoot in defeating Chaos. They do this by mocking the Knights solemnly guarding the Tomb, sneaking over the fence to break chunks of marble off as souvenirs, and frolicking on the picnic grounds 'neath the giant vallenwood trees with similarly inclined and often similarly named kender.

A visit to Solace is not enough for some kender, though, and many have taken to tracing Tasslehoff's journeys during his days as a Hero of the Lance, hoping to recapture the excitement of his encounters with dragons and draconians, gully dwarves and wooly mammoths. From Pax Tharkas to the Gates of Thorbardin, they travel. Of course, the dwarves will not actually let the kender into Thorbardin, and the kender have no way to follow Tas's journeys into the Abyss, but they do what they can. So began the kender trips to Icewall.

Once kender began trekking to Icewall, it was only a matter of time before one wayward traveler happened upon the melting terminus of Gimmenthal Glacier. The "discovery" of Gimmenthal Glacier (the locating of huge geographic features well-known and mapped by both the Ice Nomads and the dwellers on the Plains of Dust amounts to a "discovery" to a kender) would have occasioned no great fuss if it had not been for the items found there. For, y'see, the melting glacier gives up the stuff of kender dreams: random junk. Coins, weapons, bones of all sorts, rings, pots, canteens, half-rotted hats, belt-buckles, boots, utility knives, pouches, teeth, mangled and frayed rope, and on and on and on.

Apparently, at some time long forgotten, there was a battle between two mighty armies in the heights from which Gimmenthal Glacier flows. The battle remnants were quickly covered with endless snow. The snow compacted over eons into the hard ice of the glacier, and the battlefield items slowly wound their way down to the Plains of Dust to be revealed at the melting terminus of the glacier.

Not surprisingly, Gimmenthal—quickly dubbed "Gimme Glacier" by the excited "discoverer"—became a stopping point for curious kender on the way to Icewall. A constant stream of kender flock over the mudpiles, dredge the ponds of melt-off, sift through the piles of mounded gravel, and even mine the irregular icy edges and smaller fissures of the glacier itself, searching for buried treasure—well, treasure to kender anyway. Though the recovered items are mostly mundane items of metal or other sturdy construction, they are from an unknown and ancient time. One can never tell what wonders might be found. Better yet, the pickings are plentiful and, at first, no pesky sheriff or angry shopkeeper kept guard over the items, shooing kender away.

Then something happened, so they say.

Once he had heard of Gimme Glacier, there was no keeping Finderkeeper Rumplton away. A thirteenth cousin, twice removed, of Tasslehoff Burrfoot himself, Finderkeeper was determined to uphold the family honor, which of course meant wandering to as many places and finding as many things as he possibly could. Following in the steps of his famous ancestor—he was constantly looking down to see if he could actually see the steps of his famous ancestor—Finderkeeper had, at first, debated whether he should take the sidetrip to Gimme Glacier before or after visiting Icewall fortress. But when he heard from passing travelers that magic had recently been discovered among the items of Gimme Glacier, he made for the site straight away. Never mind that nobody knew what the magic did or if it would still work in these days of uncertain magical effects. Never mind that flocks of kender were already swarming all over the glacier, the gravel mounds, and the mudpits. Never mind that Finderkeeper wouldn't know what to do with a magic item if he found one. Here was an opportunity not to be missed. He whistled at his good fortune, twirled his topknot three times around in excitement, and headed for Gimme Glacier with a look of acquisitiveness so determined that it caused a passing merchant to check his pouch twice.

The scene at Gimme Glacier was chaos itself, or at least what remnants of Chaos had survived Tasslehoff's noble sacrifice at the end of the Fourth Age of Krynn. Kender plunged headfirst into muddy pools searching in the slimy muck at the bottom for artifacts. Gravel flew everywhere as mounds were enthusiastically plundered for treasure. Picks thudded regularly into the face of Gimme Glacier as impatient kender attempted to hurry the impassive ice into revealing its secrets. Tripods, pulleys, and ropes dangled over crevasses on the face of the ice sheet itself as suspended kender attempted to inspect areas that might not melt for years to come. Gaggles of kender oohed and ahhed over mud-encrusted items, trying to figure out what they were. Disappointment showed when the items turned out to be mere armor buckles or stones, but not too much disappointment.

Finderkeeper threw himself into the fray. After numerous conversations with his incredibly talkative yet refreshingly truthful cousins, and some complex calculations, he picked a spot where he judged a sensible mage would have positioned himself in relation to the main line of battle. He climbed up onto the icy surface of the glacier and made his way almost thirty feet from the soft, melting edge. No one was looking here yet. After all, so far nothing had been found near this spot. He set to exploring the crevasses—already more than ten feet deep even so close to the melting edge of the glacier.

It was dangerous. A slip into the crevasse and he would fall until it narrowed enough to pin him. Then the ice would quickly drain away heat from his body, most likely too quickly for him to be saved, even if his fellow kender were paying enough attention to hear his cries for help above the hubbub and commotion.

Late the next afternoon, however, he found his prize: an odd piece of smooth, pinkish stone with a rounded knob at one end, tapering to a flat oval at the other. No bigger than a small skipping stone, it seemed to glow from within as it lay frozen in the crevasse wall, suffusing a rosy hue to the ice-blue of the fresh chasm. An hour later, his fingers numb from digging at the frozen wall with his dagger, Finderkeeper held the object in his hands. His fingers warmed from its mere touch. This must be magic. Given the age of the other relics that had been found here, Finderkeeper Rumplton was sure that this was lost Irda magic.

He couldn't contain himself. Faster than a shopkeeper blocks the entrance to his store at the sight of an approaching kender, Finderkeeper leaped up from his mining crevasse and hollered, "I found Irda magic!" He might have been trampled in the excited onrush of treasure-fevered kender had not a squad of Knights of Neraka been busily rounding up the treasure-seekers for search and interrogation. Instead, the few nearest kender were the only ones to run over and marvel over Finderkeeper's discovery.

News of magic travels *fast*. Finderkeeper had arrived at Gimme Glacier only a day before the Knights of Neraka. Sensing, as did the mages of Krynn, the waning power of their magic, the great dragons sought magic artifacts over all else. Their lackeys, the Knights of Neraka, did their bidding, tracking down and taking all magic that they could find. Just as Finderkeeper had been loosing the Irda magic from the glacier's chilly grip, the Knights had arrived and taken charge of the search for magic at Gimmenthal Glacier.

Vern Hasterck, Commander of the squad of Knights, found no joy in his assignment to Gimmenthal Glacier. It was bad enough that the squad had to do a three-day forced march over the Plains of Dust to arrive quickly, but the southern reaches of the Plains would now be better called the Plains of Mud. Melt-off from the encroaching glacial fingers of Icewall had created a myriad of streams, ponds, and lakes—all unmapped and numbingly cold to cross. The swampy terrain yielded naught but swarms of accursed mosquitoes and biting flies, yet here he was to remain indefinitely, camped in the muck at the foot of a giant slab of ice, trying to corral kender into work details until something useful to his magic-craving dragonmaster could be found. Then and only then could he leave this frozen wasteland.

He could scarcely believe his good fortune when, mere hours after arrival, he heard one of the feckless kender cry out, "I found Irda magic!"

"Seize that kender!" he shouted to his troops. Finderkeeper heard the order and, after looking quickly over his shoulder to see who the nasty-looking Knight Commander might be talking about, uttered a squeak and backed away. "Take all his goods and bring them to me!"

While being seized is an annoying bother to most kender, the words "take all his goods" are the closest that non-afflicted kender know to actually inspiring fear, or at least aggravation.

"It's mine! I found it!" protested Finderkeeper as he continued backing away from the squad of Knights moving through the milling kender.

A tumult of protest arose from the kender. Murmurs and shouts of "He's right!" "Leave him alone!" "Find your own magic!" and "Run for it, boy!" erupted from all sides. The commotion was rising, and a fullscale kender riot threatened to break out at any moment. Hasterck was not about to let his chance of getting out of this assignment be missed because of mere kender.

"Kill anyone who gets in your way—anyone who helps him." Hasterck joined his men in rushing toward Finderkeeper.

Finderkeeper's squeak was even louder than before, as he turned his heels on the Knights and headed south, up the flowing river of ice. Fortunately, the Knights were tired from their forced march and, though longer of stride than the scampering Finderkeeper, they were unable to gain ground on their quarry.

Hasterck cursed as the quick solution to his unhappy situation scampered upslope, out of reach of his lumbering soldiers. He could not let this opportunity slip away, but he also had to see to the kender camp. Something else, something better and more readily taken might be found. As twilight fell, Hasterck divided the squad into two segments. The majority turned back under his Second-in-Command to question, search, and organize the kender that had not taken the chance to skedaddle during their temporary reprieve from the reaches of authority.

Looking back, Finderkeeper was disappointed to see that the second segment included the two largest Knights and the Knight Commander and that they had set up camp on his trail. It seemed like a lot of fuss and bother. Sure, he had found Irda magic, but he didn't know what it did or what it used to do. Still, it was his magic and he meant to keep it.

Finderkeeper tried to push on, but it was difficult in the dark. The solitary moon had not yet risen to guide him, and the crevasses grew deeper, wider, and more assuredly deadly as he progressed up the glacier. He angled toward the western edge in the hope that it would be less dangerous, when he was suddenly grabbed by his topknot and hoisted into the air.

"Look what I found, Thrak!" bellowed the large, sinewy Ice Nomad holding Finderkeeper aloft. "If huntin' don't improve, we can always take this varmint back for roasting."

"Put him down, Bodar," ordered a taller, lankier Ice Nomad on the rocky crags at the edge of the glacier. "That's no way to teach Garn hospitality on his first hunting trip." He nodded toward a nearby overhang, where a young boy sat sharpening a spear as he huddled for warmth.

Finderkeeper did his best to retain his composure and not flail about as Bodar carried him by his topknot to the edge of the glacier and set him down upon a large boulder covered with lichens. After gingerly smoothing his topknot, Finderkeeper stuck out his hand toward Thrak, obviously the native with the greatest intelligence, or at least the greatest respect for kender hair.

"Finderkeeper Rumplton, adventurer extraordinaire," he said in as formal a tone as the gregarious kender could muster.

"Thrak D'Nar, my son Garn, and I think you have already met Bodar."

"There's 'met' and there's 'well met,' " intoned the kender. "He would do well to work on the latter."

"Sorry, Rumpled Bum," said Bodar gruffly. "You haven't scared off all the game have you? Mammoth are hard enough to find these days, without the likes of you running them off."

"Rumplton. Finderkeeper Rumplton. And, no, I didn't see any mammoths, though I very much would like to do so. Do you think any are nearby? Is that what you eat for food?"

"During the winter we dig up hibernating lemmings and ground squirrels because it's so hard to travel most times," volunteered Garn.

"Arrr, boy, don't be telling him we eat frozen rodents," Bodar interrupted. "We're hunters. Don't you worry, Thrak and me, we'll find you a mammoth. You just be ready, boy. Do what you need to do. That's what a hunter does to feed his family."

Thrak looked at Bodar sternly, but without anger. "And if he needs to dig up hibernating lemmings, that's what a hunter does to feed his family, too, Bodar."

"Bazfaz!" muttered the Ice Nomad as he turned away and sought out a good place to sit amongst the jumble of rock.

Finderkeeper fidgeted a bit in the ensuing silence. "I would be happy to share some of the provisions I have with me if, in the morning, you could point me in the direction of a good passage to Ice Mountain Bay. I understand that there might be a trail along the shore that I can take . . . er . . . away from this place."

"Provisions or no, the knowledge is yours for the asking. We—all of us—appreciate the hospitality."

"All the same," gruffed Bodar, "mind your possessions Garn. Once something finds its way into a kender's hands, 'tis seldom seen again."

The cold hardtack and jerky that the kender had tucked into one of his pouches long ago were surprisingly well received by the Ice Nomads. Finderkeeper found a ready listener to his tales of adventure in Garn and soon after they had eaten, all were fast asleep.

The nights are short in Icewall in the summer, however, and Finderkeeper was distraught to realize that it was fully light when he awoke. He hastily gathered up his meager belongings and was approaching Thrak for directions when he heard a cry from Bodar, high on the rocky cliff above him. "Warriors! On the ice. Three of them."

Thrak jumped onto a nearby tumble of rocks and looked in the direction that Bodar pointed. Garn joined him. The Knights had seen the Ice Nomads and were headed toward them.

"I, perhaps, should have mentioned that my haste to leave this lovely land was motivated by the compelling circumstance that these Knights, which Bodar has so cleverly located are, erp, well, they are seeking to murder me and take my possessions, which could be interesting . . . being murdered, I mean, not having my possessions taken—that's happened before. Somehow, being murdered sounds exciting but vaguely unpleasant and terribly permanent, so if you don't mind I will just be heading on my way. If you could kindly point me on my way to Ice Mountain Bay, I will thank you very kindly for your gracious hospitality. I am very sorry for any trouble I have caused."

"Did you steal from them, little one?"

"I, Finderkeeper Rumplton, am not a crook! These . . . these . . . ruffians are seeking to seize a valuable artifact legitimately mined from the ice of this very glacier. I dug it out of the ice with these very fingers!" exclaimed the kender, holding out his bruised and scratched hands. "Hmmm. I wonder where that nail-clipper I got from that gnomish merchant is?"

Garn stepped up close to Thrak. "If you are truly on the run from bandits, whatever uniform they wear, honor demands that we protect you. Right, father?"

"You have learned well, son." Thrak looked at the armor and weapons of the well-equipped and muscular Knights. "But, perhaps, we could negotiate a purchase of your item for your pursuers." He stood and signaled the Knights that he wished to parley.

Commander Hasterck was even more cranky today than yesterday, if that were possible. A cold night hunkered down on a slab of ice will do that to a warrior. The fact that his armor was as frigid as the glacier

beneath him did not help. The fact that he had to tra-
verse gaping chasms in the ice and that his leather boots
slipped and slid on the wet sheen of the glacier as the
sun rose did not help either. Finding that the elusive
kender had found refuge with the natives of this
accursed iceland really set him off.

"Zeke, Dirk," Hasterck growled, "take no prisoners."

"And the hunters become the hunted," mumbled
Thrak. "They do not seem inclined to talk. Garn,
Bodar. Over the ridge as quick as you can."

Bodar grumbled something about meeting their foes
in noble battle, but deferred to Thrak's judgment to
make a run for it. After all, Garn was too young to hold
his own in a fight, and a father had to protect his son.

Finderkeeper started to apologize for all the trouble
he was causing them, but Thrak turned and headed up
the ridge. "Hurry. Dragon's Throat is our only chance."

Finderkeeper's apologies died on his somewhat
bluish lips. "Dragon's Throat? Sounds interesting, but
is that really the most advisable co— Yipe!" Bodar,
muttering to himself about how he liked Knights of
Neraka even less than kender, snatched his topknot
yet again to set him on his way. Looking down the rock-
strewn mountain-side at the pursuing Knights and back
up at his potential saviors, Finderkeeper decided that
the odds were considerably better if he kept up with the
Ice Nomads' trek over the mountain pass that they kept
belittling by calling a ridge. Besides, the Ice Nomads
might have something interesting in their pouches to
trade. The Knights, on the other hand, did not look
inclined to bargain. Yessiree, the Ice Nomads were the
best bet in his current ignoble situation.

Moving westward up the steep, granite slope, Finderkeeper could see that the ridge was the dwindling spine of a considerable upthrust of mountainous terrain to the south from which glaciers spilled to either side.

At midday, they reached the crest of the ridge. To the west was a green valley littered with boulders and clear, round pockets of water. A stream meandered along the surprisingly flat valley floor. Apparently the glacier that Finderkeeper could barely make out far to the south had once reached this far down the valley and had gouged the terrain flat between two spiny mountain ridges. Ice Mountain Bay glittered beyond the next ridge. Finderkeeper searched the sky and the rocky crags for dragons, nesting or flying, but found none. Instead hundreds of terns wheeled in the sky and roosted in holes along the cliff-face.

The way down was quicker than the way up. Following the lead of Thrak and Garn before him, Finderkeeper leaped zigzaggedly from side to side of the goat path, letting gravity do the work, while the loose shale and gravel absorbed some of the speed and allowed him to control his descent. It was tiring all the same and the spongy valley floor was a welcome relief from the sharp corners and loose shale of the descent. The kender expected a mad dash across the valley floor, then another arduous climb over the next ridge separating them from Ice Mountain Bay. Instead, Thrak turned southward, up the valley toward the distant Icewall.

Perhaps, the kender thought, reinforcements live in this lovely valley. Thrak said nothing, but trudged onward. Garn looked about with interest at the surroundings. It became clear to Finderkeeper that the boy had never been here before. So much for reinforcements.

Finderkeeper ran to catch up with Thrak and pulled on his goat's-wool tunic. "Excuse me, D'Nar, but they'll catch us eventually on flat ground." Already he could see the Knights of Neraka scrambling down the slope behind them—fortunately not as expertly or quickly as the Ice Nomads and the kender had done.

Thrak did not turn his gaze from the wall of ice far ahead. He looked only at it and at the stream gurgling along on the valley floor. "They won't catch us before we reach the ice. That's not what I am afraid of," stated Thrak. "Garn. You be ready. If I say 'Go', you run as fast as you can to the near cliffs and climb as fast and as high as you can. Don't wait for anything, you understand, boy? Not me, not Bodar, and not the kender. And don't stop climbing, no matter what. You, Rumplton, do the same. Not that it is likely to help, not with your short legs." With that, Thrak picked up the pace and Finderkeeper trudged along, too breathless to ask more questions. It was a peaceable valley. What was all the worry?

As they got closer to the wall of ice at the head of the valley, Finderkeeper began to hear rumbles from far ahead, like an approaching thunderstorm. But no cloud appeared in the sky. A particularly sharp crack caused Thrak to stop for a moment and stare. Bodar collided with the back of Finderkeeper as the kender also paused. "I don't understand," stammered the kender to his topknot tormenter. "Is it going to storm?"

"Nah, little one," growled the hunter. "The Dragon's just coughing a bit. Now move along. No time to dawdle here."

Zeke, Dirk, and Knight Commander Vern Hasterck also enjoyed the soft and relatively clear level ground of the valley floor. The insect pests were admittedly more of a problem here, but not as bad as on the plains approaching Gimmenthal Glacier. Here the pools of water were clear and briskly cold. Wildflowers dotted the valley floor. As the area went, Hasterck thought that this was a good place to settle. That worried him. The Ice Nomads could find reinforcements, though none of them had been able to see any settlement in the flats from their earlier high vantage point.

"Ice folk are too stupid to live in a green valley," smirked Zeke. "They want to shiver on the ice where they are safe from animals and enemies."

"Cowards, everyone of them," agreed Dirk. "Look at them scamper away. When the battle comes, they'll freeze for sure."

Both laughed heartily at that, but Vern Hasterck wasn't so sure. Something was going on. Something he didn't understand.

It was almost dark as they approached the towering wall of ice filling the valley from spiny edge to edge. Thrak led them to the western cliff-face from whence the ice flowed down, and they climbed high up along the edge of the glacial spill. Finderkeeper looked longingly at the verdant green valley floor below—a better place to sleep if it hadn't been for the Knights pursuing them. The Knights obviously agreed, as they had made a camp in the valley, complete with a roaring fire for warmth, by the time that the Ice Nomads and the kender stopped climbing.

Finderkeeper was ready to sleep, but Thrak and Bodar obviously still had plans for the evening. "The Dragon's almost ready," Finderkeeper overheard Thrak say.

"Aye, you're right about that. I heard the coughing myself."

"We need to tickle her throat a bit. That's all there is to it. I'll be the one."

"No, Thrak. I'll go. You've much to teach Garn yet."

With that, Bodar picked up his axe and headed down the rocks to the top of the wall of ice.

"If you don't mind my asking," interjected Finderkeeper as Thrak watched Bodar depart. "What is this Dragon's Throat you keep talking about? If I am going to die, I might as well die well informed."

Thrak just turned away, but Garn spoke up. "The valley below is the Dragon's Throat. I've heard of it before, but never seen it. You see, the glacier from the western edge here is not at the head of the valley. The valley continues far back south, where sits another glacier, providing a good bit of melt-off due to how the western winds come through the mountain passes. The glacier here advances down into the valley each winter, crossing it and grinding up against the eastern ridge. The advancing ice completely blocks the water from the melt-off up-valley and a lake forms behind the dam of ice."

Scratching his head, Finderkeeper peered into the darkness to the south. Indeed, he could see a huge lake almost even with the top of the ice dam extending far to the south.

"As the spring and summer come, the ice dam begins to melt and the blocking glacier begins to retreat. At some point, the rising water begins to spill over the ice dam—a trickle at first, but quickly and fiercely erosive. Within minutes the water begins to cut through the ice dam. In less than an hour, the Dragon roars and the entire lake empties out down the valley. That's why no one lives there. It's not safe."

329

"But where did Bodar go?"

Thrak, who had listened approvingly to Garn's explanation, interrupted. "She's not quite ready, but with Bodar's help, she'll go by dawn."

Indeed, in the distance, Finderkeeper could hear the methodical wet smack of Bodar's ice pick on the top of the ice dam. If the Knights heard it, they paid it no mind. Thrak could see their flickering campfire below.

Hasterck was up at dawn. Today they would catch the Ice Nomads and the kender, and the Irda magic, whatever it was, would be his—or at least his master's. He took care of his morning ablutions and then squatted at the stream to fill his canteen with the clear, cold water that flowed from the edge of the glacier. It must be warming slightly, he thought. The stream looked higher than he remembered from the evening before.

Suddenly there was a sharp crack, as if lightning had struck nearby. He turned to see a huge slab of ice break off the face of the ice wall several hundred yards up-valley. Though startling, it did not immediately frighten him. Their camp was far enough back that the slab would do it no harm.

What did frighten him severely an instant later was the cascade of water flowing rapidly over the scarred edge of the ice that had just calved. The glint of the crystal water rushing over the deep cobalt of the freshly exposed ice flank was beautiful, but he also knew it was deadly. He ran as fast as he could to the western cliff, yelling for Zeke and Dirk to awake and follow. He knew that they would not make it in time. He was unsure if he would. He climbed as if his life depended on it, because it did.

———◆●◆———

Bodar's arms ached with a weariness he had never known. His hands no longer responded to his commands. They were fixed in a death grip on the handle of his axe. The freezing water dulled the pain that had fired through his hands for the first few hours, but he knew that the best he could hope for from his evening's activities was that both his hands would turn black—frozen more solidly than the hibernating lemmings they dug up for food. As the early dawn approached, his efforts had grown more and more fevered. Finally, he had completed the narrow trench, and the water had begun to flow.

It all happened so fast after that. One moment, he had been hacking through still water of the makeshift trench in the top of the ice dam. The next moment, the water was moving swiftly through the trench, doubling its depth in seconds. Then the water seeped into unseen cracks with a gushing force that opened them ever wider. A rumble caused the trench to fork and he realized, too late, that he stood on the most unstable portion of the dam. A sharp crack and the huge V-shaped slab of ice on which he stood broke free of the dam and plummeted down the face of the ice cliff. A torrent of frigid water raced the berg.

He knew as he died that the Dragon had roared in time.

———◆●◆———

Thrak, Garn, and Finderkeeper had watched through the night, sleeping only fitfully. They worried as they saw the Commander of the Knights awake and begin to break camp. Then they, too, heard the crack of the glacier's thunder. For a moment, they glimpsed Bodar, upright, before the ice sheeted off beneath him and the water started its tumultuous rampage.

A moment before, the tremendous lake behind the ice dam had been a placid mirror, reflecting the red and purple of the sun rising above the snow-capped spires of the eastern ridge of the valley. The wake of a water bird spread out over the calm surface and lapped gently at the top of the dam as a loon heralded daybreak in the distance. But Bodar's trench was more than a mere slit in the ice dam, it gave the coursing water a way into a multitude of cracks and fissures in the melting glacier. The surface of the lake lurched downward and crashed into the valley below. Rumbles quickly became pops and huge, thunderous claps, as the disintegrating glacial dam shuddered and broke into giant, tumbling slabs of ice.

The tumultuous surge carved off tremendous, unstable bergs of ice and created a wall of rushing, foaming, angry water and house-sized chunks of ice that inundated the peaceful green valley at more than twice the speed of a galloping horse. Birds nesting in the valley grasses squawked as they wheeled upward, abandoning their eggs. Tremendous boulders littering the valley floor, perhaps from the aftermath of prior onslaughts, were picked up by the force of the water and tossed about like an angry child's marbles. Cliffsides collapsed into the torrent as the ice-slabs and rushing water eroded their underpinnings.

In less than a minute, the camp of the Knights was flung down the valley by rushing, freezing water. In two minutes, the water at the camp was a boiling, turbulent flow of fearsome waves and white-water spray. In five minutes, the wall of water hurtling down the valley was creating a roar so tremendous that they could not hear each other yelling in fear.

Everything on the valley floor was shattered and destroyed. In ten minutes, the valley was filled with water more than fifty feet deep. The edges of the spiny ridges that confined the flow were stripped clean of vegetation. The terns had fled, and outcroppings of rock were falling into the roiling, stampeding water below.

In less than twenty minutes, a lake seven miles long and more than one hundred and twenty feet deep had almost completely emptied. The ice dam was gone, leaving nothing but a stump of glacier flowing down from the western ridge, dangling precariously over the open space where the dam once held back the waters from up-valley. The Dragon had roared, and Finderkeeper now knew just a little bit of what his afflicted cousins had felt at the fall of Kendermore. The destruction was demoralizing in its speed and completeness.

The sight had been wondrous and frightening. It had saved life, and it had caused death. The rocks on which they sat, high above the devastation, had rumbled and complained. When it was over, they remained alive, each with their own thoughts on nature, sacrifice, knowledge, existence, and death. Thrak said a few words for Bodar. Garn's eyes filled with tears, but he made no sound. Finderkeeper decided that his hair-tormentor was a pretty good guy, after all.

They heard the Knight Commander before they saw him. His incessant cursing gave him away. Somehow he had made it far enough up the western ridge to escape the worst, and he held on above the cauldron of freezing, roiling death, the adrenaline building a rage in him that mirrored the destruction of the Dragon's roar itself. The remaining three companions knew that their adventure was not yet over and hastened up the ridge, for the chase was on again.

It was possible that they might defeat the Knight Commander in a battle. He was but one and they were three. But the long spears that Garn and Thrak carried for use against the mammoths were of little help in a close quarters battle, and Finderkeeper had naught but a dagger that he had been holding for his Uncle Botheragain. The Knight was armored and well-weaponed with longsword and mace. Not to mention that he was enraged . . . really, really enraged.

There is little to say of the climb and descent that followed. The bright sun shone down on a narrow arm of the Ice Mountain Bay northwest of them as they reached the crest of the last ridge. The glacial fields that had spawned the ice dam lay west and south. They headed toward the bay as the tide turned and the water seeped away from their approach. By the time they had reached the shore many, many hours later, the tide was low and mud flats stretched from edge to edge across the finger of water.

"If we can make it across the flats before the tide turns," sputtered a weak and weary kender, "maybe the water will cut off our truly dedicated but thoroughly exasperating pursuer."

"No," said Thrak. "We stand here." He turned to Garn. "No matter what befalls, do not venture onto the flats."

"I know, Father. I know."

Finderkeeper was befuddled but too tired to want to run across several miles of open mudflats. Besides, he wasn't sure how soon the tide would be turning anyhow. Drowning did not really sound like an interesting way to die. They said you just drifted off into unconsciousness, but he couldn't figure out how they would really know that. Didn't only dead people really know, one way or the other?

"Maybe if we just give him the magic thing," he volunteered weakly, taking the small carved item out of the scroll case in which he had put it for safekeeping.

"Too late," said Thrak, and then the Knight Commander was upon them.

Like the onslaught they had just witnessed at dawn, the Commander rushed at them without subtlety or tactics, but with amazing brute force. Both Thrak and Garn managed to stab at him as he charged at the group, but the force of his rush was so great that he struck the spear out of Garn's hands before it had penetrated the leather joint in his armor. Thrak held on to his weapon, driving his spear into the upper arm of the Commander, but it slashed through muscle without striking bone, and tore out the side. There was no chance to regroup before the roaring maniac was atop them.

Thrak did his best to shield Garn from immediate harm, but not so much as to diminish the boy's honor in this, his only battle. Finderkeeper drew Uncle Botheragain's dagger, but found no opening. As quick as the hands of a kender are, he was no match for a fully armored and well-muscled human. Trying to keep his wits about him, Finderkeeper stabbed at the Knight's boots, but the leather was sturdy and thick, and Uncle Botheragain's blade was really not up to the task.

Suddenly, the tidal bore—a small, perhaps twelve inch inch high, wall of water that marked the turning of the tide—could be seen entering the narrow bay at its seaward end.

"Quickly!" said Garn, grabbing the kender. "Give me the scrollcase!"

Finderkeeper did as he was told. "But it doesn't—"

Before he could say more, Garn grabbed the scrollcase and held it up. "You want the magic?" he cried hoarsely at the top of his lungs. "Then get it before the sea takes it!" He flung the scroll case out onto the mudflats, where it landed and rolled to a stop about forty feet offshore.

Perhaps Garn hoped that the Knight Commander would go after the magic and they would escape. Perhaps Garn knew only that he would be able by this maneuver to avenge his own death.

Vern Hasterck looked at the scrollcase and the approaching tidal bore. He looked at the three staggering defenders. There was enough time.

Focusing his remaining strength, the Knight Commander feinted back to gain room to swing. With a bellowing roar, he slashed in a wide, horizontal arc. He deliberately swung just over the boy's head, overbearing Garn's hasty effort to parry with his spearshaft, so that the boy could see his father die first. He need not have bothered, for Thrak threw himself into the slashing blade in a desperate attempt to purchase his son's life at the cost of his own, with a final thrust of his hunting knife at the head of their berserk attacker. His blade glanced noisily off the helm of the Knight, gouging the thick metal with its force but causing little real damage.

Finderkeeper followed Thrak's lead. Too short to reach the head or heart, he stepped into the stride of the rampaging Knight in an attempt to cripple his enemy's mobility with a thrust into the crease of his leg-armor. But Hasterck recognized the gambit and let the force of his arcing blow against Thrak carry his left leg up and into the side of the closing kender. Finderkeeper went down, falling hard onto the smooth stone pebbles and rocks on the shore of the bay. Although, in any other situation, Finderkeeper would have taken a moment to pick out several of the best weathered rocks for his pouch, in this particular situation he grabbed the armored leg that had connected with his ribcage and held on for dear life. Even Finderkeeper's full weight and strength did not slow the rampaging warrior.

Hasterck reversed his sword stroke and lunged at Garn, aiming lower this time. Before the boy's body had even fallen to the blood-soaked beach, Hasterck dropped his sword and reached down for the kender. Finderkeeper spit in the Knight's face. Uncle Botheragain had taught him that, when he was but a wee one back in Kendermore, but he had never had much use for spitting, until this particular instance.

Putting one hand on the kender's chin and wrapping the other around Finderkeeper's tangled topknot, Hasterck gave a sudden twist. Finderkeeper's last thought was that the sound of splintering bone, combined with a sudden subsiding of all pain, was really quite interesting. Then, the kender thought no more.

Before Finderkeeper's limp body once again hit the smooth stones he would never finger, Hasterck sprinted onto the mudflats to retrieve the scroll case.

The mud was soft and sucked at his legs during his rapid strides, but his momentum carried him out to the scrollcase. He stopped to pick it up. Immediately he sank in the soft saltwater mud to mid-thigh, the mud releasing a flood of water as he sank. It was only then he realized that as the mud released water, it gripped his legs in a viselike hold. He did not sink further, but he could not free himself. As if held by stone, his legs would not move—not an inch, not at all. He grabbed his dagger and cut at the bindings to his leg armor, feeling certain that cutting away the inflexible and weighty material would allow him to move. It was to no avail.

He tried not to panic. Grab the scrollcase so the magic does not flow away when the tidal bore hits, he thought. Remove the armor, so when the water comes, you can just float away to safety.

It was a plan. It should work. He grabbed the scrollcase, his prize, as the tidal bore broke over his waist with the stabbing feel of a thousand icy, vengeful knives. He waited as the shock subsided. Certainly the mud, infused now with water, would loosen around his legs. It would be unpleasant, even dangerous, but he could still float away.

But the mud did not loosen. It gripped him tighter. Soon he could not feel his legs, whether from the death grip of the accursed mud or the numbing coldness of the water of Ice Mountain Bay he did not know. The tide was quickly moving up his body. The cold was so great that he was unsure if his chest would refuse to take breath even before his head was covered by the water.

Perhaps the magic could save him. It was insane to think so, but he had to try. He opened up the scrollcase and found it empty. That bastard had tricked him! The magic was probably in one of the kender's accursed pockets. The swearing that had occurred earlier on the face of the cliff while the Dragon roared was tame in comparison to what spewed forth from the Commander's blue lips now.

The water crept higher. His breath came in ragged, shallow gasps. His body was numb. His lips quivered in the cold. His thoughts slowed and became confused. He had to do something, but what? He wanted to rest, to give in, but his training permeated through his murky thinking.

Perhaps, he thought, he could use his dagger to cut off his legs and somehow struggle to shore. The numbing effect of the water could be a blessing in disguise. He vaguely realized that there was some problem or danger or difficulty in this, but couldn't fathom what it might be. It was a plan. It should work.

He mustered all his waning strength to the effort, to the plan, but his numbed fingers fumbled with the blade. At the last, he realized that he could not even tell if he held the knife any longer, if he might even be cutting into his own flesh.

The bard finished his tale as the tribe of Ice Nomads glanced at one another. The weeping of Thrak's widow pierced the quiet of the night upon the ice fields. A small boy, however, tugged at the brightly colored tunic of the traveling bard. "But how," he asked, "do you know the tale is true, if none survived?"

"Sometimes," whispered the bard, fingering an oddly shaped, pinkish stone, "they say, the truth is not the noblest thing about a tale."

Author's Footnote: Both the Dragon's Throat and the gripping mudflats (alluvial mud) are actual features that have been found in arctic regions. During the peak of one past *jokulhlaup,* as it is known, at Lake George, as much as 150 million gallons of water drained from the 25 square mile lake each minute. Every year, people are caught in the alluvial mud in Cook Inlet. Some are not rescued in time and eventually must be abandoned as the frigid water closes over them.

The War of Souls
THE NEW EPIC SAGA FROM
MARGARET WEIS & TRACY HICKMAN

The New York Times bestseller —now available in paperback!

Dragons of a Fallen Sun
The War of Souls • Volume I

Out of the tumult of a destructive magical storm appears a mysterious young woman, proclaiming the coming of the One True God. Her words and deeds erupt into a war that will transform the fate of Krynn.

Dragons of a Lost Star
THE WAR OF SOULS • VOLUME II

The war rages on . . .
A triumphant army of evil Knights sweeps across Krynn and marches against Silvanesti. Against the dark tide stands a strange group of heroes: a tortured Knight, an agonized mage, an aging woman, and a small, lighthearted kender in whose hands rests the fate of all the world.

The tales that started it all ...

New editions from DRAGONLANCE creators
Margaret Weis & Tracy Hickman

The great modern fantasy epic – now available in paperback!

THE ANNOTATED CHRONICLES

Margaret Weis & Tracy Hickman
return to the Chronicles,
adding notes and commentary
in this annotated edition of the
three books that began
the epic saga.

SEPTEMBER 2001

THE LEGENDS TRILOGY

Now with stunning cover art by award-winning fantasy artist Matt Stawicki,
these new versions of the beloved trilogy will be treasured for years to come.

Time of the Twins • War of the Twins • Test of the Twins

FEBRUARY 2001

New characters,
strange magic,
wondrous creatures.

ADVENTURE THROUGH THE HISTORY OF KRYNN
WITH THESE THREE NEW SERIES!

THE BARBARIANS
PAUL B.THOMPSON & TONYA C. COOK
Follow a divided brother and sister as they lead rival tribes of
plainsmen amidst the wonders and dangers of ancient Krynn.

Volume One: *Children of the Plains*
Volume Two: *Brother of the Dragon*
Volume Three: *Sister of the Sword*
August 2002

THE ICEWALL TRILOGY
DOUGLAS NILES
Journey with an exiled elf to the harsh, legendary land known as Icereach,
where human tribes battle for life and ogres search to reclaim lost glories.

Volume One: *The Messenger*
Volume Two: *The Golden Orb*
January 2002

THE KINGPRIEST TRILOGY
CHRIS PIERSON
Discover for the first time the dynastic history of the Kingpriest
and how his religious-political rule of Istar influenced the world
of DRAGONLANCE for generations to come.

Volume One: *Chosen of the Gods*
November 2001

CLASSICS SERIES

THE INHERITANCE
Nancy Varian Berberick

The companions of Tanis Half-Elven knew of their friend's tragic heritage—how
his mother was ravaged by a human bandit and died from grief.
But there was more to the story than anyone knew.

Here at last is the story of the half-elf's heritage: the tale of a captive elven princess,
a merciless human outlaw, a proud elven prince, the power of love, and how
tragedy can change a life forever.

THE CITADEL
Richard A. Knaak

Against a darkened cloud it comes, soaring over the ravaged land: the flying
citadel, mightiest power in the arsenal of the dragon highlords. An evil wizard has
discovered a secret that may bring all of Ansalon under his control, and it's up
to a red-robed mage, a driven cleric, a kender, and a grizzled war veteran to
stop him before it's too late.

DALAMAR THE DARK
Nancy Varian Berberick

Magic runs like fire through the blood of Dalamar Argent, yet his heritage
denies him its use. But as war threatens his beloved Silvanesti, Dalamar will
seize the forbidden power and begin a quest that will lead him to a dark and
uncertain future.

MURDER IN TARSIS
John Maddox Roberts

Who killed Ambassador Bloodarrow? In a city where everyone is a suspect, time
is running out for an unlikely trio of detectives. If they fail to solve the mystery,
their reward will be death.